The Thing in the Tank

They had captured it when it came through the portal and imprisoned it in a glass-walled tank, sealed away from human contact. But it knew they were out there—and now it was trying to escape!

It formed into a pearly sphere at the bottom of the tank, resting briefly on the blood-slimed sand. Its myriad flickering cilia propelled it to the feeding tube . . . and *into* the pipe. The vampire-thing dropped into the feeding tank—outside its glass prison.

Its keeper, Agursky, stared at it bewildered. Then he opened the container and gently touched the vampire-egg with the tip of one finger.

In that instant the vampire struck. And Agursky was no longer human.

TOR BOOKS BY BRIAN LUMLEY

THE NECROSCOPE® SERIES
Necroscope
Necroscope II: Vamphyri!
Necroscope III: The Source
Necroscope IV: Deadspeak
Necroscope V: Deadspawn
Blood Brothers
The Last Aerie
Bloodwars
Necroscope: The Lost Years
Necroscope: Resurgence
Necroscope: Invaders
Necroscope: Defilers
Necroscope: Avengers

THE TITUS CROW SERIES
Titus Crow Volume One: The Burrowers Beneath & Transition
Titus Crow Volume Two: The Clock of Dreams &
Spawn of the Winds
Titus Crow Volume Three: In the Moons of Borea & Elysia

THE PSYCHOMECH TRILOGY
Psychomech
Psychosphere
Psychamok

SHORT STORY COLLECTIONS
Fruiting Bodies and Other Fungi
The Whisperer and Other Voices
*Beneath the Moors and Darker Places**

OTHER BOOKS
Demogorgon
The House of Doors
Maze of Worlds
*The Brian Lumley Companion**

*forthcoming

Brian Lumley

NECROSCOPE III:

THE SOURCE

TOR
HORROR

A TOM DOHERTY ASSOCIATES BOOK
NEW YORK

This is a work of fiction. All the characters and events portrayed in this book are either products of the author's imagination or are used fictitiously.

THE SOURCE: NECROSCOPE® III

Copyright © 1989 by Brian Lumley
Necroscope® is a registered trademark of Brian Lumley

Cover art by Bob Eggleton

A Tor Book
Published by Tom Doherty Associates, LLC
175 Fifth Avenue
New York, NY 10010

www.tor.com

Tor® is a registered trademark of Tom Doherty Associates, LLC.

ISBN 0-812-52127-7
EAN 978-0-812-52127-6

First edition: September 1989

Printed in the United States of America

20   19   18   17   16   15   14   13   12

This one
is for Mr MacAlan,
Peter Tremayne and Professor
Berresford Ellis—good
friends of mine,
all three.

Chapter One
Simonov

THE AGENT LAY ON A PATCH OF SNOW IN A JUMBLE OF white boulders on the eastern crest of what had once been the Perchorsk Pass in the mid-Ural'skiy Khrebet. He gazed down through nite-lite binoculars on almost two acres of curved, silvery-grey surface covering the floor of the ravine. By the light of the moon that surface might easily be mistaken for ice, but Mikhail Simonov knew that it was no glacier or frozen river; it was a mass of metal some four hundred feet long by something less than two hundred wide. Along the irregular edges of its length, where its gently curving dome met the rocky walls of the gorge, and at both ends, where the arcing metal came up flush against massive concrete barriers or dams, the stuff was "only" six inches thick, but at its centre the moulded mass was all of twenty-four inches through. That was what had registered on the instruments of the American spy-satellites, anyway, and also the fact that this was the biggest man-made accumulation of lead anywhere in the world.

It was like looking down on the three-quarters buried, lead-wrapped neck of some giant bottle, thought Mikhail Simonov. A magic bottle—except that in this case the cork had already been pulled and the genie flown, and Simonov was here to discover the nature of

1

that very dubious fugitive. He gave a quiet snort, pushed his flight of fancy to the back of his mind, focused his eyes and concentrated his attention on the scene below.

The bottom of the ravine had been a watercourse subject to severe seasonal flooding. Up-river, above the "wet" dam wall, an artificial lake was now full, its surface flat and likewise leaden—but only its surface. Channelled under the great roof of lead through unseen sluices, the water reappeared in four great shining spouts issuing from conduits in the lower wall. Spray rose up from that deluge, froze, fell or drifted back to coat the lower ravine in snow and ice, where for all the apparent volume of water only a stream now followed the ancient course. Under the shield of lead, four great turbines lay idle, bypassed by the hurtling waters bled off from the lake. They'd been at rest like that for two years now, since the day the Russians had tested their weapon for the first—and the last—time.

Despite all the USSR's technological camouflaging countermeasures, that test, too, had been "seen" by the American spy-satellites. What *exactly* they saw had never been made public or even hinted at outside of higher-echelon and correspondingly low-profile government departments, but it had been sufficient to jolt America's SDI or "Star Wars" concept into real being. In very small, very powerful and highly secretive defence circles throughout the Western World there had been worried discussions about APB (Accelerated Particle Beam) "shields," about nuclear- or plasma-powered lasers, even about something called a "Magma Motor" which might theoretically tap the energy of the small black hole believed by some scientists to lie at Earth's core, simultaneously feeding upon and fuelling the planet; but all such discussions had been purely conjectural. Certainly nothing substantial—other than the evidence provided by the satellites—had leaked out of Russia herself; nothing, that is, in the way of normal intelligence reporting. No, for the Ural Mountains in the region of Perchorsk had been for some time far more security-sensitive than even the Baikonur Space Centre in the days of the Sputniks. And it was a sensitivity which, in the aftermath of that single, frightful test, had suddenly increased fourfold.

Simonov shivered in his white, fur-lined anorak, carefully demisted his binoculars, flattened himself more rigidly to the frozen ground between the boulders as scudding clouds parted and a nearly full moon blazed treacherously down on him. It was cold in the so-called "summer" up here, but in the late autumn it was a kind of frozen hell. It was autumn now; with a bit of luck Simonov would escape suffering through another winter. No, he mentally corrected himself, that would take a *lot* of luck. A hell of a lot!

The scene below turned silver in the flooding moonlight, but the special lenses of Simonov's binoculars made automatic adjustment. Now he turned those lenses on the pass proper, or what had been the pass until the Perchorsk Projekt had got underway some five years ago.

Here on the eastern side of the ravine, the pass had been eroded through the mountain's flank by one of the sources of the Sosva River on its way down to Berezov; on the western side, it had been dynamited through a deep saddle. Falling steeply from the mountains, its road roughly paralleled the course of the Kama River for two hundred and fifty miles to Berezniki and Perm on the Kirov-Sverdlovsk rail link.

In the forty years prior to the Projekt, the pass had been used chiefly by loggers, trappers and prospectors, and for the transportation of agricultural implements and produce both ways across the range. In those days its narrow road had been literally carved and blasted from the solid rock, and so it had remained until recently: a rough and ready route through the mountains. But the Perchorsk Projekt had brought about drastic changes.

With the construction of the Zapadno rail link to Serinskaja in the east, and the extension of the railway from Ukhta to Vorkuta in the north, the high pass had long since fallen out of favour as a route through the mountains; it had only remained important to a handful of local farmers and the like, whose livelihoods hardly mattered in the greater scheme of things. They had simply been "relocated." That had taken place four and a half years ago; then, with all the speed, ingenuity and muscle that a superpower can muster, the pass had been re-opened, widened, improved and given a two-lane system of good metalled roads. But not as a public highway, and certainly not for the use of the far-scattered "local" communities. Indeed, their use of the pass had been strictly forbidden.

In all the project had taken almost three years to complete, during which time the Soviet intelligence services had leaked innocuous details of "a pass in the Urals which is undergoing repair and improvement." That had been the official line, to forestall or confuse the piecing together of the true picture as seen by the USA from space. And if additional proofs of the innocence of the Perchorsk Projekt were required, it could also be seen that gas and oil pipelines had been laid in the pass between Ukhta and the Ob gasfields. What the Russians couldn't conceal or misrepresent was the construction of dams and the movement of heavy machinery, the incredibly massive lead shield built up in layers over the erstwhile bed of a powerful ravine torrent, and perhaps most important, the gradual build-up of troop movement into the area to a permanent military presence. There had been a deal of blasting, excavation and/or tunnelling, too, with many thousands of tons of rock moved out by truck or simply dumped into local ravines, plus the installation of large quantities of sophisticated electrical equipment and other apparatus. Most of which had been seen from space, and all of which had intrigued and irritated the West's intelligence and security services almost unendurably. As usual, the Soviets were making life very difficult. Whatever they were up to, they were doing it in an almost inaccessible, steep-sided ravine nine hundred feet deep, which meant that a satellite had to be almost directly overhead to get anything at all.

Conjecture in the West had gone on unabated. The alternatives were many. Perhaps the Russians were attempting to carry out a covert mining operation? It could be that they'd discovered large deposits of high-grade uranium ore in the Urals. On the other hand, maybe they were concerned with the construction of experimental nuclear installations under the very mountains themselves. Or could it be that they were building and making ready to test something quite new and radically different? As it happened—*when* it happened, at that time just two years ago—advocates of the third alternative were seen to have guessed correctly.

Once again Mikhail Simonov was drawn back to the present, this time by the low rumble of diesel-engined transports that echoed up hollowly from the gorge to drown out the wind's thin keening. Just as the moon slipped back behind the clouds, so the headlight beams of a convoy of lumbering trucks cut a swath of white light in the darkness where they stabbed out from the gash of the pass in the deep V of the western saddle. The huge, square-looking trucks were just under a mile away across the ravine and some five hundred feet below the level of Simonov's vantage point, but still he flattened himself more yet and squirmed back a little into his nest of gaunt boulders. It was a controlled, automatic, almost instinctive reaction to possible danger, in no way a panicked retreat. Simonov had been very well trained, with no expense spared.

As the convoy came through the pass and turned its nose down the steeply descending ramp of a road cut from the face of the ravine, so a battery of spotlights burst into brilliant life, shining down from the sheer wall and lending the well-gritted road excellent illumination. Fascinated, Simonov listened to the great diesels snarling into low gear, watched the routine of a well organized reception.

Without taking the nite-lite from his eyes, he reached into a pocket and drew out a tiny camera, snapping it into position in the lower casing of the binoculars. Then he pressed a button on the camera and continued watching. Whatever he saw would now be recorded automatically, one frame every six seconds for a total of four and a half minutes, forty-five tiny stills of near-crystal clarity. Not that he expected to see anything of any real importance: he already knew what the trucks contained and the camera shots were simply to certify that this was indeed their destination—for the satisfaction of others back in the West.

Four trucks: one of them containing all the makings of a ten-foot electrified fence, two more carrying the component parts and ammo for three twin-mounted, armour-piercing, 13mm. Katushev cannons, and the fourth and last loaded with a battery of diesel-powered generators. No, what was being hauled wasn't the question. The question was this: if the Russians were going to defend the Perchorsk Projekt, who were they defending it against?

Who . . . or what?

Simonov's camera clicked almost inaudibly away; his eyes took in all that was happening below; he was aware that he mustn't stay here more than another ten or fifteen minutes at the most, because of the high radiation count, but part of his mind was already somewhere else. It was back in London just two months short of two years ago. Shooting the arrival of the trucks had done it, set Simonov's mind working on that other film he'd been shown by MI6 and the Americans in London. A real film, however short, and not just stills. He relaxed just a fraction. He was doing all that was expected of him, could afford a little mental meandering. And actually, once you'd seen that film, it was difficult not to keep going back to it.

The film was of something that had happened just seven weeks after the Perchorsk Incident (called "pi") and had earned itself the acronym "pi II" or "Pill." But it had been one hell of a pill to swallow. It had come about like this.

. . . Early morning of a bright mid-October day along the eastern seaboard of the USA; but along the "obsolete" Canadian DEW-line things have been stirring for some three hours, since a pair of spysats with overlapping windows on the Barents and Kara seas, and from Arkhangel'sk across the Urals to Igarka, flashed intruder reports down across the Pole to listeners in Canada and the USAF bases in Maine and New Hampshire. Washington has been informed, and low-key alert status has already been notified to the missile bases in Greenland and the Foxe Peninsula base on Baffin Island. Other DEW-line subscribers have been notified; Great Britain has shown mild interest and asked for updates, Denmark is typically nervous (because of Greenland), Iceland has shrugged and France has failed to acknowledge.

But now things begin to speed up a little. The original spies-in-the-sky have lost the intruder (an "intruder" being any aerial object passing east to west across the Arctic Ocean) out of their windows, but at the same time it's been picked up by DEW-line proper crossing the Arctic Circle on a somewhat irregular course but generally in the direction of Queen Elizabeth Island. What's more, the Russians have scrambled a pair of Mig interceptors from their military airfield in Kirovsk, south of Murmansk. Norway and Sweden join Denmark in an attack of the jitters. The USA is hugely curious but not yet narrow-eyed (the object is too slow to be a serious threat) but nevertheless an AWACS reconnaissance aircraft has been diverted from routine duties to a line of interception and two fighters are scrambled up from a strip near Fort Fairfield, Maine.

It is now four hours since the—UFO?—was first sighted over Novaya Zemlya, and so far it has covered a little more than nine hundred miles, having passed west of Franz Josef Land on what now seems a beeline for Ellesmere Island. Which is where the Migs draw level with it, except that doesn't quite show the whole picture. Geographically they've caught up with it, but they're at max. headroom and the UFO is two miles higher! Then . . . apparently they see it—and at the same time it sees them.

What happens then isn't known for a certainty, for the Kirovsk base has ordered radio silence, but on the basis of what will be seen to happen later we can take a broad stab at it. The object descends, puts on speed, attacks! The Migs probably open fire on it in the seconds before they are reduced to so much confetti. Their debris is lost in snow and ice some six hundred miles from the Pole and a like distance short of Ellesmere . . .

And now the intruder really is intruding! Its speed has accelerated to around three hundred and fifty miles per hour and its course is straight as an arrow. The AWACS has reported the Migs lost from its screens, presumed down, but a hotline call from Washington to Moscow fails to produce anything but the usual ambiguities: "What Migs? What intruder?"

The USA is a little peeved: "This aircraft came out of your airspace into ours. It has no right being there. If it sticks to its present course it will be intercepted, forced to land. If it fails to comply or acts in any way hostile, there's a chance it will be shot down, destroyed . . ."

And unexpectedly: "Good!" from the Russians. "Whatever it is you have on your screens, it is nothing of ours. We renounce it utterly. Do with it as you see fit!"

8

Far more detailed Norwegian reports are now in from the Hammerfest listening station: the object is believed to originate from a region in the Urals near Labytnangi right on the Arctic Circle, give or take a hundred miles or so. If they had given or taken three hundred miles south, then the reports would have been more nearly correct; for the Perchorsk Pass was just that far away from the source they'd quoted. Alas, in the other direction, north of Labytnangi, lay Vorkuta, the USSR's most northerly missile site, supplied by rail from Ukhta. And now the Americans go from mildly irritated to extremely narrow-eyed. Just what in hell are the Reds up to? Have they loosed some sort of experimental missile from Vorkuta and lost it? If so, does it have a warhead?

How *many* warheads?

Alert classifications go up two notches and Moscow comes under fire in some very heated hotline exchanges. Still the Soviets deny all knowledge, however nervously.

Better, clearer reports are coming in. We now have the thing on satellite, on ground radar, on AWACS. No physical, human sightings as yet but everything else. The spysats say it could be a dense flock of birds—but what sort of birds fly in excess of three hundred mph five miles high across the Arctic Circle? Collision with birds *could* have taken out the Migs, of course, but . . . The top-secret high-tech radar sites along the older DEW-line say it's either a large airplane or . . . a space-platform fallen out of orbit? Also that it's impossibly low on metal content—namely, it doesn't have any! But intelligence won't admit of any aircraft (not to mention space-stations) two hundred and some feet long and constructed of canvas. AWACS says that the thing is flying in a series of spurts or jets, like some vast aerial octopus. And AWACS is more or less right.

It is now one hour since the American interceptors scrambled. Flying at close to Mach II, they have crossed the Hudson Bay from the Belcher Islands to a point about two hundred miles north of Churchill. In so doing they've just overtaken the AWACS and left it a few minutes behind. The AWACS has told them that their target is dead ahead, and that he's come down to 10,000 feet. And now, finally, just like the Migs before them, they spot the intruder.

That had been the narrative, the scenario that the CIA and MI6 had set for Simonov before showing him the AWACS film; and as the Briefing Officer had spoken those last three words, "spot the intruder," so the film had started to roll. All very dramatic, and deservedly so . . .

"Spot the intruder," thought Simonov now, the words bitter on his tongue so that he almost spat them out loud. By God, yes! For that was the name of the game, wasn't it? In security, intelligence, spying: *Spot the Intruder*. And all sides playing it expertly, some a little better than others. Right here and now he was the intruder: Michael J. Simmons, alias Mikhail Simonov. Except he hadn't been spotted yet.

Then, as he re-directed all of his concentration back down onto the scene in the ravine, he sensed or heard something that didn't belong. From somewhere behind and below him had come the *chink* of a dislodged pebble, then lesser clatterings as the tumbling stone picked up smaller cousins on its way down the side of the mountain. The last leg of the climb had been along a steep, terraced ridge of rock, more a scramble than a real climb, and there had been plenty of loose scree and stony debris littered about. It could be that in his passing he'd left a pebble precariously balanced on some ledge, and that a strong gust had dislodged it. Simonov fancied that was all there was to it, but—

What if it was something else? He'd had this feeling recently—a sort of uneasy, half-formed suspicion—that someone, somehow, was aware of him. Someone he'd rather was not aware of him. He supposed this was a feeling spies learned to live with. Maybe it was just that everything had seemed to be going so smoothly, so that now he'd started to invent difficulties. He hoped that was all it was. But just to be sure . . .

Without looking back or changing his position, he unzipped his anorak, reached inside and came out with a blocky, wicked-looking short-barrelled automatic, its stubby silencer already attached. He checked the magazine, and silently eased it up again into the grip. And all of this done one-handed, with practiced ease, without pausing in the filming of the trucks in the ravine. Maybe the last couple of frames would be a bit off-centre. No big deal. Simonov was satisfied with what he'd got.

The tiny camera attached to Simonov's nite-lite clicked one last time and gave a warning *whir*, signalling that the sequence was complete. He unclipped the camera and put it away. Then he wedged his binoculars securely in the base of a boulder, carefully cocked his pistol, squirmed about face and got to his knees. Still concealed, he peered cautiously through the V formed where the tops of two rounded boulders leaned together. Nothing back there. Nothing he could see, anyway. Steep cliffs falling away for a thousand feet, with spurs extending here and there, and thinly drifted snow lying white and gleaming on all flat surfaces. And way down there, obscured by the night, the tree-line and gentling lower slopes. Everything motionless and monochrome in dim starshine and occasional moonlight, where only the thin wind scattered little flurries of snow from the spurs and high ledges. There were plenty of places where men could hide themselves, of course—no one knew that better than Simonov, himself an expert in concealment—but on the other hand, *if* he'd been followed, why would they want to come up here? Easier to wait for him below, surely? Yet still the feeling persisted that he was not alone, that feeling which had

11

grown in him increasingly over his last two or three visits to this place.

This place, this spawning ground for utterly alien monsters . . .

He got back down into his original position, recovered the nite-lites and brought them to his eyes. In the ravine, where the steep road hugged the face of the defile down to the towering twin walls of the dam and the curved lead surface between them, a cavernous opening in the cliff blazed with light. The last truck turned left off the road onto a level staging area, then passed in through huge, wheeled, steel-framed lead doors. A gang of yellow-clad traffic controllers flagged the truck rumbingly inside and out of sight, then followed it into the blaze of illumination under the cliff. Other men came hurrying down the road, gathering up flashing beacons. The great doors had clanged shut by the time they reached them, but a wicket-gate thick as the door of a vault had been left open, issuing a square beam of yellow light. It swallowed up the men with the traffic beacons, then was closed. The floodlights over the pass snapped out and left stark blackness in their wake. Only the dammed watercourse and the great lead shield were left to reflect the starshine.

But all of that lead down there. And these poisoned heights, a little more than mildly radioactive. And that *Thing* filmed by the AWACS as it did battle with the USAF jet fighters. Simonov couldn't suppress a small shudder, which this time wasn't due to the intense cold. He folded his nite-lites into a flat, leather-cased shape which he slipped inside his anorak with the strap still round his neck. Then for a moment longer he just lay there, his eyes staring into the enigmatic gulf below, his mind superimposing on the darkness the sequence of events he'd witnessed in London, recorded on that flickering AWACS film . . .

But even remembering it, he cringed away from it. Bad enough that he still occasionally saw it in his dreams! But could that . . . that . . . whatever it had been, could it really have come from here? A monstrous mutation? A gigantic, hideous warrior clone conjured in some crazed geneticist's incredible experiment? A "biological" weapon outside all of man's previous experience and understanding? That was what he was here to find out. Or rather, it was what he was here to prove conclusively: that indeed this was where that *Thing* had been born—or made. That seething, pulsing, writhing—

Snow crunched softly, compacted by a stealthy footfall!

Simonov thrust himself to his feet, turning as he rose, and saw a head and staring eyes outlined briefly above the low jumble of rocks. His automatic was in his hand as he launched himself into a dive to the left of the boulders, his right arm outstretched, ready to target his weapon. A man in a pure white parka was crouched behind the boulders, with a gun in his hand which he even now lifted to point at Simonov. In the instant before Simonov came down on his side in the snow he snapped off two shots; the first one struck the man in the shoulder, snatching him upright, and the second slammed into his chest, flinging him backwards and down onto the patchy snow.

The dull *phut, phut,* of Simonov's silenced weapon had caused no echoes, but he'd scarcely caught his breath when there came a hoarse, gasping grunt from close at hand and silver glinted in a sudden flood of moonlight. The snow on Simonov's left-hand side, not eighteen inches away, erupted in a spray of frantic activity. "Bastard!" a voice snarled in Russian as a massive hand reached out to grasp Simonov's hair and an ice-axe came arcing down, its spike impaling his gun-hand through the wrist and almost nailing it to the stony ground.

The Russian had been lying in a snow-filled depression, waiting. Now he sprawled forward, trying to hurl his bulk on top of Simonov. The agent saw a dark face, a white bar of snarling teeth framed in a beard and a ruff of white fur, and drove his left elbow into it with as much force as he could muster. Teeth and bone crunched and the Russian gave a gurgling shriek, but he didn't release his grip on Simonov's hair. Then, cursing through blood and snot, the massive Soviet drew back his ice-axe for a second swipe.

Simonov tried to bring his gun to bear. Useless— there was no feeling in his hand, which flopped like a speared fish. The Russian hunched over him, dripped blood on him, changed his grip to Simonov's throat and drew back his axe menacingly.

"Karl!" came a voice from the shadows of other boulders. "We want him alive!"

"How *much* alive?" Karl choked the words out, spitting blood. But in the next moment he dropped the axe and instead drove a fist hard as iron to Simonov's forehead. The spy went out like a light, almost gladly.

A third Russian figure came out of the night, went to his knees beside Simonov's prone form. He felt the unconscious man's pulse, said: "Are you all right, Karl? If so, please see to Boris. I think this one put a couple of bullets into him!"

"Think? Well, I was closer than you, and I can assure you he did!" Karl growled. Gingerly touching his broken face with trembling fingertips, he went to where Boris lay spreadeagled.

"Dead?" the man on his knees beside Simonov inquired, his voice low.

"As a side of beef," Karl grunted. "Dead as that one should be," he pointed an accusing finger at Simonov. "He's killed Boris, messed up my face—you should let me twist his fucking head off!"

"Hardly original, Karl," the other tut-tutted. He stood up.

He was tall, this leader, but slender as a rod even in his bulky parka. His face was pale and thin-lipped, sardonic in the moonlight, but his sunken eyes were bright as dark jewels. His name was Chingiz Khuv and he was a Major—but in his specialized branch of the KGB the wearing of uniforms and the use of titles and rank were to be avoided. Anonymity increased productivity, ensured longevity. Khuv forgot who'd said that, but he agreed wholeheartedly: anonymity did both of those things. But at the same time one must make sure it did not detract from authority.

"He's an enemy, isn't he?" Karl growled.

"Oh, yes, he's that all right—but he's only one and our enemies are many. I agree it would be very satisfying to squeeze his throat, and who knows but that you'll get your chance—but not until I've squeezed his brain."

"I need attention." Karl held snow tenderly to his face.

"So does he," Khuv nodded at Simonov. "And so does poor Boris." He went back to his hiding place in the rocks and brought out a pocket radio. Extending its aerial, he spoke into the mouthpiece, saying: "Zero, this is Khuv. Get the rescue chopper up here at once. We're a kilometer up river from the Projekt, on top of the eastern ridge. The pilot will see my torch . . . Over."

"Zero: at once, Comrade—out," came back the answer, tinny and with a touch of static. Khuv took out a heavy-duty torch and switched it on, stood it upright on the ground and packed snow around its base. Then he unzipped Simonov's anorak and began to turn out his pockets. There wasn't much: the nite-lites, spare clips for the automatic, Russian cigarettes, the slightly crumpled photograph of a slim peasant girl sitting in a field of daisies, a pencil and tiny pad of paper, half a dozen loose matches, an "official" Soviet Citizen's ID, and a curved strip of rubber half an inch thick by two inches long. Khuv stared at the block of black rubber for long moments. It had indentations that looked like—

"Teeth marks!" Khuv nodded.

"Eh?" Karl mumbled. He had come to see what

15

Khuv was doing. He spoke through a handful of bloody snow with which he staunched the wounds to his nose and lips. "What? Did you say teeth marks?"

Khuv showed him the rubber. "It's a makeshift gumshield," he informed. "I'd guess he puts it in at night—to keep from grinding his teeth!"

They got down on their knees beside Simonov where Karl could work on his jaws. The unconscious man groaned and twitched a little but finally succumbed to the pressure of the Russian's huge hands. Karl forced his mouth wide open, said: "There's a pencil torch in my top pocket." Khuv fumbled the torch out of the other's pocket, shone it into Simonov's mouth. Lower left, at the back, second forward from the wisdom tooth—there it was. A capped tooth at first glance, but on closer inspection a hollow tooth containing a tiny cylinder: Part of the enamel had worn away, showing bright metal underneath.

"Cyanide?" Karl wondered.

"No, they've got a lot better stuff than that these days," Khuv answered. "Instantaneous, totally painless. We'd better get it out before he wakes up. You never know, he might just want to be a hero!"

"Turn his face left-side down on the ground," Karl grunted. He had put both Simonov's and Boris's guns in a huge pocket; now he took them out and used the butt of Simonov's weapon as a wedge between his jaws. His dead comrade's gun had a barrel that was long and slender. "This is *not* going to hurt me more than it hurts him!" Karl grunted. "I think Boris would like it that I'm using his gun."

"What?" Khuv almost shouted. "You'd shoot it out? You'll ruin his face and the shock might kill him!"

"I would *love* to shoot it out," Karl answered, "but that isn't my intention." He poised the heel of his free hand over the weapon's butt.

Khuv looked away. This part of it was for such as Karl. Khuv liked to think he stood a little above sheer animal brutality. He looked out over the rim of the ridge, gritted his own teeth in a sort of morbid empathy as he heard Karl's hammer hand come down with a smack on the butt of the gun. And:

"There!" said Karl with some satisfaction. "Done!" In fact he'd got two teeth, whole, the one with the cylinder and its neighbour. Now he used a grimy finger to hook them out of Simonov's bloody mouth. "All done," Karl said again, "and I didn't break the cylinder. See, the cap's still secure on the top. He was just about to wake up, I think, but that bit of additional pain should keep him under."

"Well done," said Khuv with a small shudder. "Pack some snow in his mouth—but not too much!" He inclined his head, added, "Here they come."

Dim, artificial light washed up from the gorge like the pulse of a far false dawn. It brightened rapidly. With it came the slicing *whup, whup, whup*, of a helicopter's rotors . . .

Jazz Simmons was falling, falling, falling. He'd been on top of a mountain and had somehow fallen off. It was a very high mountain and it was taking him a long time to hit the bottom. Indeed, he'd been falling for so long that the motion now seemed like floating. Floating in air, frog-shaped, free-falling like an expert parachutist waiting for the right moment to open his chute. Except Jazz had no chute. Also, he must have hit his face on something as he fell, for his mouth was full of blood.

Nausea and vomiting woke him up from nightmare to nightmarish reality. He *was* falling! In the next moment, remembering everything, the thought flashed through his mind:

God! They've tossed me into the ravine!

But he wasn't falling, only floating. At least that part of his dream was real. And now as his brain got in gear and shock receded a little, so he felt the tight grip of his

17

harness and the down-draft of the helicopter's great fan overhead. He craned his neck and twisted his body, and somehow managed to look up. Way up there a chopper, its spotlights probing the depths of the ravine, but directly overhead . . .

Directly overhead a dead man twirled slowly on a second line, a hook through his belt, his arms and legs loosely dangling. His dead eyes were open and each time he came round they stared into Jazz's eyes. From the splashes of crimson on his white parka Jazz supposed it was the man he'd shot.

Then—

Shock returned with a vengeance, weightlessness and vertigo and cold, blasting air and noise combining to put him down a second time. The last thing he remembered as he fell into another ravine, the night black pit of merciful oblivion, was to wonder why his mouth was full of blood and what had happened to his teeth.

Mere moments after he'd passed out the helicopter lowered him to the flat top of the upper dam wall and yellow-jacketted men removed him and his harness complete from his hook. They took Boris Dudko down, too, a heroic son of Mother Russia. After that . . . their handling of Jazz Simmons wasn't too gentle, but he neither knew nor cared.

Nor did he know that he was about to experience the dream of every intelligence boss in the western world: he was about to be taken inside the Perchorsk Projekt.

Getting out again would be a different thing entirely . . .

Chapter Two
Debrief

THOUGH LENGTHY, THE DEBRIEFING WAS THE VERY GEN-
tlest affair, nothing nearly so cold and clinical as
Simmons had imagined this sort of interrogation would
be. Of course, in his case it had to be gentle, for he'd
been close to death when his friends had smuggled him
out of the USSR. That had been several weeks ago—or
so they told him—and it seemed he was a bit of a mess
even now.

Gentle, yes, but on occasion irritating, too. Especially the way his Debriefing Officer had insisted on
calling him "Mike," when he must surely have known
that Simmons had only ever answered to Michael or
Jazz—and in Russia, of course, to Mikhail. But that
was a very small grievance compared to his freedom
and the fact that he was still alive.

Of his time as a prisoner he'd remembered very little,
virtually nothing. Security suspected he'd been brain-
washed, told to forget, but in any case they hadn't
wasted too much time on that side of it; the important
thing had been his work, what he'd achieved. Perhaps
at one time the Reds had intended to keep him, maybe
even try to reprogramme him as a double agent. But
then they'd changed their minds, ditched him, tossed
his drugged, battered body into the outlet basin under

the dam. He'd been picked up five miles down-river from Perchorsk, floating on his back in calm waters but gradually drifting toward falls which must surely have killed him. If that had happened . . . nothing remarkable about it: a logger and spare-time prospector, one Mikhail Simonov, falls in a river, is exhausted by the cold and drowns. An accident which could happen to anyone; he wasn't the first and wouldn't be the last. The West could make up its own mind about the truth of it, if they ever found out about it at all.

But Simmons hadn't drowned; "sympathetic" people had been out looking for him ever since his failure to return to the logging camp; they'd found him, cared for him, given him into the hands of agents who'd got him out through an escape route tried and true. And Jazz himself remembering only the scantiest details of it, brief, blurry snatches from the few occasions when he'd been conscious. A lucky man. Indeed a *very* lucky man . . .

His days were uncomplicated during that long period of recuperation. Uncomfortable but uncomplicated. He would wake up to slowly increasing pain, a pain which seemed to stem from his very veins as much as from any identifiable limb or organ. Immobile, his lower half encased and (he suspected) in some sort of traction, his left arm splinted and swathed and his head similarly wrapped, waking up was like moving from some darkly surreal land to an equally weird world of grey shadows and soft external movements.

Light came in through the bandages, but it was like trying to see through inches of snow or a heavily frosted window. His entire face had been very badly bruised, apparently, but the doctors had managed to save his eyes. Now he must rest them, and the rest of his body, too. Simmons had never been vain; he didn't ask about his face. But he did wonder about it. That was only natural.

His dreams disturbed him most, those dreams he

could never quite remember, except that they were deeply troubled and full of anxiety and accusation. He would worry about them and puzzle over them in the period between waking and the pain starting, but after that his only concern would be the pain. At least they'd given him a button he could press to let them know he was awake. "Them": the angels of this peculiar hell on earth, his doctor and his Debriefing Officer.

They would come, shadows through the snow of his bandages; the doctor would feel his pulse (never more than that) and cluck like a worried hen; the Debriefing Officer would say: "Easy now, Mike, easy!" And in would go the needle. It didn't put him out, just took away the pain and made it easy to talk. He talked not only because the DO wanted him to and because he knew he must, but also out of sheer gratitude. That's how bad the pain could get.

He'd been told this much: that while he was badly banged about he wasn't beyond repair. There'd been some surgery and more to come, but the worst of it was over. The pain-killer they'd used had been highly addictive and now they had to wean him off it, but his dosage was coming down and soon he'd be on pills alone, by which time the pain wouldn't be nearly so bad. Meanwhile the DO had to get everything he knew—every last iota of information—out of him, and he had to be sure he was getting the truth. The "damned Johnnie-Red" might have inserted stuff in there that wasn't real, "don'tcha know." With the methods they used these days they could alter a man's memory, his entire perception of things, "the damned boundahs!" Jazz hadn't known there were people who still talked like that.

And so, to ensure they were digging out the "gen stuff," they'd started right back at the beginning before Simmons had ever been recruited by the Secret Service, indeed before he'd been born . . .

* * *

21

Simonov hadn't been such a hard name to adopt, for it was his father's name. Back in the mid-1950s Sergei Simonov had defected to the West in Canada. He had been a trainer with a team of up-and-coming young Soviet skaters. A disciplinarian and cool head on the ice, off it he'd been quick-tempered and given to hasty and ill-considered decisions. Afterwards, in calmer mood, he'd often enough change his mind, but there are some things you can't easily undo. Defection is one of them.

Sergei's love affair with a Canadian ice-star fizzled out and he found himself stranded. There had been offers of work in America, however, and total freedom was still something of a heady experience. Coaching an ice-troupe in New York, he met Elizabeth Fallon, a British journalist in the USA on assignment, and they fell in love. They had a whirlwind engagement and got married; she arranged work for him in London; Michael J. Simmons had been born in Hampstead nine months to the day after the first meeting of his parents in a wild Serbian restaurant in Greenwich Village.

Seven years later on the 29th October 1962, a day or so after Khruschev had backed out of Cuba, Sergei walked into the Russian embassy and didn't come back out. At least, not when anyone was watching. His elderly parents had been writing to him from a village just outside Moscow, where they'd been having less than a grand time of it; Sergei had been in a mood of depression over his marriage, which had been coming apart for some time; his belated double-defection was another typically hasty decision to go home and see what could be recovered from the wreckage. Elizabeth Simmons (she had always insisted on the English version of the name) said, "good riddance, and I hope they send him where there's plenty of ice!" And it later turned out that "they" did just that. In the autumn of 1964, the week before Jazz's ninth birthday, his mother got word from the government department responsible that Sergei Simonov had been shot dead after killing a guard during an attempted escape from a prison labour camp near Tura on the Siberian Tunguska.

She cried a few tears, for the good times, and then got on with it. Jazz, on the other hand . . .

Jazz had loved his father very much. That dark, handsome man who used to speak to him alternately in two languages, who taught him to skate and ski even as a small child, and spoke so vividly of his vast homeland as to seed in him a deep-rooted and abiding interest in all things Russian—an interest which had lasted even to this day. He had spoken bitterly of the injustices of the system, too, but that had been in the main beyond Jazz's youthful understanding. Now, however, at the age of only nine years, his father's words had come back to him, had assumed real importance and significance in his mind, conflicting with his thirst for knowledge. The father Jazz had loved and always known would return was dead, and the Russia Sergei Simonov had loved was his murderer. From that time forward Jazz's interest became centered not so much in the sweeping grandeur and the peoples of his father's homeland as in its oppressions.

Jazz had attended a private school since before he was five and his special subject, requiring private tuition as well as his father's constant guidance, was of course Russian. By the time he was twelve it was obvious that he had a linguist's grasp of the language, which proved to be the case when he obtained almost 100 per cent marks in a specially set examination. He attended university and at seventeen held a first in Russian; by the time he was twenty he'd added to this a second in Mathematics, a subject towards which his brilliantly clear mind had always leaned. Only a year later his mother died from leukemia; uninterested in an academic career, he took a job as an industrial interpreter/translator. After that all of his spare time was spent in winter sports, which he would pursue world-wide wherever the climate and whenever the financial situation permitted. There were several girlfriends, none of them serious affairs.

Then, holidaying in the Harz when he was twenty-three, Jazz had met a British Army Major on a Winter Warfare course. This new friend was a member of the Intelligence Corps serving in BAOR and the meeting proved to be a big turning point. A year later Jazz was in Berlin as an NCO of that same low-profile corps. But Berlin and BRIXMIS hadn't suited him, and by then the Secret Service had its eye on him anyway and didn't want him over-exposed; he was field agent material and should now start to learn the real tricks of the trade. His demobilization was arranged, as would be the next six years of his life, all greatly to Michael J. Simmons's satisfaction.

From then on it had been training, and training, and more training. He trained in surveillance, close protection, escape and evasion, winter warfare, survival, weapons handling (up to marksman), demolition and unarmed combat. The only thing they couldn't give him was experience . . .

Jazz had been all set to fly to Moscow as a "diplomatic interpreter" when Pill came up, or "went down" as the CIA had it. His original task was reassigned (it had in any case been little more than a training exercise) and he was given Operation Pill. The Service had been setting it up ever since the Soviets got the Perchorsk Projekt underway, and "local services" were all well established and in full working order. Jazz was briefed from head to heels, went out to Moscow 2nd Class as Henry Parsons, an ordinary tourist, got issued with his Russian ID within an hour of de-planing. An intelligence agent already in the USSR would assume his Parsons identity (along with his passport, etc.) and use his return flight back to London. "One in, one out, and shake it all about!" as Jazz's Chief Briefing Officer had explained. "Like the hokey-cokey except there are no left feet, only right ones."

24

Jazz hadn't known much about the Moscow end of the network; he'd been deliberately kept in the dark on that, just in case. Ditto for the Magnitogorsk set-up, which had a line on shipments by rail destined for the Perchorsk Projekt. He hadn't quite been able to figure out why his DO should feel peeved that he didn't know more about these things. That was definitely the impression that came over: that even though he'd given as much detail as he could, still the DO would have liked him to have known more. But the simple fact was that all of that stuff had been on a need-to-know basis, and Jazz hadn't needed to know.

As for "local services": he'd known all about them! And during the many debriefing sessions, Jazz had told everything.

Back in the 1950s Khruschev had broken up a politically suspect pocket of Ukranian Jewish peasants and "resettled" them from an area near Kiev to the eastern slopes and valleys of the upper Urals. Maybe he'd hoped the cold would kill them off. There they'd been allocated land and a work quota. The business: logging, and in winter trapping, all generally to be carried out under the supervision and guidance of old-guard "Komsomol" officials from the West Siberian oil and natural gas fields. It wasn't quite a forced labour camp, but in the beginning it wasn't a hell of a lot better.

But the Ukranian dissidents were a funny lot; they stuck it out, filled their quotas, made a going concern of it and actually settled the district. Their success, coupled with the rapid expansion of the far more important oil and natural gas industries in the east, made strict control of the Jewish settlements unwieldy, even unnecessary. Their overseers had better things to do. It could plainly be seen how a previously untamed region was now productive of timber and skins, making good use of natural assets and giving work to the people; Khruschev's ploy had apparently worked, making good conscientious Russian citizens from what had been an idle pack of troublesome political pariahs. He should have been so lucky in other fields! Anyway, visits from controlling officialdom fell off in direct proportion to the scheme's success.

In fact, all the Jews had wanted was a little peace to follow their own whims and ways of life. The climate might change but they never would. There in their logging camps at the foot of the mountains they were now more or less content. At least they were not pestered and there was always more than enough left over to make the living good. Hard but good. They had all the timber they needed to build with in the summers and burn through the winters, meat aplenty, all the vegetables they could grow for themselves, even a growing fund of roubles from forbidden trading in furs. There was a little gold in the streams, for which they prospected and panned, occasionally with some success; the hunting and fishing were good, flexible work rosters ensured a fair distribution of labour, and everyone had a share in what was available of "prosperity" and the good things of life. Even the cold worked in their favour: it kept busybodies out and interference to a minimum.

Several of the settlers were of Romanian stock with strong family ties in the Old Country. Their political views were not in accord with Mother Russia's. Nor would they ever be—not until all oppression was removed and people could work and worship in their own way, and restrictions lifted so that they might emigrate at will. They were Jews and they were Ukranians who thought of themselves as Romanians, and given freedom of choice they might also have been Russians. But mainly they were people of the world and belonged to no one but themselves. Their children were brought up with the same beliefs and aspirations.

In short, while many of the resettled families were simple peasants of no distinct political persuasion, there were a good many in the new villages and camps who were anti-Communist and budding, even active fifth-columnists. They clung to their Romanian links and contacts, and similar groups in Romania had well-established links with the West.

Mikhail Simonov—fully documented as a city-bred hothead and troublemaker, who'd been given the choice of becoming a pioneering Komsomol, or else—had gone to just such a family, the Kirescus of Yelizinka village, for employment as a lumberjack. Only old man Kazimir Kirescu himself, and his oldest son, Yuri, knew Jazz's real purpose there at the foot of the Urals, and they covered for him to give him as much free time as possible. He was "prospecting" or "hunting" or "fishing"—but Kazimir and Yuri had known that in actual fact he was spying. And they'd also known what he was after, his mission: to discover the secret of the experimental military base down in the heart of the Perchorsk ravine.

"You're not only risking your neck, you're wasting your time," the old man had told Jazz gruffly one night shortly after he took up lodgings with the Kirescus. Jazz remembered that night well; Anna Kirescu and her daughter Tassi had gone off to a women's meeting in the village, and Yuri's younger brother Kaspar was in bed asleep. It had been a good time for their first important talk.

"You don't have to go there to know what's going on in that place," Kazimir had continued. "Yuri and I can tell you that, all right, as could most of the people in these parts if they'd a mind to."

"A weapon!" his great, lumbering, giant-hearted son, Yuri, had put in, winking and nodding his massive shaggy head. "A weapon like no one ever saw before, or ever could imagine, to make the Soviets strong over all other people. They built it down there in the ravine, and they tested it—and it went wrong!"

Old Kazimir had grunted his agreement, spitting in the fire for good measure and for emphasis. "Just a

27

little over two years ago—'' he said, gazing into the heart of the flames where they roared up the sprawling cabin's stone chimney, ''—but we'd known something was in the offing for weeks before that. We'd heard the machinery running, do you see? The big engines that power the thing.''

"That's right," Yuri had taken up the story again. "The big turbines under the dam. I remember them being installed more than four years ago, before they put that lead roof on the thing. Even then they'd restricted all hunting and fishing in the area of the old pass, but I used to go there anyway. When they built that dam—why, the fish *swarmed* in that artificial lake! It was worth a clout and a telling-off if you got caught there. But about the turbines: *hah!* I was stupid enough then to think maybe they were going to give *us* the electricity. We still don't have it . . . but what did they need all that power for, eh?'' And he'd tapped the side of his nose.

"Anyway," his father continued, "it's so still on certain nights in these parts that a shout or the bark of a dog will carry for miles. So did the sound of those turbines when they first started to use them. Despite the fact that they were down in the ravine, you could hear their whining and droning right here in the village. As for the power they produced, that's easy: they used it for all of their mining and tunnelling, for their electric drills and rock-cutting tools, their lights and their blasting devices. Oh, and for their heating and their comfort, too, no doubt, while here in Yelizinka we burned logs. But they must have taken thousands of tons of rock out of that ravine, so that God only knows—you'll forgive me—what sort of warrens they've burrowed under the mountain!''

Then it had been Yuri's turn again: "And that's where they built the weapon—under the mountain! Then came the time when they tested it. My father and me, we'd been setting a few traps and were late getting

28

home that night. I remember it clearly: it was a night much like tonight, bright and clear. Where it was darkest in the woods, we could look through the treetops and see *aurora borealis* shimmering like a strange pale curtain in the northern sky . . .

"The humming of the turbines was the loudest it had ever been, so that the air seemed to throb with it. But it was a distant throbbing, you understand, for of course the Projekt is about ten kilometres from here. My father and me, we were somewhere in the middle, maybe four or five kilometres from the source. Anyway, that should give you some sort of idea of the raw power they were drawing from the river."

"At the top of Grigor's Crest," Kazimir took up the thread, "we stopped and looked back. A wash of light, like the aurora, was playing all along the rim of the Perchorsk ravine. Now, I was one of the first men to settle this place—one of the first victims of Khruschev's scheme, you might say—and in all those years I'd seen nothing like this. It wasn't nature, no, it was the machine, the weapon! Then—" he shook his head, momentarily lost for words, "—what happened next was awesome!"

At this point Yuri had grown excited and once again took over. "The turbines had wound themselves up to a high pitch of whining," he said. "Suddenly . . . it seemed there was a great gasp or sigh! A beam of light—no, a *tube* of light, like a great brilliant cylinder—shot up from the ravine, lit up the peaks bright as day, went bounding into the sky. But fast?—lightning is slow by comparison! That's how it seemed, anyway. It was a *pulse* of light; you didn't actually see it, just its after-image burning on your eyeballs. And in the next moment it was gone, fired like a rocket into space. Lightning in reverse. A laser? A giant searchlight? No, nothing like that—it had been more nearly solid."

At that Jazz had smiled, but not old Kazimir. "Yuri is right!" he'd declared. "It was a clear night when this

29

happened, but within the hour clouds boiled up out of nowhere and it rained warm rain. Then there blew a hot wind, like the breath of some beast, outwards from the mountains. And in the morning birds came down out of the peaks and high passes to die. Thousands of them! Animals, too! No beam of simple light, no matter how powerful, can do all that. And that's not all, for right after they'd tested it—after the bar of light shot up into the sky—then there came that smell of burning. Of electrical burning, you know? Ozone, maybe? And after that we heard their sirens."

"Sirens?" Jazz had been especially interested. "From the Projekt?"

"Of course, where else?" Kazimir had answered. "Their alert sirens, their alarms! There'd been an accident, a big one. Oh, we heard rumours. And during the next two or three weeks . . . helicopters flying in and out, ambulances on the new road, men in radiation suits decontaminating the walls of the ravine. And the word was this: blow-back! The weapon had discharged itself into the sky, all right—but it had also backfired into the cavern that housed it. It was like an incinerator; it melted rock, brought the roof down, nearly took the lid off the whole place! They took a lot of dead out of there over the next week or so. Since then it hasn't been tried again."

"Now?" Yuri had had to have the last word. He shrugged his massive shoulders. "They run the turbines now and then, if only to keep 'em in trim; but as my father says, the weapon's been quiet. No more testing. Maybe they learned something from that first trial, and maybe it was something they'd rather not know. Myself, I reckon they know they can't control it. I reckon they're finished with it. Except that doesn't explain why they're still there, why they haven't dismantled everything and cleared off."

At which Jazz had nodded, saying: "Well, that's one of the things I'm here to find out. See, a lot of very important, very intelligent men in the West are worried about the Perchorsk Projekt. And the more I learn about it, the more I believe they have good reason to be . . .''

One night when they gave Jazz his pills, he didn't take them. He pretended to, stuck them in a corner of his mouth, drank his water without washing them down. It was partly an act of rebellion—against what amounted to physical, even mental imprisonment, however well-intended—and partly something else. He needed time to think. That was the one thing he never seemed to have enough of: time to think. He was always either asleep or taking pills to *put* him to sleep, in pain or dopey from the needle that killed the pain and helped him talk to the Debriefing Officer, but never left alone to just lie there and think.

Maybe they didn't want him to think. Which made him wonder: *why* didn't they want him to think? His body might be a bit banged-up, but there didn't seem a deal wrong with his brain.

When he was alone (after he'd heard them go out of his room and close the door) he turned his head a little on one side and spat the pills out. They left a bad taste, but nothing he couldn't live with. If the pain came he could always ring his bell; the button was right there beside his free right hand, requiring only a touch from his index finger.

But the pain didn't come, and neither did sleep, and at last Jazz was able to just lie there and think. Better still, in a little while his thinking grew far less fuzzy; indeed, in comparison to the mental slurry he'd recently been accustomed to, it became like crystal. And he began to ask himself all over again those questions he *had* been asking, but which he'd never found the time to answer. Like:

Where the hell were his friends?

He'd been out of Russia . . . what, two weeks now? And the only people he'd seen (or rather, the only ones

31

who'd seen him) were a doctor, a DO, and a nurse who grunted a little but never spoke. But he did have *friends* in the Service. Surely they would know he was back. Why hadn't they been to see him? Was he *that* banged-up? Did he look *that* bad?

"I don't feel that bad," Jazz whispered to himself.

He moved his right arm, clenched his right fist. The hole through his wrist had healed and new skin had knitted over the punctures front and back. It was pure luck that the point of the ice axe had slipped between the bones and managed to miss the arteries. The hand was a little stiff and out of practice, that was all. There was some pain, but nothing he couldn't survive. Come to think of it, there wasn't much of pain in anything right now. But of course he couldn't move everything— could he? Jazz decided he'd better not try.

What about sight? Would his room be in light or darkness? The "snow" of his bandages was thick and dark. They said they'd saved his sight. From what? Had his eyes been hanging out or something? "Saved his sight" could mean anything. That he'd be able to see for instance—but how well?"

Suddenly, for the first time since he'd been here, he knew real panic. They might have kept something back until he'd been fully debriefed, so as not to discourage or distract him: where there's life there's hope, sort of thing. How about that? What if they hadn't told him everything?

Jazz got a grip on himself, gave a derisive snort. *Huh!* Told him everything? Christ, they hadn't told *him* anything! He was the one who'd been doing all the—

Talking . . .

His new clarity of mind was leading him in a frightening new direction, and it was all downhill going; the more he considered the possibilities, the faster he went and the more frightening it got; bits of a puzzle he hadn't known existed until now were starting to fall into place. And the picture they made was one of a clown, a puppet, with his name on it. Michael J. Simmons: dupe!

He bent his right elbow, lifted his hand to his bandaged head, began picking at the bandages where they covered his eyes. But carefully; he only needed a peephole, nothing more than that. A narrow gap between strips of bandage. He wanted to see without being seen.

In a little while he believed he'd succeeded. It was hard to tell with any degree of certainty. The snow was still there, but if he narrowed his eyes to slits the light (there wasn't a lot of it) became more nearly natural. It was like when he was a child: he'd used to lie in bed with his eyes slitted, simulating the slow, regular breathing of sleep. His mother would come in and put the light on, stand there looking at him, and she was never quite sure if he was asleep or awake. But now, with these bandages swathing his face, it should be so much easier.

He straightened his arm again, found his button and pressed it. Now his nurse would know he was still awake, but the principle would be the same: when she came in he'd be able to look at her and she wouldn't know it. He hoped!

In a little while soft, unhurried footsteps sounded. Jazz pressed his head back into his pillows, waited in the near-darkness of his room. Around him the air-conditioning hummed faintly; the air had a mildly antiseptic smell; his sheets felt somehow coarse to those parts of his body which were exposed. And he thought:

It doesn't feel like a room in a hospital. Hospitals feel artificial, unreal, at best. But this one feels like fake artificial . . .

Then the door opened and the light came on.

Jazz squinted straight up; only the fact that his eyes were shuttered saved them from dazzle from the naked light bulb where it hung on its flex from the ceiling. As for that ceiling itself: that was of dark grey stone, pocked from blasting and patterned with folded, tightly packed strata. Jazz's hospital room was a man-made cave, or at least it was part of one!

Too stunned to move, he lay there frozen as his nurse came to the side of his bed. Then, fighting the anger and revulsion he felt welling inside, he slowly turned his head to look at her. She scarcely glanced at him, merely reached down to feel his pulse. She was short and fat, wore her hair straight and short-cropped, like a medieval knight, also wore the uniform and starched cap of a nurse. But not a British nurse. A Soviet nurse. And all of Jazz's worst fears were realized.

He felt her fingers on his wrist, at once snatched his hand away. She gasped, took a pace to the rear, and the heel of one of her square black shoes came down hard on something that crunched. She stood still, glanced at the floor, looked hard at Jazz and frowned. Her green eyes narrowed where they tried to penetrate the slit in his bandages. Maybe she saw the steely glint of his grey eyes in there; anyway, she gasped a second time and her hand flew to her mouth.

Then she went down on her knees, gathered up fragments of tablet, came upright with fury written right across her pudgy face. She glared at Jazz, turned on her heel and headed for the door. He let her get there, then called out: "Comrade?"

She paused instinctively, whirled and thrust out her jaw, glowered her hatred of the spy, then rushed out and slammed the door behind her. She had left the light on in her hurry to go and report all of this.

I have about two minutes before things start to warm up, Jazz thought. *I suppose I'd better put them to some use.*

He looked to his left, his alleged "dead" side, and saw a deep saucer of pale yellow fluid standing on a bedside table. Inclining his head and stretching his neck as far as he could in that direction, he inhaled deeply, smelled a strong antiseptic odour. How easy it was to create a hospital atmosphere: rubber tiles on the floor to deaden footfalls, a saucer of TCP for the too-clean smell, and a constant flow of sterile, temperate air. Simple as that.

The walls of Jazz's room (his cell?) were of corrugated metal sheets bolted to vertical steel stanchions. There'd be laminated padding, too, Jazz supposed, to keep the room soundproofed and isolated. Or it could be the case that in fact this entire area *was* a hospital, built to serve the staff of the Projekt. After the Perchorsk Incident, they'd probably decided it was advisable. A hospital area would be handy for periodic check-ups and would probably be situated alongside a decontamination facility—assuming, that is, that there was still an atomic pile down here. Back in the West they were pretty sure that there had been one. Anyway, Jazz had already spotted an excess-radiation warning device on the wall; at present it was green, with just a tinge of pink showing in the aperture.

The uneven rock ceiling was maybe nine feet high on average; it looked very hard stuff and there were no fractures, not even small ones, that Jazz could see. Still (and even taking into account the massive steel stanchions) he felt just a touch of claustrophobia, something of the enormous weight of a mountain pressing down on him. For by now there was no doubt at all in his mind but that that was where he was: under the Urals.

Running footsteps sounded and the door was thrown open. Jazz lifted his head as far as restrictions would allow and stared at the people who came panting into the room. Two men, and behind them the fat nurse. Hot on their heels came a third man; his white smock and the hypodermic in his hand gave him away at once: Jazz's favourite pulse-feeler, the clucking doctor. Well, and maybe now he'd have something worth clucking about.

"Mike, my boy!" the man in front, dressed in casual civilian clothes, motioned the others back. He approached the bed alone, said: "And what's all this that Nursie's been telling us? What? You didn't take your pills? Why ever not? Wouldn't they go down?'' The ingratiating voice was that of Jazz's DO.

Jazz nodded stiffly. "That's right, 'old boy,' " he answered harshly, "they sort of stuck in my craw.'' He lifted his right hand and tugged at his fake bandages, tore them from his eyes. He stared at the four where they stood frozen as if they were insects trapped in amber.

After a moment the doctor muttered something in Russian, took an impatient pace forward and gave his needle a brief squirt. The second man into the room, also dressed casually, caught his arm and dragged him to a halt. "No," Chingiz Khuv told the doctor curtly, in Russian. "Can't the two of you see that he knows? Since he's awake, aware and with all his wits about him, let's keep him that way. Anyway, I want to talk to him. He's all mine now.''

"No," Jazz told him, staring straight at him. "I'm all mine—now! If you want to speak to me you'd better let him dope me up. It's the only way I'm going to do any talking.''

Khuv smiled, stepped right up to the bed and looked down on Jazz. "Oh, you've already talked enough, Mr. Simmons," he said, without a trace of malice. "Quite enough, I assure you. Anyway, I don't intend to *ask* you anything. I intend to tell you a few things, and maybe show you a few things. And that's all.''

"Oh?" said Jazz.

"Oh, yes, really. In fact I'm going to tell you the things you most want to know: all about the Perchorsk Projekt. What we were attempting to do here, and what we actually did. Would you like that?''

"Very much," said Jazz. "And what is it you're going to show me? The place where you make your bloody monsters?''

Khuv's eyes narrowed, but then he smiled again. And he nodded. "Something like that," he said. "Except there's one thing you should know right from the start: we don't make them.''

"Oh, but you do!'' Jazz also nodded. "That's one thing we're pretty sure about. This is the source. This is where it was born—or spawned.''

Khuv's expression didn't change. "You're wrong,'' he said. "But that's only to be expected, for you only know half the story—so far. It *came* from here, yes, but it wasn't born here. No, it was born in a different world entirely.'' He sat down on Jazz's bed, stared at him intently. "It strikes me you're a survivor, Mr. Simmons.''

Jazz couldn't resist a snort of derision. "Am I going to survive this one?''

"Maybe you will at that.'' Khuv's smile was very genuine now, as if in anticipation of something quite delicious. "First we must get you up on your feet again and show you round the place, and then—''

Jazz moved his head enquiringly.

"And then . . . then we'll see just what sort of a survivor you really are.''

Chapter Three
The Perchorsk Projekt

THE COMPLEX BUILT INTO THE BASE OF THE RIVEN MOUN-tain at the bottom of the Perchorsk ravine was vast, and it wasn't without a degree of Russian pride in achievement that Chingiz Khuv took Michael J. Simmons on a tour of inspection—but neither did Khuv lack respect for Jazz's considerable talent for destruction. On their walkabouts, the British agent was literally strait-jacketed in a garment which effectively disabled him from the waist up, and as if that weren't enough Karl Vyotsky was invariably present, surly bodyguard to his KGB boss.

"Blame all of this on the technology-gap, if you must have any sort of scapegoat at all," Khuv told the British agent. "The Americans with their microchips, spy-satellites, complicated and oh-so-clever electronic listening systems. I mean, where's the security if they can tap-in on any phone call anywhere in the whole wide world, eh? And these are only a handful of the ways in which sensitive information may be obtained. The art of spying," (a sideways glance at Jazz, but without enmity) "takes a great many forms and encompasses some formidable, one might even say terrifying talents. On both sides, I mean, East and West alike. High-tech on the one hand, and the supernatural on the other."

"The supernatural?" Jazz raised an enquiring eyebrow. "The Perchorsk Projekt looks solid enough to me. And anyway, I'm afraid I don't much believe in ghosts."

Khuv smiled and nodded. "I know," he said, "I know. We've checked on that—or perhaps you don't remember?"

Jazz looked blank for a moment, then frowned. Come to think of it, he did remember. It had been part of his "debriefing," but at the time he hadn't paid it a lot of attention. Actually, he'd thought his "DO" was pulling his leg: to ask what he knew about INTESP, or E-Branch, which used Extra Sensory Perception as a tool for espionage. Indeed ESPionage! As it happened, Jazz had quite genuinely known nothing at all about it, and he probably wouldn't have believed it even if he had.

"If telepathy was feasible," he told Khuv, "they wouldn't have needed to send me, would they? There wouldn't *be* any more secrets!"

"Quite right, quite right," Khuv answered after a moment's pause. "Those were my feelings exactly— once upon a time. And as you rightly point out, all of this," he waved an arm expansively about, "is obviously solid enough."

"All of this" was the gymnasium area, where for the past week Jazz had been getting himself back in shape following the fortnight he'd spent on his back. The fact that they'd so easily emptied him of all he had known still didn't sit too well with him. Here, as they paused a while to let Karl Vyotsky strip off his pullover and work out for a few minutes with the weights, Jazz thought he'd try a little pumping of his own.

He had no doubt that whatever questions he put to Khuv, they'd be answered in a truthful, straightforward manner. In this respect the KGB Major was entirely disarming. But on the other hand, why shouldn't he be open? He had nothing to lose. He knew that Jazz wasn't going anywhere outside of this place, ever. He'd known that right from square one. That's the way *they* had it figured out, anyway.

"You surprise me," he said, "complaining about American know-how. I was supposed to be about 75 per cent proof against brainwashing, but you pulled my plug and I just gurgled away. No torture, not even a threat, and I'm pentathol-resistant—but I couldn't hold a thing back! How the hell did you do that?"

Khuv glanced at him, went back to watching Vyotsky handling weights as if they were made of papier-maché. Jazz looked at Vyotsky, too.

Khuv's underling was huge: seventy-five inches and a little over two hundred pounds, and all of it muscle. He hardly seemed to have any neck at all, and his chest was like a barrel expanding out of his narrow waist. His thighs were round and tight inside light-blue trousers. He felt Jazz's eyes on him, grinned through his black beard and flexed biceps that would shame a bear. "You'd like to work out with me, British?" He finished his exercises and dropped the weights clanging to the floor. "Bare-fisted, maybe, in the ring?"

"Just say the word, Ivan," Jazz answered, half-smiling, his voice low. "I still owe you for a couple of teeth, remember?"

Vyotsky showed his own teeth again, but not in a grin, and put on his pullover. Khuv turned to Jazz, said: "Don't push your luck with Karl, my friend. He can give you twenty pounds and ten years of experience. On top of which he has some ugly little habits. When we caught you on that mountain he knocked your teeth out, yes, but believe me you were lucky. He wanted to pull your head off. And it's possible he could do it, with a little effort. I might even have let him try, except that would have been a terrible waste, and we've already had enough of that around here."

They began to walk again, passed through the gymnasium and out into a room containing a small swimming pool. The pool wasn't tiled; it had simply been blasted out of the bedrock along a natural fault. Here, where the uneven, veined ceiling was a little higher, several of the Projekt's staff were swimming in the pool's heated water; the room echoed to the slapping sounds of flesh on plastic as two women open-handed a ball to and fro between them. A thin, balding man was practicing jack-knives from a springboard.

"As for your 'debriefing,' " said Khuv, shrugging, "well, there's high-tech and there's high-tech. The West has its miniaturization, its superb electronics, and we have our—"

"Bulgarian chemists?" Jazz cut him short. The tiled walkway at the side of the pool was wet and his feet were slipping; he stumbled, and Vyotsky caught his arm in a powerful grip, steadied him. Jazz cursed under his breath. "Do you know how uncomfortable it is walking round in this thing?" He was talking about his strait-jacket.

"A necessary precaution," said Khuv. "I'm sorry, but it really is for the best. Most of the people here aren't armed. They're scientists, not soldiers. Soldiers guard the approaches to the Projekt, certainly, but their barracks are elsewhere; not far away, but not here. There are some soldiers here, as you'll see, but they are specialists. And so, if you were to get loose—" again his shrug. "You might do a lot of damage before you met up with someone like Karl here."

At the end of the pool they passed out through another door into a gently curving corridor which Jazz recognized as the perimeter. That was what they called it, "the perimeter": a metal-clad, rubber-floored tunnel which enclosed the entire complex about its middle level. From the perimeter, doors led inwards into all the Projekt's many areas. There were still a few doors Jazz hadn't been through, the ones which required special security access. He'd seen the living areas, hospital, recreation rooms, dining hall and some of the laboratories, but not the machine itself, if there was such a beast. Khuv had promised him, however, that today he was to visit "the guts" of the place.

Khuv led the way, Jazz following, with Vyotsky bringing up the rear. People came and went around them, dressed in lab smocks, overalls; some with millboards and notes, others carrying pieces of machinery or instruments. The place could easily be some high-tech factory anywhere in the world. As Jazz and his escort proceeded, so Khuv said:

"You asked me about your debriefing. Well, you're right about our Bulgarian friends: they really have a knack for brewing potent stuff—and of course I'm not just talking about their wine. The pills were to cause you pain; they cramp muscles, heighten sensitivity. The shots are part truth-drug, part sedative. They have the effect of making you susceptible to suggestion. It's not so much that you can't refuse, more that you're far more likely to believe—anything that we tell you! Your Debriefing Officer not only speaks very good English, but he's a top-rank psychologist, too. So don't blame yourself that you let your side down. You really had no choice. You thought you were home and dry, and that you were only doing your duty."

Jazz merely grunted for reply. His face was void of emotion, which was the way he'd kept it most of the time since discovering he'd been duped.

"Of course," Khuv continued, "your own British, er, 'chemists' are rather clever men in their own right. That capsule in your mouth, for instance: we weren't able to analyse its contents here at the Projekt. Hardly surprising; we aren't equipped with a full range of analytical facilities—that's not what the Perchorsk Projekt is about—but even so we were at least able to conclude that your little tooth capsule contained a remarkably complex substance. That's why we've sent it to Moscow. Who can say, maybe there's something in it we can use, eh?"

While he spoke to Jazz, Khuv kept glancing back at

him, checking him up and down as he'd done so often during the course of the past few weeks. He saw a man only thirty years of age, upon whose shoulders his secret service masters in the West had placed an awesome weight of responsibility. They obviously respected his abilities. And yet for all Simmons's training, his physical and mental fitness, still he was inexperienced. Then again, how "experienced" can a field agent in the secret service be? Every mission was a flip of a coin: heads you win, and tails . . . you lose your head? Or as the British agent himself might have it, a game of Russian roulette.

For all Simmons's expertise in his many subjects, still they were only theoretical skills, as yet untested under "battle" conditions. For on his very first assignment the dice had rolled against him, the cylinder had clicked into position with its bullet directly under the firing pin. Unfortunate for Michael J. Simmons, but *extremely* fortunate for Chingiz Khuv.

Again the KGB Major's dark jewel eyes rested on Simmons. The Englishman stood just a fraction under six feet tall, maybe a half-inch less than Khuv himself. During the time he'd spent in his role as a logger he'd grown a red beard to match his unruly shock of hair. That had gone now, revealing a square jaw and slightly hollow cheeks. He'd be a little underweight, too, for apparently the British liked their agents lean and hungry. A fat man doesn't run as fast as a thin one, and he makes a much easier target.

For all that he was young, Simmons's brow was deeply lined from frowning; even taking into account his present circumstances, he did not seem a particularly happy man, or even one who'd ever been especially happy. His eyes were keen, grey, penetrating; his teeth (with the exception of the ones Karl had removed) were in good order, strong, square and white; about his sturdy neck he wore a small plain cross on a silver chain, which was his only item of jewellery. He had hands which were hard for all that they were long and tapered, and arms which seemed a little long, giving him a sort of gangling or gawky appearance. But Khuv was well aware that appearances can be deceptive. Simmons was a skilled athlete and his brain was a fine one.

They reached an area of the perimeter Jazz had not seen before. Here the coming and going of staff was far less frequent, and as the three turned the curve of the long corridor so a security door had come into view, blocking it entirely. On the approach to this door the ceiling and walls were burned black; great blisters were evident in the paintwork; closer to the door the very rock of the ceiling appeared to have melted, run down like wax and solidified on the cool metal of the artificial walls. The rubber floor tiles had burned right through to naked metal plates, which were buckled out of alignment. It seemed somehow paradoxical that a Russian Army flame-thrower stood on a shelf against the exterior wall, clamped in position there. In surroundings like these Jazz might well have expected a fire extinguisher—but a flame-thrower? He made a mental note to ask about it later, but right now:

"The Perchorsk Incident," he said, watching Khuv for his reaction.

"Correct." The Russian's expression didn't change. He faced Jazz eye to eye. "Now we are going to take that strait-jacket off you. The reason is simple: down in the lower levels you will need some freedom of movement. I don't want you to fall and hurt yourself. However, should you attempt anything foolish, Karl has my permission—indeed he has my instructions—to hurt you severely. Also I should tell you that if you got lost down there, you could well find yourself in an area of high radioactivity. Eventually we may get around to decontaminating all the hotspots, but it's unlikely. Why should we when we won't have cause to use those areas again? And so, depending on how long it took you to surrender, or how long it took us to flush you out, you would almost certainly jeopardize your health—perhaps even fatally. Do you understand?''

Jazz nodded. ''But do you really think I'd be stupid enough to make a run for it? Where to, for God's sake!?''

''As I explained before,'' Khuv reminded him while Vyotsky unfastened the restraining straps on his straitjacket, ''we aren't too concerned that you'll try to escape. That would be sheer suicide, and you no longer have reasons to wish to die—if you ever did. What we are concerned about is the damage you might do, maybe even large-scale sabotage. And that could have very grave consequences indeed. Not only for everyone here, but for the entire world!''

For once Jazz's expression changed. He slanted his mouth into a humourless smile, laughed gratingly. ''A bit melodramatic, aren't we, Comrade? I think maybe you've been watching too many decadent James Bond films!''

''Do you?'' said Khuv, his slightly slanted eyes narrowing a fraction and becoming that much brighter. ''Do you indeed?''

He took a key from his pocket, turned to the heavy metal door. It was equipped with a lock set centrally in a steel hand-wheel, like a locking device on a bank vault. As Khuv went to insert his key, so the wheel turned through quarter of a circle and the edges of the door cracked open. Khuv stepped back. Someone was coming through from the other side.

The door opened fully toward the three where they waited, and a handful of technicians and two men dressed in smart civilian clothes came through. One of the two was fat, beaming, jovial: a VIP visitor from Moscow. The other, grave-faced, was small and thin; his face was badly scarred and the hair was absent from the left half of his face and yellow-veined skull. Jazz had seen him before; he was Viktor Luchov, Direktor

45

of the Perchorsk Projekt—a survivor of Perchorsk Incidents One and Two.

Brief greetings were exchanged between Khuv and these two men, and then the larger party went on its way. Then Jazz and his escorts passed through the door and Khuv locked it behind them.

Beyond the door the complex took on an entirely different aspect. By comparison, the damage on the approach to this area had been superficial. Jazz stared and tried to make sense of the chaos he saw there. The evidence of terrific heat was apparent everywhere: stanchions were blackened and in places eaten half-way through; the floor-plates were missing entirely, had been replaced with timbers; the face of the exterior rock wall—literally the mountain itself—was black, dull and lumpy, like lava frozen in its course. A metal chair or desk—difficult to tell which—and a steel cabinet projected in twisted ruin half out of a massive nodule of lava which was in turn welded to the wall; and above this anomalous nodule a cylindrical shaft maybe twelve feet in diameter had been drilled through the rock upwards at an angle of forty-five degrees, from the lip of which the lava could be seen in large part to have issued.

Jazz looked again at the dark throat of the shaft, wondered how it could have been cut and where it went. He reached up a hand to touch the side of the rim where the shaft opened into the corridor; the rock was smooth as glass, not lumpy like the volcanic flow from the shaft's lip . . . Aware that Khuv was watching him, Jazz shot him an inquisitive glance.

"I'm told that used to have a square cross-section, whose sides were something less than two metres," Khuv informed. "Also that it was lined with a perfect mirror of a very high density glass on impervious ceramic, giving almost 100 per cent reflectivity. After what you have termed the Perchorsk Incident, this is what remained of the shaft. I suppose you might say that this is what comes of trying to pass a round peg through a square hole, eh?" And before Jazz could answer: "Of course, I wasn't here when this happened. You see, I have my own job, Michael—you'll forgive my familiarity?—with a branch of the Service whose work you would find entirely unbelievable. It is that E-Branch of which we've already spoken."

Jazz said nothing, continued to glance all about, tried to take in all he was seeing and hearing. What good that would do him, he couldn't say, but it was all part of his training. "E-Branch, yes, Michael," Khuv went on. "You English have an E-Branch, too, you know—which is why we were so interested to know if you were a member of that organization. If you had been—" he shrugged "—then we would have been obliged to dispose of you from the outset."

Jazz raised his customary eyebrow.

"Oh, yes," said Khuv, casually, "for we couldn't allow you to transmit—neither telepathically nor any other way—knowledge of this place to the outside world. That, too, could be very dangerous; so much so that it might even conceivably bring about World War III!"

"More melodramatics," Jazz murmured.

Khuv sighed deeply. "You will understand—eventually," he said. "But first find yourself a place to sit for a while, and I'll tell you everything you were sent here to discover. You see, I actually *want* you to understand everything. You'll know why later."

Khuv perched himself on a knob of black rock while Jazz found a seat on the side of the steel cabinet where it leaned out of the lava nodule. Vyotsky remained standing, saying nothing, merely watching. The Projekt's air-conditioning whispered faintly, distantly, and apart from this and Khuv's voice, all was silent. Khuv spoke very softly and the effect was eerie: like a whisper echoing in some deeply buried alien vault.

"You must blame all you see here primarily on the USA's SDI or Star Wars scenario," he began. "Of

47

course, those terms hadn't been thought of as early as that, but the idea was there sure enough. We knew that much from standard intelligence sources. As for the Perchorsk Projekt: it was little more than a clever theory until America started dreaming up its space defence initiative. But after that it was the same old story: we had to have an even better defence system. As with bigger and better bombs, so with defence systems. If Star Wars could mean the loss of 95 per cent of our nuclear capability, then we had to have something which cancelled out the West's strike capability utterly.

"Perchorsk was to have been the first step, the proving ground. If it had worked, then similar installations would have been constructed all around Russia's borders. The satellite countries might perhaps have to fend for themselves in any future holocaust, but the Soviet heartland would be defended—completely! Do you follow me so far?"

Jazz cocked his head on one side. "You're telling me that this," he glanced here and there, all about, "wasn't intended as a weapon, right?"

"Exactly," Khuv nodded. "It was to have been the opposite of a weapon: a shield. An impenetrable umbrella over the head of the central Soviet Union. Ah! But now I see how interested you are; finally we have a little animation! Well, and should I proceed?"

"By all means," said Jazz at once. "Do go on."

Khuv settled into his story:

"Don't ask me about the mechanics of the thing; I'm a—well, a 'policeman,' not a physicist! Franz Ayvaz was the brains and driving force behind Perchorsk, and Viktor Luchov was his second-in-command. Ayvaz, as you may already know, was our top man in Particle Beam Acceleration and various associated fields of research; in his younger days he'd been a leading pioneer of laser technology; his credentials were impeccable, and his theory—on paper at least—seemed to be exactly what the defence staff was looking for. A dual-purpose force-field to shut out incoming missiles and render their nuclear capacity entirely harmless.

"That's how the Perchorsk Projekt was born five years ago, and this is where it died three years later. Ayvaz died with it, and Luchov is still here gathering information, piecing it all together and seeing if there's anything that can be salvaged. As to what happened exactly:

"What was *supposed* to happen was this:

"A beam was to be generated down below in the lower levels. That's where most of the hardware used to be. Accelerated to the limits of tolerance and excited by atomic bombardment, it would be released up this shaft and emitted like an enormous laser into the ravine. Where the shaft emerged into the ravine, a nest of mirrors would divide the beam into a fan shape which would be waved across the sky and into space. It was to be a test, that's all. The very first of a series.

"Alas, there was a failure in the motors which governed the movement of the exterior mirrors. They jammed in the worst possible position at the worst possible moment. Also, the scientists here had been under pressure; their work had been hurried and performed in conditions which weren't the best; a full range of failsafe devices had not been incorporated. Do you know what happens, Michael, if you plug the barrel of a gun, load it and pull the trigger? But ridiculous to ask a question like that of a man who is an expert in firearms! Of course you know what happens.

"Well, and that's what happened here. There was a colossal blow-back. Energies sufficient to fill an arc of space covering from Afghanistan to Franz Josef Land were trapped and confined within the shaft and redirected back to their source. There was a collision of awesome forces, the instantaneous generation of incredible temperatures, and in the immediate vicinity of the beam matter itself underwent some radical changes. Now of course that is my non-technical layman's explanation. You will need to talk to Luchov if you want more—but I guarantee you wouldn't understand him. Not unless there's a lot more to you than we've discovered, anyway.

"So . . . that was the Perchorsk Incident, or 'pi' as your people in the West have christened it. The shambles you see here is not one hundredth part of the devastation which occurred down below, where we'll be going in a moment. And as for loss of life: we paid a terrible toll for our haste, Michael, a terrible toll. But not so terrible as the toll we may still have to pay . . ."

With those enigmatic words still echoing, Khuv abruptly stood up. "Let's go deeper," his words were clipped, urgent, "right now! Two levels down, where perhaps you'll be able to get the feel of what it was really like." Jazz got to his feet and followed on, and once again Vyotsky formed their tail along the perimeter a little way, then down wide, heavy-beamed wooden stairs into what could only be termed a region of sheer fantasy.

With one hand lightly on the rail, Jazz stared into the dim recesses of a great disorder, a weird chaos. The lighting was poor here, perhaps deliberately so, for certainly what little could be seen was—to say the least—disconcerting, even frightening. Down through a tangle of warped plastic, fused stone and blistered metal they passed, where on both sides amazingly consistent, smooth-bored tunnels some two or three feet in diameter wound and twisted like wormholes through old timbers, except they cut through solid rock and crumpled girders.

And the thought came to the British agent that something, some vast force, had attempted to bring about a certain homogeneity here, had tried to make every different thing into one similar thing. Or had tried to deform everything beyond recognition. It was not so much that the various materials had been fused by heat and fire, rather that they seemed to have been folded-in, like the ingredients of dough, or different coloured plasticines in some monstrous child's hands.

"It gets worse," said Khuv quietly, leading the way lower still. "Those strange tunnels there were not 'cut' through the magmass—that's what Viktor Luchov calls this jumble of matter, incidentally, a 'magmass'—they were *eaten* into it by energy shearing off from the blow-back! We can only guess at the extent of the damage if the installation had been built on the surface."

The stairs descended to a veritable bed of magmass, only levelling out when they reached a vertical wall of unbroken rock like the face of a cliff. Here the timbers underfoot formed a walkway which turned to the right through an angle of ninety degrees and ran parallel with the foot of the looming wall of rock. Under the boards the floor was chaotically humped and anomalous, where different materials had so flowed into each other as to become unrecognizable in their original forms. And through all the congealed mass of this earthly and yet unfamiliar material ran those irregular wormhole energy channels, very like the indiscriminate burrows of rock-boring crustaceans in the sea, but on a gigantic scale.

" 'Eaten,' " Jazz pondered over the word. "You said these holes were 'eaten' into this stuff—but by what?"

"Rather, shall we say, 'converted'?" Khuv glanced at him. "Perhaps that paints a truer picture, to say that the material was converted into energy. But if you'll be patient I can show you a far better example. We are going to the place where the pile used to be. That, too, was eaten—or converted, if you prefer."

"Pile?" For the moment Khuv's meaning didn't register in Jazz's confused thoughts.

"The atomic pile which was the Projekt's main source of power," the Russian explained. "The backlash ate it—utterly. Yes, and then it seems it ate itself!"

Jazz might have questioned that statement, too, but now looming on the left of the walkway a huge, perfectly circular hole appeared in the face of the black wall of rock. Light issued from this tunnel where it angled steeply downward, and Jazz didn't need telling that this was a continuation of the shaft seen in the upper level, which once—and only once—had carried a fearsome beam of energy to the outside world.

The walkway turned left into the mouth of the shaft, became a stairway once again. Blinding white light was painful after the comparative gloom of the two levels through which the party had descended. Ahead and below, the far end of the shaft was a white disk of glaring brilliance, with its lower rim blacked out by the walkway's platform. Jazz shielded his eyes, saw a young Russian soldier in uniform leaning against the curved wall. The man at once came upright, snapped to attention, slapped the stock of his Kalashnikov rifle in salute.

"At ease," said Khuv. "We need some glasses."

The soldier leaned his rifle against the wall, groped in a satchel slung over his shoulder. He produced three pairs of tinted cellophane spectacles with cardboard rims, like the glasses Jazz had once been issued to view a 3-D film.

"For the light," Khuv explained, though there was hardly any need. "It can be blinding until you're used to it." He put on his glasses.

Jazz did the same, followed Khuv down the stairway built through the glass-smooth cylindrical shaft. From behind them came a clatter as the soldier's rifle toppled over when he went to pick it up, then Karl Vyotsky's husky, threatening voice hissing: "Idiot! Dolt! Would you like to do a month of nights?"

"No, sir!" the young soldier gasped. "I'm sorry, sir. It slipped."

"You damn well should be sorry!" Vyotsky rasped. "And not only for the rifle. What the hell are you here for anyway? To check passes for security, that's what! Do you know that man in front, and me, and the man with us?"

"Oh, yes, sir!" the young soldier quavered. "The man in front is Comrade Major Khuv, sir, and you too are an officer of the KGB. The other man is . . . is . . . a friend of yours, sir!"

"Clown!" Vyotsky hissed. "He is *not* my friend. Nor yours. Nor anyone's in the whole damned place!"

"Sir, I—"

"Now hold that rifle out in front of you," Vyotsky snapped. "Arm's length, finger through the trigger-guard, finger under the backsight. *What the hell . . . ?* Arm's length, I said. Now hold it, and count to two hundred, slowly! Then get back to attention. And if I ever catch you slacking off again, I'll feed you into that white hell down there dick first, got it?"

"Yes, sir!"

Following Khuv toward the white glare at the end of the shaft, Jazz murmured sourly: "A disciplinarian, our Karl."

Khuv glanced back, shook his head. "Not really. Discipline isn't his strong point. But sadism is. I hate to admit it, but it does have its uses . . ."

At the end of the shaft there was a railed landing where the stairs levelled out and turned to the left. Khuv paused on the landing with Jazz alongside. Waiting for Vyotsky, they gazed down on a fantastic scene.

It was like being in a cavern, but there was no way it could be mistaken for any ordinary sort of cave. Instead, Jazz saw that the rock had been hollowed out in the shape of a perfect sphere, a giant bubble in the base of the mountain—but a bubble at least one hundred and twenty feet in diameter! The curving, shiny-black wall all around was glass-smooth except for the wormholes which riddled it everywhere, even in the domed ceiling. The mouth of the shaft where Jazz and Khuv stood pointed downward at ninety degrees directly at the centre of the space, which also happened to be the source of the light. And that was the most fantastic thing of all.

For that central area was a ball of light some thirty feet across, and it was apparently suspended there, mid-way between the domed ceiling and the upward curving floor. A sphere of brilliance hanging motionless within a sphere of air, and the whole trick neatly buried under the foot of a mountain!

Narrowing his eyes against the glare, which was powerful even through the tinted lenses of his spectacles, Jazz slowly became aware that the spherical cavern contained other things. A spidery web of scaffolding had been built half way up the wall and all around the central blaze. The scaffolding supported a platform of timbers which circled the weird light source, reminding Jazz vaguely of the ring system round Saturn. Leading inwards from the ring, a walkway proceeded right to the edge of the sphere of light.

Externally, backed up against the black, wormhole-riddled walls—evenly spaced around the perimeter and massively supported on a framework of stanchions—three twin-mounted Katushev cannons pointed their muzzles point-blank at the blinding centre. Crews were in position, their sights aligned on the sphere, their faces white and alien-looking with headset antennae and insect goggle-eyes trained on the dazzling target.

Between the guns and the sphere stood a ten-foot high electrified fence, with a gate where the timber walkway spanned the gap between the Saturn rings and the centre. There was some motion down there, nervous and jumpy, but not much; the stench of fear was so thick in the supposedly conditioned air that Jazz could almost feel it like slime on his skin.

He gripped the wooden rail, let the entire scene print itself indelibly on his brain, said: "What in the name of all that's . . . ?" He turned his head to stare at Khuv. "I saw the arrival of those guns that night you caught me. The electrified fence, too. I thought they were meant to defend Perchorsk against attack from the outside, which struck me as making no sense. But from the *inside*? Christ, that doesn't make much sense either! I mean, what *is* that thing? And why are those men down there so desperately afraid of it?''

And suddenly, without any prompting, he knew the answer before it came. Not all of the answer but enough. Suddenly everything fitted: all he'd seen, and all Khuv had told him. And especially the flying monstrosity that the American fighters had burned to hell and sent crashing to earth in a ball of flame from high over the west coast of the Hudson Bay. And speaking of flames, wasn't that a four-man flame-thrower squad down there on the Saturn's-rings platform? Yes, it was.

Vyotsky had come up quietly behind Jazz and Khuv where they stood at the rail. He put a huge hand on Jazz's shoulder, causing him to start. "As to what it is, British," he said, "it's some sort of gate or door. And as such we're not frightened of it." But Jazz noted how for once Vyotsky's tone was muted, perhaps even a little awed.

"Karl is right," said Khuv. "No, we're not frightened of the Gate itself—but I defy any sane person not to fear the things that sometimes come through it!"

Chapter Four
The Gate To . . . ?

THEY STARTED DOWN THE FINAL FLIGHT OF WOODEN STAIRS to the Saturn's rings of spiderweb platform, then moved round the central sphere until they approached the walkway leading to its coldly incandescent heart. Ten feet away from the gate in the electric fence Khuv halted, turned to Jazz and said: "Well, what do you make of it?" He could only be talking about the glaring yet enigmatic globe which stood on the other side of the gate, maybe seven paces away. It was quite motionless, it made no sound, and yet it was menacing.

"You said that this was where the atomic pile stood," Jazz answered. "What, in mid-air? No, OK, I'm being facetious. So what you mean is that after the blow-back everything within sixty-five feet or so of the centre of that . . . that—whatever it is—was vaporized out of existence, right?"

"That would have been my explanation, too," Khuv nodded, "but incorrectly. As I've already pointed out, conversion is the word. According to Viktor Luchov, the energy of the trapped beam was attracted by the latent energy—or the energy in action—in the pile. You could compare it to the way a nail is drawn to a magnet. In the final fusing there was no explosion. Perhaps there was an implosion, I don't know any more

about that than Luchov himself. But the matter which
had formed the floor of this place, and the pile itself
along with its fuel—yes, and all the machinery, too,
which had filled this area—*all* of these things, outwards
from the centre to the spherical wall which now you
see, were eaten, transformed, converted. Men, too.
Seventeen nuclear physicists and technicians died instantly, leaving no trace.''

Jazz was impressed, if not by Khuv's telling of the
story, certainly by its content. ''And radiation?'' he
said. ''There must have been a massive release of—''

Khuv shook his head, bringing Jazz to a halt. ''In
relation to what was available, there was very little in
the way of escaped radiation. The tips of those wormholes, fifteen to twenty feet into the rock, some of those
were hotspots. We did what we could, then sealed them
off. In the levels above there are dangerous places still,
but again mainly sealed off. And in any case those
levels are no longer in use and will never be used again.
You have seen something of the magmass, but you
have not seen all of it. Metal and plastic and rock were
not the only materials which flowed together insepara-
bly in that blast of alien energy, Michael. But rock and
metal and plastic do not rot! You understand my meaning, I'm sure . . .''

Jazz grimaced, said: ''How did they . . . clean the
place up? It must have been a nightmare.''

''It still is,'' Khuv told him. ''That's why the lighting is muted up there. Acid was used. It was the only
way. But it left moulds in the magmass which are
utterly hideous to look upon. Pompeii must be something similar, but there at least the figures are still
recognizably human. Not elongated or twisted or . . .
reversed.''

Jazz thought about it, enquired no further as to Khuv's
exact meaning.

Vyotsky had been growing restless for some little
time. ''Do we have to stand here like this?'' he sud-

denly growled. "Why must we make targets of ourselves?"

Jazz's dislike for the man was intense, amounting to hatred. He'd hated him from the moment he first laid eyes on him, and couldn't resist jibes whenever the opportunity for such surfaced. Now he sneered at the huge Russian. "You think their fingers are likely to slip?" he nodded in the direction of the crew manning the closest Katushev. "Or maybe they've a grudge against you, too, eh?"

"British," said Vyotsky, taking a threatening pace closer, "I could happily toss you on that fence there and watch you fry! You've been advised to mind your mouth. But me?—I hope you go on pushing your luck till you push yourself right over the edge!"

"Calm yourself, Karl," Khuv told him. "He's looking for your measure, that's all." And to Jazz: "He doesn't mean that sort of target," he said. "Or rather he does, but not in the way you think. It's simply that if anything—anything at all strange—comes out of that ball of light there, those crews have orders to open fire immediately and destroy or *try* to destroy it. And those orders take absolutely no account of the fact that we happen to be standing here, right in the arc of fire."

"But if it did happen," Vyotsky added, "and if what *could* come through *did*, then I personally would be glad to stop a bullet!"

Khuv gave a little shiver, said, "Let's get out of here. Karl is quite right: we are stupid to stand here tempting fate. It has happened five times before, and there's no guarantee it won't happen again."

As they turned away and headed back toward the stairs, Jazz asked, "Do you have it on film? I mean, if it's a regular occurrence—"

"Not regular," Khuv corrected him. "Five—shall we call them, 'emergencies'—in two years can hardly be called frequent. But I take your point. Oh, yes, Michael, we learned our lessons quickly. After the first two encounters we fitted cameras, and now there are also cameras mounted on these guns. They are triggered when the weapons themselves are triggered. What the gunners see, the cameras capture—on film, anyway. As for the thing your side has code-named 'Pill': that was the first. Nobody here was ready for it. The second one was smaller, but we weren't ready for that, either. After that the cameras were put in.''

"Any chance of seeing what we're talking about?" Jazz might as well go for broke; there was little or no chance of him getting out of here, but still he'd try to discover what he could of this mess if only on the off-chance.

"Certainly," said Khuv without hesitation. "But if you prefer I can show you something far more interesting than mere films." There was something about the way he said it that warned Jazz to be careful, but nevertheless he answered:

"Well, by all means, let's keep me interested."

Vyotsky's grimly sardonic chuckle sounding from behind made him wonder if he'd made the right choice . . .

They went back up through the quiet but disquieting magmass levels to the perimeter, and along it to the secure area which housed the Projekt's laboratories. Passing through two guarded security doors, they arrived finally at a steel door bearing a stencilled scarlet skull and the stark warning:

CAUTION!
KEEPER AND SECURITY
CLASSIFIED PERSONS
ONLY!

Jazz couldn't help but think: *more melodramatics?* But Khuv and Vyotsky had gone very quiet, and perhaps it would be as well if he followed suit. He held his tongue, wondered about the word "keeper." Keeper of what?

Khuv had a plastic ID tag which he inserted in a slot in the door. The card was accepted, "read" and given back; mechanisms whirred and the door opened with a click. Before pushing it all the way open, Khuv motioned to Vyotsky who turned down the lights in the anteroom. As the lights dimmed Jazz noticed Vyotsky's face: it was pale and shiny with cold sweat. Also, his Adam's apple bobbed noticeably. There could be little doubt that the big Russian was both hard and cruel, but it seemed there were some things that could get to him. It also appeared that Jazz was about to meet one of them.

Khuv, though, was cool as ever. Now he pushed the heavy door open and motioned Jazz through it. With some misgivings, the British agent stepped inside the dark room. Vyotsky followed close behind him, and Khuv came last, closing the door after him.

The darkness was almost complete: only a series of small red lights the size of flashlight bulbs glowed in the ceiling. Revealed by their dim glow, the rectangular shape of a glass case stood against one wall like a huge tropical fish tank. Khuv's voice came soft out of the darkness. "Are you ready, Michael?"

"When you are," Jazz answered. But even as the words left his mouth, he knew he wasn't here to admire goldfish.

A sharp click sounded and the lights came on.

Something moved in the tank and reared up!

Behind Jazz, Vyotsky made a choking sound. He'd seen this before, had known what was in here, but if anything the knowledge had only served to precipitate his instinctive reaction to it. And now that Jazz saw it he could readily understand why.

The thing was something like the moulds in the magmass which Khuv had *not* described but Jazz had pictured. It was like that, and yet not like that, for it was alive. Twisting, flowing, it glared out through the thick glass of the tank with eyes that were sheer hell. It

60

was the size of a large dog, but it was not a dog. It wasn't anything Jazz could have possibly imagined but a composite of most of his worst nightmares. It didn't stay still long enough for him to even try to decide what it was. And worst of all, it didn't seem to know itself!

Flattening itself for a moment against the glass of the tank, the thing might have been a leech. Its underside was corrugated and shaped like a huge, elongated sucker. But its four hands, its tail and its head were parts that might readily fit on a giant rat! That was how it looked— for a split-second. Then—

The head and hands changed, underwent a swift metamorphosis, became manlike. An almost human face crushed itself to the glass, gazing flatly, almost pitifully out into the room. It grimaced: an expression that was part smile, part scowl, part snarl, and then its human jaws yawned inhumanly open. Inside that mouth was a hell of teeth worthy of some monster piranha!

Jazz stepped back, gasping, and bumped into Vyotsky. The big Russian grasped his shoulders, steadied him. And in the tank the thing's hands sprouted hooks that scrabbled at the glass; its face collapsed to a black leathery mask with a convoluted snout and huge, hairy pointed ears, like a great bat; webs grew between its limbs and body, forming wings. It sprang high, thudded against the tough glass ceiling of its tank, flopped down on the deep sandy bed.

Jazz was vaguely aware that someone—possibly Khuv, he thought; yes, even Khuv—had murmured, *"My God!"* In that same moment the thing had elongated into a worm with a spade head, rammed itself head-first down into the sand and burrowed out of sight. There was a finaly flurry of sand and . . . all was still.

After long moments of silence Jazz expelled his breath in a great sigh. "Christ almighty!" he said, in a small voice. Then all three men drew air deeply into starved lungs. Jazz closed his gaping mouth, looked at the two

61

Russians. "And you're telling me this—*thing*—came out of that ball of light, right?"

Khuv, pale in the bright lights, with eyes that were dark blue blots in his doughy face, nodded. "Through the Gate, yes," he said.

Jazz shook his head in bewilderment. "But how in hell did you *catch* it?" It seemed a very reasonable question.

"As you can see," Khuv answered, "it doesn't like bright lights. And for all that it can change its shape at will, still it seems very primitive in its mental processes—if it has any worth considering as such. It could be that it's all sheer animal instinct. We think it probably *attacked* the Gate on the other side; it would have been night in that world, and the glaringly bright sphere must have seemed like an enemy, or even prey. But when it burst through to our side—into the hollow sphere of rock down there—it was bright as day. Luckily for the people who were there, it headed straight down one of the wormholes—to escape from the light, do you see? And someone had his wits about him sufficiently to put the open end of a steel cabinet over the mouth of the hole. When it tried to come back out it was trapped."

"How long have you—" Jazz found the greatest difficulty in concentrating on what he was saying, found it almost impossible to take his eyes off the tank, "—had this thing?"

"Eighteen months," Khuv answered. "This was the third encounter."

"Of the too close kind," Jazz had finally got himself together.

"Pardon?" Khuv stared at him blankly.

"Nothing," Jazz shook his head. "But tell me: what does it eat?" He didn't know why he'd asked that. Maybe it was the memory of all those teeth, and Khuv's talk of prey.

Khuv's eyes narrowed. Not defensively but thoughtfully. He opened the door, switched off the lights and beckoned Jazz and Vyotsky to come out. They went back to the perimeter and Khuv led the way to his own quarters. On the way Jazz asked: "I take it it does eat?"

Khuv remained silent but Vyotsky answered for him: "Oh, yes, it eats. It doesn't need to, apparently, but it does when food's on offer. It eats people—or anything else with good red salty guts! Or it would if it could. Its keeper feeds it on blood and offal which is pumped through a tube to it. He knows exactly how much to give it. Too much and it gets bigger and stronger. Too little and it shrivels, hibernates. When they've worked out a way to handle it safely, then they'll try to find out what makes it tick."

"They?"

"The specialists from Moscow," said Vyotsky, shrugging. "The people from—"

"Karl!" Khuv stopped him with a word. And Jazz thought: *so even though I'm a prisoner, and for all Khuv's "glasnost," still there are sensitive areas, eh?*

"Specialists," said Khuv, "yes. If they can find out about it, maybe they'll also discover something of its world."

Something else was bothering Jazz. "What about these flame-throwers I keep seeing?"

"Isn't it obvious?" Vyotsky scowled. "Are you stupid after all, British?"

"Concentrated fire kills them," said Khuv. "Up to now it's about the only thing that does. That we've discovered, anyway."

Jazz nodded. Things were beginning to shape up in his head. "I'm starting to see the potential," he said, drily. "And no need to tell me where your 'specialists' come from. The Department for the Study of Chemical and Biological Warfare on Protze Prospekt, right?"

Khuv made no answer. His mouth had fallen aslant in a twisted smile.

Jazz nodded. His own expression was a mixture of

63

sarcasm and revulsion. ''And how would *that* be for a biological weapon, eh?''

They had reached Khuv's quarters. He opened the door, said: ''Would you like a drink, or should I let Karl take you back to your cell and toss you around a little to improve your manners?'' His voice crackled like thin ice underfoot. Jazz had touched a tender spot. The British agent was much quicker on the uptake than Khuv had given him credit for.

Jazz looked at Vyotsky's grinning face, said: ''Oh, I think I'd prefer the drink every time.''

''Very well, but try to remember: you are in no position to criticize anything. You are a spy, a murderer, a would-be saboteur. And remember this, too: you don't know everything. *We* don't know everything! Weapons? Like . . . like that? Personally I would rather close the place down, concrete it in, lock the Gate shut forever—if that's at all feasible. So would Viktor Luchov. But the Projekt was sponsored—indeed it was ordered —by the Defence Agency. We don't control anything, Michael, but are ourselves controlled. Now make up your mind: we can be 'friends,' or I can have someone else, someone a lot less sympathetic, complete your briefing. It's up to you.''

Briefing? For some reason Jazz didn't like the way Khuv had used the word. A slip of the tongue, obviously. Briefing didn't really apply here, did it? *Why are you being given the treatment?* a voice asked in the back of his mind. *What's in it for them?* He didn't have the answers and so put the question aside, said:

''OK, I accept that. We all do what we have to. We all have our orders. But just answer me one more thing and after that I won't interrupt you again.''

Khuv ushered Jazz and Vyotsky into his living area. ''Very well,'' he said, ''what is it?''

''That thing in the glass tank, your intruder from another world,'' Jazz wrinkled his nose in disgust. ''You say it has a keeper? Someone who looks after it, feeds it, studies it? It's just that I can't imagine what kind of a man he would be. He must have nerves of steel!''

"What?'' Vyotsky gave a snort that was half-way a laugh. "Do you think he volunteered? He's a scientist, a small man with thick spectacles. A man dedicated to science—also to the bottle.''

Jazz raised an eyebrow. "An alcoholic?''

Khuv's expression didn't change. "Very soon,'' he said after a moment's pause. "Yes, I'm afraid he will be . . .''

Three hours later, at about 7:30 P.M.—after Jazz had had delivered to him in his cell a cup of tepid, flavourless coffee and a cold meat sandwich, standard evening fare, and after he'd consumed both—he lay on his back on his metal army bed and yet again turned over in his mind all the facts Khuv had given him. The Russian had talked almost nonstop for an hour and a half, during which time the British agent had remained true to his word and had not once interrupted him. Once Khuv was underway Jazz hadn't wanted to stop him anyway, partly because the Russian's flow of words and images had been smooth and required no deep explanation, but mainly because his story had been completely fascinating.

And now, yet again, Jazz recapped:

The Perchorsk Incident or "pi'' had been the disastrous test run of Franz Ayvaz's sub-atomic shield. After that mess, cleaning up had almost been completed when "Pill'' happened, which Khuv referred to as Encounter One; but from what the KGB Major had told Jazz, it hadn't been so much an encounter as a downright nightmare!

The—creature?—which had come through the sphere of light on that occasion had been . . . well, it had been the monstrosity Jazz had seen on the film shot by the AWACS reconnaissance aircraft over the Hudson Bay, which now he realized was like nothing so much as the Big Brother of the thing in the glass tank. But when Big Brother had squeezed its bulk into this world from its own . . .

Khuv's description of Encounter One as he himself had heard it from people present at the time had been graphic:

"You've seen it, Michael, on that film you told us about. You *know* what it was like. Ah, but that was only after it had escaped through the shaft into the ravine and got itself airborne! On the ground it had been far worse; oh, yes, and I'll tell you about it from first-hand accounts! First, however, I'll try to explain how the Gate works. Or I'll describe what happens *when* it works. The 'skin' of the sphere—its 'surface' as we see it—is in itself a contradiction of physics as we understand that science. Viktor Luchov has likened it to an 'event horizon.' We see things on it after, and even in advance of, any given event! In the former case as a sort of retinal after-image printed in the sphere, and in the latter as a gradual emergence until the—whatever—breaks through.

"They actually saw that thing coming—but they didn't know what they were seeing! Remember, it was the first. They saw it in the sphere: a gradual darkening of part of the surface up near the sphere's dome. The dark patch became a shape, the shape a sort of misty three-dimensional picture, and the image—in a little while—reality. They saw the head and face of a bat four or five feet across: like a hologram but slowly, oh so slowly, changing. It was all in slow-motion, a fascinating thing to witness. So they thought. The wrinkling of the convolute snout, which perhaps took half a minute; the leaning forward of the ears—a flicker of motion in real-time—lasting all of five seconds; the baring of the needle teeth, each one of them six inches long, which was accomplished with the speed of a yawn.

"Now think of it: they had guns! There were actually

a handful of soldiers down there with weapons—not for any specific purpose, but simply because soldiers sometimes have guns. But who would think to shoot at such a thing, eh? After the fact, maybe—but at the time? Listen to me: do we shoot off guns at pictures on a screen? That was what this was like, a 3-D film.

"Also, Viktor Luchov was there. Do you think he would have let them shoot at it? Not a chance! He didn't even know what the sphere was yet. But . . . it might well be his redemption! In Franz Ayvaz's absence he had still to answer for the Perchorsk Incident, and now out of nowhere this . . . phenomenon!

"Its clarity had been improving for about an hour. All the misty edges had firmed up until the image had the brilliance of a TV picture. People had run to fetch cameras and were actually filming it, like tourists filming ancient monuments or views of outstanding beauty! After all, they knew it couldn't be real. What? A bat with a head as huge as an elephant's?

"Then—quite suddenly, without warning—the impossible happened. They realized that the snout had pushed *through* the 'skin' of the sphere. The monster was no longer just an image on a screen. It sniffed, inhaled sharply several times—and in the next instant the nightmare was upon them!

"The event horizon slows things down, Michael. But once the Gate is breached, then all reverts to normal. But 'normal' for that obscenity was total hell for the people face to face with it! I say it sniffed—a huge bat sniffing its prey—and it scented them! *And it changed!* The face and head that came through the skin were those of a vast wolf. You saw the thing in the tank metamorphose? It was like that, the very same. The giant wolf's head came through, and then its shoulders—but pushing them forward was a leathery bat's body, and great bat wings unfurling as wide as the sphere itself!

"Panic? There was such panic as men rarely experience in a lifetime. And to make it worse, the thing didn't come into this world silently but screaming. Ah, and what a voice it had!

"It came howling its rage at the bright lights, its hunger for the blood it had scented, its fear of an alien environment. And it slew. But while it was doing this, *still* it continued to emerge from the sphere. Now the rear end of the thing was like a vast centipede, stampeding through the Gate and threshing everywhere. It changed endlessly, became a dozen different hybrids in as many moments, and each and every one of them murderous!

"It snapped cables in its blind blundering—blind, yes, for it couldn't bear the lights. And a mercy it *was* blind, for if not the carnage would have been that much worse. But as it damaged the power supply many of the lights failed and its vision improved accordingly. Now it picked its victims with more deliberation, and devoured them whole with a deal more dexterity.

"But now, too, the soldiers were shooting at it—those with the nerve for it, anyway. They couldn't tell if their bullets hurt, but the massed gunfire certainly alarmed it. It headed for the darkest place it could find: the dimly lighted shaft, of course. By now it had changed into something very like the squirting squid-like thing your AWACS air-crew filmed. Vast—amazingly *vast*—it squeezed and squirted its way through the magmass levels. Indeed, in the way its plastic body flowed it was not unlike the magmass; and as it went so it put out extrusions with mouth and with eye and with . . . oh, appendages for which there is really no description. Imagine a leg sprouting from its side, and then the leg itself becoming a scuttling spider-thing, and you may have some idea of what I'm talking about.

"But finally it was out into the ravine, and in its wake a trail of death and destruction filled with the screams of the dead and the dying, and the empty spaces which were all that remained of those who had vanished forever. For a second time the Perchorsk Projekt was a shambles, and somewhere in the world outside that monstrosity was on the loose and rampaging. And no one had the faintest idea what to do about it.

"If we Russians have faults, Michael, they are these: we tend to be too well regimented in our thinking, and we are not accustomed to failure. So that when things go disastrously wrong we stand stunned, uncomprehending, like small children waiting for Mama to tell us what to do next. It was like that for Khruschev when Kennedy faced him down, and again for the—shall we say—'responsible authorities' over that stupid affair of the Korean airliner. If there are any more disasters in the offing, it will doubtless be the same all over again— just as it was here at Perchorsk.

"Eventually the military were alerted, and they in turn told Moscow. But can you imagine the reaction? 'What? Something has got loose from Perchorsk in the Urals? What sort of something? What are you talking about?' But at last Migs were sent up from Kirovsk, and the rest you already know. Indeed, you know more than I do about that part of it! But at least I know why the Russian fighters failed while the USAF planes succeeded. We've learned that much from the other . . . encounters. It's the reason for the flamethrowers.

"That's right: the American aircraft were equipped with experimental Firedevil air-to-air missiles which not only explode on impact but hurl searing flames all about. Less bulky than napalm but ten percent more effective. That is what stopped that thing over the Hudson Bay—fire! Fire and light—sunlight! Until the American fighters contacted it, the thing had flown through or under fairly dense cloud cover, and the sunlight wasn't strong yet. But as the sun rose so the creature descended, seeking protection for itself. They are cold things, Michael, and they are things of darkness.

"You've described what you saw on that AWACS film: clouds of vile gasses boiling off the creature's surface in the bright sunlight, and the way its vast, flattened, airfoil body shrank from the sun. Ah, yes! It wasn't so much that the Migs failed, but that other, *natural* forces assisted the Americans in their success. The thing was half-beaten before it met the Americans, and their Firedevils finished it off.

"Well, and that was the end of Encounter One . . .

"Now a sort of anticlimax: Encounter Two was a wolf!

"It came through in just the same way as the first thing, but by comparison it was so small—and so normal—that it almost went unnoticed. But not quite. A soldier spotted it first, put a bullet in it the moment it came limping through the Gate. That stopped it, but not fatally. It was examined, but oh so cautiously, and found to be . . . a wolf! It was old, mangy, almost blind and close to starving. They saved its life, caged it, fed and cared for it and subjected it to every test in the book. Because they weren't quite sure they could trust it, do you see? But . . . it *was* a wolf. In every respect a brother of the creatures which even today hunt in the great forests of these parts. By the time it died nine months ago, of old age, the animal was quite tame.

"And so they thought: perhaps the world on the other side isn't so very different from this one after all. Or: perhaps this gateway we've opened leads to many other worlds. Viktor Luchov thinks that as a physical phenomenon—or as a phenomenon of physics—it lies somewhere between a black hole and a white hole. Black holes sit out in the deeps of space and gobble up worlds, and not even light can escape from their fantastic gravitational attraction; white holes are the theoretical melting pots that give birth to galaxies; both are gateways to and from other space-times. Likewise our sphere of white light—but not nearly so violent! Which is why Luchov calls it a 'grey hole,' a gateway in *both* directions!''

At this point Khuv had held up a warning hand. "Don't break the thread now, Michael, for we're doing so well. You can ask your questions later." And when Jazz had relaxed again:

"Myself, I've no interest in the 'holes' of advanced physics theory—I simply call it a monstrous threat! But that aside . . .

"You've seen Encounter Three and I've told you about it. As for Four: that was another anticlimax, but not quite so ordinary or acceptable as the wolf. It was a bat, order *Chiroptera,* genus *Desmodus.* Strangely, *Vampyrum* is the false vampire, while *Desmodus* and *Diphylla* are the true blood-suckers. This one had a wing-spread of point seven of a metre: quite a large one of its species, I'm told, but by no means a giant. It was seen coming well in advance, of course, and no chances were taken with it. As it emerged, in that self same moment, they shot it dead. But just as the wolf was a true wolf, so the bat was a true bat. Curiously, the vampire bat is a creature of South or Central America. Perhaps our grey hole was a gateway not only to other worlds but also to other parts of this world.

"Anyway, I was here by this time; the rest of this account is first-hand. Oh, and I can show you film of the bat's emergence, if you like. Not that you'll learn anything more than I've already told you, for it is exactly as I've described it. Ah, but the Fifth Encounter . . . that was something entirely different."

At this juncture Jazz had noted how Vyotsky, behind his dark beard, had gone very pale again. He, too, had been present for that Fifth Encounter. "Get it over with," the big KGB man had stood up, gulped down his drink, started to pace the floor. "Tell him about it, or show him the film, but get done with it."

"Karl doesn't like it," Khuv's comment was entirely superfluous, his smile cold and grim. "But then, neither do I. Still, likes and dislikes change nothing. They can't alter the facts. Come, I'll show you the film."

In a second small room Khuv had something of a study. There were bookshelves, a tiny desk, steel chairs, a modern projector and small screen. Vyotsky made no attempt to join Jazz and his senior officer but poured himself another drink and stayed behind in Khuv's living-room. Jazz knew, however, that that was the only way out of Khuv's quarters, and that only a few scant paces and a bit of flimsy door panelling separated him from the huge KGB bully.

Now, too, he had seen that his coming here had not been a spontaneous occurrence; Khuv had prepared himself in advance; all he had to do was dim the lights and roll the film. And whatever Jazz had expected, it certainly had *not* been what he saw.

The film was in colour, had a sound track, was very professional in every way. At one side of the screen a dark, fuzzy, out of focus shadow proved to be the side of a Russian soldier, with a glinting Kalashnikov braced against his thigh. Centre screen was the sphere of white light, or "Gate" as Jazz now thought of it, and imposed on its dazzling surface—the bottom of the "picture" coming just inches higher than the boards of the walkway where it spanned the gap between the Saturn-rings platform and the sphere—was the image . . . *of a man!*

The camera had then zoomed in, turning the entire screen white and therefore that much less dazzling, with the image of the man central. He "strode" straight ahead, looking directly into the camera. His movements were so painfully slow that each pace took long seconds, and Jazz had found himself wondering if he'd ever get here. But then Khuv had warned:

"See how the picture clears? A sure sign that he's about to come through. But if I were you I wouldn't wait for that. Study him now, while you can!" And obligingly, the camera had closed on the man's face.

The forehead was sloped, and the skull shaved except for a central lock of hair like a thick black stripe on the pale, almost grey flesh. Swept back like a mane and tied in a knot, the lock bobbed at the back of the man's neck. His eyes were small and close together, and very startling. They glared out from under thick black eyebrows that met in a tangle across the bridge of a squat or flattened nose. The ears were slightly pointed and had large lobes; they lay flat to the head above hollow, almost gaunt cheeks. The lips were red and fleshy, in a mouth slanted to the left and set with a sort of permanent sneer or snarl. The man's chin was pointed, made to look even more so by a small black beard waxed to a point. But the face's main feature was that pair of small, glaring eyes. Jazz had looked at them again: red as blood, they'd gleamed in deep black orbits.

As if sensing Jazz's needs, the camera had then drawn back to show the entire man again. He wore a short pelmet of cloth about his loins, sandals on his feet, a large ring of golden metal in his right ear. His right hand was gloved in a gauntlet heavy with spikes, blades and hooks—an incredibly cruel, murderous weapon!

After that Jazz had only sufficient time to note the man's leanness, the ripple of his fine-toned muscles, and his wolf's lope of a walk before he stepped out of the sphere onto the walkway—and then everything had speeded up!

The British agent came back to the present, gripped the edge of his bed and drew himself into a sitting position. He swung his feet to the floor and put his back to the metal wall. The wall was cool but not cold; through it, Jazz could feel the life of the subterranean complex, the nervous, irregular coursing of its frightened blood. It was like being below decks in a big ship, where the throb of the engines comes right through the floor and walls and bulkheads. And just as he'd be aware of the life in a ship, so he was aware of the terror in this place.

There were men down there in that unnatural cavern

in the heart of the mountain, men with guns. Some of them had seen for themselves, and others had been shown on films like the one Jazz had seen, what could come through the Gate they guarded. Little wonder the Perchorsk Projekt was afraid.

He gave a small shiver, then a grim chuckle. He'd caught the Projekt's fever: its symptom was this shivering, even when it was warm. He'd seen them all doing it, and now he did it, too.

Jazz deliberately gave himself a mental shake, forced himself to return to the film Khuv had shown him . . .

Chapter Five
Wamphyri!

THE MAN CAME RIGHT OUT THROUGH THE SPHERE ONTO THE walkway—and then everything speeded up!

He shuttered his red eyes against the sudden light, shouted an astonished denial in a language Jazz halfway understood or felt he should understand, and fell into a defensive crouch. Then the film had suddenly come alive. Before, the sounds had seemed muted: the occasional low cough, nervous conversation, feet shuffling in the background, and now and then the springs of weapons being eased or tested and the unmistakable metallic clatter of magazines slapped into housings. But all of it seeming dull and a little out of tune, like the first few minutes of a film in a cinema, where your ears are still tuned to the street and haven't yet grown accustomed to the new medium of wall to wall sound.

Now, however, the sound was very much tied to the film. Khuv's voice, shouting: "Take him alive! *Don't shoot him!* I'll court martial the first man who pulls a trigger! He's only a man, can't you see? *Go in and capture him!*"

Figures in combat uniforms ran past the camera, caused the cameramen and therefore the film to jiggle a little, burst into view on the screen and almost blotted out the picture. Having been ordered not to shoot, they

75

carried their weapons awkwardly, seemed not to know what to do with them. Jazz could understand that: they'd been told that hideous death lurked in the sphere, but this seemed to be just a man. How many of them would it take to cow just one man? With an assortment of weapons at their fingertips, they must feel like men swatting midges with mallets! But on the other hand, some damned weird things had come out of that sphere, and they knew that, too.

The man from the sphere saw them coming, straightened up. His red eyes were now at least partly accustomed to the light. He stood waiting for the soldiers, and Jazz had thought: *this lad has to be six and a half feet if he's an inch! Yes, and I'd bet he can look after himself, too.*

And certainly he would have won his bet!

The walkway was maybe ten feet wide. The first two soldiers approached the near-naked man from the sphere on both sides, and that was a mistake. Shouting at him to put his hands up in the air and come forward, the fastest of the two reached him, made to prod him with the snout of his Kalashnikov rifle. With astonishing speed the intruder came to life: he batted the barrel of the gun aside with his left hand, swung the weapon he wore on his right hand shatteringly against the soldier's head.

The left side of the soldier's head caved in and the hooks of the gauntlet caught in the broken bones of his skull. The intruder held him upright for a moment, flopping uselessly like a speared fish. But it was all nervous reaction, for the blow must have killed him instantly. Then the man from the Gate snarled and jerked his hand back, freeing it, and at the same time shouldered his victim from the walkway. The soldier's body toppled out of sight.

The second soldier paused and looked back, his face bloodless where the camera caught his indecision. His comrades were hot on his heels, outraged, eager to bring this unknown warrior down. Made brave by their numbers, he faced the intruder again and swung his rifle butt-first toward his face. The man grinned like a wolf and ducked easily under the blow, at the same time swinging his gauntlet in a deadly arc. It tore out the soldier's throat in a scarlet welter and knocked him sideways. He went sprawling, got to his knees—and the intruder brought his weapon down on top of his head, caving in his fur hat, skull and all!

Then the rest of the combat-suited figures were surging all around the warrior, clubbing with their rifles and kicking at him with booted feet. He slipped and went down under their massed weight, howling his hatred and fury. The yelling of the soldiers was an uproar, over which Jazz had recognized Khuv's voice shouting: "Hold him down but don't kill him! We want him alive—*alive*, do you hear?"

Then Khuv himself had come into view, advancing onto the walkway and waving his arms frantically over his head. "Pin him down," he yelled, "but don't beat him to a pulp! We want him . . . in one piece?" The final three words were an expression of Khuv's astonishment, his disbelief. And watching the film Jazz had been able to see why, had understood the change in Khuv's voice, had almost been able to sympathize with him.

For the strange warrior had quite genuinely slipped when he went down—possibly in blood—and that was the *only* reason he'd gone down. The five or six soldiers where they crowded him, hampered by their weapons and desperate not to come in range of that terrible mincing-machine he wore on his right hand, weren't even a match for him! One by one they'd rear up and back, clutching at torn throats or mangled faces; two of them went flying over the rim of the walkway, plunging sixty-odd feet to the basin-like magmass floor; another, hamstrung as he turned away, was kicked almost contemptuously into empty air by the warrior—who finally stood gory and unfettered, and *alone*, on the red-slimed boards of the walkway. And then he had seen Khuv, and nothing between them but four or five swift paces across the planking.

"Flame-thrower squad!" Khuv's voice was hoarse, almost a whisper in the sudden, awed silence of the place. "To me—*quickly!*" He hadn't looked back, dared not for a moment take his eyes off the menacing man from the sphere.

But the warrior had heard him speak. He cocked his head on one side, narrowed his red eyes at Khuv. Perhaps he took the KGB Major's words for a challenge. He answered: a short, harshly barked sentence—probably a question—in a language which once again Jazz had felt he should understand, a question which ended in the word "Wamphyri?" He took two paces forward, repeated the enigmatic, vaguely familiar words of the sentence. And this time the last word, "Wamphyri?", was spoken with more emphasis, threateningly and with something of fierce pride.

Khuv went down on one knee and cocked an ugly, long-barrelled automatic pistol. He pointed it waveringly at the warrior, used his free hand to beckon men urgently forward from behind him. "*Flame-thrower squad!*" he croaked. There had been no spittle in his throat, nor in Jazz's throat, by the time the film had reached this point.

And then the warrior had loped forward again, only this time he hadn't looked like stopping; and the look on his face and the way he held his deadly gauntlet at the ready spoke volumes for his intentions. The clatter of booted feet sounded and figures darkened the sides of the screen where men hurried forward, but Khuv wasn't waiting. His own orders about the use of weapons were forgotten now, so much hot air. He held his automatic in both trembling hands, fired point-blank, twice, at the menacing human death-machine from the other side.

His first shot took the warrior in the right shoulder, under the clavicle. A dark blotch blossomed there like an ugly flower in the moment that he was thrown backwards, sent sprawling on the boards. The second shot had apparently missed him entirely. He sat up, touched the hole in his slumped shoulder, stared in open astonishment at the blood on his hand. But pain didn't seem to have registered at all—not yet. When it did, a second later—

The warrior's howl wasn't a human sound at all. It was something far more primal than that. It came from night-dark caverns in an alien world beyond strange boundaries of space and time. And it was shocking and frightening enough to match the man himself.

He would have hurled himself at Khuv, indeed he crouched down and made ready to do so, but the three-man flame-thrower squad was in the way. The machine they handled wasn't the small man-pack variety that can be carried on one man's back; it was a weighty thing consisting of a fuel tank on a motorized trolley which one man controlled while another walked alongside with the flame-projector. The third member of the squad held a large flexible asbestos shield, fragile protection against blow-back.

The man from the sphere, wounded though he was, smashed his gauntlet weapon through the asbestos shield and almost succeeded in knocking it from the keeper's hands. Before he could withdraw the gauntlet, which seemed to be stuck, Khuv shouted: "Show him your fire! But only *show* it to him—don't burn him!"

Perhaps they were a little too eager: a jet of flame lashed out, lapped at the warrior's side where he screamed his rage and terror and turned away. And when the fire was snuffed out at its source, still chemical flames leaped up the man's body from his side, burning away his beard, eyebrows, and setting fire to the single lock of black hair on his head.

He began to blister, screamed in agony and beat at

the flames with his left hand. Then he snatched the asbestos shield from the soldier who held it and hurled it at the squad. Before they could recover from this, he turned and staggered, still smoking, back toward the shiny white sphere.

"Stop him!" Khuv shouted. "Shoot him—but in the legs! Don't let him go back!" He began firing, and the man jerked and staggered as bullets smashed into the back of his naked thighs and lower legs. He had almost reached his objective when a lucky shot hit him behind the right knee and knocked him down. But he was close enough to the sphere to try hurling himself into it. Except—

—It threw him back! It was as if he'd tried to dive through a brick wall.

And at that moment, watching the film, Jazz had known—as those who had been present had known, and everyone who'd seen the film since—that the Gate was a mantrap. Like the pitcher plant, it allowed its victims access, then denied them egress. Once through the Gate, the creatures from the other side were stuck here. And Jazz had wondered: *would it be the same for someone going through from this side?* Except of course there was no way anyone was ever going to find out— was there?

"Now he *has* to come quietly!" Khuv was jubilant. As the firing ceased he ran down the walkway toward the flame-thrower squad, stood behind them watching the pitiful antics of the man from the Gate. At that moment Jazz had found himself feeling sorry for the weird visitor, but the moment had not lasted long.

The man sat up, shook himself dazedly, reached out a hand toward the shining sphere. His hand met resistance, could not proceed. He got to his knees, turned to face his tormentors. His scarlet eyes opened wide and glared his hatred at them; he *hissed* at them, spat his contempt onto the walkway. Even with great yellow blisters bursting and seeping their fluid all down his right side, crippled and—helpless?—still he defied them.

Khuv stepped to the fore, pointed at the gauntlet on the warrior's right hand. "Take it off!" he made unmistakable gestures. "Get rid of it—now!"

The man looked at his gauntlet and, incredibly, struggled to his feet. Khuv backed away, aimed his gun. "Take that bloody thing off your hand!" he demanded.

But the man from the sphere only smiled. He looked at Khuv's gun, at the flame-projector whose nozzle pointed directly at him, and smiled a twisted smile. It was a strange expression, combining triumph, unbearable irony, even sardonic sadness or melancholy. But never a sign of fear. "Wamphyri," the man thumbed his chest, lifting his head in pride. Then . . . he laid back his head and literally howled the word: *"Wamphyri!"*

As the echoes of that cry died away, he thrust his face forward and glared once more at the men on the walkway, and there was that in his look which said: "Do your worst. You are nothing. You *know* nothing!"

"The gauntlet!" Khuv cried again, pointing. He fired a shot in the air for emphasis, aimed his gun at the warrior's heart. But in the next moment he inhaled sharply, audibly, and let his air out in a gasp.

Standing there on the walkway, swaying a little from side to side, the man from the sphere had opened his jaws, opened them impossibly wide. A forked tongue, scarlet, lashed in the cavern of his mouth. The gape of his jaws expanded more yet; they visibly elongated, making a sound like tearing sailcloth. And because all else was total silence and the rest of the tableau was frozen, the sight and sounds of his metamorphosis were that much more vivid.

Jazz had held his breath as he watched; and now, in his cell, he held it again at the very memory of what he'd seen:

The warrior's fleshy lips had rolled back, stretching until they split, spurting blood and revealing crimson gums and jagged, dripping teeth. The entire mouth had resembled nothing so much as the yawning muzzle of a rabid wolf—but the rest of the face had been as bad if not worse! The squat, flattened nose had grown broader, developed convoluted ridges like the snout of a bat, whose oval nostrils were shiny-black flaring pits in dark, wrinkled leather. The ears, previously flat to the head, had sprouted patches of coarse hair, growing upward and outward to form scarlet-veined and nervously mobile shapes like fleshy conchs; and in this respect, too, the effect was batlike. Or perhaps demoniac.

For certainly hell was written in those outlines, was limned in the nightmarish expression of that face: a visage which was part bat, part wolf, and all horror! And still the change was incomplete.

The eyes, which before were small and deep-sunken, had now grown large as gorged leeches until they bulged crimson in their sockets. And the *teeth* . . . the teeth gave a new meaning to nightmare. For growing and curving up through the lacerated ribbons of the creature's gums, those bone daggers had so torn his mouth that it filled to overflowing with his own blood; and his teeth snarled *through* the blood like the awesome fangs of some primal carnivore!

As for the rest of his body, that had remained mercifully anthropomorphic; but through all of his metamorphosis his ravaged trunk and legs had taken on the dull gleam of lead, and every inch of his body had vibrated with an incredible palsy. But finally—

—Finally it was done. And knowing what *he* was doing, at last the man, or *thing,* from the sphere reached out its arms and took one more, stumbling step forward. And with that last lurching step in Khuv's direction, the creature gurgled: *"Wamphyri!"*

Khuv had thought the thing was human, and he'd scarcely had time to recover from the shock of his error. His nerves, legs, voice—all of these things almost failed him. And that would have been a fatal malfunction. But in the last moment he stepped back out of range and croaked: "Burn him—it! God, *burn the whore's bastard to hell!*"

That was all the man with the hose had been waiting for; he needed no further urging, and it required only the pressure of his forefinger on the trigger. A yellow jet of flame with a searing white core roared out from the nozzle, broadened, enveloped the horror from the Gate. For long seconds the squad hosed the thing down with chemical fire, and it simply stood there. Then the shape in the heart of the fire crumpled, seemed to melt down into itself, collapsed into a sitting position.

"Stop!" Khuv covered his face with a handkerchief. The roaring stream of fire continued for a second or two, hissed into silence as it was shut off at source. But the alien warrior continued to burn. Fire leaped up from him, rising six or seven feet above the black oval core which was his melting head, and there turned to foul, stinking smoke. Jazz hadn't been able to smell it, but still he'd known how it must have stank.

The flames burned lower, hissing and crackling, and the slumped shape shrank as its juices bubbled and boiled. Something that might have been a long, tapering arm rose up from the tarry remains in the fire, undulated like a crippled cobra in the clouds of smoke, began a violent shuddering which ceased when it collapsed back into the mess on the burning walkway.

"One more burst," said Khuv, and the squad obliged. And in a very short space of time it was finished . . .

Then the film had come to an end and the screen flickered with white light, but Jazz and Khuv had continued to sit and stare at the scenes burned in their minds. Only after the last inch of film clattered from its free-spinning reel had Khuv moved, reaching to switch off the projector and turn up the lights.

After that . . . it had been time for another drink. And rarely in Jazz's life had alcohol been more welcome . . .

* * *

While Michael J. Simmons sat on his bunk and thought about all the things he'd seen and heard, gradually the heartbeat or pulse of the complex slowed and took on something of a soft regularity. Outside it was night, and so in here it was a time for sleeping. But not all of the Projekt's staff and supporting units slept (there were, for instance, those who guarded the Gate, who were very much awake) and as for the one creature in the complex which was neither human nor anything else of Man's world: that hardly seemed to sleep at all.

So thought its keeper, Vasily Agursky, where he sat with his chin and drawn cheeks cupped in the palms of his too-large hands, gazing at Encounter Three through the thick glass wall of its tank. Agursky was a small man, no more than five-three in height, slender, slope-shouldered and with a large head whose dome came shiny and pointed through its uneven halo of dirty-grey down. Behind thick lenses his magnified eyes were light-brown in a pale face; they were red-rimmed, tiredly mobile under thin but expressive eyebrows. Thin-lipped and big-eared, he looked somehow gnomish in a para-doxically uncomical sort of way.

The red lighting of the thing's room was turned low so as not to frighten it down out of sight beneath the sand of its tank; it "knew" Agursky and rarely became excited in his presence; while he sat observing the thing, with his skinny legs astride a steel chair and his elbows on the backrest, so it sprawled on the floor of its tank watching him. At present it was a leech-thing with a rodent face. A pseudopod, sprouting from a spot on its rear left-hand side, moved slowly on starfish feet, independently examining pebbles and lumps of crusted sand, then laying them aside. The pseudopod's single rudimentary eye was alert and unblinking.

The creature was hungry, and Agursky—unable to sleep despite the half-bottle of vodka he'd consumed—had decided to come down here and feed it. The queer

thing (one of many queer things) was this: that lately
he'd noticed how its moods seemed to affect him.
When it was restless, so was he. Likewise when it was
hungry. Tonight, despite the fact that he'd eaten fairly
well during the day, he had *felt* hungry. And so he'd
known that it must be hungry, too. It didn't really need
to eat, not that he'd been able to discover, but it did
like to. Offal from the cookhouse, blood of slaughtered
beasts, the matted hides and hooves, eyes and brains
and guts which men scorned—all of these things were
grist for its mill. Ground up, they'd all go in through its
feeder tube, and the thing in the tank would devour the
lot.

"What the hell are you?" Agursky asked the creature
for what must have been the thousandth time since it
came into his care. Frustrating to say the least, for if
anyone should have known the answer to his question it
was Agursky himself. Zoology and psychology were
his "A" subjects; he'd been brought in specifically to
study the thing and find out what made it tick, but all
he'd discovered so far was that it ticked. After he'd
worked with it for only a month or so other scientists,
supposedly better qualified, had come to see it. Agursky
had been slacking, apparently. But they'd looked at it,
studied his notes, shaken their heads and gone away
baffled. And he'd been left to get on with it. But get on
with what? He knew the creature as intimately as any
man could possible wish to know it, and still he didn't
know it.

Its blood was similar to the blood of all Earth's
myriad animals, but sufficiently dissimilar to any of
them as to make it alien. On the scales of intelligence it
was not a higher species—not in comparison with Man,
the dolphins, canines, apes—and yet it did have a
certain sly intelligence. Its eyes, for example, were
near-hypnotic. Every now and then Agursky had to stop
staring it down and look away, or he was liable to go to
sleep. The thing had put him to sleep on several occa-

sions. And nightmares had invariably brought him gibbering awake.

It could be taught but resisted learning; it knew, for instance, that when its keeper showed it a white card food was coming. Also that a black card meant it was in danger of receiving an electrical shock. It had learned, painfully, that white and black cards together meant: "Don't touch the food until the black card is taken away." But to show it those cards together would produce a great fury in it. When food was available it did not like being denied it, or threatened through it. These were a few of the things Agursky had learned about the creature, but he would get the uncomfortable feeling just looking at it that it had learned far more about him. Another thing he knew about it was this: that it had a capacity for hate. And he knew who it hated.

"Feeding time," he told it. "I'm going to pump some vile, rancid, gone-off shit in there with you. And you're going to slurp it up like mother's milk and honey sweet from the comb—you bloody *thing*!" Doubtless it would prefer a live white rat or two, but the sight (even the thought) of that had already given Agursky too many bad dreams. For that was something else he'd learned about the thing in the tank: that while it would take dead, clotted blood readily enough, it in fact preferred it straight from a perforated, pulsing artery. Namely, that it was a vampire.

As Agursky stood up and began to prepare the feeding apparatus, he remembered the first time he'd tried the thing with a live rat. That had meant first drugging the creature in the tank and putting it well and truly to sleep. A small amount of blood containing a massive dose of tranquilizing agent had seen to that; after the thing had groggily retreated beneath the sand of its tank to sleep, then the heavy lid had been unclamped and lifted, and the wriggling rat inserted. Three hours later (a remarkably short spell for the drug dosage) the thing had regained its senses and surfaced to see what was going on.

The rat hadn't stood a chance. Oh, it had fought as only a cornered rat can fight, but to no avail. The vampire had held it down, bitten through its neck and siphoned off its living blood. And it had formed a pair of fleshy, needle-tipped tubes to do so, actual siphons which it had slid into the rat's severed vessels.

The "meal" had taken only a minute or two to complete, and Agursky had never seen the creature so avid for its food. After that . . . occasionally the thing would take on certain rodent characteristics, which its keeper assumed it had "learned" from the creature it devoured. Nor was "devoured" too strong a word for it; for after leeching the rat's blood, then the creature had consumed skin, bones, tail and all!

From this and subsequent meals of living food, Agursky had drawn several conclusions, however unproven. Encounter One had been a vampire; or if not vampiric, certainly it had been a carnivore. It had been seen to devour men whole before it fled the complex. Encounter Two, the wolf, was also a predator, a flesh-eater. Four was a bat—but specifically a *vampire* bat. And five . . . he had declared himself to be Wamphyri. Was there anything at all in that world beyond the Gate which was not vampiric or savagely carnivorous? Agursky's conclusion: that world was not one he would care to visit to find out at first hand.

Another speculation or line of thought which might lead to a number of unthinkable conclusions was this: that three of the five encounters—the five incursions from beyond—had been shape-changers, creatures which were not bound to one form. The thing in the tank, having examined and eaten a rat, could now assume an imperfect rodent identity. Would it also be able to emulate a man? Which in turn begged the question, was the Wamphyri warrior a man with the ability to change his shape, or had he *been* something else which now merely imitated a man?

Morbid thoughts and questions such as these had driven Agursky to drink, and thinking them again now made him wish he had a bottle with him right here, right now. But he didn't. The sooner he could get done with this, the sooner he'd be able to get back to his quarters and drink himself to sleep.

Just inside the door stood a trolley with the creature's food in a lidded container. The container was hooked up to an electric pump. Agursky wheeled the trolley closer to the tank and plugged in to the power supply. He coupled up the container's outlet to a feeder tube in the end wall of the tank, turned the valves on the container and tank to the open position and started the motor. The electric motor was quietly efficient; with a cough and a gurgle, glutinous liquids commenced to flow.

As he worked, Agursky had been aware that the thing was watching him. Strangely, it had not turned toward the food supply but remained in the position in which he'd left it. Only its eyes had swivelled to follow his movements. Agursky was puzzled. Dark red lumps of minced meat in a stream of semi-clotted beast-blood were jetting in sporadic spurts into the tank, forming a foul heap of guts on the sand at that end of the thing's "lair." And still it hadn't moved.

Agursky frowned. The creature could consume half its own weight at a time, and it hadn't been fed for four days. Could it be sick? Was its air supply OK? And *now* what the hell was it doing?

He went back to his chair and seated himself as before, with his arms folded on the backrest and his chin resting on the back of his left hand. The creature stared back at him through eyes which now seemed very nearly human. Its face, too, had lost much of its rodent identity and had taken on more nearly human outlines. The leech-like body sack was elongating, losing its dark colour and corrugations. Legs were developing, and arms—and breasts?

"What?" Agursky hissed the single word from between clenched teeth. *"What . . . ?"*

The spurious pebble-examining member shrank, was withdrawn into the main mass of the body. That body was now very nearly human, in shape if nothing else. It was like a girl, even had a girl's flowing hair. But on the creature's head that mass of hair was coarse and lacklustre, like the false hair of a poorly made doll. The breasts were lumpy and without nipples, like pallid blobs of flesh stuck on a flat male chest. The size, too, was wrong, for the thing only had the mass of a large dog, which even remodelled made for a very small woman.

With every passing second the expression on Agursky's face grew that much more disgusted. The creature was attempting to resemble a woman, but it was making a nightmarishly horrific job of it. Its "hands" had now shaped themselves into appendages very like human hands, but the nails on the too-slender fingers were bright scarlet and far too long. Worse, its "feet" were also hands: the creature couldn't discriminate. Then . . . the thing's simpering, idiot face smiled at Agursky, and suddenly he knew where he'd seen that smile before.

It was the face and smile, even the hair, of that sex-starved hag Klara Orlova, a spindly theoretical physicist who was fascinated by the creature and occasionally came in here to admire it! It had seen her face, her hands with their brightly painted nails, the upper roundness of her bosom where she wore that gown of hers unbuttoned to titillate the common soldiers—but it didn't know she had nipples, and it hadn't seen her feet at all. It had simply assumed that her feet were like her hands!

Agursky checked himself: no, for that would be to grant the thing too high a level of intelligence, and he had already satisfied himself that it was not especially bright. This mimicking was like the mindless, human-seeming cry of a parrot, or the ape wearing spectacles to "read" a book. Indeed it was less than the latter, for it was purely instinctive. Like the colour change of a chameleon, or better still the chameleon's colour control *plus* the elasticity of the octopus.

Even while he was thinking these thoughts the thing had been ironing out certain imperfections. The skin tone was more nearly correct, as was the painted Cupid's bow of the mouth. The vampire's nose and dark nostrils, however, were still ugly and alien, ridged, convoluted and quivering. In its natural environment (wherever the hell that was) its sense of smell might well be its most important tool for survival; to change that organ's shape would be to drastically degrade its function. In any event, the final image which the thing presented— for all that it was still wrong, still grotesque—was at least something of . . . an attempt?

But an attempt at what?

Suddenly, unreasonably, Agursky felt fury surging in him. Was this . . . this damned, flesh-eating *slime* actually trying to seduce him?

"Damn you—you *thing!*—that's it, isn't it?" he cried, jumping to his feet. "You know the difference between us—or at least you sense it. And you'd like to use it! You think I'll be a little nicer to my plastic, blood-guzzling, alien little whore if I think I can maybe make love to it, eh? By God!—have *you* got the wrong man!"

Like a playful cat the thing stretched, rolled on its back, thrust its pale, useless breasts at him. There was no navel in its belly, but a little below where a navel should be was a protuberant, pulsing tube of flesh that could only be the thing's conception of a human vulva. The sexual implications turned Agursky white with rage in a moment. The thing *was* trying to seduce him! He yanked a black card from the pocket of his smock, showed it to the half-smiling, half-grimacing thing.

"You see this, you motherless monstrosity? How'd you like to dance for uncle, eh? You don't like that, do you?" But it was a bluff and the creature knew it. Its limpid eyes looked through the glass, this way and that all around the room, but Agursky hadn't brought the shock-box with him. He was impotent to carry out his threat.

The gurgling, crimson mess from the feeder tube continued to pump into the tank. The container was almost empty, and still the thing hadn't been tempted to start feeding. But now, as Agursky tremblingly took his seat again, a stream of scarlet seepage from the pile of offal found a zigzag route to the creature and touched its side. The metamorphosis which took place in it then was rapid indeed.

Its neck twisted round at an impossible angle to allow its quasi-human face to peer at the blood spreading round its flank. Then the face turned back and Agursky saw that the thing's eyes had taken on the hue of the blood it had observed. Hell glared out of those eyes at him. The grotesque, imitation face began to melt into another shape, another form. The mouth widened until it spanned almost the entire face, opened to display a cavernous gape where crooked, needle-sharp teeth lined a scarlet throat as far back as Agursky cared to look. And a forked snake's tongue vibrated in there, the tips of the fork flickering this way and that between the slime-dripping lips of the thing.

"That's more like it!" Agursky cried, feeling that he'd achieved something of a victory. "Your little plan didn't work, so now let's see you as you really are."

Contact with the raw red pulp had triggered the thing's hunger, ripped away its mask. In the face of instinctive urges it was incapable of keeping up the deception. Except . . . for all the time he'd spent with the creature, Agursky had never seen anything quite like this before. Its food was there and the thing from beyond the Gate knew it, but more than just hunger and blood-lust had been triggered. And again the scientist wondered: *is it ill? Is it suffering? And if so, from what?*

For as if the vibration of the tongue had been only the start of it, the catalyst, now the thing's entire body was beginning to tremble. The human paleness of its protoplasm (Agursky could scarcely bring himself to think of it simply as "flesh") was turning a slaty, almost leprous colour and tufts of coarse hair were sprouting everywhere. Limbs retracted, withering back into the main mass, and the vibrations of the whole began to come in regular, almost seismic spasms.

Watching it—fascinated despite himself, so that he was unable to take his eyes off it—Agursky's lips drew back from his yellow teeth in a silent snarl of loathing. God, the thing resembled nothing so much as a vast, diseased placenta—with a head!

But its crimson eyes still glared at him, and even as he continued to observe it so the thing curled back its forked tongue to reach far back into its own throat. Its spasms became retching movements, until finally the creature coughed its tongue back into view. Balanced in the slightly upward curving fork was a quivering, misted-pearl sphere about as big as a small boy's marble.

Agursky quickly stood up, went to the tank, crouched down and stared hard at the strange blob of matter in the creature's gaping mouth. Whatever it was, he could see that it was alive! Its surface was aswim with a pearly film, but Agursky believed he could see rows of flickering cilia around its circumference, causing the sphere to turn vertically on its own axis where it rested in the fork of the thing's tongue.

"Now what—?" he started to say—but at that precise moment the creature thrust its head forward and its tongue uncoiled, hurling the pearly sphere directly at the scientist's face!

Agursky automatically jerked back, went sprawling on his backside. A ridiculous reaction, for of course the creature could do him no harm while the thick glass of the tank separated them. That was where the shimmering blob of matter had landed, flattening itself to the glass wall and clinging there. But even as Agursky stood up and shakily dusted himself down, so the sphere was on the move.

It slipped down the inner wall of the tank, came to rest—however briefly—on the blood-slimed sand and pebbles. Then it resumed its spherical shape, floating like a pearly bubble on the film of blood. And with its myriad flickering cilia propelling it, it swiftly followed the stream back to its source beneath the feeder tube. Then, an astonishing thing:

Like a ping-pong ball riding a jet of water, the spheroid *climbed* the last thick trickle of gore to the tube's inlet and disappeared inside. Frowning, jaw hanging slack, Agursky stepped to that side of the tank. The valves were still open, of course, and . . . it would be wonderful to isolate this thing, this—parasite? Is that what it was? Some parasitic creature inhabiting the alien's body? Perhaps, but—

All sorts of ideas, words, were going through Agursky's mind. He had likened the creature itself to a placenta in the moment before it coughed this thing up. Maybe the connection he'd made there hadn't been too wild after all. The creature had seemed to undergo a sort of cataplasia, a reversion of its cells and tissues to a more primitive, almost embryonic form. Placenta, cataplasia, embryo—protoplast?

Egg?

Agursky turned off the valves and pump, pulled the trolley close and lifted the heavy lid of the food container. Inside, central on the bottom of the container, floating on a film of blood amidst a few lumps of red gristle and unidentifiable debris, the pearly sphere whirled in a blur of almost invisible cilia. Agursky stared at it and shook his head in bewilderment.

In a moment of carelessness, fascinated and simply

forgetting what he was dealing with here, he reached into the container and gently nudged the thing with the digit finger of his right hand. In the moment of contact he realized the folly of his action, but it was already too late.

The spheroid turned blood red in a moment—and ran up his hand under the cuff of his white laboratory smock. Agursky gave a gurgling cry, rearing up and back, away from the trolley. He could feel the spheroid wetly mobile on his forearm, moving swiftly to his upper arm, his shoulder. In a moment it was on his neck, coming out from under his collar. Dancing like a maniac, he cursed and slapped at the thing, felt it damp against his palm and for a single instant of time believed he'd crushed it. But then it was on the back of his neck.

Which was exactly where it *wanted* to be! The vampire egg soaked like quicksilver through Agursky's skin and settled on his spinal column.

Incredible pain at once filled his body, his limbs, his brain. Out of sheer reaction, like a man grasping a live cable, he bounded, bounded again and again. He crashed into a wall, lurched dizzily away from it, crumpled to his knees. Somehow he forced himself upright again, waded across the room through an ocean of pain. He must *do* something; but this hideous . . . this unbearable . . .

Red rockets were bursting, burning in his brain. Someone—some*thing*—was dripping acid on nerveendings which were as raw as if recently severed. Agursky screamed, and as the entire world began to turn crimson saw his only possible salvation: the black alarm button in its red-framed glass box on the wall.

Even as he passed out he summoned sufficient strength to throw a punch at the glass box . . .

Chapter Six
Harry Keogh: Necroscope

HARRY SAT ON THE RIM OF THE RIVER AND TALKED TO HIS mother. He believed he was alone and unobserved, but it would make no difference anyway: no one would object to a crazy hermit sitting on a riverbank talking to himself. He suspected that a handful of locals thought of him that way, as an eccentric recluse: someone to be regarded warily, but mainly harmless. He suspected it and didn't much care one way or the other. In their position he'd probably feel the same way about it.

Indeed he sometimes wished he *was* in their position: normal, common-or-garden, everyday people. *Homo sapiens,* with normal lives to lead. But he wasn't in their position, he was in his, and it could hardly be described as normal. He was a Necroscope* and as far as he knew he was the only Necroscope in the world. There should be at least one other like him, his son, but Harry Jr. was no longer in the world. Or if he was, Harry didn't know where.

Harry looked down between his knees and dangling legs at his own face mirrored on the surface of the water. He watched its blank expression turn to a cynical scowl. "His own face," indeed! For to complicate

Necroscope: Tor, 1988.

matters, it wasn't his face at all! Or it was—now. But it *had been* the face of Alec Kyle, one-time head of British E-Branch. And yet Harry also seemed to see himself—the Harry Keogh he'd once been—superimposed over the stranger's face, making up a composite mask which wasn't really strange at all. Not any longer. But it had taken him eight long years to get used to it. Eight years of waking up in the mornings, of looking in the mirror and thinking: *Jesus! Who's this?* Until in the end the question has been merely academic. He'd known who it was: himself, in mind if not in body.

"Harry?" his mother's suddenly anxious voice broke in on his mental paradox. "You know you really shouldn't worry any more about things like that. That side of your life is over, done with. You were called to do a job and you did it. You did more than any other man could possibly have done. And for all that there have been . . . well, changes, you know that you're still you."

"But in another man's body," he answered, wryly.

"Alec was dead, Harry," she made the point bluntly, for there was no other way to make it. "He was worse than dead, for there was nothing left of his mind at all—not even of his soul. And anyway, you had no choice."

Harry's thoughts, spurred by his mother's words, carried him back, back to that time eight years ago:

Alec Kyle had been on a mission to Romania—to destroy the remains of a human vampire in the ground there.* Thibor Ferenczy had been dead, but he'd left part of himself in the earth to pollute it, and to pollute anyone who went near it. Kyle had succeeded, burned the thing, and was on the point of returning to England when Soviet espers had picked him up. Flown in secrecy to Russia, to the Château Bronnitsy, the then HQ of Soviet E-Branch, he'd been subjected to a particu-

---

Necroscope II: Vamphyri!, Tor, 1989.

larly horrific method of brain-washing. His mind had been electronically drained, his brain literally emptied of knowledge. *All* knowledge. It wasn't merely a question of hot white lights, the rubber hose, truth-drugs and the like: the very *contents* of his mind had been forcibly, needlessly extracted, like a good tooth, and thrown away. And in the process Soviet telepaths had stolen the bits that were useful to them, all the secrets of their enemies, the British espers. When they'd finished with Kyle he'd been alive—been kept alive, for the time being—but his brain had been completely vacant, dead. Taken off life-support, his body too would die. And that had been the intention of his tormentors: to let him die and have his corpse dumped in West Berlin. There wouldn't be a pathologist in the whole wide world who could state with any certainty what had killed him.

That was to have been the scenario. Except . . . while Alec Kyle had been a husk, an empty mind in a living body, the then Harry Keogh had been mind alone! Incorporeal, a bodiless inhabitant of the Möbius Continuum, Harry had searched for Kyle, found him, and the rest had been almost beyond his control. Nature abhors a vacuum, whether in the physical or metaphysical worlds. The normal universe had no use for an incorporeal being. And Kyle's brain had been an aching void. Thus Harry's mind had become one with Kyle's body.

Since then . . . a great deal had happened since then.

Harry forced the scowl from his face, stared harder at his image in the calm river water. His hair (or Alec's?) was russet-brown, plentiful and naturally wavy; but in the last eight years a lot of the lustre had disappeared, and streaks of grey had become very noticeable. It would not be too long before the grey overtook and ruled the brown, and Harry not yet thirty. His eyes, too, were honey-brown; very wide, very intelligent, and (strange beyond words) very innocent! Even now, for all he'd seen, experienced and learned, innocent. It could be argued that certain murderers have the same look, but in Harry the innocence was mainly genuine. He had not asked to be what he was, or to be called upon to do the things he'd done.

His teeth were strong, not quite white, a little uneven; they were set in a mouth which was unusually sensitive but could also be cruel, caustic. He had a high brow, which now and then he'd search for freckles. The old Harry used to have freckles, but no longer.

As for the rest of Harry's body: it had been well-fleshed, maybe even a little overweight, once. With its height, however, that hadn't mattered a great deal. Not to Alec Kyle, whose job with E-Branch had been in large part sedentary. But it had mattered to Harry. He'd trained his new body down, got it to a peak of condition. It wasn't bad for a forty-year-old body. But better if it was only thirty, like Harry himself.

"You're at odds with yourself again, Harry," said his mother. "What's bothering you, son? Is it Brenda still, and little Harry?"

"No use denying it," he gruffly answered, with something of an irritable shrug. "You never met him, did you? He'd have been able to talk to you too, you know. But . . . I *still* can't get over the way he did it. It's one thing to lose somebody—or even two some-bodies—but quite another to be left wondering why. He could have told me where he was taking her, could have explained his reasons. After all, it wasn't my fault she was like she was—was it? Maybe it was," (again his shrug,) "I don't know any more . . ."

His mother had heard all of this before; she knew what he meant, intimately understood his otherwise vague words and expressions, even his tone of voice. For while he didn't need to, he usually spoke out loud to her. He didn't need to because he was a Necroscope, (no, *the* Necroscope, the man who communicated with the dead) and also because she *was* dead, and had been since Harry was an infant. She was down there, where she'd been for more than twenty-seven years, in the mud and the weeds of the river, murdered all that time ago by Harry's stepfather. Yes, and now that same traitor was down there with her, put there by Harry, but he'd stopped speaking to anybody long ago.

"Why not look at it from their point of view?" his mother said, reasonably. "Brenda had been through an awful lot for a small village girl. Maybe she simply . . . well, wanted to get away from it all. For a while, anyway."

"For eight years?" There was a brittle edge to Harry's voice.

"But having made the break," his mother hurriedly went on, at her diplomatic best, "she found she was happier. And he could see she was happier, and so they didn't come back. After all's said and done, your main concern was for their happiness, wasn't it, Harry? And you'd be the first to admit that you weren't the man she'd married. Well, not exactly. *Oh!*" And he could picture her hand flying to her mouth, even though he knew she no longer had either of those things. Alas, she'd stumbled over her own argument, speaking not only her mind but Harry's, too. "I mean—"

"It's all right," he stifled her. "I know what you mean. And you're right—as far as you go." But because she had tried to be diplomatic, she hadn't gone far enough. And Harry knew that, too.

What had happened back then, eight years ago, was this:

In the Möbius Continuum, Harry had discovered by chance the elements of an insidious plot which was unfolding in the mundane world. The vampire Thibor Ferenczy had set in motion a gradual metamorphosis in a child as yet unborn. He had physically (and psychically, spiritually) defiled an innocent unsuspecting mother-to-be, causing something of himself to attach and cling to her foetal child. Now that child was grown to a youth, Yulian Bodescu, and as he had developed so his potential for evil had outstripped his human side to achieve a monstrous vampire dominance.

The task of the British E-Branch had been twofold: to seek out and destroy whatever remained of lingering vampire influences (especially what remained of Thibor) in the USSR and her satellites, and so ensure that the "Bodescu situation" could never arise again; also to destroy Yulian Bodescu himself through whom Thibor had determined to terrorize the world anew.

But Bodescu had discovered the covert workings of E-Branch, specifically their plot and determination to put him down, and had turned his awesome emerging vampire powers and cold, cruel fury upon them. His principal adversary in the Branch had been the incorporeal Harry Keogh, who at the time was trapped in the psyche of his own infant son. Kill Harry Jr. and Bodescu would also rid himself of Harry. After that . . . the remaining members of E-Branch could be tracked down and picked off one by one, at the vampire's discretion.

This was a scheme monstrous enough in itself, but the true horror of the situation would lie in the aftermath of such a bloodbath; for then there would be no stopping Bodescu, who could create almost at will an army of undead followers which would spread like a dark plague across the face of the entire earth! And this was a very real possibility, for while Bodescu had become one of the Wamphyri, he did not have their self-discipline. They were essentially territorial; they had their cold pride; they were solitary and cautious, and usually firmly in control of their own destinies. Most of all, they were jealous of their powers, deviously protective of their Wamphyri nature and history, aware and appreciative of human skills and ingenuity. Only let mankind become aware that they were real and not merely creatures of myth and legend, and men would strive to hunt them down and destroy them forever! But Yulian Bodescu was "self-taught";

he had had no Wamphyri instruction. He was none of the things which had made them what they were and possessed none of their dubious qualities. He was only a vampire, and he was insane!

Brenda and her months-old infant son Harry Jr. were living in a garret flat in Hartlepool on the north-east coast of England when matters finally came to a head. Leaving a trail of bloodshed and destruction behind him, Bodescu evaded E-Branch's attempts at entrapment, fled his home in Devon and travelled north. Having inherited his mentor's expertise in hideous necromancy, he could "examine" the desecrated corpses of his victims and read in their brains and blood and guts all of their innermost secrets. This was his intention in respect of the two Harrys, father and son: to murder them and steal the secrets of the Necroscope, and so discover the nature and properties of the metaphysical Möbius Continuum.

E-Branch, closing on the Devon house to destroy it, missed their main quarry but discovered unthinkable horror there. Bodescu's aunt, uncle and cousin had been tortured and vampirized; his huge black dog was something more than a mere dog; a semi-plastic *thing* inhabited the earth under the extensive cellars, and Bodescu's mother was quite out of her mind from the unbearable knowledge of what Yulian had become. The house and all who dwelled in it were put to the torch.

E-Branch had men in Hartlepool, physically talented people who were keeping a low profile in and around the Edwardian building which housed Brenda's flat. The local police and Special Branch had also been informed (however guardedly, so as not to panic the populace) that the woman and child in the garret rooms were possible targets for an "escaped lunatic." Their presence hardly deterred the vampire; he invaded the building, killed all who stood before him mercilessly and with dreadful efficiency, and finally reached his objective. But where the incorporeal Harry Keogh himself had been impotent, his infant son was anything but. His father's freakish powers had come down to him; he could talk to the dead, could even call them up from their graves in the cemetery across the road from the house.

Harry Sr. had considered himself "trapped" in the baby's psyche, but this had not been the case. The infant had held him there for one reason only: to explore Harry's mind and learn from it. Physically he was a baby, apparently helpless, but mentally—

Harry Jr.'s talents were already vaster far than anything his father possessed or ever dreamed of achieving. And his potential was enormous. All the theory was there in the child's mind and only practical application, experience, was missing. But not for long.

Brenda, attempting to protect her infant son from the incredible nightmare which was Yulian Bodescu, had been tossed aside by the vampire. Unconscious, she had not seen the final confrontation. Thinking back on that scene in the flat now, Harry remembered it as vividly as if it were yesterday:

The two Harrys had looked out through the infant's eyes into the face of terror itself, the face of Yulian Bodescu. Crouched over the baby's cot, the leering malignancy of his eyes spoke all too clearly of his intentions.

Finished! Harry had thought. *All done, and it ends like this.*

No, another voice, not his own, had spoken in his mind. *No it doesn't. Through you I've learned what I had to learn. I don't need you that way any more. But I do still need you as a father. So go, save yourself.*

It could only have been one person speaking to him, doing it now, for the first time, when there was no longer any time to question the hows and whys of it. Then . . . Harry had felt the child's restraints falling from him like broken chains, leaving him free again. Free to will his incorporeal mind into the safety of the

Möbius Continuum. He could have gone, right there and then, leaving his son to face whatever was coming. He *could* have gone—but he couldn't!

Bodescu's jaws had yawned open like a pit, revealing a snake's tongue flickering behind gleaming dagger teeth.

Go! little Harry had said again, with more urgency.

You're my son! Harry had cried. *Damn you. I can't go! I can't leave you to this!*

Leave me to this? It had been as if the infant couldn't follow his reasoning. But then he had, and said: *But did you think I was going to stay here?*

The beast's taloned hands were reaching for the child in his cot. Little Harry had seen the lust in the monster's eyes; he turned his small round head this way and that, seeking a Möbius door. A door had appeared, floating up out of his pillows. It was easy, instinct, in his genes. It had been there all along. His control over his mind was awesome; over his body, much less certain. But he'd been able to manage this much. Bunching inexpert muscles, he'd curled himself up, rolled into and through the Möbius door. The vampire's hands and jaws had closed on thin air!

After that it had been all up for Yulian Bodescu. Harry had not called up the dead from the local graveyard, but his son had. For the dead had learned to love this child who talked to them, who *had* talked to them even from the womb! They loved him even as they loved and trusted his father; and if Harry Jr. was in trouble, that was all the incentive they needed to move limbs stiffened by death, to will back into pseudolife tissues and sinews long turned to leather and ravaged by the worm.

They had pinned the vampire down, staked him out between their own yawning graves, lopped his harshly screaming head from his body and burned him to ashes. And Harry Sr., no longer prisoned but once more master of the Möbius Continuum, had watched them do it and instructed them when they faltered.

Later . . . Harry had discovered that his infant son had not only saved his own life but also removed his unconscious mother from danger. The child had used Möbius or Zöllnerist metaphysics to move both himself and Brenda to a place of safety—indeed, to the safest possible place: E-Branch HQ in London! And Harry had been left to pursue his own destiny and inhabit the shell of the once-Alec Kyle.

This he had done, and in the process destroyed the KGB's new toy, the Soviet espionage centre at the Château Bronnitsy.

After that . . . it should have been a time for relaxation, a time to pause and take stock, make adjustments, realign lives. But the staff of E-Branch, jubilant over their triple success—the elimination of Yulian Bodescu, the termination of residual vampire sources abroad, and the destruction of Russia's KGB-corrupted esper corps—hadn't fully appreciated the stresses Harry and his family had suffered. Now that the job was done they wanted the entire thing pegged out, mapped, recorded, studied and more fully understood; and the only man who understood all of it was Harry. For a month he gave them what they wanted, even considered taking on the job of Director of E-Branch; but over that same period of time it had become increasingly apparent that all was not well with Brenda. As Harry's mother had so recently pointed out, there was hardly any mystery that anyone could attach to that; indeed Brenda's breakdown was only to have been expected, might even have been anticipated.

After all, she'd only recently been a mother and was still recovering from an uncomfortable confinement and difficult birth. Indeed, for a little while the doctors had thought they'd lost her. Add to this the fact of her husband's talents (that he was a Necroscope) which she had known and which had preyed on her mind for months; the fact that her infant child seemed to possess similar and even more frightening powers, so that even in the midst of E-Branch men, who were themselves ESP-endowed, he was looked upon as something of a freak; the fact that Harry was now (literally) a different person, a person who *was* Harry, was all of his past, his memories and mannerisms, but living in a total stranger's body; the fact of the absolute *terror* she had endured through that night, face to face with the monster Yulian Bodescu, whose like she couldn't possibly have imagined even in her worst nightmares . . .

Little wonder the poor girl's mind had started to give way under the strain! On top of all of which she hated London and couldn't return to Hartlepool; her old flat was poison to her now, where monstrous memories dwelled. And gradually, as her mental connections with the real world were eroded, so her visits to various specialists and psychiatric clinics increased—until one morning she and the baby . . .

"They'd gone!" Harry said it out loud. "They weren't there. They weren't anywhere that I've been able to discover. And what gets to me most is that there was no warning, no hint. He simply up and took her . . . somewhere. And you know, he never spoke to me? After that first time in the flat, when Yulian Bodescu almost had us, he never *once* spoke to me! He could have; he'd look at me in that way babies have, and I knew he could have spoken to me. But he never did." Harry sighed, shrugged. "So maybe he blamed me, too. Maybe they both did. And who can say they weren't right to blame me? If I hadn't been the way I was—"

"Oh?" his mother was angry now. She didn't like the tone of self-pity which had started to creep into Harry's voice. Where was all that quiet strength he'd used to have? "If you hadn't been what you were? And Boris Drogosani still alive in Russia? And Yulian Bodescu, spreading heaven-only-knows what evil through the world? And the myriad dead, cast off and forgotten, lost and lonely, thinking their dead thoughts forever in the cold earth and never knowing that they weren't really alone at all? But you've changed all that Harry. And there's no way back. *Hah!* If you weren't what you are, indeed!''

He nodded to himself, thinking that of course she was right, then picked up a pebble and tossed it in the water so that its ripples shivered his image into ribbons. ''Still,'' he said as his face slowly reformed. ''I'd like to know where they went. I'd like to be sure they're OK. Are you certain, Ma, that you haven't heard anything?''

''From the dead? Harry, there's not one of us who doesn't want to help. Believe me, if Brenda and little Harry were . . . with us, you'd be the first to know of it. Wherever they are, they're alive, son. You can rely on that.''

He frowned and tiredly rubbed at his forehead. ''You know, Ma, I can't figure it out. If anyone could find them it has to be me. And I haven't even found a trace of them! When they disappeared, I got those people at E-Branch on it. They couldn't find them. A couple of them even approached me cautiously with the idea— and with a little sensitivity, you understand—that maybe Brenda and the baby were dead. By the time I handed the job over to Darcy Clarke six months later, everyone seemed *sure* they were dead.

''Now E-Branch has people who could find anybody anywhere—spotters who can pick up psychic emanations on the other side of the world—but they couldn't find my son. And little Harry's talent was far and away greater than mine. But your people,'' (he was talking about the Great Majority, the countless dead,) ''they say they're alive, that they have to be alive because they don't number amongst the dead. And I know that none of you would ever lie to me. So I think to myself: if they're not dead, and they're not here where I can

106

find them—*then where the hell are they?* That's what's eating away at me.''

He could sense her nod, feel how sad she was for him. "I know, son, I know."

"And as for physically searching for them—" he went on, as if he hadn't heard her, "—is there anywhere in this world where I didn't look? But if E-Branch couldn't find them, what chance did I stand?"

Harry's mother had heard all this before. It was his obsession now, his one passion in life. He was like a gambler hooked on roulette, whose one dream is to find "the system" where none exists. He'd spent almost five years searching, and nearly three more planning the various stages of the search. To no avail. She had tried to help him every step of the way, but so far it had been a long, bitterly disappointing road.

Harry stood up, dusted a little soil from his trousers. "I'm going back to the house now, Ma. I'm tired. I feel like I've been tired for a long time. I think I could use a good long rest. Sometimes I think it would be good if I could just stop thinking . . . about them, anyway."

She knew what he meant: that he'd reached the end of the road, that there was nowhere else he could look.

"That's right," he said, turning away from the riverbank, "nowhere else to look, and not much purpose to it anyway. Not much purpose to anything any more . . ."

Head down, he bumped into someone who at once took his arm to steady him. At first Harry didn't recognize the man, but recognition quickly followed. "Darcy? Darcy Clarke?" Harry began to smile, only to feel the smile turning sour on his face. "Oh, yes—Darcy Clarke," he said, more slowly this time. "And you wouldn't be here if you didn't want something. I thought I'd already made it clear to you people. I'm through with all of that."

Clarke studied his face, a face he'd known well from

the old days, when it had belonged to someone else. There were more lines than there used to be, and there was also something more of character. Not that Alec Kyle had been without character, but Harry's had gradually imprinted itself on the flesh. Also, there was weariness in that face, and signs that there'd been a lot of pain, too.

"Harry," Clarke said, "did I hear you telling yourself just now that there's no purpose to anything? Is that how you're feeling?"

Harry glanced at him sharply. "How long were you spying on me?"

Clarke was taken aback. "I was standing there by the wall," he said. "I wasn't spying, Harry. But . . . I didn't want to disturb you, that's all. I mean," he nodded toward the river, "this is where your mother is, isn't it?"

Harry suddenly felt defensive. He looked away, then looked back and nodded. He had nothing to fear from this man. "Yes," he said, "she's here. It was my mother I was talking to."

Without thinking, Clarke glanced quickly all about. "You were talking to—?" Then he looked once more at the quiet flowing river and his expression changed. In a lowered voice, he said: "Of course, I'd almost forgotten."

"Had you?" Harry was quick off the mark. "You mean that isn't what you come to see me about?" Then he relented a little. "OK, come on back to the house. We can talk as we go."

As they made their way through brittle gorse and wild bramble, Clarke unobtrusively studied the Necroscope. Not only did Harry seem a little vacant, abstracted, but his style in general seemed to have suffered. He wore an open-necked shirt under a baggy grey pullover, thin grey trousers, scuffed shoes on his feet. It was the attire of someone who didn't much care. "You'll catch your death of cold," Clarke told him, with genuine concern. The E-Branch head forced a smile. "Didn't anyone tell you? We'll soon be into November . . ."

They walked along the riverbank toward the large Victorian house brooding there behind its high stone garden wall. The house had once belonged to Harry's mother, then to his stepfather, and now it had come down naturally to Harry. "Time's not something I worry about a lot," Harry eventually answered. "When I feel it's getting colder I'll put more clothes on."

"But it doesn't matter much, right?" said Clarke. "There doesn't seem to be much purpose to it. Or to anything. Which means you haven't found them yet. I'm sorry, Harry."

Now it was Harry's turn to study Clarke.

The head of E-Branch had been chosen for that job because after Harry he was the obvious candidate. Clarke's talent guaranteed continuity. He was what they called a "deflector," the opposite of accident-prone. He could walk through a minefield and come out of it unscathed. And if he did step on one it would turn out to be a dud. His talent protected him, and that was all it did. But it would ensure that he'd always be there, that nothing and no one would ever take him out, as two heads before him had been taken out. Darcy Clarke would die one day for sure—all men do—but it would be old age that got him.

But to look at Clarke without knowing this . . . no one would ever have guessed he was in charge of anything, and certainly not the most secret branch of the Secret Service. Harry thought: *he's probably the most perfectly nondescript man!* Middle-height (about five-eight or -nine,) mousey-haired, with something of a slight stoop and a tiny paunch, but not overweight either: he was just about middle-range in every way. And in another five or six years he'd be just about middle-aged, too!

Pale hazel eyes stared back at Harry from a face much given to laughter, which Harry suspected hadn't laughed for quite some little time. Despite the fact that Clarke was well wrapped-up in duffle coat and scarf, still he looked cold. But not so much physically as spiritually.

"That's right," the Necroscope finally answered. "I haven't found them, and that's sort of killed off my drive. Is that why you're here, Darcy? To supply me with a new purpose, a new direction?"

"Something like that," Clarke nodded. "I certainly hope so, anyway."

They passed through a door in the wall into Harry's unkempt back garden which lay gloomy in the shade of gables and dormers, where the paint was flaking and high windows looked down like frowning eyes in a haughty face. Everything had been running wild in that garden for years; brambles and nettles grew dense, crowding the path, so that the two men took care where they stepped along the crazy-paving to a cobbled patio area, beyond which sliding glass doors stood open on Harry's study. The room looked dim, dusty, foreboding: Clarke found himself hesitating on the threshold.

"Enter of your own free will, Darcy," said Harry—and Clarke cast him a sharp glance. Clarke's talent, however, told him that all was well: there was nothing to drive him away from the place, no sudden urgency to depart. The Necroscope smiled, if wanly. "A joke," he said. "Tastes are like attitudes, given a different perspective they change."

Clarke stepped inside. "Home," said Harry, following him and sliding the doors shut in their frames. "Don't you think it suits me?"

Clarke didn't answer, but he thought: *well your taste was never what I would have called flamboyant. Certainly the place suits your talent!*

Harry waved Clarke into a cane chair, seated himself behind a blocky oak desk dark with age. Clarke looked all about and tried to draw the room into focus. Its gloom was unnatural; the room was meant to be airy, but Harry had put up curtains, shutting out most of the light except through the glass doors. Finally Clarke could keep it back no longer. "A bit funereal, isn't it?" he said.

Harry nodded his agreement. "It was my stepfather's room," he said. "Shukshin—the murdering bastard! He tried to kill me, you know? He was a spotter, but different to the others. He didn't just smell espers out, he hated them! Indeed, he wished he *couldn't* smell them out! The very feel of them made his skin crawl, drove him to rage. Drove him in the end to kill my mother, too, and to have a go at me."

Clarke nodded, "I know as much about you as any man, Harry. He's in the river, isn't he? Shukshin? So if it bothers you, why the hell do you go on living here?"

Harry looked away for a moment. "Yes, he's in the river," he said, "where he tried to put me. An eye for an eye. And the fact that he lived here doesn't bother me. My mother's here, too, remember? I've only a handful of enemies among the dead; the rest of them are my friends, and they're good friends. They don't make any demands, the dead . . ." He fell silent for a moment, then continued:

"Anyway, Shukshin served his purpose: if it hadn't been for him I might never have gone to E-Branch— and I mightn't be here now, talking to you. I might be out there somewhere, writing the stories of dead men."

Clarke, like Harry's mother, felt and was disturbed by his gloomy introspection. "You don't write any more?"

"They weren't my stories anyway. Like everything else, they were a means to an end. No, I don't write any more. I don't do much of anything." Abruptly, he changed the subject:

"I don't love her, you know."

"Eh?"

"Brenda," Harry shrugged. "Maybe I love the little fellow, but not his mother. See, I remember what it was like when I did love her—of course I do, because *I* haven't changed—but the physical me is different. I've a new chemistry entirely. It would never have worked, Brenda and me. No, that's not what's wrong with me, that isn't what gets to me. It's not knowing where they are. Knowing that they're there but not knowing where. That's what does it. There were enough changes in my life at that time without them going off, too. Especially him. And you know, for a while I was part of him, that little chap? However unwillingly—unwittingly?—I taught him much of what he knows. He got it from my mind, and I'm interested to know what use he's made of it. But at the same time I realize that if they hadn't gone, she and I would have been finished long ago anyway. Even if she'd recovered fully. And sometimes I think maybe it's best they did go away, and not only for her sake but his, too.''

All of this had flooded out of Harry, poured out of him without pause. Clarke was pleased; he believed he glimpsed a crack in the wall; maybe Harry was discovering that sometimes it was good to talk to the living, too. "Without knowing where he'd gone, you thought maybe it was the best thing for him? Why's that?'' he said.

Harry sat up straighter, and when he spoke his voice was cold again. "What would his life have been like with E-Branch?'' he said. "What would he be doing now, aged nine years old, eh? Little Harry Keogh Jr.: Necroscope and explorer of the Möbius Continuum?''

"Is that what you think?'' Clarke kept his voice even. "What you think of us?'' It could be that Harry was right, but Clarke liked to see it differently. "He'd have led whatever life he wanted to lead,'' he said. "This isn't the USSR, Harry. He wouldn't have been forced to do anything. Have we tried to tie you down? Have *you* been coerced, threatened, made to work for us? There's no doubt about it that you'd be our most valuable asset, but eight years ago when you said enough is enough . . . did we try to stop you from walking? We *asked* you to stay, that's all. No one applied any pressure.''

"But he would have grown up with you." Harry had thought it all out many, many times before. "He'd have been imprinted. Maybe he could see it coming and just wanted his freedom, eh?"

Clarke shook himself, physically shrugged off the mood the other had begun to impose upon him. He'd done part of what he came to do: he'd got Harry Keogh talking about his problems. Now he must get him talking, and thinking, about far greater problems—and one in particular. "Harry," he said, very deliberately, "we stopped looking for Brenda and the child six years ago. We'd have stopped even sooner, except we believed we had a duty to you—even though you'd made it plain you no longer had one to us. The fact is that we really believed they were dead, otherwise we'd have been able to find them. But that was then, and this is now, and things have changed . . ."

Things had changed? Slowly Clarke's words sank in. Harry felt the blood drain from his face. His scalp tingled. They had *believed* they were dead, but things had changed. Harry leaned forward across the desk, almost straining toward Clarke, staring at him from eyes which had opened very wide. "You've found . . . some sort of clue?"

Clarke held up placating hands, imploring restraint. He gave a half-shrug. "We *may* have stumbled across a parallel case—" he said, "—or it may be something else entirely. You see, we don't have the means to check it out. Only you can do that, Harry."

Harry's eyes narrowed. He felt he was being led on, that he was a donkey who'd been shown a carrot, but he didn't let it anger him. If E-Branch did have something . . . even a carrot would be better than the weeds he'd been chewing on. He stood up, came round the desk, began pacing the floor. At last he stood still, faced Clarke where he sat. "Then you'd better tell me all about it," he said. "Not that I'm promising anything."

Clarke nodded. "Neither am I," he said. He glanced

with disapproval all about the room. "Can we have some light in here, and some air? It's like being in the middle of a bloody fog!"

Again Harry frowned. Had Clarke got the upper hand as quickly and as easily as that? But he opened the glass doors and threw back the curtains anyway. Then: "Talk," he said, sitting down carefully again behind his desk.

The room was brighter now and Clarke felt he could breathe. He filled his lungs, leaned back and put his hands on his knees. "There's a place in the Ural Mountains called Perchorsk," he said. "That's where it all started . . ."

Chapter Seven
Möbius Trippers!

DARCY CLARKE GOT AS FAR AS PILL—THE MYSTERIOUS object shot down over the Hudson Bay, but without yet explaining its nature—when Harry stopped him. "So far," the Necroscope complained, "while all of this has been very interesting, I don't see how it's got much to do with me; or with Brenda and Harry Jr."

Clarke said, "But you will. You see, it's not the sort of thing I can just tell you part of, or only the bits you're going to be interested in. If you don't see the whole picture, then the rest of it will be doubly difficult to understand. Anyway, if you do decide you'd like in on this, you'll need to know it all. I'll be coming to the things you'll find interesting later."

Harry nodded. "All right—but let's go through to the kitchen. Could you use a coffee? Instant, I'm afraid; I've no patience with the real thing."

"Coffee would be fine," said Clarke. "And don't worry about your instant. Anything has to be good after the gallons of stuff I drink out of that machine at HQ!" And following Harry through the dim corridors of the old house, he smiled. For all the Necroscope's apparently negative response, Clarke could see that in fact he was starting to unwind.

In the kitchen Clarke waited until Harry brought the

coffee to the large wooden kitchen table and seated himself, then started to take up the story again. "As I was saying, they shot this thing down over the Hudson Bay. Now—"

"Wait," said Harry. "OK, I accept that you're going to tell it your own way. That being the case, I'd better know the bits round the edges, too. Like how your lot got interested in Perchorsk in the first place?"

"Actually, by accident," Clarke answered. "We don't automatically get called in on everything, you know. We're still very much the 'silent partner,' as it were, when it comes to the country's security. No more than half-a-dozen of Her Majesty's lads in Whitehall—and one lady, of course—know that we even exist. And that's how we prefer to keep it. As always, it makes funding difficult, not to mention the acquisition of new technology toys, but we get by. Gadgets and ghosts, that's always been the way of it. We're a meeting-point— but only just—between super-science and the so-called supernatural, and that's how we're likely to stay for quite some little time.

"But since the Bodescu affair things have been relatively quiet. Our psychics get called in a lot to help the police; indeed, they're relying on us more and more all the time. We find stolen gold, art treasures, arms caches; we even supplied a warning about that mess at Brighton, and a couple of our lads were actually on their way down there when it happened. But by and large we're still very much low-key. So we don't tell everything, and alas we don't get told everything. Even the people who do know about us have difficulty seeing how computerized probability patterns can work alongside precognition. We've come a long way, but let's face it, telepathy isn't nearly as accurate as the telephone!"

"Isn't it?" Harry's sort—with the dead—was one hundred percent accurate.

"Not if the other side knows you're listening in, no."

"But it is more secret," Harry pointed out, and

Clarke sensed the acid in his tone. "So how did you 'accidentally' learn about Perchorsk?"

"We got to know about it because our 'Comrades' at Perchorsk didn't want us to! I'll explain: do you remember Ken Layard?"

"The locator? Of course I remember him," Harry answered.

"Well, it was as simple as that. Ken was checking up on a bit of Russian military activity in the Urals—covert troop movements and what-not—and he met with resistance. There were opposed minds there, Soviet espers who were deliberately smothering the place in mental smog!"

Now a degree of animation showed in Harry's pale face, especially in his eyes, which seemed to brighten appreciably. So his old friends the Russian espers had regrouped, had they? He nodded grimly. "Soviet E-Branch is back in business, eh?"

"Obviously," said Clarke. "Oh, we've known about them for some time. But after what you did to the Château Bronnitsy they've not been taking any chances. They've been even more low-key than we are! They have two centres now: one in Moscow, right next door to the biological research laboratories on Protze Prospekt, and the other in Mogocha near the Chinese border, mainly keeping a wary eye on the Yellow Peril."

"*And* this lot at Perchorsk," Harry reminded him.

"A small section," Clarke nodded, "established there purely to keep us out! As far as we can tell, anyway. But what on earth can the Soviets be doing there that rates so high on their security list, eh? After Pill, we decided we'd better find out.

"The MI branches owed us favours; we learned that they were trying to put one of their agents—a man called Michael J. Simmons—in there; and so we, well, we sort of hitched a lift."

"You got to him?" Harry raised an eyebrow. "How?

And more to the point, since he's one of ours anyway, why?''

"Quite simply because we didn't want him to know!" Clarke seemed surprised that Harry hadn't fathomed it for himself. "What, with Soviet espers crawling all over the place, we should openly establish a telepathic link with him or something? No, we couldn't do that, for their psychics would be onto him in a flash—so we sort of bugged him instead. And since he was in the dark about it, we decided not to tell his bosses at MI5 either! Let's face it, you can't talk about what you don't know about, now can you?''

Harry gave a snort. "No, of *course* not!" he said. "And after all, why should the left hand tell the right one what it's doing, eh?''

"They wouldn't have believed us, anyway," Clarke shrugged off the other's sarcasm. "They only understand one sort of bugging. They couldn't possibly have understood ours. We borrowed something belonging to Simmons for a little while, that's all, and gave it to one of our new lads, David Chung, to work on.''

"A Chinaman?" Again the raised eyebrow.

"Chinese, yes, but a Cockney, actually," Clarke chuckled. "Born and raised in London. He's a locator and scryer, and damned good at it. So we took a cross Simmons wears and gave it to Chung. Simmons thought he'd mislaid it, and we arranged for him to find it again. Meanwhile David Chung had developed a 'sympathetic link' with the cross, so that he would 'know' where it was at any given time and even be able to see or scry through it, like using a crystal ball. It worked, too—for a while, anyway.''

"Oh?" Harry's interest was waning again. He'd never thought much of espionage, and he considered ESPionage the lowest of all its many forms. Yet another reason why he'd left E-Branch. Deep down inside he thought of espers who used their talents that way as psychic voyeurs. On the other hand he knew it was

better that they worked for the common good than
against it. As for his own talent: that was different. The
dead didn't consider him a peeping Tom but a friend,
and they respected him as such.

"The other thing we did," Clarke continued, "was
this: we convinced Simmons's bosses that he shouldn't
have a D-cap."

"A what?" Harry wrinkled his nose. "That sounds
like some sort of family planning tackle to me!"

"Ah, sorry!" said Clarke. "You weren't with us
long enough to learn about that sort of thing, were you?
A D-capsule is a quick way out of trouble. A man can
find himself in a situation where it's a lot better to be
dead. When he's suffering under torture, for instance,
or when he knows that one wrong answer (or right
answer) will compromise a lot of good friends. Simmons's mission was that kind of job. We have our
sleepers in Redland, as you know. Just as they have
theirs over here; your stepfather was one of them. Well,
Simmons would be working through a group of sleepers
who'd been activated; if he was caught . . . maybe he
wouldn't want to jeopardize them. The initiative to use
his death capsule would be Simmons's own, of course.
The capsule goes inside a tooth; all a man has to do is
bite down hard on it, and . . ."

Harry pulled a face. "As if there aren't enough of the
dead already!"

Clarke felt he was losing Harry, that he was driving
him further from the fold. He speeded up:

"Anyway, we convinced his bosses that they should
give him a fake D-cap, a capsule containing complex
but harmless chemicals, knock-out drops at the worst."

Harry frowned. "Then why did they give him one at
all?"

"Incentive," said Clarke. "He wouldn't know it was
a fake. It would be there as a reminder to watch his step!"

"God, the *minds* of you people!" Harry felt genuine
disgust.

And Clarke actually agreed. He nodded glumly. "You haven't heard the worst of it. We told them that our prognosticators had given him a high success rating: he was going to come back with the goods. Except . . ."

"Yes " Harry narrowed his eyes.

"Well, the fact is we'd given him no chance at all; we *knew* he was going to be picked up."

Harry jumped up, slammed his fist down on the table so hard that he made it jump. "In that case it was criminal even to let them send him!" he shouted. "He'd get picked up, spill the beans under pressure, drop the people who'd helped him right in it—to say nothing of himself! What the hell's been happening in E-Branch over the last eight years? I'm damned sure Sir Keenan Gormley wouldn't have stood for any of this in his day!"

Clarke was dead white in the face. The corner of his mouth twitched but he remained seated. "Oh, yes he *would* have, Harry. This time he really would have." Clarke made an effort to relax, said: "Anyway, it isn't as black as I've painted it. See, Chung is *so* good that he'd know the minute Simmons was taken. He *did* know, and as soon as he said so we passed it on. As far as we're aware MI5 has alerted all Simmons's contacts over there and they've taken action to cover their tracks or even get the hell out of it."

Harry sat down again, but he was still coldly furious. "I've just about had it with this," he said. "I can see now that you've got yourself in a hole and you've come to ask me to dig you out. Well, if that's the case, then the rest of what you have to tell me had better be good because . . . frankly, this whole mess pisses me off! OK, let's recap. Even knowing Simmons would get picked up, you fixed him up with a dummy D-cap and let him get himself sent on an impossible mission. Also—"

"Wait," said Clarke. "You still haven't got it right. As far as we were concerned, that *was* his mission: to get picked up! We knew he was going to be anyway."

His expression was as cold as Harry's but without the other's fury.

"I can't see this improving," said Harry in a little while. "In fact it gets worse and *worse!* And all of this to get a man inside the Perchorsk Projekt, so that your scryer Chung could spy through him. But . . . didn't it dawn on you that the Soviet espers would pick Chung up, too? His ESP?"

"Eventually they would, yes," Clarke nodded. "Even though Chung would use his talent in the shortest possible bursts, they'd crack him eventually—and in fact we believe they have. Except we'd hoped that by that time we'd know exactly what was going on in there. We'd have proof, one way or the other, about what the Soviets were making—*or breeding*— down there!"

"Breeding—?" Harry's mouth slowly formed an "O." And now his tone was very much quieter. "What the hell are you trying to tell me, Darcy?"

"The thing they shot down over the Hudson Bay," Clarke said, very slowly and very clearly, "was one hellish thing, Harry. Can't you guess?"

Harry felt his scalp tingling again. "You'd better tell me," he said.

Clarke nodded and stood up. He put his knuckles on the table-top and leaned forward. "You remember that thing Yulian Bodescu grew and kept in the cellar? Well, that's what it was, Harry, but big enough to make Bodescu's creature look tiny by comparison! And now you know why we need you. You see, it was the biggest, bloodiest vampire anybody could possibly imagine—and it came out of Perchorsk!"

After a long, long moment Harry Keogh said, "If this were someone's idea of a joke, it would be just too gross to—"

"No joke, Harry," Clarke cut in. "Down at HQ we have film of the thing, shot from an AWACS before the fighters got it and burned it out of the sky. If it wasn't a

121

vampire—or at least made of the stuff of vampires—
then I'm in the wrong business. But our people who
survived that raid on Bodescu's place, Harkley House
in Devon, they're a lot more qualified than I am; and
they all say it was exactly like that, which to my mind
means there's only one thing it could possibly be.''

"You think the Russians may be experimenting, making them—*designing* them—as weapons?'' It was plain
that the Necroscope found it incredible.

"Didn't that lunatic Gerenko have exactly that in
mind before you . . . dealt with him?'' Clarke was
persistent.

Harry shook his head. "I didn't kill Gerenko,'' he
said. "Faethor Ferenczy did it for me.'' He fingered his
chin, glanced again at Clarke and said, "But you've
made your point.''

Harry put his head down, clasped his hands behind
him, walked slowly back through the brooding house to
his study. Clarke followed him, trying to contain himself and not show his impatience. But time was wasting and he desperately needed Keogh's help.

It was mid-afternoon and streamers of late autumn
sunlight were filtering in through the windows, high-
lighting the thin layer of dust that lay everywhere.
Harry seemed to notice it for the first time; he trailed
his finger along a dusty shelf, then paused to consider
the accumulation of dark, gritty fluff on his fingertip.
Finally he turned to Clarke and said: "So really, there
was no 'parallel case' after all. That was just to
make sure I'd listen to you, hear you out?''

Clarke shook his head. "Harry, if there's one person
in the world I would never lie to, you're it! Because I
know you hate it, and because we need you. There's a
parallel case, right enough. You see, I remembered
how you put it that time eight years ago when your
wife and child disappeared—before you quit E-Branch.
You said: 'They're not dead, and yet they're not here—so

where *are* they?' I remembered it because it seems the same thing has happened again.''

"Someone has disappeared? In the same way?" Harry frowned, made a stab at it: "Simmons, do you mean?"

"Jazz Simmons has disappeared, yes, in the same way," Clarke answered. "They caught him something less than a month ago and he was taken into Perchorsk. After that contact was difficult, very nearly impossible. David Chung reckoned it was (a) because the complex is at the foot of a ravine; the sheer bulk of matter blocks the psychic view (b) because it's protected by a dense lead shield, which has the same effect; and (c) mainly because there are Soviet espers mind-blocking the place. Even so, Chung was able to get through on occasion. What he has seen or 'scried' in there isn't reassuring.''

"Go on," said Harry, his interest waxing again.

"Well," Clarke continued, and immediately paused and sighed. "This isn't easy, Harry. I mean, even Chung found it difficult to explain, and I'm only repeating him. But . . . he's seen something in a glass tank. He says he can't describe it better than that because it never seems to be the same. No, don't ask me." He quickly held up his hands, shook his head. "Personally I haven't the foggiest idea. Or if I have an idea then I don't much care to voice it.''

"Go ahead," said Harry. "Voice it."

"I don't have to," Clarke shook his head. "I'm sure you know what I mean . . .''

Harry nodded. "OK. Is there anything else?"

"Only this: Chung says he sensed fear, that the complex was full of dread, living in terror. Everyone in the place was desperately afraid of something, he said. But again, we don't know what. So that was how things stood until just three days ago. Then—''

"Yes?"

"Then no more contact. And not just Soviet 'static' either—literally *no* contact! Simmons's cross, and presumably Simmons himself, were—well, no longer there. No longer anywhere, in fact.''

"Dead?" Harry's face was grim.

But Clarke shook his head. "No," he said, "and that's what I meant when I called it a parallel case. It's so like your wife and child. Chung himself can't explain it. He says he *knows* the cross still exists—that it hasn't been broken up or melted down or in any other way destroyed—and he believes that Simmons still has it. But he doesn't know where it is. It defies his talent to find it. And he's angry about it, and frustrated. In fact his feelings are probably a lot like yours: he's come up against something he doesn't understand and can't figure out, and he's blaming himself. He even started to lose faith in his scrying, but we've tested that and it's OK."

Harry nodded and said, "I can understand the way he must feel. That's exactly what it's like. He knows that the cross is still extant, and Simmons still alive, but he doesn't know where they are."

"Right," Clarke nodded. "But he does know where the cross isn't. It isn't on this Earth! Not according to David Chung, anyway."

Lines of concentration etched themselves in Harry's brow. He turned his back on Clarke and stared out of a window. "Of course," he said, "I can very quickly discover if Simmons is dead or not. Quite simply, I can check with the dead. If an Englishman called Michael 'Jazz' Simmons has died recently in the upper Urals, they'll be able to tell me in . . . why, in no time at all! It's not that I doubt your man Chung is good—not if you say he is—but I'd like to be sure."

"So go ahead, ask them," Clarke answered. But he couldn't suppress a shiver at the matter-of-fact way the Necroscope talked about it.

Harry turned to face his visitor and smiled a strange, wan smile. His brown eyes had turned dark and very bright, but even as Clarke looked at them their colour seemed to lighten. "I just did ask them," he said. ''They'll let me know as soon as they have the answer . . .''

That answer wasn't long in coming: maybe half an hour, during which time Harry sat deep in his own thoughts (and who else's thoughts? Clarke wondered) while the man from E-Branch paced the floor of the study to and fro. The sun's light began to fade, and an old clock ticked dustily in a corner. Then—

''He's not with the dead!'' Harry breathed the words like a sigh.

Clarke said nothing. He held his breath and strained his ears to hear the dead speaking to Harry—and dreaded to hear them—but there was nothing. Nothing to hear or see or feel, but Clarke knew that Harry Keogh had indeed received his message from beyond the grave. Clarke waited.

Harry got up from behind his desk, came and stood close. ''Well,'' he said, ''it looks like I'm recruited—again.''

''Again?'' Clarke spoke to cover the feeling of relief he felt must be emanating from his every pore in tangible streams.

Harry nodded. ''Last time it was Sir Keenan Gormley who came to get me. And this time it's you. Maybe you should take warning from that.''

Clarke knew what he meant. Gormley had been eviscerated by Boris Dragosani, the Soviet necromancer. Dragosani had gutted him to steal his secrets. ''No,'' Clarke shook his head, ''that doesn't really apply. Not to me. My talent's a coward called Self Preservation: first sign of anything nasty, and whether I want to or not my legs turn me about face and run the hell out of there! Anyway, I'll take my chances.''

''Will you?'' The question meant something.

''What's on your mind?''

''I left stuff of mine at E-Branch,'' Harry said.

"Clothes, shaving kit, various bits and pieces. Are they still there?"

Clarke nodded. "Your room hasn't been touched except to clean it. We always hoped you'd come back."

"Then I won't need to bring anything from here with me. I'm ready when you are." He closed the door to the patio.

Clarke stood up. "I've two rail tickets here, Edinburgh to London. I came from the station by taxi, so we'll need to call a—" And he paused. Harry wasn't moving, and his smile was a little crooked, even devious. Clarke said: "Er—is there something?"

"You said you'd take your chances," Harry reminded him.

"Yes, but . . . what sort of chances are we talking about here?"

"It's been a long time," Harry told him, "since I went anywhere by car or boat or train, Darcy. That way wastes a lot of time. The shortest distance between two point is an equation—a Möbius equation!"

Clarke's eyes went wide and his gasp was quite audible. "Now wait a minute, Harry, I—"

"You came here knowing that when you'd told me your story I wouldn't be able to refuse," Harry cut him off. "No risk to you or to E-Branch; your talent takes care of you and the Branch looks after its own, but plenty of trouble for Harry Keogh. Where I'm going— *wherever* I'm going—I'm sure there'll be times I wish I hadn't listened to you. So you see, *I* really am taking my chances. I'm trusting you, trusting to luck and to my talents. So how about you? Where's your faith, Darcy?"

"You want to take me to London . . . your way?"

"Along the Möbius strip, yes. Through the Möbius Continuum."

"That's perverse, Harry," Clarke grimaced. He still wasn't convinced that the other meant it. The thought of the Möbius Continuum fascinated him, but it frightened him, too. "It's like forcing a scared kid to take a ride on a figure-of-eight. Like bribing him to do it, with an offer he can't refuse."

"It's worse than that," Harry told him. "The kid has vertigo."

"But I don't have—"

"—But you will!" Harry promised.

Clarke blinked his eyes rapidly. "Is it safe? I mean, I don't know anything about this thing you do."

Harry shrugged. "But if it isn't safe, your talent will intervene, won't it? You know, for a man who's protected as you are, you don't seem to have much faith in yourself."

"That's my paradox,' Clarke admitted. "It's true—I still switch off all the power before I'll even change a lightbulb! OK, you win. How do we go about it? And . . . are you sure you know the way there? To HQ, I mean?" Clarke was starting to panic. "And how do you know you can still do it, anyway? See, I—"

"It's like riding a bike," Harry grinned, (a natural grin, Clarke was relieved to note.) "Or swimming. Once you can do it, you can always do it. The only difference is that it's almost impossible to teach. I had the best teacher in the world—Möbius himself—and it still took me, oh, a long time. So I won't even try to explain. Möbius doors are everywhere, but they need fixing for a second before they can be used. I know the equations that fix them. Then . . . I could push you through one!"

Clarke backed away—but it was purely an instinctive reaction. It wasn't his talent working for him.

"Let's dance," said Harry.

"What?" Clarke looked this way and that, as if he searched for an escape route.

"Here," Harry told him, "take my hand. That's right. Now put your arm round my waist. See, it's easy."

They began to waltz, Clarke taking mincing steps in the small study, Harry letting him lead and conjuring flickering Möbius symbols on the screen of his mind. "One, two-three—one, two-three—" He conjured a door, said: "Do you come here often?" It was the closest Harry had come to humour for a long time. Clarke thought it would be a good idea to respond in the same vein:

"Only in the mating—" he breathlessly began to answer.

And Harry waltzed the pair of them through the otherwise invisible Möbius door.

"—S-season!" Clarke husked. And: "Oh, Jesus!"

Beyond the metaphysical Möbius door lay darkness: the Primal Darkness itself, which existed before the universe began. It was a place of absolute negativity, not even a parallel plane of existence, because nothing existed here. Not under normal conditions, anyway. If there was ever a place where darkness lay upon the face of the deep, this was it. It could well be the place from which God commanded *Let There Be Light*, causing the physical universe to split off from this metaphysical void. For indeed the Möbius Continuum was without form, and void.

To say that Clarke was "staggered" would be to severely understate his emotion; indeed, the way he felt was almost a new emotion, designed to fit a new experience. Even Harry Keogh had not felt like this when he first entered the Möbius Continuum; for he had understood it instinctively, had imagined and conjured it, whereas Clarke had been thrust into it.

There was no air, but neither was there any time, so that Clarke didn't need to breathe. And because there was no time, there was likewise no space; there was an *absence* of both of these essential ingredients of any universe of matter, but Clarke did not rupture and fly apart, because there was simply nowhere to fly to.

He might have screamed, *would* have, except he held Harry Keogh's hand, which was his single anchor on Sanity and Being and Humanity. He couldn't see Harry for there was no light, but he could feel the pressure of his hand; and for the moment that was *all* he could feel in this awesome no-every-place.

And yet, perhaps because he had a weird psychic talent of his own, Clarke was not without an understanding of the place. He knew it was real because Harry made use of it, and also because he was here; and he knew that on this occasion at least he need not fear it, for his talent had not prevented him being here. And so, even in the confusion of his near-panic, he was able to explore his feelings about it, at least able to conjecture upon it.

Lacking space it was literally nowhere; but by the same token lacking time it was every-where and -when. It was both core and boundary, the interior *and* the exterior. From here one might go anywhere if one knew the route—or go nowhere forever, which would be Clarke's fate if Harry Keogh deserted him. And to be lost here would *mean* lost forever; for in this timeless, spaceless non-environment nothing ever aged or changed except by force of will; and there was no will here, unless it were brought here by someone who strayed into this place, or someone who came here and knew how to manipulate it—someone like Harry Keogh. Harry was only a man, and yet the things he could achieve through the Möbius Continuum were amazing! And if a superman—or god—should come here?

Again Clarke thought of The God, who had wrought a Great Change out of a formless void and willed a universe. And the thought also occurred to Clarke: *Harry, we shouldn't be here. This isn't our place . . .* His unspoken words dinned like gongs in his brain, deafeningly loud! And apparently in Harry's, too.

Take it easy, said the Necroscope. *No need to shout here.*

Of course not, for in the total absence of everything else, even thoughts had extraordinary mass. *We're not meant to be here,* Clarke insisted. *And Harry, I'm scared witless! For God's sake, don't let go of me!*

Of course not, came the answer. *And no need to feel afraid.* Harry's mental voice was calm. *But I can feel and I understand what it's like for you. Still, can't you also feel the magic of it? Doesn't it thrill you to your soul?*

And as his panic began to subside, Clarke had to admit that it did. Slowly the tension went out of him and he began a gradual relaxation; in another moment he believed he could sense matterless forces working on him. *I feel . . . a pull, like the wash of a tide,* he said.

Not a pull, a push, Harry corrected him. *The Möbius Continuum doesn't want us. We're like motes in its immaterial eyes. It would expel us if it could, but we won't be here that long. If we stayed still for long enough, it would try to eject us—or maybe ingest us! There are a million million doors it could push us through; any one of them could be fatal to us, I fear, in one way or another. Or we could simply be subsumed, made to conform—which in this place means eradicated! I discovered long ago that you either master the Möbius Continuum, or it masters you! But of course that would mean us standing still for an awfully long time—forever, by mundane terms.*

Harry's statement didn't improve Clarke's anxiety. *How long are we staying here?* he wanted to know. *Hell, how long have we been here?*

A minute or a mile, Harry answered, *to both of your questions! A light-year or a second. Listen, I'm sorry, we won't be here long. But to me, when I'm here, questions like that don't have much meaning. This is a different continuum; the old constants don't apply. This place is the DNA of space and time, the building-blocks of physical reality. But . . . it's difficult stuff, Darcy. I've had lots of "time" to think about it, and even I don't have all the answers. All of them? Hah! I have only a*

*handful! But the things I can do here, I do them well.
And now I want to show you something.*

Wait! said Clarke. *It's just dawned on me: what
we're doing here is telepathy. So this is how it feels for
the telepaths back at HQ!*

Not exactly, Harry answered. *Even the best of them
aren't as good as this. In the Möbius Continuum,* he
explained, *thoughts have matter, weight. That's because they are in fact physical things in an immaterial
place. Consider a tiny meteorite in space—which can
punch a hole through the skin of a space-probe! There's
something of a similarity. Issue a thought here and it
goes on forever, just as light and matter go on forever
in our universe. A star is born, and we see it blink into
life billions of years later, because that's how long it
took its light to reach us. That's what thought is like
here: long after we're gone, our thoughts will still exist
here. But you're right to a degree—about telepathy, I
mean. Perhaps telepaths have a way of tapping in—a
mental system which they themselves don't understand—to
the Möbius Continuum!* And Harry chuckled. *There's
"a thought" for you! But if that's the case, how about
seers, eh? What about your prognosticators?*

Clarke didn't immediately grasp his meaning. *I'm
sorry—?*

*Well, if the telepaths are using the Möbius Contin-
uum, however unconsciously, what of the forecasters?
Are they also "tapping in," to scry into the future?*

Clarke was apprehensive again. *Of course,* he said,
I'd forgotten that. You can see into the future, can't you?

Something of it, Harry answered. *In fact I can go
there! In my incorporeal days I could even manifest
myself in past and future time, but now that I have a
body again that's beyond me—so far, anyway. But I
can still follow past and future time-streams, so long as
I stick to the Möbius Continuum. And I can see you've
guessed it: yes, that's what I want to show you—the
future and the past.*

131

Harry I don't know if I'm ready for this. I—

We're not actually going there, Harry calmed him. *We'll just take a peek, that's all.* And before Clarke could protest, he opened a door on future time.

Clarke stood with Harry on the threshold of the future-time door and his mind was almost paralysed by the wonder and awe of it. All was a chaos of millions —no, billions—of lines of pure blue light etched against an otherwise impenetrable background eternity of black velvet. It was like some incredible meteor shower, where all of the meteors raced away from him into unimaginable deeps of space, except their trails didn't dim but remained brilliantly printed on the sky—printed, in fact, on time! And the most awesome thing was this: that one of these twining, twisting streamers of blue light issued outwards from himself, extending or extruding from him and plummeting away into the future. Beside Clarke, Harry produced another blue thread. It ribboned out of him and shot away on its own neon course into tomorrow.

What are they? Clarke's question was a whisper in the metaphysical Möbius ether.

Harry was also moved by the sight. *The life-threads of humanity,* he answered. *That's all of Mankind—of which these two here, yours and mine, make up the smallest possible fraction. This one of mine used to be Alec Kyle's, but at the end it had grown very dim, almost to the point of expiring. Right now, though—*

It's one of the brightest! And suddenly Clarke found himself completely unafraid. Even when Harry said:

Only pass through this door, and you'd follow your life-thread to its conclusion. I can do it and return— indeed I have done it—but not to the very end. That's something I don't want to know about. I'd like to think there isn't an end, that Man goes on forever. He closed the door, opened another. And this time he didn't have to say anything.

It was a door to the past, to the very beginning of

human life on Earth. The myriad blue life-threads were there as before; but this time, instead of expanding into the distance, they contracted and narrowed down, targetting on a far-away dazzling blue origin.

Before Harry could close that door, too, Clarke let the scene sear itself into his memory. If from this time forward he got nothing else out of life, this adventure in the Möbius Continuum was something he wanted to remember to his dying day.

But finally the door on the past was closed, there was sudden swift motion, and—

We're home! said Harry . . .

Chapter Eight
Through the Gate

A FOURTH AND FINAL DOOR WAS OPENED AND CLARKE felt himself urged through it. But the abrupt sensation of speed in motion had alarmed and shaken him, and as yet he hadn't recovered.

Harry? he said, the thought trembling like a leaf in the immaterial void of the Möbius Continuum. "Harry?"

Except the second time it was his voice he heard not just his thoughts. He stood with Harry Keogh in his office at E-Branch HQ, in London. Stood there for a moment, stumbled, and reeled!

The real, physical world—of gravity, light, all human sensation and especially sound, most *definitely* sound—impressed themselves forcefully on Clarke's unprepared person. It was signing-off time for most of the staff; many had already left, but the Duty Officer and a handful of others were still here. And of course the security system was in operation as always. Bleepers had started to go off all over the top-floor complex as soon as Clarke and Keogh appeared, quietly at first but gradually increasing in pitch and frequency until they would soon become unbearable. A monitor screen in the wall close to Clarke's desk stuttered into life and printed up:

MR. DARCY CLARKE IS NOT AVAILABLE
AT PRESENT. THIS IS A SECURE AREA.
PLEASE IDENTIFY YOURSELF IN YOUR
NORMAL SPEAKING VOICE, OR LEAVE IM-
MEDIATELY. IF YOU FAIL TO—

But Clarke had already regained partial control of
himself. "Darcy Clarke," he said. "I'm back." And in
case the machine hadn't recognized his shaky voice—
not waiting for it to print up its cold mechanical
threats—he staggered to his desk keyboard and punched
in the current security override.

The screen cleared, printed up: DO NOT FORGET
TO RE-SET BEFORE YOU LEAVE, and switched
itself and the alarm off.

Clarke flopped into his chair—in time to give a great
start as the intercom began to buzz insistently. He
pressed the receive button and a breathless Duty Officer's voice said: "Either there's someone in there, or
this is a malfunction . . .?" A second voice behind the
first growled:

"You'd better *believe* there's somebody in there!"
One of the espers obviously.

Harry Keogh pulled a wry face and nodded. "This
place was no great loss," he said. "None at all!"

Clarke pressed the command button and held it down.
"Clarke here," he said, talking to the entire HQ. "I'm
back—and I've brought Harry with me. Or he's brought
me! But don't all rush; I'll see the Duty Officer, please,
and that'll be all for now." Then he looked at Harry.
"Sorry, but you can't just—well, *arrive*—in a place
like this without people noticing."

Harry smiled his understanding—but there was something of his strangeness in that smile, too. "Before they
gang up on us," he said, "tell me: how long did you
say it was since Jazz Simmons disappeared? I mean,
when did David Chung first notice his absence?"

"Three days ago in—" Clarke glanced at his watch,

"—just six hours time. Around midnight. Why do you ask?"

Harry shrugged. "I have to have some place to start," he said. "And what was his address here in London?"

Clarke gave him the address, by which time the Duty Officer was knocking at the door. The door was locked and Clarke had the key. He got up, unsteadily crossed the room to let in a tall, gangling, nervous-looking man in a lightweight grey suit. The Duty Officer had a gun in his hand which he returned to its shoulder-holster as soon as he saw his boss standing there.

"Fred," said Clarke, closing and locking the door against other curious faces where they peered along the corridor, "I don't believe you've ever met Harry Keogh? Harry, this is Fred Madison. He—" But here he noticed the look of astonishment on Madison's face. "Fred?" he said; and then they both looked back into the room. Which apart from themselves was quite empty!

Clarke took out a handkerchief and dabbed at his brow. And in the next moment Madison was steadying him where he suddenly slumped against the wall. Clarke looked slightly unwell. "I'm alright, it's OK," he said, propping himself up. "As for Harry—" he glanced again all around the office, shook his head.

"Darcy?" said Madison.

"Well, maybe you'll get to meet him some other time. He . . . he never was desperately fond of this place . . ."

Something less than four days earlier, inside the Perchorsk Projekt: Chingiz Khuv, Karl Vyotsky and the Projekt Director, Viktor Luchov, stood at the hospital bedside of Vasily Agursky. Agursky had been here for four days, during which time his doctors had recognized certain symptoms and had started to wean him off alcohol. More than that: already they believed they had succeeded. It had been remarkably easy, all considered; but from the moment Agursky had been freed from the responsibility of tending the thing in the tank, so his dependency on local vodka and cheap slivovitz had fallen off. He had asked for a drink only once, when he regained consciousness on the first day, since when he'd not mentioned alcohol and seemed hardly the worse for the lack of it.

"You're feeling better then, Vasily?" Luchov sat on the edge of Agursky's bed.

"As well as can be expected," the patient replied. "I had been on the verge of a breakdown for some time, I think. It was the work, of course."

"Work?" Vyotsky seemed unconvinced. "The thing about work—any kind of work—is that it produces results. On the strength of that, it's rather difficult to see how you could be exhausted, Comrade!" His bearded face scowled down on the man in the bed.

"Come now, Karl," Khuv tut-tutted. "You know well enough that there are different sorts of work exerting different pressures. Would you have liked to be the keeper of that thing? I hardly think so! And Comrade Agursky's condition was not strictly exhaustion, or if it was then it was nervous exhaustion, brought on by proximity to the creature."

Luchov, who carried maximum responsibility in the Perchorsk complex and therefore wielded maximum authority, looked up at Vyotsky and frowned. Physically, Luchov would not have made half of the KGB man, but in the Projekt's pecking order he stood head and shoulders over him, even over Khuv. The contempt he felt for the bully was obvious in his tone of voice when he said to Khuv:

"You are absolutely correct, Major. Anyone who thinks Vasily Agursky's duties were light should try them and see. Do I see a volunteer here, perhaps? Is your man telling us he'd make a better job of it?"

KGB Major and Projekt Direktor looked in unison, pointedly at Vyotsky. Khuv smiled his dark, deceptive smile but Luchov's scarred face showed no emotion at

137

all and certainly not amusement. Evidence of his annoyance was apparent, however, in the throbbing of the veins on the hairless left half of his seared skull. The quickening of his pulse was a sure sign that he disapproved of someone or something, in this case Karl Vyotsky.

"Well then?" said Khuv, who had been at odds recently with his underling's boorishness and bad temper. "Perhaps I was wrong and you would like the job after all, Karl?"

Vyotsky swallowed his pride. Khuv was just perverse enough to let it happen. "I . . ." he said. "I mean, I—"

"No, no!" Agursky himself saved Vyotsky from further embarrassment. He propped himself up on his pillows. "It is quite out of the question that anyone else takes over my job, and ridiculous even to suggest that an unqualified person should assume such duties. This is not stated in any way to slight you personally, Comrade," he glanced indifferently at Vyotsky, "but there are qualifications and there are qualifications. Now that I've overcome two problems—my breakdown, and my absurd . . . *obsession*, for I refuse to call it an addiction, with drink—the third will not be difficult, I promise you. Given the same amount of time as I've already spent, that creature *will* give up its secrets to me, be sure. I know that so far my results have not been promising, but from now on—"

"Take it *easy*, Vasily!" Luchov put a hand on his shoulder, stemming an outburst which was quite out of character for the hitherto retiring Agursky. Obviously he was not yet fully recovered. For all his doctors' assurances that he was fit enough to be up and about again, his nerves were still on the mend.

"But my work is important!" Agursky protested. "We have to know what lies beyond that Gate, and this creature may carry the answers. I can't find them if I'm to be kept on my back in here."

138

"Another day won't hurt," Luchov stood up, "and I'll also see to it that from now on you have an assistant. It can't be good for a man to have to deal with a creature like that on his own. Some of us—" he glanced meaningfully at Vyotsky, "—would have broken long ago, I'm sure . . ."

"Another day, then," Agursky lay down again. "But then I really *must* get back to my work. Believe me, what lies between me and that creature has now become a very personal thing, and I won't give in until I've beaten it."

"Get your rest then," Luchov told him, "and come and see me when you're up and about. I'll look forward to that."

Agursky's visitors left the ward and at last he was on his own. Now he could stop acting. He smiled a sly and yet bitter smile—a smile composed in part of success, in that he'd deceived everyone who'd seen him, and partly of his terror of the unknown, and the fact that he was now on his own—which died on his face as quickly as it was born. It was replaced by a nervous anxiety which showed in his pale, trembling lips, and in the tic that jerked the flesh at the corner of his mouth. He had fooled his doctors and visitors, yes, but there was no fooling himself.

His doctors had examined him thoroughly and found nothing except a little stress and maybe physical weariness—not even Vyotsky's "exhaustion"—and yet Agursky *knew* that there was a lot more than that wrong with him. The thing in the tank had put something into him, something which had hidden itself away for now. But wheels were turning and time ticking away, and the question was: how long would it remain hidden?

How long did he have to find the answer and reverse the process, whatever the process was? And if he couldn't find the answer, what would it do to him, physically, while it lived and grew in him? What would it be *like* when it finally surfaced? So far no one knew about it but him, and from now on he must watch himself closely, must know before anyone else knew if . . . if anything strange were to happen. Because if they knew first—if they discovered that he nurtured within himself something from beyond that Gate—if they even suspected it . . .

Agursky began to shudder uncontrollably, gritted his teeth and clenched his fists in a spasm of absolute terror. They *burned* those things from the Gate, hosed them down with fire until they were little heaps of congealed glue. And would they burn him, too, if . . . if—

What would he be like after those slowly turning inner wheels had turned full circle? That was the worst of it, not knowing . . .

Out on the perimeter and having separated from Luchov who had gone his own way, Khuv and Vyotsky were making for their own place of duty with the Projekt's esper squad when one of the latter came panting to meet them. He was a fat and especially oily man called Paul Savinkov, who prior to Perchorsk had worked in the embassies in Moscow. An unnatural predilection for male, junior members of foreign embassy staff had made him something of a risk in that employment. His transfer to Perchorsk had been swift; he was still trying to ooze his way out of the place, primarily by doing his very best to keep Khuv happy. He was sure he could convince his KGB watchdog that there were places where his talent could be far more effectively and productively employed. His talent was telepathy, in which he was occasionally very proficient.

Savinkov's fat, shiny baby-face was worried now as he bumped into Khuv and Vyotsky in the sweeping outer corridor. ''Ah, Comrades—the very men I seek! I was on my way to report . . .'' He paused to lean against the wall and catch his breath.

''What is it, Paul?'' said Khuv.

"I was on duty, keeping an eye—so to speak—on Simmons. Ten minutes ago they tried to get through to him! I cannot be mistaken: a strong telepathic probe was aimed directly at him. I sensed it and managed to scramble it—certainly I interfered with it—and when I could no longer detect it, then I came to find you. Of course I left two of the squad there in my place in case there should be a recurrence. Oh, and on my way here I was given this to relay to you" He handed Khuv a message from Communications Centre.

Khuv glanced at it—and his forehead at once wrinkled into a frown. He read it again, his dark eyes darting over the printed page. *"Damn!"* he said, softly—which from him meant more than any explosion. And to Vyotsky: "Come, Karl. I think we should go at once and talk to Mr. Simmons. Also, I intend to bring our plans for him forward a little. Doubtless you'll be sad to learn that from tonight you'll no longer be able to taunt him, for he won't be here." He tucked the message from Comcen into his pocket, dismissing the fawning Savinkov with a wave of his hand.

Vyotsky almost had to jog to keep up with Khuv where his boss now diverted and made for Simmons's cell. "What is it, Major?" he said. "Where did that message come from and what was in it?"

"This telepathic sending we've just had reported to us," Khuv mused, almost as if he hadn't heard the other's questions. "It isn't the first, as you're aware . . ." He strode urgently ahead, with Vyotsky close at heel. "Most of them have been merely inquisitive: the work of various groups of foreign seers or scryers trying to discover what's going on here. But they were very weak because the alien espers can't precisely pinpoint our location—that is, they have no definite point of focus—and also because we're protected by the ravine. Our own psychics have been able to break them up or block them easily enough. Ah, but if a foreign power could actually get an ESP-endowed agent *inside* this place, then it might be a different story entirely!''

"But Simmons isn't talented that way," Vyotsky protested. "We are certain of that beyond any reasonable doubt."

"That's entirely true," Khuv growled his answer, "but I believe they've found a way to use him anyway. In fact this message in my pocket confirms it." He chuckled grimly, like a man who has just lost a piece in a game of chess. "It can only be the British, for they're the most advanced in this game. The people in their E-Branch are a clever lot! They always have been—and extremely dangerous, as our espers learned to their cost at the Château Bronnitsy."

"I don't follow you," Vyotsky scowled through his beard. "Simmons didn't worm his way in here; we *caught* him, and he certainly wasn't coming quietly!"

"Right again," Khuv nodded sharply. "We caught him, and we brought him here—but believe me we can no longer afford to keep him here. That's why he must go—tonight!"

They had arrived at Simmons's cell. Outside the door an armed, uniformed soldier lounged, coming to attention as Khuv and Vyotsky approached him. In a cell next door to the prisoner's, a pair of espers in plainclothes sat at a table wrapped in their own thoughts and mental pursuits. Khuv went in and spoke to them briefly: "You two—I suppose Savinkov has told you what's happened? That calls for extra security. Be alert as never before! In fact I want the entire squad—all of you, Savinkov included—on the job from now on. Full time! These measures won't be in force for long, probably only a matter of hours, but until I say otherwise that's how I want it. Pass it on, and make sure the rosters are adjusted accordingly."

He rejoined Vyotsky and the soldier on duty let them into Jazz's cell. The British agent was sprawled on his bunk, hands behind his head. He sat up as they entered, rubbed his eyes and yawned. "Visitors!" he said, displaying his accustomed sarcasm. "Well, well! Just as I was beginning to think you two had forgotten all about me. To what do I owe the honour?"

Khuv smiled coldly. "Why, we're here to talk to you about your D-cap, Michael—among other things. Your very interesting, very ingenious D-cap."

Jazz fingered the left side of his face, his lower jaw, and worked it from side to side. "Sorry, but I'm afraid you've already got to it," he said, a little ruefully. "And the tooth next door, too. But we're healing nicely, thanks."

Vyotsky advanced menacingly. "I can very quickly stop you from healing nicely, British," he growled. "I can fix bits of you so they'll never heal again!"

Khuv restrained him with an impatient sigh. "Karl, sometimes you're a bore," he said. "And you know well enough that we need Mr. Simmons fit and alert, or our little experiment won't be worth carrying out." He looked pointedly at the prisoner.

Jazz sat up straighter on his bed. "Experiment?" he tried to smile enquiringly and failed miserably. "What sort of experiment? And what's all this about my D-cap?"

"Let's deal with that first," Khuv answered. "Our people in Moscow have analyzed its contents: very complex but completely harmless drugs! They would have put you to sleep for a few hours, that's all." He watched the other's reaction very closely. Jazz frowned, displayed open disbelief.

"That's ridiculous," he finally replied, "Not that I'm the sort who'd ever have used it—at least I don't think so—but those capsules are lethal!" His eyes narrowed. "What are you up to, Comrade? Some silly scheme to lure me over to your side?"

Again Khuv's smile. "No, for I'm afraid we've no use for you, Michael—certainly not now that you've seen the inside of Perchorsk Projekt! But don't be so scornful of the possibility. I don't see that our side could be any worse than yours. After all, they haven't treated you too well so far, now have they?''

"I don't know what you're talking about," Jazz shook his head, stopped acting the comedian. "Why don't you tell me why you're really here?''

"But I have," Khuv answered. "Part of it, anyway. As for what I'm talking about: I'm telling you that your people *expected* you to be caught! They couldn't be sure what sort of reception you'd get, however, and they had to be sure that you wouldn't kill yourself too soon.''

Jazz's frown deepened. "Too soon for what?''

"Before they could use you, of course.''

The frown stayed. "What you're saying feels like it's making sense even though I know it can't be making any sense," said Jazz. "That is *if* what you're saying is true!''

"Your confusion is understandable," Khuv nodded, "and very reassuring. It tells me you weren't a party to it. Your D-Cap was meant to fool you—ensure you'd play out your part to the full—just as it was meant to fool us! It was designed to slow us down as much as possible. I would guess your espers, British E-Branch, rigged the whole thing. And sooner or later they would also find a way to get through to you, if they had the time. But they haven't. Not any more.''

"E-Branch? ESP?" Jazz threw up his hands. "I've already told you I don't know anything about that sort of thing. I don't even *believe* in that sort of thing!''

Khuv sat down on a chair besides Jazz's bed, said: "Then let's talk about something you do believe in.'' His voice was very quiet, very dangerous now. "You believe in that space-time Gate down in the magmass bowels of this place, don't you?''

"I can accept the evidence of my own five senses, yes," Jazz answered.

"Then accept this also: tonight you go through that Gate!''

Jazz was stunned. "I *what?*"

Khuv stood up. "It was my intention all along, but I wanted to be sure you were one hundred percent recovered from your injuries before using you. Another three or four days at most." He shrugged. "But now we've had to bring it forward. Whether you believe in that sort of thing or not, the world's E-Branches are very real. I am the appointed monitor and watchdog over just such a group of psychics, and several of my espers have been deployed here with me. Your people in the West are trying to use you as a 'mirror' on our work here; so far they have not been successful; tonight we will ensure that they never are."

Jazz jumped to his feet, stepped toward Khuv. Vyotsky put himself in the way, said: "Come on then, British, try me."

Jazz backed off a pace. He would dearly love to "try" the big Russian, but in his own time, his own place. To Khuv he said: "You force me through that damned Gate and you're no more than a murderer!"

"No," Khuv shook his head. "I am a patriot, devoted to my country's welfare. *You* are the murderer, Michael! Have you forgotten Boris Dudko, the man you killed on top of the ravine?"

"He tried to kill me!" Jazz protested.

"He did not," Khuv shook his head, "—but if he had tried at least he would have had the right." And here Khuv feigned outrage. "What? An enemy agent engaged in espionage, deep inside a peaceful country's borders? Of course he had the right! And we also have the right to take your life."

"That's against every convention!" Jazz knew he had no argument, but anything was worth the shot.

"On this occasion," Khuv answered evenly, "there are no conventions. We *must* dispose of you, surely you can see that? And in any case, it will not be murder."

"Won't it?" Jazz flopped down again on his bed. "Well, you can call it an experiment if you want to, but

I call it murder. Jesus! You've *seen* what comes through that sphere or Gate or whatever! What chance will one man have in the world they come from?''

"A very small one," Khuv answered, "but better than none at all."

Jazz thought about it, tried to imagine what it would be like, tried to get his suddenly whirling thoughts into order. "A man alone," he finally said, "in a place like that. And I don't even know what 'like that' means."

Khuv nodded. "Sobering, isn't it? But . . . not necessarily a man alone . . ."

Jazz stared at him. "Someone's going in with me?"

"Sadly, no," Khuv smiled. "Shall we say instead that someone—three someones—have already gone?"

Jazz shook his head. "I can't keep up with you," he admitted.

"The first was a convicted thief and murderer, a local man. He was given a choice: execution or the Gate. Not much of a choice, really, I suppose. We equipped him, as we'll equip you, and sent him through. He had a radio but never used it, or if he did the Gate was a barrier. But it was worth a try; it would have been something of a novelty to receive radio transmissions from another universe, eh? He also had food concentrates, weapons, a compass and—most important —a great desire to live. His equipment was all of the very highest quality, and there was plenty of it—far more than I've mentioned here. You shall have no less, maybe even more. It's all a question of what you can carry, or what you're willing to carry. Anyway, after a fortnight we wrote him off. If there was a way back, he didn't find it—or maybe something found him first. I say we've written him off, but of course he may still be alive on the other side. After all, we don't know what it's like there.

"Next we tried an esper—ah, yes! One of our very own élite! His name was, perhaps still is, Ernst Kopeler, a man with the astonishing power to see something of the future. What a waste, you are thinking, to send such a man through the Gate! Alas, Kopeler could never see eye to eye with our way of life. Twice he tried to—how do you say it—defect? That's how *you* say it, yes, but we call it vile treachery. The fool; with a talent like his, he expected freedom, too! His real reasons in the end were most ironic: he had apparently looked into his future—and had found it monstrous, unbearable!''

Jazz considered that. ''He knew he was going through the Gate,'' he said.

Khuv shrugged. ''Possibly. But, how do the Spanish say it? *Que será será?* Men cannot avoid their tomorrows, Michael. The sun sets, and it rises again for all of us.''

''Except me, eh?'' Jazz gave a snort of self-derision. ''What about your third, er, 'volunteer'? Another traitor?''

Khuv nodded. ''Perhaps she was, yes, but we can't be sure.''

''She?'' Jazz found it hard to believe. ''Are you telling me you actually sent a woman through there?''

''I am telling you exactly that,'' Khuv answered. ''And a very beautiful woman at that. A great pity. Her name was or is Zek Föener. Zek is short for Zekintha. Her father was an East German, her mother a Greek. In her time she had been the most proficient esper of them all but . . . something happened. We can't be certain what changed her, but she lost her talent—or so she said. And she kept saying it for all of the six years she spent in a mental institution, where she was troublesome to a fault. Then she spent two more years in a forced labour camp in Siberia, where espers kept an eye on her. They swore that she was still a telepath, and she as vehemently denied it. All very annoying and a terrible waste. She had been a brilliant telepath, now she was a dissident, refused to conform, demanded the right to emigrate to Greece. In short, she had become a problem in far too many ways. So—''

''You got rid of her!'' Jazz's tone was scornful.

Khuv ignored the acid in the other's eyes. ''We told

her: Go through the Gate, use your telepathy to tell us what it's like on the other side—for we've people here who will hear you, be sure—and if you're successful and after you've done all these things to our satisfaction, then we'll bring you back!''

Jazz stared coldly at Khuv, said: "But you didn't know *how* to bring her back!''

Again Khuv's shrug. "No, but she didn't know that,'' he said.

"So we are talking about murder after all," Jazz nodded. "Well, if you'd do that to one of your own, I can't see how I can expect any better. You people are . . . hell, you're *shit!*''

Vyotsky grunted a warning, or a challenge, came forward with his huge hands reaching. Khuv laid a hand on his arm, stopped him. "My patience is also used up, Karl. But what does it matter? Save your energy. Anyway, we're all through here. Believe me, I'm just as sick of Mr. Simmons as you are, but I still want him to go through the Gate in one piece.''

They went to the door; Khuv knocked and it was opened for them; but on the point of leaving, suddenly the KGB Major said: "Ah, but I had almost forgotten! By all means show Michael your dirty pictures, Karl. If we are shit, then by all means let's behave like shit!''

Khuv went through the door, disappeared without looking back. Vyotsky turned and looked at Jazz, grinned, and produced a small manila envelope from his pocket. "Remember your friends at the logging camp? The Kirescus? As soon as we caught you your friends in the West tipped them off. We'd had our suspicions about them for some time, and we were watching them when they made a run for it. I can't imagine where they thought they could run to! Anna Kirescu will go to a forced labour camp, and the boy Kaspar to an orphanage. Yuri put up a fight and had to be shot—fatally, naturally. That leaves only two of them.''

"Kazimir and his daughter, Tassi? What about them?''

148

Jazz stood up. He could almost feel himself leaning in Vyotsky's direction. God, how he *wanted* the bully!

"Why, we have them, of course! There are so many things they can tell us. About their contacts here in Russia, and in the old country. But since they're a bit unsophisticated, our methods for extracting information needn't be so devious. We can allow ourselves to be more . . . direct? Do you follow me?"

Jazz took a short pace forward. His emotions and temper were on the boil. He knew that if he took another step he'd have to go all the way, hurl himself at Vyotsky. Which was probably what the KGB thug hoped he'd do. "An old man and a girl?" he grated the words out. "Are you saying you'd torture them?"

Vyotsky licked his rough, fleshy lips, flipped the envelope across the cell, accurately onto Jazz's bed. "There's torture and there's torture," he said, his voice husky with inner lust. "For example, these photographs will be torture for you. I mean, you and your little Tassi quite enjoyed each other, didn't you?"

Jazz felt the blood draining from his face. He looked at the envelope, then back to Vyotsky. He was torn two ways. "What the hell—?" he said.

"See," Vyotsky drawled, "the Major knows how I enjoy taunting you, so he said it would be OK if we had a little photographic session, me and the girl. I hope you like them. Very artistic, I think."

Jazz flew at him.

Vyotsky stepped backward through the door and slammed it in Jazz's face.

Inside the cell Jazz skidded to a halt. He glared at the door, his breathing ragged in his chest and throat. At that moment he could have happily performed an operation on Vyotsky's intestines with a rusty penknife and no anaesthetic. But the photographs . . .

Jazz stepped to the bed and took five small pictures from their envelope. The first was a little crumpled; Jazz knew it well: Tassi, sitting in a field of dasies.

She'd once given the picture to him. The next photograph showed her . . . naked, manacled to a steel wall. Her hands were chained over her head, her legs spread wide. The girl's eyes were squeezed tightly shut—and Vyotsky towered beside her, grinning, weighing her left breast in the palm of his hand.

The third picture was worse and Jazz didn't even look at the others. He screwed them into a tight ball and hurled them away from him. And then he curled up on his bed and concentrated on pictures of his own. They centered on Vyotsky's intestines again, but this time there was no penknife. Just Jazz's fingernails.

Outside the cell door Vyotsky stood for a moment with his ear to the cold steel. Nothing. Absolute silence. And Vyotsky thought: *his blood must be water!* He banged on the door. "Michael," he called out. "Khuv says that tonight, after we're rid of you, then I can amuse myself with her for an hour or two. Life has its little moments, eh? I thought maybe you'd like to tell me how she likes it? No . . . ?" Still silence.

The grin slipped from Vyotsky's face. He scowled and walked away.

Curled up tightly on his bed, Jazz Simmons gave a low moan where he bit his lip until it bled. His blood wasn't water but liquid fire . . .

Over the space of the next five or six hours Jazz had a good many visitors. They came to his cell with various pieces of equipment whose functions were all minutely explained and demonstrated. He was even allowed to handle, take to pieces and reassemble them; and he worked hard at it, for they were survival. But the tiny flamethrower came minus its gallon of fuel, and instead of the small caliber sub-machine gun he got only a handbook.

The young soldier who turned up later that evening with the handbook also brought with him an ammunition box half full of condemned rounds and rusting magazines. This was so Jazz could practice magazine loading. In a combat situation, the faster you can load a magazine the longer you live. Jazz had fumbled the first load, then concentrated, speeded up and succeeded in loading a second magazine in very quick time. The young soldier had been impressed, but after that he'd yawned and lost interest. Jazz had continued to load and unload magazines for another half-hour.

"What are you in for?" the soldier had asked eventually.

"You mean why am I a prisoner? Espionage," said Jazz. He saw little or no reason to hide the fact. Not now.

"Me," the youth thumbed himself in the chest, "it'll be mutiny if I don't get some sleep soon! There was a practice alert at the barracks last night, and I've been on duty ever since. I'm dead on my feet!" He frowned. "Did you say espionage?"

"Spying," Jazz nodded. He tossed the old magazines and a handful of discoloured, brass-jacketed shells into the ammo-box and slammed the lid, then fastened its hasps. Then he dusted his hands on his trousers and stood up. "There, I think I can manage that well enough now."

"Not much good, though, knowing how to load a magazine," the soldier grinned, "if you don't have a gun!"

Jazz had grinned back. "You're right," he said. "Are you going to bring me one?"

"*Hah!*" the youth had laughed out loud. "Mutiny is one thing, but madness is something else again! Bring you a gun? Not me, friend. You'll get that later . . ."

Now was the "later" that the soldier had been talking about: 2 A.M. in the outside world, but inside the subterranean Perchorsk Complex the hour was of no real consequence. Things didn't change a great deal down here day or night. Not on a normal night, anyway. But tonight was different.

151

Below the nightmare magmass levels, in the core of the place, Michael "Jazz" Simmons stood on the Saturn's-rings platform and allowed himself to be kitted-up in his gear. In any case, he didn't have much choice about it. But he still hadn't been given the fuel tank for his mini-flamethrower, and he was still minus his SMG. That was in the very capable hands of Karl Vyotsky, who cradled the lightweight weapon like a baby in his great arms. Vyotsky was to be Jazz's escort along the walkway.

At last the agent had everything he could carry and still move with a degree of efficiency. He had refused a parka, and a huge woodsman's knife which must have weighed all of three pounds. But he'd taken a small, razor-honed hatchet which would serve both as a weapon and as a most useful tool.

Finally Khuv had stepped forward through the circle of people who'd been attending to Jazz, said: "Well, Michael, this is it. If I thought you would accept them, now would be the time to offer you my best wishes."

"Oh?" Jazz looked him up and down. "Personally I wouldn't offer you shit, Comrade!"

The corners of Khuv's mouth turned down. "Very well," he said, "so *be* hard! And stay hard, Michael. Who knows but that way you might even survive. But if you do find a way to come back through, we'll be waiting. And then I'll look forward to hearing all about it. Eventually, you know, we'll be obliged to put an army through there; any advance knowledge would be a big help." He nodded to Vyotsky.

"Let's go, British," the big Russian prodded him with the business end of the SMG.

Jazz moved inwards across the planking, glanced back once, shrugged and faced the sphere. Dark glasses protected his eyes from something of its glare, but even so the very *plainness* of the sphere's surface was a pain in itself; it was like looking at a dead channel on a live TV screen. Now the Saturn's-rings platform was left behind and Jazz went forward along the neck of the walkway. Scorched timbers underfoot told him that this was where the warrior had died, and it seemed he heard again that creature's cry: *Wamphyri!* Then—

—They had reached the sphere. Jazz came to a halt, put out a hand. His fingers passed easily into the white light; there was no resistance, until he withdrew his hand again; but then he felt a weird viscosity, felt the sphere tugging at him. It didn't like to let go, not even from the first moment of penetration. He pulled his hand free, but not without a little effort.

"Hold it," said Vyotsky from right behind him. "Don't be too eager, British. You'll need these." He hung a cylindrical aluminium bottle on Jazz's harness at the rear: the fuel for his flamethrower. Then he said, "Turn around."

Jazz obeyed him. Vyotsky grinned at him and said: "You're very pale, British! Feels queer, does it?"

"A little," Jazz answered truthfully. Now that it was inevitable it did feel a little queer. It would be a lot worse except he wasn't concentrating on his feelings but something else entirely.

Vyotsky searched his face for a moment, said: *"Huh!* I don't know if you're a hero or just plain stupid! Whichever, this is yours." He removed the magazine from the SMG and handed the weapon to Jazz. Then, chuckling, he said, "Wouldn't you like this, too, British?" He shook the magazine in his hand until it rattled. "A lot handier right now than the ones you have in your pack, eh?"

The other's drawn face was all concentration, showing no emotion whatever; and suddenly Vyotsky thought: *something's wrong here!* He stopped grinning, took a single backward step.

Jazz's right hand snatched at a pocket of his one-piece combat suit, came out holding a rusty but serviceable magazine. In a single fast-flowing movement he slapped

153

the magazine into its housing and cocked the weapon. "Stand still!" he snapped at Vyotsky.

Vyotsky froze. Jazz closed the distance between, stuck the muzzle of his gun up under the Russian's chin. And he grated: "Funny, but you're looking a bit pale, Ivan! Is something bothering you?"

Khuv came running from the Saturn's-rings platform. "Hold your fire!" he yelled—not to Jazz but to the soldiers on the perimeter where all weapons were aimed at the British agent. Khuv skidded to a halt a good ten feet away. "Michael," he panted. "What's on your mind?"

"Isn't it obvious?" Jazz was almost enjoying this. "Ivan the Terrible here is coming with me." He took a firm grip on Vyotsky's beard, pushed the SMG harder under the Russian's chin, backed toward the sphere.

Vyotsky was white as death. "No!" he gurgled; but he didn't dare to struggle, not and risk the Englishman putting too great a pressure on that trigger.

"Oh yes you are, Ivan—or you die right here!" Jazz told him. "Me, I've nothing to lose." He could feel the outer skin of the gate tugging at him.

Khuv came closer, and Jazz was struck with an even better scenario. "You too, Major," he said, "or I shoot right through this bastard and into you."

Khuv was fast; he was in motion on the instant Jazz's words registered, falling flat to the walkway and screaming: "Fire, fire, *fire!*"

Jazz tumbled backwards into the sphere, yanking the stumbling Vyotsky after him. And—

—It was *white* in there! It was pure white, a solid white background against which Jazz and Vyotsky formed the only imperfections. They rolled on a solid-seeming floor, made invisible because it too was pure white! Shots were screaming overhead in a deafening barrage of rumbling thunder—which ceased in another moment as Khuv's voice, slowed down to an almost unrecognizable drone, howled as if from an infinity away:

"C-e-a-s-e f-i-r-e! *C-e-a-s-e f-i-r-e!*" Now that they were inside the sphere and he was safe, he didn't want any further harm to befall them.

Jazz stood up, looked back. Through a thin film of milk, "outside," all motion seemed slowed down almost to a standstill. It was a two-way effect. Khuv was half-way to his feet, one arm and hand raised high overhead as he signalled the ceasefire.

Jazz waved at him, then turned and pointed his gun at Vyotsky where he sprawled, terrified. "Up you get, Ivan," he said, and his voice came out sounding perfectly normal. "Let's move it, shall we?"

Vyotsky looked around, came to his senses. His shoulders slumped. He slowly got to his feet, said: "*Fuck you, British!*" and made a dive toward Khuv.

Or attempted to. Useless, for from now on this was a one-way trip! He hit against an invisible barrier, slid to his knees clawing at thin air. And as the truth dawned on him, then he did what Jazz expected him to do: he started screaming for help!

Jazz watched him grovelling there for a moment, then said: "Suit yourself, Ivan. Stay here and scream and gibber, and in the end die."

Vyotsky's head turned swiftly. "Die?"

Jazz nodded. "Of starvation, or exhaustion . . ." Then he turned his back on the view beyond the Gate—of Khuv, against a backdrop of magmass walls and slow-motion soldiery—and started forward into what looked and felt like an aching white immensity.

From behind him Vyotsky snarled, "But why? *Why?* What good am I to you, here?"

"None at all," Jazz called back. "But you'd have been even less good to Tassi . . ."

Chapter Nine
Beyond the Gate

MAJOR CHINGIZ KHUV OF THE KGB FACED HIS UNDERLING, Karl Vyotsky, across a distance of no more than ten feet and through a fine white milky film so thin it was almost invisible—yet they were worlds apart. Khuv could take two or three paces forward, reach out and shake Vyotsky by the hand. He *could* do it, but dared not. For in his present condition Vyotsky might just hold on, and while the Major couldn't drag Vyotsky out of there, Vyotsky was certainly capable of dragging him in. They could still converse, however, albeit laboriously.

"Karl," Khuv called out. "There's no way you can get back right now, and you can't just go on kneeling there like a lost waif. Or you can, but it won't do you any good. Oh, we can feed you—of course we can— simply by rushing food through to you! Simmons was quite wrong about that. It was something he hadn't thought out, that's all. But he was right when he said you'll die. You *will* eventually, Karl! How long that will be depends on how long you've got before Encounter Six. Do you follow me?"

Khuv waited for Vyotsky's reply. Communicating through the gate was a frustrating business, but eventually Vyotsky nodded and got to his feet. Just doing that took him all of two minutes and more, and meanwhile the figure of the British agent was dwindling into the distance, oh-so-slowly vanishing from sight. Then Vyotsky's face and mouth began to work grotesquely, and his words came in a dull, distant, slow-motion booming. Khuv made him out to say: "What do you suggest?"

"Simply this: that we kit you out exactly like Simmons, give you all we can of equipment and concentrated food. Then at least you'll have the same chance as he has."

Eventually the answer came back: "No chance, is that what you mean?"

"A slim chance," Khuv insisted. "You won't know unless you try it." He called forward an NCO from the squad of soldiers at his rear, issued sharp, rapid orders. The man went off at a run. "Now Karl, listen," Khuv continued. "Is there anything you can think of that might be useful to you—other than what Simmons has?"

Again Vyotsky's slow nod, and at last, "A motorcycle."

Khuv's jaw fell open. They had no idea what the terrain would be like. He said so, and:

"So if I can't ride it, then I'll ditch the bloody thing!" Vyotsky answered. "For God's sake, is it too much? If I could fly a helicopter I'd ask for that instead!"

Khuv issued more instructions; but all of this taking time, and Simmons now a dot on the white horizon, gradually drawing away like an ant across the face of a sand dune.

The equipment began to arrive, and a trolley to carry it. The trolley was loaded and pushed into the sphere, and Vyotsky commenced the endless business of kitting-up. He was working as fast as he could, but to Khuv and the other observers it was like watching the progress of a snail. The paradox was this: that it was just as bad for Vyotsky. He felt that *he* was the one moving at speed, and they were the flies stuck in treacle! While to them even the droplets of sweat falling from his brow took seconds to strike the invisible floor where he stood.

At last his motorcycle arrived: a heavy military model but in good working order, with about two hundred and fifty miles of fuel in her belly. The bike was put on its stand on a second trolley and wheeled through. On the other side, Vyotsky began the incredibly slow process of mounting the machine, kick-starting its engine into life. But whatever might be wrong with time in there, the rest of the physical spectrum seemed in order. The bike coughed, made a noise like great hammers on oak, where the beat of each piston was a distinct, individual sound, and Vyotsky lifted his feet off the ground. And slowly, oh-so-slowly—but still a great deal faster than Simmons—so Vyotsky and his machine dwindled into the white distance and finally disappeared from view. Two empty trolleys were all that was left . . .

After Vyotsky had gone, Khuv continued to watch the sphere until his eyes began to hurt. Then he turned and crossed the walkway to the Saturn's-rings platform, and started up the wooden stairs to the shaft through the magmass. There on the landing at the mouth of the shaft Viktor Luchov was waiting for him. Khuv came to a halt, said:

"Direktor Luchov, I notice you distanced yourself from this experiment. Indeed you were conspicuous by your absence!" His tone was neutral, or if anything even a little defensive.

"As I shall continue to absent myself from such . . . *acts!*" Luchov answered. "*You* are the KGB here, Major, and I am a scientist. You call it an experiment, and I call it an execution. Two executions, it would seem! I thought it would be over by now else I'd not have been here, but unfortunately I was in time to see that lout Vyotsky take his departure. A brutal man, yes, and yet now I pity him. And how will you explain *this* to your superiors in Moscow, eh?"

Khuv's nostrils flared a little and he grew slightly

paler, but his voice remained even as he replied: "My reporting procedures are my business, Direktor. You are right: you are a scientist and I am KGB. But you will note that when I say 'scientist' I do not make it sound like pig-swill. I would advise caution how you emphasize your use of the term KGB. Does the fact that I am able to perform certain thankless tasks better than you make me any less useful? I should have thought the very opposite. And can you truthfully tell me that as a scientist you are not fascinated by the opportunity we have here?"

"You perform these 'tasks' better than me because I would *not* perform them!" Luchov almost shouted. "My God, I . . . I—!"

"Direktor?" Khuv raised an eyebrow; the line of his mouth was tight, thin and ugly now.

"Some people never learn!" Luchov stormed. "Man, have you forgotten the trials at Nuremberg? Don't you know we're still bringing people to justice for—" He saw the look on Khuv's face and stopped.

"You compare me with Nazi war criminals?" Khuv was now deathly white.

"That man," Luchov pointed a trembling finger at the sphere, "was one of our own!"

"Yes, he was," Khuv snapped. "He was also psychotically brutal, devious, insubordinate and dangerous to the point of being a downright liability! But haven't you wondered why I never reprimanded him? You think you know it all, don't you, Direktor? Well, you don't. Do you know who Vyotsky worked for before me? He was a bodyguard to Yuri Andropov himself—and we still don't know exactly how *he* died! But it's a fact they didn't get on, and that Andropov intended to demote him. Oh yes, you can believe it—Karl Vyotsky was implicated! Very well, and now I'll tell you why he was sent here—"

"I . . . I don't think that's necessary," Luchov grasped the landing's hand rail to steady himself. All of the blood had drained from his face until he was as white as Khuv. "I think I already know."

Khuv lowered his voice. "I'll tell you anyway," he whispered. "But for his misadventure tonight, Karl Vyotsky was to have been our next 'volunteer'! So don't cry for him, Direktor—he had only a month left anyway!"

Luchov gazed aghast at Khuv where he turned away and climbed the steps through the shaft. "And he didn't know?" he said.

"Of course not," Khuv answered without looking back. "If you were in my shoes, would *you* have told him?"

Jazz plodded on.

No use hurrying and wasting energy needlessly, and it wasn't as if anyone or thing was going to sneak up on him. Not here. But certainly he must try to conserve his strength. He didn't know how far he had to go, another mile or ten or a hundred. He felt like a man crossing a vast lake of salt, whom the sun had already blinded. Yes, it was like that: as if he marched blindly, endlessly under a blazing sun, but one which held no heat. Only light. He sweated, yes, but purely from his efforts and not from any external source of heat. It was neither hot nor cold in this white tunnel between the worlds; the temperature seemed constant and was no problem; one might actually live here, except one couldn't possibly *live* here. No one could ever really live here; not in a place where he was the only reality and everything else was . . . white!

Twice he'd taken a swig from his water bottle, replacing lost moisture, and twice he'd thought to himself: *is this all there is, this emptiness? What if it doesn't go anywhere?*

But then, where had the bat and the wolf come from, and the magmass creatures, and the warrior? No, it had to go somewhere.

He had also paused to take the rusty magazine off his SMG and throw it away, and fit a good one from his packs. If he had to use the weapon, the last thing he wanted to happen was for a duff round to jam itself in the breach.

It was then, just after he'd fitted the new magazine, that he learned something else about this weird Gate place. Fastening the straps of his pack, he'd looked up—and discovered that he didn't know which direction was which. He had a compass on his wrist, but it was a little late for that; he should have checked it immediately after entering the sphere. He'd looked at it anyway—and seen the hand circling aimlessly, just as lost as he was! And then again he'd looked all about him, slowly turning in a full circle, or what he believed was a full circle. But he couldn't even be sure of that.

It was all the same everywhere he looked: whiteness stretching as far as the eye could see in every direction. Even a white floor and a white sky, making no distinction anywhere, no horizon, nothing but himself. Himself and gravity. And thank God for gravity, for without the sensation that there was something solid underneath him—he knew he would have very quickly gone mad. With it . . . at least he knew which way was up!

Then he'd looked back over his shoulder. Had he really come from over there? Or from over there? Difficult to tell. How did he know he was still heading in the right direction? What the hell was "direction" in this God-forsaken place?

But when he tried to move off again there had been resistance, a wall of invisible foam that pushed him back with a force equal to that which he mustered against it. To the right it wasn't so bad, but still difficult, and to the left likewise. There was only one way to go, which meant that that had to be the right way. That was why he hadn't noticed it before; because he'd automatically chosen, or been guided, along the path of least resistance.

And after that there'd been more plodding, more sweating, until now—time for another swig at his bottle. Staring ahead, and as he pulled at the bottle and let the water cool his mouth, Jazz suddenly realized that things were no longer pure white. That came as a shock, so that he almost choked on his water. Now what the hell . . .? There in the distance . . . mountains? Silhouettes of crags? A dark-blue sky and . . . stars? It was like looking through a sea-fret; better, like looking down a tunnel at a misty morning. Or at a scene faintly etched on a white silk screen. But how far away?

Jazz plodded on, more eagerly now—and at the same time somewhat more apprehensively. The scene came closer, growing brighter as the stars blinked out and were replaced by weak beams of sunlight seeming to strike *through* the mountains to the right of the picture's frame. And that was when Jazz heard the sound.

At first he associated it with the emerging scene, but then he realized that it came from behind him. And no sooner that than he recognized it for what it really was: a motorcycle! He turned and looked back.

Karl Vyotsky rode with the sling of his SMG across his right shoulder, the gun itself hanging under his arm, muzzle forward. As yet he couldn't see the distant scene that Jazz had spotted, but he could see Jazz. The big Russian gritted his teeth into a snarling grin, guided the bike with his left hand and his knees and took the handgrip of the gun in his right fist. He laid his index finger along the trigger-guard, turned up the throttle and felt the bike surge forward. "British," he grunted to himself, "your time's up. Kiss it all goodbye!"

For a moment Jazz was stunned. A motorcycle! And here he'd been knocking himself out walking it! The problem was, how to turn Vyotsky's advantage into a disadvantage? But as he'd walked, so Jazz had been giving the Gate's weird physics a thought or two. Now he believed he had the answer. "OK, Ivan," he murmured to himself, "so let's see if you're as smart as you think you are."

Vyotsky rode closer, revved up until sixty showed on his clock and the bike throbbed under him. The ride was smooth as silk, but even so, aiming the SMG would not be easy. It would be, literally, hit or miss. But he did have the element of surprise, or if not surprise, shock at least. What must the Englishman be thinking now, he wondered, to see this powerful machine bearing down on him?

He's a little less than half a mile away, Jazz was thinking. *Thirty seconds*. He got down on one knee, turned his body side-on so as to decrease his target silhouette, turned his gun in Vyotsky's direction. Not that he intended to shoot at him, just make him a little nervous.

A quarter mile to go, and Vyotsky's face a mask of hatred where he thundered to the attack. But . . . suddenly his quarry had grown smaller, he'd gone down on one knee. And at the same time Vyotsky saw the scene on the other side of the Gate. For a moment it threw him, but then he returned his concentration to what he was doing, namely: hunting down this British bastard to the death! He began to move his knees, shift his bodyweight, give the bike something of a slow wobble; and at the same time he commenced firing single shots in Jazz's direction.

One hundred and fifty yards, and Jazz held his fire. He hadn't even released the safety-catch, hadn't cocked the weapon. It seemed obvious that the crazy Russian intended to run him down; Vyotsky was relying on Jazz losing his nerve and making a run for it, trying to get out of the way. But Jazz had some ideas of his own. Finally he clicked off the safety-catch, cocked the weapon, resighted and . . . waited. For if he was correct it would be useless to fire anyway.

Fifty yards, and Vyotsky firing an automatic, a stream of lead that buzzed and plucked at the air all about Jazz, too close for comfort. And at the last possible moment he hurled himself to one side. Vyotsky's bike careened by him; its rider threw it into a steep, banking turn; *the bike stood on its nose and hurled him out of the saddle!*

Then machine and rider were somersaulting in different directions, and Jazz walked carefully forward toward them, and toward the scene looming on the other side of the Gate. Miraculously, Vyotsky came to the end of his skidding and tumbling and found himself virtually unharmed. The "ground" here was obviously different. He had bruises and one sleeve of his combat suit was torn where he'd put his elbow through it, but that was all. He climbed shakily to his feet, stared unbelievingly at the Englishman maybe fifteen paces away where he walked toward him. "Hello there, Ivan!" Jazz called out. "I see you got here the easy way."

Vyotsky grabbed up his weapon, checked it was undamaged, aimed at his oncoming enemy. Why was the stupid bastard grinning like that? Because of the accident? He'd found it amusing? The bike must have blown a tyre or something, but Simmons, *he* must have blown his mind! He wasn't even defending himself; he merely cradled his gun in his arms, came forward at a casual stroll.

"British, you're dead!" said Vyotsky. He deliberately lowered his aim—to chew up the other's thighs, groin and belly—and squeezed the trigger. The weapon was on automatic. It fired three stuttering shots before Vyotsky's finger was jerked from the trigger, which happened when the gun slammed into his chest and sent him crashing backwards to sprawl on the floor. Vyotsky felt as if his chest had caved in, as if his ribs were broken; possibly one or two of them were.

Lying there hugging himself, gritting his teeth and murmuring, *"Ah! Ah!"* from the pain, he looked at Jazz. In the distance between them, three bullets were plainly visible lying on the floor. The SMG had "fired" them insofar as they'd escaped from its barrel, but only just. And that had resulted in three mighty mule-kicks coming in rapid succession, blows which even the huge Russian's bulk hadn't been fully able to absorb.

Vyotsky made an effort to reach the smoking gun where it lay, but that was in Jazz's direction, which was the wrong way. He tried harder, and of course failed. The SMG was all of fifteen inches beyond his straining fingertips—hardly a great distance—but it might have been a mile, or not there at all. The motorcycle, too, lay in the wrong direction.

Jazz reached the bike, hauled it upright, stood astride the front wheel and wrenched the handlebars back into position from where they'd been knocked slightly askew. He ignored Vyotsky's groaning. Then he wheeled the bike forward and picked up the Russian's gun. And at last he spoke:

"Sound and light are the only things that seem to work in both directions here," he said. "We can hear each other, talk to each other, and even though you're ahead of me—toward the other end of the Gate, I mean—your words get back to me. Likewise your picture, for I can see you. But while we're standing like this, nothing solid can ever come from you to me. Reverse our positions, and sure enough I'd be dead, except that isn't the case. So there's no way you could have harmed me, Ivan: no bullets, no sticks or stones, nothing. These three rounds—" he kicked the three projectiles aside, "—*they* fired the gun! If you weren't so burned-up with hate, you'd have worked it out for yourself."

It all sank in, and finally Vyotsky scowled and nodded. Then, still holding his chest, he sat up. "So get it over with," he said. "What are you waiting for?"

Jazz looked at the other and grimaced. "God, what a wanker you are! Hasn't it dawned on you yet that we may be the only human beings this side of Earth? You and me? Not that I'm much for male companionship but I can't see myself killing off half the human population just for the fun of it. Last time that happened it was Cain and Abel!''

Vyotsky was finding it hard to follow Jazz's logic. He wasn't even sure it was logic. ''What are you saying?'' he said.

''I'm saying that, against my better judgement, I'm giving you your life,'' Jazz told him. ''See, I'm not the sort of murderous lunatic that you appear to be. Yesterday, in my cell—if I'd had you then in this position— things might be different. And your own fault because you worked me up to it. But I'm damned if I can kill you here and now.''

Vyotsky tried to sneer, managed only a wince. ''Lily-livered chicken-shit son of a—'' He jerked himself to his feet.

Jazz lowered his own SMG and put a single round between Vyotsky's feet. It *whupped* where it ricochetted off the ground. ''Sticks and stones,'' he reminded, ''can't hurt *my* bones, but names can certainly do yours a hell of a lot of damage!'' He got on his bike and kicked it into life.

''You're leaving me here, without my gun?'' Vyotsky was suddenly alarmed. ''Then you might as well kill me after all!''

''You'll find your gun waiting for you when you come through the Gate,'' Jazz told him. ''But remember this: if I ever catch you on my trail again, it'll be a story with a different ending. I don't know how big that world is up front, but from here at least it looks big enough for the two of us. It's your decision. So that's all from me, Comrade. Here's hoping I won't be seeing you.''

He put the bike in gear and rolled forward past Vyotsky, upped the gear and picked up a little speed, looked back once, briefly. The big Russian was watching him go. It was hard to say what sort of an expression he was wearing. Jazz sighed, climbed through the remaining gears and headed for the sunlit scene ahead. But in the back of his mind something kept telling him he'd made a bad mistake . . .

Another mistake was this: failing to recognize where the Gate ended and the strange world beyond it began!

Jazz had been riding only three or four minutes, had kept his speed even at maybe twenty, twenty-five miles per hour, when without warning he breached the sphere's outer skin. For it was a sphere on this side, too, he realized as he tumbled in mid-air. The trouble was that on this side the sphere seemed parked in the throat of what looked like a crater, and the crater's rim was three feet higher than the surrounding terrain.

The bike fell, Jazz too, managing somehow to kick himself free of the rotating machine, and both of them collided jarringly with hard earth and scattered rocks. Winded, Jazz lay there for a moment and let his senses stop reeling. Then he sat up and looked all about. And *then* he knew how lucky he'd been.

The dazzling white sphere was perhaps thirty feet across, and all around its perimeter, penetrating the earth and the crater walls alike to a radius of maybe seventy feet, magmass wormholes gaped everywhere. Jazz had landed between two such holes, and he knew it was only a matter of good fortune that he'd not been pitched headlong down the throat of either one of them. Their walls were glass smooth and very nearly perpendicular, and their depth entirely conjectural; once in, it would be a hell of a job to climb out again.

Jazz glanced at the sphere, turned his face away before the dazzle blinded him. A giant, illuminated golf ball plopped down in wet mortar and left to dry out. That's what it looked like. "But who the hell drove it here?" Jazz muttered to himself. "And why didn't he shout 'fore'?"

He stood up and checked himself, finding only bumps and bruises. Then (and despite the fact that he felt almost compelled to stand still and simply *gape* at the weird world he'd entered) he went to the bike and examined it for damage. Its front forks were badly twisted and the wheel jammed immovably between them. If he had a spanner he could get the wheel off, then he might be able to straighten the forks one at a time using brute strength. But . . . he had no spanner.

So . . . what about tools in general?

He released catches on the bike's seat and tilted it back . . . the tool compartment underneath was empty. Now the machine was doomed to lie here until it rusted. So much for transport . . .

Now Jazz gave a thought to Karl Vyotsky. The Russian was maybe one and a half to two miles behind him. Forty minutes at the outside, even weighed down with equipment. The last thing Jazz wanted was still to be here when Vyotsky arrived. But he must do one more thing before he moved off.

He had a small pocket radio, a walkie-talkie that Khuv had insisted he bring with him. Now he switched it on and spoke briefly into the mouthpiece: "Comrade bastard Major Khuv? This is Simmons. I'm through to the other side, and I'm not going to tell you a bloody thing about how I got here or what it's like! How does that grab you?"

No answer, not even static. Or perhaps the very faintest, far-distant hiss and crackle. Nothing that remotely constituted an answer, anyway. Jazz hadn't really expected anything; if the others hadn't been able to get through, why should he be different? But:

"Hello, this is Simmons," he tried again. "Anyone out there?" Still nothing. The radio, for all that it weighed only a pound, was now "dead" weight, useless to him. "Balls!" he said into the mouthpiece, and pitched it into one of the magmass holes where it slid from view.

And now . . . now it was time to take a deep breath and really have a good look at where he'd landed.

Jazz was glad then that he'd dealt with things in their

correct order of priority. For the fact was he could have just stood and gaped at the world on this side of the Perchorsk Gate for a very, very long time. It was in part familiar and fascinating, in part strange and frightening, but it was all fantastic. The eye was quite baffled by contrasts which might well be compared to a surreal landscape, except that they were all too real.

Jazz dealt first with the familiar things: these were the mountains, the trees, the pass that lay like the void of a missing tooth in stone fangs that reared up from scree bases and forested slopes, through the tree-line to gaunt, vertical buttresses of grey stone that seemed to go up forever. In awe of their grandeur, Jazz was drawn by the mountains away from the sphere maybe a hundred yards, and there he paused and put up a hand to his eyes to guard them from lingering sphere-glare; and he stared at the marching mountains again.

Even if he had not known he was in an alien world, he might have guessed that these were not Earth's mountains. He had skied on the slopes of Earth's mountains, and they had not been like these. Rather than born of some vast geological heaving, they seemed to have been *weathered* into being; and while this could scarcely be called a rare feature in Jazz's own world, still he had never imagined it on a scale such as this. An incredible feat even for an alien Nature: to have sculpted a fortress range of planet-spanning mountains right out of the virgin rock! So high, jagged, sheer and dramatically awesome—why, only take away the trees under the timber-line, and these could well be the mountains of the moon!

The mighty range ran (Jazz glanced at his compass, which appeared to be working again) east to west, in both directions, as far as the eye could see. Its peaks marched away to far horizons and merged with them, passing into purple, indigo and velvet distances and disappearing at the very rim of the world. And apart from this pass, where in ages past the mountains had cracked open, their march seemed entirely unbroken.

Now, with the sphere behind him, Jazz stared at the "sun"—or what he could see of it. Those weak beams he had seen when he was passing through the Gate, which came from the right of the picture to give light to this land, had been filtered through the pass from the rim of the distant sun. But that was all it was, a rim.

There at the other side of the pass, a blister of red light was rising (or setting, perhaps, for there'd been no enlargement of it while Jazz had been here) and shooting its feeble rays through the wall of the mountains. But it was the sun, or *a* sun, however weakly it shone; its light felt good on Jazz's face and hands where he shielded his wondering eyes. As for what lay beyond the mountains on that far, as yet unseen sunlit side: impossible to tell. But on *this* side . . .

To the west there was only the wooded flank of the mountain range, and at the foot of the range a plain stretching northwards, turning blue then dark blue into the apparently featureless distance. Directly to the north, to the far north beyond the dome of the sphere, all was darkness, where stars glittered in unknown constellations like diamonds in the vaulted jet of the skies. And under those stars, dimly reflective and reflecting too the far-flung beams of the blister-sun, the surface of what might be a sullen ocean, or more likely a sheet of glacial ice.

A chill wind was now blowing from the north, which was gradually eating its way through Jazz's clothing to his bones. He shivered and knew that "north" was a very inhospitable place. And instinctively he began to pick his way across the plain of rocks and boulders toward the pass in the mountains.

But . . . this was strange. If the mountains ran east and west, and the—icelands?—were north, then the sun was due south. And still that blister of light and warmth hadn't moved. A sun lying far to the south, apparently motionless there? Jazz shook his head in puzzlement.

And now, finally he paused to let his gaze turn eastward, which was where anything real or vaguely familiar came to an abrupt end and the unreal or at best surreal took over. For if Jazz had wondered at the seismic or corrosive forces of nature which had created the mountains, what was he to make of the spindly towers of mist-wreathed rock standing to the east: fantastically carven, mile-high aeries that soared like alien sky-scrapers up from the boulder plain in the shadow of the rearing mountains? All the time he'd been here, Jazz had been aware of these structures, and yet he'd managed to keep his eyes averted; another sign, perhaps, that his choice of direction—the pass, and through the pass—was a good one.

Possibly these columns or stacks had been fretted from the mountains, to be left standing there like weird, frozen sentinels as the mountains themselves melted from around them. Certainly they were a "natural" feature, for it was impossible to conceive of any creature aspiring or even requiring to build them. And yet at the same time there was that about them which hinted of more than nature's handiwork. Especially in the towers and turrets and flying buttresses of their crowns, which looked for all the world like . . . castles?

But no, that could only be his imagination at work, his need to people this place with creatures like himself. It was a trick of the spectral light, a mirage of the twining mists which wreathed those great menhirs, a visual and mental distortion conjured of distance and dreams. Men had not built these megaliths. Or if they had, then they were not men as Michael J. Simmons understood them.

So . . . what sort of men? Wamphyri? Flight of fancy it might well be, but again, in his mind's eye, Jazz saw the warrior burning on the walkway, and heard his voice raised in savage pride and defiance: "Wamphyri!"

Mile-high castles: the aeries of the Wamphyri! Jazz

gave a snort of grim amusement at his own imaginings, but . . . the idea had taken hold of his mind and for the moment was fixed there.

Suddenly a mood was on him; he felt as lonely—more lonely—than he'd ever felt in his life. And the thought struck him anew that he *was* alone, and totally friendless in a world whose denizens . . .

. . . What denizens? Animals? Jazz hadn't seen a one!

He looked at the sky. No birds flew there, not even a lone kite on the lookout for an evening meal. Was it evening? It felt like it. Indeed it felt like the evening not only of a place but of an entire world. A world where it was always evening? With the sun so low in the sky, that was possible. On this side of the mountains, anyway. And on the other side . . . morning? Always morning?

Reverie had taken hold, out of phase with Jazz's character, from which he must forcibly free himself. He gave a sigh, shook himself, set out with more purpose toward the opening of the pass and the blister-sun beyond it. The pass didn't lie level but climbed toward the crest of a saddle; and so Jazz, too, must climb. He found the extra effort strangely exhilarating; also, it kept him warm and was something he could concentrate on. Along the way grew coarse grasses and stunted shrubs, even the occasional pine, and above the scree the steep slopes were dense with tall trees. Just here the place was so like parts of the world he knew that . . . but it wasn't the world he knew. It was alien, and he'd had proof enough that it housed creatures whose natures were lethal.

Twenty-five minutes or so later, pausing to lean against a great boulder, Jazz turned and looked back.

The sphere was now a little less than two miles behind and below him, and he had actually entered the mouth of the ''V'' where it lay like a slash through the mountain range. But back there on the rock-littered plain . . .

172

the sphere was like a brilliant egg half-buried in its magmass nest. And a dark speck moved like a microbe against its glare. It could only be Vyotsky. A moment more—and Jazz nodded sourly. Oh, yes, that was Vyotsky all right!

The *crack* of a single ringing shot came echoing up to Jazz, bouncing itself from wall to wall of the pass. The Russian had found his gun where Jazz had left it for him; now he was telling this alien world that he was here. "So look out!" he was saying. "A man is here, and one to be reckoned with! If you know what's good for you, don't try fooling around with Karl Vyotsky!" Like a superstitious peasant whistling in the dark. Or maybe he was just saying: "Simmons, it's not over yet. This is just to warn you: keep looking back!"

And Jazz promised himself that he would . . .

Down beside the sphere, Vyotsky quit cursing, laid aside his gun and turned to the bike. He saw the seat laid back on its hinges and his face twisted into a grin. Tucked loosely into a pocket of one of his packs he had a small bag of tools. It was the last thing they'd given him on the other side, and he'd been in such a hurry that he hadn't stored his tools away under the seat. Then the sneering grin slid from his face and he breathed a sigh of relief. He'd not once thought of those tools since Simmons took the bike off him. If he had, then for sure he'd have thrown them away somewhere in the last couple of miles.

Now he unhooked a small kidney-pack from his back harness, got the tools out and loosened the front wheel. He stood on one of the forks with his foot wedged under the wheel, bent his back and hauled on the other fork one-handed until he could feel it giving, then slid the wheel free. Now it was only a question of straightening the forks. He picked up the front end of the bike, half-dragged, half-wheeled it over to a pair of large boulders where they leaned together. If he could jam the twisted forks into the gap between the boulders, and apply the right amount of leverage in the right direction . . .

He upended the bike and got the forks in position, began to exert leverage—and froze! He stopped panting from his exertions, stopped breathing, too. *What the hell was that?* Vyotsky raced for his gun, grabbed it up and cocked it, looked wildly all about. No one. Nothing. But he'd heard something. He could have sworn he'd heard something. He went warily back to the bike, and—

There it was again! The big Russian's skin prickled, broke out in goose-flesh. Now what—? A tiny voice? A tinny, metallic calling? A cry for help? He listened hard, and yet again he heard the sound. But it wasn't a whisper, just a tiny, distant voice. A *human* voice—and it came from one of the magmass wormholes!

That wasn't all—Vyotsky recognized the voice. Zek Föener's voice, breathless and yet full of desperate hope, eager to communicate with someone, with anyone human in this entirely alien world.

He flung himself face-down beside the wormhole, peered over its rim. The smooth shaft was perfectly circular, about three feet in diameter, curving sharply inward toward the buried face of the sphere and so out of sight. But just where the shaft disappeared from view . . . there lay a small radio like the one Vyotsky carried in his own pocket! Obviously it had been Simmons's, and he'd discarded it. Every time Föener's voice came, so a little red monitor light flickered on and off on the control panel. It warned of reception, that light: it advised its operator to turn up the volume.

"Hello?" Zek Föener's voice came again. "Hello? Oh, *please* answer! Is anyone there? I heard you speaking but . . . I was *asleep!* I thought I was dreaming! Please, *please* —if there's anyone out there—please say again who you are? And where you are? Hello? Hello?"

"Zek Föener!" Vyotsky breathed, licking his lips as

he pictured her. Ah, but a different woman now from the acid-tongued bitch who'd spurned his advances at Perchorsk! This world had seen to that. It had changed her. Now she craved companionship. Any sort!

Vyotsky took out his own radio, switched it on and yanked up the aerial. There were only two channels. He systematically transmitted on both of them, and this was his message:

"Zek Föener, this is Karl Vyotsky. I'm sure you'll remember me. We've discovered a way to neutralize the one-way drag effect of the Gate. I've been sent to seek out any survivors of through-Gate experiments and bring them back. Find me, Zek, and you find your way out of here. Do you hear me?"

As he finished speaking, so the red light on his set began to flicker and blink. She was answering, but he couldn't hear her. He turned up the volume and got broken, crackling static. He shook the set, glared at it. Its plastic casing was cracked, and the miniature control panel in the top was badly dented. It must have got damaged when he was flung from the bike. Also, its proximity to Simmons's discarded radio was jamming reception on that set, too.

"Shit!" he hissed from between clenched teeth.

He set the broken radio aside and lowered his head, one arm and shoulder into the wormhole. He gripped its rim with his free hand and hooked one foot round a knob of rock. And he stretched himself down and around, inching his fingers toward Simmons's radio. Its antenna was fully extended, formed a slender, flexible half-hoop of telescoping metal sections where it had some-how jammed against the sides of the shaft to halt the radio's descent. Vyotsky's straining fingers touched the antenna—dislodged it!

Damn!

The set went clattering out of sight into unknown depths below.

Vyotsky snatched himself viciously up and out of the

175

hole and jumped to his feet. Of all the bloody luck! He picked up his own set again, said: "Zek, I can't hear you. I know you're out there and you can probably hear me, but I can't hear you. If you get my message you'll most likely want to start looking for me. Right now I'm at the sphere but I won't be staying here. Anyway, I'll be keeping my eyes peeled for you, Zek. It looks like I'm your one hope. How's that for a novel situation?"

The red light on his set started flickering again, a brief, unintelligible morse message that wasn't intended to be understood. He couldn't tell if she was pleading with him or screaming her defiance. But sooner or later she would have to search him out. He'd been lying when he said he was her one chance, but of course she couldn't know that. She might suspect it, but still she couldn't afford to ignore him.

Vyotsky grinned, however nervously. At least there was one thing in the world he could appreciate. And would appreciate. Still grinning, he switched his radio off . . .

Chapter Ten
Zek

TWO HOURS AFTER SETTING OUT FROM THE SPHERE—TWO lonely, shadowy hours, with only the grunts and groans of his own exertions for company—Jazz Simmons paused for his first real break and found a seat on a tall, flat-topped boulder which gave him good vantage over the terrain all around. He took hard biscuits from his pack and two cubes of dense black chocolate designed for sucking, not biting. Wash these down with a sip of water, and then he'd be on his way again. But now, while he sat here easing his deceptively gangly but powerful frame and catching a breather, there was time to look around a little and consider his position.

"His position." That was a laugh! It certainly wasn't an enviable position: alone in a strange land, with hardtack food sufficient to last a week, enough weaponry to start World War III, and so far nothing to shoot at, blast or burn! Not that he was complaining about that. But again the thought occurred: where were they? Where in hell were this world's denizens? And when he did eventually find them, or they found him, what would they be like? Which was to assume, of course, that there were others here *unlike* those he already knew about. Which was to hope so, anyway.

It was as if his private thoughts were an invocation.

177

Two things occurred simultaneously: first a rim of bright half-moon, rising in the west and turning the sky in that quarter a gold-tinged indigo, showed itself over the peaks on the opposite side of the gorge; and second . . . second there sounded a far, almost anguished howl, a reverberating, sustained note echoing up to the moon and down again, picked up by kindred throats and passed mournfully on up the pass into the beckoning distance.

There could be no mistaking cries like that—wolves! And Jazz remembered what he'd been told about Encounter Two. That one had been lame, blind, harmless. These weren't. Nothing that sounded like that could possibly be in anything other than extremely good health. Which didn't bode too well for his own!

Jazz finished eating, washed the gritty chocolate from the back of his throat, adjusted his pack and got down from his rock. Time he was on his way again. But—he paused, then froze in his tracks, stared directly ahead, and up, *and up!*

Before, the light from the blister-sun, however feeble, had kept the canyon walls in silhouette; they'd presented only a black, flanking frame to Jazz's eyes, with the main picture lying directly ahead. That picture had been the false horizon at the head of the saddle, the scree-littered way to it, and the thin arc of bright yellow light beyond; which, Jazz noted, had moved gradually from west to east, until now it was lying in the very corner of his picture.

When during the last two or three miles he'd turned his gaze away from the sun for a moment, turned his face to the flank and looked up, then, as they'd grown accustomed, his eyes had been able to spy the dark, forested heights, and above them the sharp silver gleam of snow. But in fact he'd had little time for sightseeing; mainly his attention had been glued to the nonexistent trail, picking a way through rocks and fallen jumble, always choosing the easiest way ahead. It had scarcely dawned on him that as he progressed, so indeed there *had* been something of a trail. In his own world he'd have expected one, and so in this world it had failed to make an impression. Until now.

But here the gorge was a great deal narrower. Where two hours earlier, at the mouth of the pass, the distance between walls had been something more than a mile, maybe even a mile and a half, here it had narrowed down to less than two hundred yards, almost a bottleneck at the foot of steep canyon walls. The crest of the saddle, as he judged it, was only a quarter-mile ahead now, when at last he'd be able to look down and spy something of the world on the sunlit side of the range.

What had caused him to freeze was this:

The moon, rising swiftly over the western side of the gorge, now shone its silvery-yellow light down on the east wall. Jazz was close to that side of the gorge, so that the previously silhouetted face seemed to tower almost directly overhead. But no longer in silhouette—no longer a vertical, soaring jut of black rock—the mighty cliff of the canyon had taken on a different aspect entirely.

Picked out now by the moon in sharp detail, Jazz saw a castle built into the vertiginous heights! A castle, yes, and no way he could be mistaken on this occasion. Where once a wide ledge had scarred the cliff's face, now the walls of a fortress rose up fantastically to meet the massy overhang of natural stone high overhead. A castle, an outpost, a grimly foreboding keep guarding the pass. And Jazz knew he'd hit upon its purpose here at the first throw: a keep guarding the pass!

Craning his neck, he took in its awesome moonlit bleakness, the gaunt soullessness of its warlike features. There were battlements, with massive merlons and gaping embrasures; and where towers and turrets were supported by flying buttresses, there yawned the mouths of menacing corbels. Stone arches formed into steps joined parts of the architecture which were otherwise inaccessible, where the natural rock of the cliff bulged or jutted and generally obstructed; flights of stone stairs rose steeply between the many levels, carved deep into the otherwise sheer rock; window holes gloomed like dark eyes in the moon-yellowed stone, frowning down on Jazz where he crouched in the shadows and gazed, and wondered.

The structure started maybe fifty feet up the cliff face, half-way to the top of a lone, projecting stack. In the chimney between cliff and pillar, stone steps were visible zig-zagging upwards to the mouth of a domed cave; presumably the cave was extensive, with its own passageways to the castle proper. Higher still, the fortifications themselves spread outward across the face of the cliff like some strange stone fungus, covering nature's bastions with the lesser but more purposeful works of . . . men? Jazz could only suppose so.

But whoever had built this aerie, they were not here now. No figures moved in the battlements or on the stairways; no lights shone in the windows, balconies or turrets; no smoke curled from the tall chimneys moulded to the face of the cliff. The place was deserted—maybe. That "maybe" was because Jazz was sure as he'd ever been that hooded eyes were upon him, studying him where he in turn held his breath and studied the cliff-fashioned castle.

The lower part of the stack where it stood mainly free of the canyon's wall was still in shadow, which gradually drew back as the moon rose higher still. Jazz was glad of that moon, for the sun was now plainly declining. When he crossed the crest of the saddle, then perhaps he'd catch up a little with the sun, earn himself maybe an hour or so more of its dim light; but here in the lee of the great grim castle, for the present the moon was his only champion. He moved swiftly forward, going at a lope because of the imagined (?) eyes, sticking to the shadows of boulders where possible and crossing the moonlit gaps between at speed. And pres-

ently he came to the base of the stack of weathered rock
where it leaned outward a little from the cliff. Or at
least, he came to the great wall which surrounded that
base.

The wall was of massive blocks; it stood maybe
twelve feet high and was crowned with merlons and
embrasures; the mouths of dragons formed spouts for
corbel chutes. But the carven dragons were not Earth's
dragons. Jazz swiftly, silently skirted the wall, came to
a gate of huge timbers studded with iron and painted
with a fearsome crest: the dragon again, with the face
and wings of a bat and the body of a wolf! He was
reminded of nothing so much as the magmass thing in
the tank back at Perchorsk. But this dragon was split
down the middle with the menacing darkness of a
courtyard—for the great gates stood open a little, inwards. As if in invitation. If so, then Jazz ignored it; he
hurried on toward the waning sun, desiring only to put
as much distance as possible between himself and this
place while there was still light enough to do so.

Minutes later he began to breathe more easily, reached
the crest and was at once bathed in warm, wan sunlight.
Shielding his eyes against the sudden light, however
hazy, he turned to look back. A quarter-mile away, the
castle had merged once more into the face of the cliff.
Jazz knew it was there for he'd seen it—had even *felt*
it—but stone was stone and the uneven cliff face was a
good disguise. And Jazz realized how glad he was to
have come past that place unscathed. Maybe there was
no one, or nothing, there after all. But still he was glad.

He took a deep breath, issued it in a long drawn-out
sigh—and gave a massive start!

Something moved close by, in the shadow of fallen
boulders where they humped darkly on his left, and a
cold female voice, speaking Russian, said: "Well, Karl
Vyotsky, it's your choice. Talk or die. Right here and
right now!"

Jazz's finger had been on the trigger of his SMG ever

since the castle. Even before the woman's voice had started speaking, he'd turned and sprayed the darkness where she was hiding. She was dead now—or would be if the weapon had been cocked! Jazz was glad it wasn't. Sometimes, with his speed and accuracy, it was as well to take precautions. On this occasion his precaution had been to leave the gun safe. It was good practice for his nerves, that's all. Shooting at shadows was a sure sign that a man was cracking up.

"Lady," he said, his voice tense, "—Zek Föener? —I'm not Karl Vyotsky. If I was you'd probably be on your way to an alien heaven right now!"

Eyes peered at Jazz from the darkness, but not a woman's eyes. They were triangular—and yellow. And much too close to the ground. A wolf, grey, huge, hungry-looking, stepped cautiously into view. Its red tongue lolled between incisors nearly an inch and a half long. And *now* Jazz cocked his weapon. The action made a typical ch-*ching* sound.

"Hold it!" came the woman's voice again. "He's my friend. And until now—maybe even now—the only friend I have." There came a scuffing of stones and she stepped out of the shadows. The wolf went to heel on her right and a little to her rear. She had a gun like Jazz's, which shook in her hands where she pointed it at him.

"I'll say it again," he said, "just in case you weren't listening: I'm *not* Karl Vyotsky." Her gun was still shaking, violently now. Jazz looked at it, said: "Hell, you'd probably miss me anyway!"

"The man on the radio?" she said. "Before Vyotsky? I . . . I recognize your voice."

"Eh?" Then Jazz understood. "Oh, yes, that was me. I was trying to give Khuv a hard time—but I doubt if he could hear me. It was Khuv sent me through the Gate, just like he did it to you. Only he didn't lie to me about it. I'm Michael J. Simmons, a British agent. I don't know how you feel about that, but . . . it looks like we're in the same boat. You can call me Jazz. All my friends do, and . . . would you mind not pointing that thing at me?"

She sobbed, a great racking gulp of a sob, and flew into his arms. He could feel her straining not to, but she had to. Her gun went clattering to the stony earth and her arms tightened round him. "British?" she sobbed against his neck. "I don't care if you're Japanese, African, or an Arab! As for my gun—it's jammed. It has been for days. And I'm out of bullets anyway. If it was working and I had the ammunition—I'd probably have shot myself long ago. I . . . I . . ."

"Easy," said Jazz. "Easy!"

"The Sunsiders are after me," she continued to sob, "to give me to the Wamphyri, and Vyotsky said there's a way back home, and—"

"He what?" Jazz held her close. "You've spoken to Vyotsky? That's impos—" And he checked himself. The antenna of a radio was sticking out of her top pocket. "Vyotsky's a liar," he said. "Forget it! There isn't a way back. He's just looking for a chum, that's all."

"Oh, God!" Her fingers were biting into his shoulders. "Oh, *God!*"

Jazz tightened his grip on her, stroked her face, felt her tears hot in the crook of his neck. He smelled her, too, and it wasn't exactly flowers. It was sweat, and fear, and more than a little dirt, too. He pushed her away to arm's length and looked at her. Even in this deceptive light she looked good. A little haggard but good. And very human. She couldn't know it, but he was just as desperately pleased to see her.

"Zek," he said, "maybe we should find ourselves a nice safe place where we can talk and exchange notes, eh? I think you can probably save me a hell of a lot of time and effort."

"There's the cave where I rested," she told him, a little breathlessly. "It's about eight miles back. I was

183

asleep when I heard your voice on my radio. I thought I was dreaming. By the time I realized I wasn't it was too late. You'd gone. So I headed for the sphere, which was where I was going anyway. And I kept calling every ten minutes or so. Then I got Vyotsky . . ." She gave a small shudder.

"OK," Jazz quickly told her. "It's all right now—or about as right as it can be. Tell me all about it on our way to this cave of yours, right?" He stooped to pick up her gun, and the great wolf went into a crouch, screwed its face into a ferocious mask and snarled a warning.

She patted the animal almost absently on its great head where its ears lay flat to the long skull, said: "It's all right, Wolf—he's a friend."

"Wolf?" Jazz couldn't help smiling, however tightly. "That's original!"

"He was given to me by Lardis," she said. "Lardis is the leader of a Traveller pack. Sunsiders, of course. Wolf was to be my protection, and he has been. We got to be friends very quickly, but he's not much of a pet. There's too much of the wild in him. Think of him in a friendly way, like a big dog—I mean really *think* of him that way, as your friend—and he won't be any trouble." She turned and began to lead the way down from the crest toward the misty orb of the sun sitting apparently motionless over the southern mouth of the pass.

"Is that a theory or a fact?" Jazz asked her. "About Wolf, I mean?"

"It's a fact," she answered simply. Then, as quickly as she'd started off, she paused and grabbed his arm. "Are you sure we can't get back through the sphere?" Her voice had a pleading quality.

"I told you," Jazz answered, trying not to sound too harsh, "Vyotsky's a liar—amongst a lot of other things. Do you think he'd still be here if he knew a way out? When they put me through the Gate I dragged Vyotsky with me. That's the only reason he's here. I figured if it was bad enough for me it was good enough for him! Khuv and Vyotsky, those people are . . . it's hard to find a word for them without being offensive.''

"Be offensive," she said, bitterly. "They're bastards!"

"Tell me," said Jazz, following her as she started off again, "why were you heading for the sphere in the first place?"

She glanced at him briefly. "When you've been here as long as I have you won't need to ask. I came in that way, and it's the only Gate I know. I keep dreaming about being able to get out that way. I wake up thinking it's changed, that the poles have reversed and the flow lies in the other direction. So I was going there to try it. At sunup, of course, which is now. One chance and only one, and if I didn't make it through, then I wouldn't be making it back to Sunside, either."

Jazz frowned. "Reversed poles and all that—is that scientific stuff? Is it supposed to mean something?"

She shook her head. "Just my fantasy," she said, "but it was worth one last shot . . ."

They walked in silence for a while, with the great wolf loping between them. There were a million questions Jazz wanted to ask, but he didn't want to exhaust her. Eventually he said: "Where the hell is everybody? Where are the animals, birds? I mean, it's nature's way that where there are trees there are animals to chew on them. Also, I saw things at Perchorsk that made me think my coming would be like rolling a snowball into hell! And yet I haven't seen—"

"You wouldn't," she cut him short. "Not on Starside, not at sunup. Now we're down toward Sunside you'll start to see animals and birds; on the other side of the range you'll see plenty of them. But not on Starside. Believe me, Michael—er, Jazz?—you really wouldn't want to see anything of what lives on Starside." She shivered, hugged her elbows.

"Starside and Sunside," he mused. "The pole is

back there, the mountains run east and west, and the sun is south.''

"Yes," she nodded her head, "that's the way it is—always." She stumbled, said: *"Oh!"* and went to one knee; Jazz reached out and caught her elbow, stopped her from toppling over. This time Wolf made no protest. Jazz helped Zek to her feet, guided her to a flat rock. He shrugged a pack from his shoulder, took out a twenty-four hour manpack: food for one man for one day. Then he dumped the pack onto the rock and made Zek sit on it.

"You're weak from hunger!" he said, pulling the ring on a tiny can of concentrated fruit juice. He took a sip at the juice to clean his mouth, handed her the can and said, "Finish it." She did, with relish. Wolf stood close by, wagging his tail for all the world like a low-slung Alsation. His great tongue was beaded with saliva. Jazz broke a cube off a block of Russian chocolate concentrate and tossed it. Before it could hit the ground Wolf's jaws closed on it crunchingly.

"It's mainly my feet," Zek said. Jazz looked at them. She wore rough leather sandals, but he could see caked blood between the toes where they projected. The mist had cleared from the sun a little, and now Jazz could take in the rest of her. True colours were still difficult, but outlines, shadows and silhouettes made readable contrasts. Her one-piece was ragged at the elbows and knees, patched at the backside. She carried only a slim roll, hooked to her harness. A sleeping-bag, Jazz correctly supposed.

"They're no kind of footgear for this terrain," he said.

"I know it now," Zek answered, "but I'd forgotten. Sunside is bad enough, but this pass is worse. And Starside is sheer hell. I had boots when I came here, like you. They don't last. Your feet harden quickly, you'll see, but some of these pebbles and rocks are sharp as knives.''

186

He gave her chocolate, which she almost snatched. "Maybe we should rest right here," he said.

"Safe enough, with the sun on us," she answered, "but I'd prefer to keep moving. Since we can't use the sphere, and we can't stay Starside, it's best we get back to Sunside as soon as we can." Her tone was ominous.

"Any special reason?" Jazz was sure he wouldn't like the answer.

"Lots of them," she told him, "and they all live back there." She nodded back the way they'd come.

"Do you feel like telling me about—them?" Jazz unhooked one of his kidney-packs; he knew it contained, among other things, a very basic first-aid kit. He took out gauze bandages, a tube of ointment, plasters. And as Zek talked he kneeled and carefully slipped the sandals off her feet, began to work on her wounds.

"Them," she echoed him, making the word sound sour; and again a shudder ran through her. "The Wamphyri, do you mean? Oh, they're the main problem, it's true, but there are other things on Starside almost as bad. Did you see Agursky's 'pet,' the thing in the tank at Perchorsk?"

Jazz looked up, nodded. "I saw it. Telling you exactly *what* I saw would be a different matter!" He tore off a strip of gauze, soaked it in water from his flask, gently wiped away the caked blood from her toes. She sighed her appreciation as he squeezed ointment from its tube and rubbed it into the splits under her toes and the pads of her feet.

"That thing you saw was what happens when a vampire egg gets into a species of local fauna," she told him. She said it as simply as that, her voice quite neutral.

Jazz stopped working on her feet, looked her straight in the eye, slowly nodded. "A vampire egg, eh? That is what you said, isn't it?" She stared at him, obstinately, until he had to look away. "OK, a vampire egg," he shrugged, began wrapping her feet in gauze. "So you're telling me that the Wamphyri are oviparous? They're egg-layers, right?"

She shook her head, changed her mind and nodded. "Yes and no," she said. "The Wamphyri are what happens when a vampire egg gets into a man—or a woman."

Jazz put her sandals on. They'd been a little loose, tending to cause burns and blisters. Now they were tighter, stopping her feet from sliding about too much. "Is that better?" he asked. He thought about what she'd just told him, decided to let her tell it all in her own time, her own way.

"That feels good," she said. "Thanks." She stood up, helped him get his packs hooked up, and they set off toward the sun again.

"Listen," he said, when they were underway. "Why don't I just listen and let you tell me everything that's happened to you while you've been here? All you've seen, learned, everything you know. So far as I can tell we've got plenty of time on our hands. Vision's good, and we don't seem in any sort of immediate danger. The sun's up ahead, and we have some good moonlight . . ."

"Have we?" Zek answered. Jazz craned his neck, looked at the moon. It had crossed the pass and already its rim touched the eastern peaks. A few more minutes and it would be gone. "The planetary rotation period is incredibly slow," she began to explain. "But on the other hand the moon's orbit is closer and much faster. A 'day' here is about a week on Earth. Oh, and incidentally, this place is 'Earth.' That's what they call it. It isn't our Earth, of course not, but it's theirs. I thought it was strange at first, but then I thought: what else would they call it?

"Anyway, this planet rotates westward very slowly, and its poles are not quite lined up on the sun. So it's like the planet has a wobble. The sun is seen to revolve west to east—anti-clockwise, if you like—in a slow, small circle. Now I'm not an astronomer or a space scientist of any sort so don't ask me the whys and wherefores, but how it works out is like this:

"On Sunside we get a 'morning' of about twenty-five hours' duration, a 'day' of maybe seventy-five hours' duration, an 'evening' of twenty-five hours and a 'night' of about forty. Midday or thereabouts is sunup, and all of the night is sundown."

Jazz looked up again, saw the moon halved now by the sharp rim of the mountains. Even as he watched its glow lessened as it prepared to slip from sight. "I'm no astronomer either," he said, "but still it's very plain we have something of a fast-moving moon up there!"

"That's right," she answered. "It has a rapid spin, too, and unlike the old moon shows both its face and its backside."

Jazz nodded. "Not shy, eh?"

She snorted. "In some ways you remind me of another Englishman I once knew," she said. "He seemed sort of naïve, too, and yet in reality he was anything but naïve!"

"Oh?" Jazz looked at her. "Who was this lucky man?"

"He wasn't *that* lucky," she said, tilting her head a little. Jazz looked at her in profile in the last rays of moonlight, decided he liked her. A lot.

"So who was he?" he asked again.

"He was a member—maybe even the head—of your British E-Branch," she answered. "His name was Harry Keogh. And he had a special talent. I have a talent, too, but his was . . . different. I don't even know if you could call it ESP. That's how different it was."

Jazz remembered what Khuv had told him about her. That sort of stuff was so much baloney as far as he was concerned, but best not to let her see his scepticism. "Oh, yes, that's right," he said. "You're a mentalist, right? You read minds. So what was this Keogh's talent, eh?"

189

"He was a Necroscope," she said, her voice suddenly cold.

"A what?"

"He could talk to the dead!" she said; and coming to a sudden, angry halt, she drew apart from Jazz.

He looked at her stubborn, bad-tempered stance, and at the great wolf standing between them, staring yellow-eyed from one to the other. "Did I do something?"

"You *thought* something!" she snapped. "You thought, 'what a load of—' "

"Christ!" said Jazz. Because that was exactly what he'd thought.

"Listen," she said. "Do you know how many years I've been hiding the truth of my telepathy? Knowing I was better than anything else they had but not wanting to work for them? Not *daring* to work for them, because I knew if I did then sooner or later I'd come up against Harry Keogh again? I've suffered for my telepathy, Jazz, and yet now—here where it doesn't matter much any more—the moment I admit the truth of it . . ."

"Show me!" he said, cutting her off. "OK, I can see how we won't get anywhere if we've no faith in each other. But we won't get far by lying or misleading each other either. If you say you can do it I have to accept it, right—certainly I know there are those who *do* believe you have this talent. But isn't there any way you can show me? You have to admit, Zek, it would have been easy just now to take a guess at what I was thinking. Not only about your telepathy but also about this Keogh bloke—about what you say *he* can do! Don't tell me you haven't met up with scepticism before, not with a gift most people would consider supernatural!"

"You're tempting me?" her eyes flashed fire. "Humouring me? Taunting me? *Get thee behind me, Satan!*"

"Oh, it's godlike, this talent of yours, is it?" Jazz

couldn't quite conceal his sneer. "Well, if you're that good, how come you didn't know who it was coming up the pass? *If* telepathy and ESP in general are real, why didn't Khuv know I'd hidden away a magazine for my SMG, which is how I came to get the chance to drag that goon Vyotsky in here with me?"

Wolf gave a low whine and his ears went flat.

"You're annoying him," Zek said, "and you're annoying me, too. Also you've missed my point. Big macho man! I say: 'I'm a telepath,' and you say 'prove it.' The next thing, you're asking me to prove I'm a woman!"

Jazz nodded, pulled a sour face. "You rate yourself pretty damned high, don't you? God knows what sort of men you're used to; but I—"

"All *right!*" she snapped. "Watch . . ."

She looked at Wolf, the merest glance, then turned and tossed her head, walked on toward the sun. She went maybe a hundred yards, and Jazz and the wolf stood still watching her. Then she stopped and looked back. "Now I'm not going to say *anything*," she called out. "So see what you think of what happens next."

Jazz frowned, thought *What the—?* But in the next moment Wolf showed him what the. The huge creature loped closer, took the sleeve of Jazz's one-piece in his great jaws—but gently—and began to tug Jazz in Zek's direction. Jazz stumbled to keep up, and the faster he went the faster the Wolf ran, until both of them were flying full tilt toward the girl where she waited. Only then did the wolf let go, when both of them drew level with her.

"Well?" she said, as Jazz came to a panting, stumbling halt.

He sucked the hole in his jaw where two teeth had once been, put up a hand and scratched his nose. "Well," he started, "I—"

"You're thinking I'm an animal trainer," she cut in. "But if you say it out loud, that's it. We go our separate ways. I've survived so far without you and I can keep right on doing it." Wolf went and stood beside her.

"Two to one," Jazz grinned, however ruefully "And since I've always believed in the democratic process . . . OK, there's no option but to believe you. You're a telepath." They carried on walking, but slightly more apart now. "So why didn't you know it was me coming up the pass? How come you challenged me as Vyotsky?"

"You saw the castle back there, the keep?"

"Yes."

"That's why."

Jazz glanced back. The cliff-hugging castle must be miles back by now. "But it was empty, deserted."

"Maybe, and maybe not. The Wamphyri want me—badly. They're not stupid, anything but. They know I came in through the sphere, the Gate, and they've surely guessed that sooner or later I'd try to get out again that way. At least, I credit them with that much intelligence. It would have been easy for them during the last sundown—during any one of many sundowns—to put a creature in there. There'll be plenty of rooms and corners in there that the sun never touches."

Jazz shook his head, held up a restraining hand. "Even if I understood all you just said, which I don't, still I wouldn't know what it has to do with me," he said.

"In this world," she answered, "you're careful how you use ESP. The Wamphyri have it—in many diverse forms—and so to a lesser degree do most of the animals. Only the true men are without it."

"You mean, if the Wamphyri left something in that castle back there—a creature?—it would have *heard* your thoughts?" Again Jazz was close to incredulous.

"It might have heard my directed thoughts, yes," she nodded.

"But that's—" he stilled his tongue before it could offend her.

"Wolf can hear them," she said, simply.

192

"And me?" Jazz gave a snort. "Does that make me an idiot or something, because I can't hear them?"

"No," she shook her head. "Not an idiot, just a true man. You're not an esper. Listen, when I came up this way I heard your thoughts, distant and strange and a little confused. But I didn't dare concentrate on you and check out your identity in case that allowed something else to pick out and identify me! Now that we're in the light of the sun, the pressure's off; but the closer I got to Starside the more careful I had to be. And because I couldn't be sure you weren't Vyotsky, so I challenged you. You said he'd probably have killed me. Maybe he would and maybe not. But then he'd have had to kill Wolf, too, which wouldn't be so easy. And if he had killed me, then he really would be on his own. It was a chance I had to take . . ."

This time Jazz accepted all she told him; he had to start somewhere, and it seemed the best way to go. "Listen," he said. "Even though I like to think I'm fairly quick on the uptake, still there's a lot you'll need to explain about what you've already told me. But before that there's one thing I'd better know right now: do I need to guard my thoughts?"

"Here in the sunlight? No. On Starside, yes—all the time—but with a bit of luck we'll never see Starside again."

"OK," Jazz nodded. "Now let's get to more immediate things. Where's this cave you told me about? I really think we should rest up. And at the same time I can do a better job on your feet. Also, you look like you could use a more substantial meal."

She smiled at him, the first time she'd done it. Jazz wished he could see her in good old down-to-earth daylight. "I'll tell you something," she said. "I long ago learned not to listen in on people's thoughts—they can be nice, I'll grant you, but when they're not nice they can be very unpleasant indeed. We sometimes think things we could never express in words. Me, too.

Among espers it was a general rule that we observe each other's privacy. But I've been lonely a long time—for a mind I could relate to, I mean. A mind from my own world. So while I've been hearing you talking, well, I've been hearing other things, too. When I've grown used to you, then I'll make an effort not to intrude. I'm trying even now, but . . . I can't help scanning you."

Jazz frowned. "So what was I thinking?" he said. "I mean, I only said we should rest up."

"But you *meant* I should rest up. Me, Zek Föener. That's nice of you, and if I really needed it I'd accept. But you've come quite a long way yourself. And anyway, I'd prefer to keep moving until we're right out of the pass. Another four miles or so and we're out of it. But as you can see, the sun is just about to touch the eastern wall. It's a slow process, but in something less than an hour and a half the pass will be in darkness again. On Sunside it's still sunup for, oh, twenty-five hours yet, and the evening is just as long. After that . . . then we'll be holed up somewhere." She shivered.

Jazz knew nothing about ESP, but he did read people very well. "You're a hell of a brave woman," he said; and then he wondered why, for passing compliments was something he wasn't good at and didn't usually do. But he knew he'd meant it. So did she, but she didn't agree with him.

"No, I'm not," she said seriously. "I think I maybe used to be, but now I'm a dreadful coward. You'll find out why soon enough."

"Before then," Jazz said, "you'd better fill me in on more immediate hazards—assuming they are immediate. You said something about the Sunsiders—Travellers? —being after you? And something about the Wamphyri being desperate to get hold of you? Now what's all that about?"

"*Sunsiders!*" she gasped, but not in answer. She stiffened to a halt, glanced wildly all about, especially in the shadows cast by the eastern cliffs. Her hand went

194

to her brow, stroked it with trembling fingers. Wolf's hackles rose; he laid back his ears and offered a low, throaty growl.

Jazz took his SMG off safe. It was already cocked. He checked that the magazine was firmly seated in its housing. "Zek?" he husked.

"Arlek!" she whispered. And: "That's what comes of holding back on my telepathy, for your sake! Jazz, I—"

But she had no time for anything else, for by then they were in the thick of it!

Chapter Eleven
Castles—Travellers—The Projekt

SOMETHING MORE THAN AN HOUR EARLIER:

Keeping alert for bats, Karl Vyotsky rode his motorcycle across the boulder-strewn plain toward the towering, fantastically carved stacks standing like weird sentinels in the east. It had been his first instinct to make for the pass and the thin sliver of sun he'd seen on the horizon in the high wide 'V' of the canyon. But half-way to the mouth of the pass the sun had gone down, leaving only its rays to form a fan of pink spokes on the southern sky.

The mountain range reaching east and west as far as the eyes could see was black in silhouette now, highlighted with patches and slices of gleaming gold where the moon's beams lit on reflective features; but the sky over the mountains was indigo shot with fading shafts of yellow, and since night was obviously falling on this world, Vyotsky preferred the open ground under the moon to the inky blackness of the pass. He had no way of knowing that on the other side of the range, the daylight would last for the equivalent of two of his old days.

And so with his headlights blazing, he had turned back and headed for the stacks instead; and as his eyes had grown accustomed to the moonlight, and as the miles sped by under his now slightly eccentric wheels, so he had gazed at those enigmatic aeries some nine or ten miles east with something more than casual curiosity. Were those lights he could see in the topmost towers? If so, and if there were people up there, what sort of people would they be? While he had been pondering that, then he'd seen the bats. But not the tiny, flying-mice creatures of Earth!

Three of them, each a metre across wing-tip to wing-tip, had swooped on him, causing him to swerve and almost unseating him. The beat of their membrane wings had been a soft, rapid *whup-whup-whup*, stirring the air with its throbbing. They seemed of the same species as Encounter Four: *Desmodus* the vampire. Vyotsky didn't know what had attracted them; possibly it had been the roar of his engine, which was loud and strange in the otherwise eerie silence of this place. But when one of the bats cut across his headlight beam—

The creature's flight had immediately become erratic, even frenzied. Shooting aloft on the instant, its alarmed, high-pitched sonar trill had echoed weirdly down to Vyotsky, to be answered with nervous queries from its two travelling companions. That had given the Russian a notion how to be rid of them. Possibly they were harmless, merely curious; vampires or not, they weren't likely to attack a man, not while he was active and mobile. But he had his time cut out controlling his machine over this rugged terrain. There were fissures in the dry, pulverized earth of the plain, and rocks and boulders scattered everywhere. He needed to concentrate on where he was going, not on what this trio of huge bats were up to.

And so he'd stopped the bike, taken a powerful hand torch from one of his packs, and waited until the bats had come close again. The one already "blinded" kept its distance, patrolling on high, but after a little while the others had moved in closer. As they circled about him, then darted at him head-on, so Vyotsky had aimed his torch and pressed its button to bathe them in dazzling light. Confusion! The two had crashed into each other, fallen in a tangle. They separated on the ground, scuttling, flopping, crying their vibrating cries of alarm. Then one had managed to flap back aloft, but the other wasn't so lucky.

Vyotsky's SMG almost chopped the thing in half, splashed its blood on nearby rocks. And when the stuttering echoes of his weapon's voice had died away, the two survivors had gone. He'd given several loud blasts on the bike's horn then, to speed them on their way . . .

That had been twenty minutes ago and he hadn't been bothered since. He'd been aware that small shadows flitted apace with him high overhead, but nothing had come within swatting distance. He was glad of that, for one thing was certain: he mustn't expend any more ammunition killing bats! Like the Englishman, Michael Simmons, he knew that there were far worse things than bats in this world.

By now, too, the other thing was certain: he'd been right about the lights atop the no longer distant aeries. The closest of these was perhaps five miles away, with others dotted irregularly over the plain behind it, fading into the distance and seeming to get smaller and hazier even in the bright light of moon. Their bases were piled with scree, fortified with walls and earthworks. In the striated, stony stem of the closest one, lights flickered and flared intermittently; smoke smudged the dark blue sky, obscuring the pale stars where it issued from various chimneys; lesser structures clung to precipitous faces where ledges had permitted precarious construction work. But the great stone buildings that crowned these massive stacks could only be described accurately in one word: castles!

Who had built them, how and why?—these things remained to be discovered; but Vyotsky felt certain they were the works of men. Warlike men! The kind of men the big Russian could do business with—he hoped. Strong men, certainly; and again his eyes were lifted to the crest of that closest tower, to the great ominous structure wrought bleak and frowning to scan the land about like some brooding watchtower.

In a little while, returning his gaze to the hazardous way ahead, Vyotsky found himself obliged to apply his brakes. A low wall of piled boulders had seemed to grow out of the littered surface, stretching left far out onto the plain, and right to extend itself into the very foothills of the mountains. The wall was maybe five feet high and a little less than that through its base. Man-made, of course, it was . . . a boundary? The Russian turned his bike south, and riding up into the foothills he searched for a break in the wall. But ahead the wall rose up to meet with a steeply inclined escarpment of smooth rock which Vyotsky knew his machine couldn't climb. And even if it could, he wouldn't. Frustrated, he turned about, pausing awhile to stare thoughtfully at the nearest stack.

From this high vantage point his view was that much better. Seated here on his bike, for a moment he found himself calculating the dimensions of these mighty columns:

At its base, this one would be maybe two hundred metres through, tapering down to about half of that as it rose all of a kilometre and a half to its turret-clad crest. Basically the tower was—well, a stone stack! Natural as any of the Grand Canyon's grotesque outcrops, its awesomeness lay mainly in its size and the structures built upon it. But as his eyes travelled up the tremendous, sky-scraping height of the thing, so he noticed what he took to be activity of some sort in the darkness of a huge cavern close to the top.

He narrowed his eyes in an attempt to bring the activity into focus. Now what was . . . *that?*

Stuffed into the bottom of his main back-pack—packed in haste, when he hadn't been thinking too clearly—

Vyotsky knew there were binoculars. All well and good, but he didn't want to waste the time necessary to retrieve them now. But staring at the stack with its many gravity-defying structures, its watchtower castle and now this bustling activity in the—

Something launched itself outwards from the high cavern!

Vyotsky's spine prickled and his fleshy lips drew back from teeth which were still sore from the battering Simmons's elbow had given them. He drew breath in a gasp, straining his eyes to make out what it was that floated now like a black boiling cloud, forming an airfoil as it circled slowly about the great stack and lost a little height.

And in the next moment all of the blood drained from the Russian's face as it dawned on him just what this flying *thing* might be—namely, the twin of Encounter One! An alien dragon in the sky of an alien land!

Vyotsky was paralysed with dread, but only for a moment. Now was not the time to go into shock. He switched off his engine, and keeping to the lee of the wall let his bike free-wheel and carry him down from the foothills back to the plain. There he found a massive outcrop of rock and parked the bike in its shadow. The moon, which seemed to be moving across the sky remarkably quickly, was now almost directly overhead, making concealment difficult. In what little shadow there was, the Russian fumbled to unhook his packs, loaded his SMG with a fresh magazine and stuffed a spare into a pocket of his one-piece. Then he primed his small flamethrower, and even though he was faithless thought: *Christ—and a lot of good this will be against that!*

"That" had meanwhile circled the titan stack a second and third time, and was now less than a thousand teet high. Suddenly it veered sharply toward the plain, then seemed to expand rapidly as it came swooping in a series of glides and dips directly toward Vyotsky's hiding place. And he knew then that it was no use pretending any longer, no use hoping that the flight of this thing was merely coincidental to his being here. The—creature?—*knew* he was here; it was looking for him!

It passed overhead a little to the north, laying a huge shadow on the plain like a vast, swiftly flowing inkblot, and Vyotsky was able to look up at it and measure its size. He saw with only a minimum of relief that it wasn't nearly as huge or terrifying as the murderous thing which had half-wrecked Perchorsk. Fifty feet long, with wings spanning a distance something greater than that, it formed a shape similar to the great mantas of Earth, with a long trailing tail for balance. Unlike the manta, however, there were huge lidless eyes on its underside, peering in as many different directions as could be imagined!

Then the thing banked left and came swooping back, dropping lower still in a controlled stall, finally set down in a fanning of fleshy wings that churned up a cloud of dust which for a little while obscured it. It landed no more than thirty or forty metres away; as the dust settled Vyotsky saw it lolling there, turning what was best described as a "head" this way and that in a manner which could only be called vacant or at best aimless.

Vacant, yes—and vacated! For now the Russian saw the thing's harness—and the empty saddle of ornately carved leather upon its back. But mainly he saw the man who stood on the ground beside the thing, staring in the direction of his hiding place. Saw enough of him, at least, to know that he wasn't a man, not entirely. For just such a "man" as this had burned to death on the walkway in Perchorsk's core: a Wamphyri warrior!

He stared hard, apparently right at Vyotsky, then began to turn in a slow circle. Before he turned away, Vyotsky saw the glint of his red eyes like small fires burning in his face. But more than the warrior's face,

201

the Russian was concerned with—concerned about—the gauntlet-like weapon he wore on his right hand. He knew the damage that weapon could do. But not to Karl Vyotsky. Not this time.

The big Russian remained quiet as a mouse in the shadows; he didn't move, didn't breathe, didn't blink an eye. The warrior completed his circling turn, then looked up and gazed for a moment at the castle on the stack. He spread his legs, put his hands on his hips, cocked his head sharply on one side. And he whistled a high-pitched, penetrating whistle that was more a throbbing on the eardrums than a real sound. Down from the sky fell a pair of familiar shapes; they circled the warrior once, then headed straight for Vyotsky where he crouched in the shadows of leaning boulders. It was so unexpected that the big Russian was caught off-balance.

One of the bats almost struck Vyotsky with a pulsing wing, so that he must duck to avoid it. The short barrel of his SMG clattered against stone, and he knew his cover was broken. The warrior faced him again, whistled to call off the bats, came striding forward. There was no uncertainty now, none. He knew where his quarry was hiding. His red eyes burned and he grinned a strange, sardonic grin; he tossed back his forelock from the side to the back of his head; he held himself proudly, chin high, shoulders pulled sharply back.

Vyotsky let him get as close as twenty paces, then stepped out into view, onto the stony plain in the yellow light of the half-moon. He pointed his weapon, called out: *"Halt!* Hold it right there, my friend, or it ends for you right here!" But his voice was shaky, and the warrior seemed to know it. He simply swerved to change his angle of approach, came head-on as before.

Vyotsky didn't want to kill him. He had to try and live here, not die in some vendetta for the death of this heathen brave. The Russian would prefer to deal, not fight, not with an entire world against him. He put his weapon on single shot, fired a round over the advancing warrior's head. The bullet plucked at the warrior's fore-lock, it passed so close. He stopped, looked up, sniffed at the air. And Vyotsky called out:

"Look, let's talk." He held up his free hand, palm open toward the warrior, lowered his SMG to point it at the stony ground. It was the best way he could think of to signal peace. But at the same time his thumb switched the weapon to rapid fire. The next time he pulled the trigger, it would be for real.

The warrior put his hand up to touch his forelock. He brought it down again, sniffed suspiciously at his fin-gers with his squat, almost swinish snout. Then his eyes widened and went as round as blood-hued coins. He snarled something Vyotsky half-recognized, which he made out or guessed to be: "What? You dare threaten?" Then the warrior's right arm rose up toward his right shoulder in a sort of salute. His gauntlet was clenched, but at the apex of the salute it sprang open and showed an arrangement of blades, hooks, claws.

He went into a crouch, affected a combat stance, made as if to hurl himself at Vyotsky. But the big Russian wasn't waiting. Over a distance of only six or seven paces he couldn't possibly miss. He squeezed the trig-ger, opened up, hosed the warrior across the body with a stream of lethal led—or should have!

But the KGB man wasn't having much luck with his gun. Of all times to have a defective round!—the weapon fired three or four shots and jammed. It had been Vyotsky's intention to stitch the warrior one way across his body, right to left and rising, then the other way, coming back down. A simple "wave" of the SMG should suffice, pouring maybe fifteen to twenty rounds at him, half of which should find their target. But the gun had only released three or four shots, none of them aimed.

The first had sliced a groove along the warrior's left side, laying open the flesh there as if he'd been slashed with a jagged toothed saw; the next had pierced his shoulder under the right collar bone at the joint with his arm; the rest, two shots at most, had missed entirely. But the two hits had been like hammer blows which would have stopped any soldier of Earth. This wasn't Earth, however, and the target wasn't just a man.

Thrown back and spun around by the force of the impact to his shoulder, he'd gone sprawling flat-out in the dust—where in the next moment he'd sat up and looked groggily all about. Vyotsky, cursing loudly, snatched the magazine from his gun, re-cocked the weapon and glanced into the chamber. A cartridge, struck but not fired, was stuck in the breach. He shook the SMG to try to dislodge the jammed, defective round; no good, it would have to be carefully prised loose. And by now the warrior was back on his feet.

Vyotsky hooked the gun to his belt to keep it out of the way, unhooked the nozzle of his flamethrower. He struck ignition and threw off the safety catch. As the wounded warrior again stumbled toward him, he made one last attempt for peace and adopted the same pose as before, showing the warrior his open palm. Perhaps the other considered it an insult; whichever, all Vyotsky got for an answer was a snarl of rage. Then, even though the warrior had been shot through his right shoulder, still he lifted his gauntlet, flexed its terrible tools and showed them to his opponent.

"Enough is enough!" the Russian growled. He let the other come to within three or four paces, aimed the nozzle of his flamethrower and squeezed the firing stud. The small, licking blue flames at its tip became a searing lance of roaring heat, lashed out and torched the warrior all down the left-hand side of his body. Burning, he screamed his shock and terror and bounded away, bounded again, then threw himself down and rolled in dust and pebbles, finally extinguishing the flames. Smoking, he staggered to his feet, went careening back toward his weird mount. But now that Vyotsky had started this, he'd decided it should be finished.

He advanced after the smoking warrior, aimed his hose a second time—and froze!

The Wamphyri warrior was calling to his mount, harsh, agonized orders which it heard and obeyed. The bulk of its grey body seemed to shrivel while its wings extended into huge sails. It beat them upon the air, flattening out even as it lifted off. Thrust aloft on what seemed to Vyotsky a nest of vast pink worms that uncoiled like springs to give it lift, it was like a huge sheet of lumpy, leprous canvas in the air. Its worm boosters retracted into it, and it came gliding overhead with its manta tail extended, lashing from side to side. As its body took back a little bulk and the wings commenced to beat, so the eyes along its belly re-formed, all of them ogling in various directions. Then they spied and fastened on the Russian.

Vyotsky backed off. The flying creature fell toward him; its fish-like shadow overtook him, black as ink; its rubbery underside opened up into a great mouth or pouch lined with barbs. Vyotsky stumbled, began to fall. With a rush of air that carried an unbelievable stench the thing was on him. A flap of flesh scooped him up, cartilege hooks caught in his clothing and cold, clammy darkness compressed him.

His finger was still on the stud of the flamethrower but he daren't squeeze it. Do that here, *inside* the creature, and he'd only succeed in frying himself! There was air to breathe but it was fetid, vile. The whole experience was a livid, living, claustrophobic nightmare that went on and on—

The creature's gasses worked on him like an anaesthetic. Hardly knowing he was losing consciousness, Vyotsky blacked out . . .

For Jazz Simmons, "in the thick of it" meant about five seconds in which to make up his mind; it was what might have been if Zek Föener hadn't been there to advise him. He'd made his mind up in two seconds, and as shadows began separating from the main shadow of the cliff was on the point of turning decision to action when she cautioned him with: "Jazz—don't shoot!"

"What!" He was incredulous. The shadows were men who came loping to surround the pair. "Don't shoot? Do you know these people?"

"I know they won't harm us—" she breathed, "that we're more valuable to them alive than dead—and that if you fire a single shot you'll not live to hear its echoes! There'll be a half-dozen arrows and spears lined up on you right now. Probably on me, too."

Jazz put up his gun, but slowly, grudgingly. "This is what's called faith in your friends," he growled, without humour. And he looked at the wary, crouching gang of men who surrounded them. One of them finally straightened up, stuck his chin out, addressed Zek. He spoke in a harsh gabble, a dialect or tongue which for all the world Jazz felt he should recognize. And Zek answered in a tongue he *did* recognize. Recognition as least, if nothing more. It was a very basic, somewhat disjointed Romanian!

"Ho, Arlek Nunescu!" she said, and: "Tear down the mountains and let the sun melt the castles of the Wamphyri, but what's this!? Do you waylay and molest fellow Travellers?"

Now that Jazz knew the tongue, he could more readily concentrate on understanding it. His knowledge of the Romantic languages was slight but not entirely without value. Some of it came from his father, a little less from his later academic studies, the rest he supposed from instinct; but he'd always had a "thing" for languages anyway.

The man Arlek—indeed, all of these men ringing them in, and others where they now came out of hiding—were Gypsies. That was Jazz's first impression: that they were Romany. It was stamped into them and just as recognizable as it would be in the world now left behind, on the other side of the Gate. Dark-haired, jingling, lean and swarthy, they wore their hair long and greased and their clothes loosely and with something of style and flair. The one thing about them that struck a wrong chord was the fact that several of them carried crossbows, and others were armed with sharpened hardwood staves. Apart from that, Jazz had seen the like of these people in countries all over the world— the old world, anyway.

Gypsies, tinkers, wandering metalworkers, musicians and . . . fortune tellers?

"Tear down the mountains, aye," Arlek answered her greeting now, speaking more slowly, thoughtfully. "You know the things to say, Zekintha, because you steal them from the minds of the Travellers! But we've been saying 'tear down the mountains' as long as men remember, which is a very long time, and they're still standing. And while the mountains are there the Wamphyri remain in their castles. And so we wander all our lives, because to remain in one place is to die. I have read the future, Zekintha, and if we shelter you you'll bring down disaster on Lardis and his band. But if we give you into the hands of the Wamphyri—"

"*Hah!*" her tone was scornful. "You're brave with Lardis Lidesci away in the west, seeking a new camp for you where the Wamphyri won't raid. And how will you explain this to him when he returns? How will you tell him you plotted to give me away? What, you'd give away a woman to appease your greatest enemies and make them stronger? The act of a coward, Arlek!"

Arlek took a deep breath. He drew himself up, took a pace toward her and raised his hand as if to strike. A dark flush had made his face darker yet. Jazz lowered the muzzle of his weapon until it touched Arlek's shoulder, pointing into his left ear. "Don't," he warned in the man's own tongue. "From what I've seen of you I don't much care for you, Arlek, but if you make me kill you I'll die, too." He hoped the words he'd used made sense.

Apparently they did. Arlek backed off, called forward two of his men. They approached Jazz and he showed them his teeth in a cold grin, showed them the gun, too.

"Let them have it," Zek said.

"I was thinking about it," he answered out of the corner of his mouth.

"You know what I mean," she said. "Please give them the gun!"

"Does your telepathy let you walk naked in lions' dens?" he asked her. One of the Gypsies had taken hold of the barrel of the SMG, the other's hand closed on Jazz's wrist. Their eyes were deep, dark, alert. Jazz was aware that crossbow bolts were trained on him, but still he asked: "Well? It's your show, Zek."

"We can't go back to Starside," she quickly answered him, "and the Travellers guard the way to Sunside. Even if we got out of this—got away from them—they'd find us again eventually. So give them the gun. We're safe for now, at least."

"Against my better judgement," he growled. "But really I suppose there's nothing else for it." He released the magazine and slipped it into his pocket, handed over the gun.

Arlek smiled crookedly. "That, too," he pointed at Jazz's pocket. "And the rest of your . . . belongings."

Hearing the language spoken, using it, was inspirational. Jazz's talent for tongues searched out and found him a few words. "You're asking too much, Traveller," he said. "I'm a free man, like you. More free, for I make no deals with the Wamphyri so that I may live."

Arlek was taken aback. To Zek he said: "Does he read the thoughts in men's heads, too?"

"I hear only my own thoughts," Jazz spoke first, "and I speak my own words. Don't talk *about* me, talk *to* me."

Arlek faced him squarely. "Very well," he said. "Give us your weapons, your various . . . things. We take them so that you may not use them against us. You are a stranger, from Zekintha's world; so much is obvious from your dress and your weapons. Therefore, why should we trust you?''

"Why should *anyone* trust *you!?*" Zek cut in, as Arlek's men began taking Jazz's equipment. "You betray your own leader while he's away seeking safe places!"

To give them their due, some of the Travellers shuffled their feet and looked a little shamefaced. But Arlek turned on Zek and snarled: "Betrayal? You speak to me of betrayal? The moment Lardis's back's turned you run off! Where to, Zekintha? Your own world, even though you've said there's no way back there? To find yourself a champion, maybe—this man, perhaps? Or to give yourself to the Wamphyri and so become a power in the world? I *would* give you to them, aye—but only in trade for the safety of the Travellers—not for my own glory!"

"Glory!" Zek scoffed. "Infamy, more like!"

"Why, you—!" He was lost for words.

Jazz had meanwhile been stripped of his packs, his weapons, but not of his pride. Strangely, now that he was down to his combat suit he felt safer; he knew he wouldn't be shot for fear of the havoc he might wreak with his awesome weapons. At least he could stand man to man now. Even if he couldn't understand all of Arlek's words—and even though many that he could understand rang true—still he didn't like Arlek's tone of voice when he spoke to Zek like that. He caught the Gypsy's shoulder, spun him round face to face. "You're good at making loud noises at women," he said.

Arlek looked at Jazz's hand bunching his jacket and his eyes opened wide. "You've a lot to learn, 'free man,' " he hissed—and he lashed out at Jazz's face with his clenched fist. His reaction had been telegraphed; Jazz ducked his blow easily; it was like fighting with a clumsy, untrained schoolboy. No one in Arlek's world had ever heard of unarmed combat, judo, karate. Jazz

209

struck him with two near simultaneous blows and stretched him out. And for his troubles he in turn was stretched out! From the side, one of the Gypsies had smacked him on the side of the head with the butt of his own gun.

Passing out, he heard Zek cry: "Don't kill him! Don't harm him in any way! He may be the one answer to all your troubles, the only man who can bring you peace!" Then for a moment he felt her cool, slender fingers on his burning face, and after that . . .

. . . there was only the cold, creeping darkness . . .

Andrei Roborov and Nikolai Rublev were lesser KGB lights. Both of them had been seconded to Chingiz Khuv at the Perchorsk Projekt—known as a punishment posting—for over-zealousness in their work; namely, Western journalists had snapped them beating-up on a pair of black-market Muscovites. The "criminals" in the case had been an aged man-and-wife team, selling farm produce from their garden in the suburbs. In short, Roborov and Rublev were thugs. And on this occasion they were thugs in serious trouble.

Khuv had sent them to "talk" to Kazimir Kirescu; it was to be their last opportunity to interrogate the old man before he went on a course of truth-drugs. It would be best if he could be persuaded to volunteer the required information (on Western and Romanian links) for the drugs weren't too good for a man's heart. The older the man, the worse their effect. Khuv had wanted information before Kirescu died, for afterwards it would be too late. This might seem perfectly obvious, but to members of the Soviet E-Branch things were rarely as obvious as they seemed. In the old days when a person died without releasing his information, then they would have called in the necromancer Boris Dragosani, but Dragosani was no more. As it happened, neither was Kazimir Kirescu.

Approaching the old man's cell to see how his men

were making out, Khuv was in time to discover the two just making their exit. Both wore the clear plastic capes or ponchos of the professional torturer, but Rublev's cape was spattered with blood. Too much blood. His rubber gloves, too, where he stripped them from shaking hands. His face was deathly white, which Khuv knew was sometimes the reaction with this sort of man when he'd done a job too well, or enjoyed it too much. Or when he feared the consequences of a gross error.

As the two turned from locking the door, Khuv met them face to face. His eyes narrowed as they took in Rublev's shaken condition, and the condition of his protective clothing. "Nikolai," he said. *"Nikolai!"*

"Comrade Major," the other blurted, his fat lower lip beginning to tremble. "I—"

Khuv shoved him aside. "Open that door," he snapped at Roborov. "Have you sent for help?"

Roborov backed off a pace, shook his long, angular head. "Too late for that, Comrade Major." He turned and opened up the door anyway. Khuv stepped inside the cell, took a long, hard look, came out again. His dark eyes blazed their fury. He grabbed the two by the fronts of their smocks, shook them unresistingly.

"Stupid, stupid—!" he gasped his rage at them. "That was nothing less than butchery!"

Andrei Roborov was so thin as to be almost skeletal. His cadaverous face was always pale, but never more so than now. There was no fat on him to shake, and so he simply rocked to and fro under Khuv's assault, rapidly blinking his large green expressionless eyes, and opening and closing his mouth. When Khuv had first met him he'd thought: *this man has the eyes of a fish—probably its soul, too!*

Nikolai Rublev on the other hand was very much overweight. His features were pink and almost babylike, and even the mildest reproof could bring him to the point of tears. On the other hand his fists were huge and hard as iron, and Khuv knew that his tears were usually tears of suppressed fury or rage. His rages, when he threw them, were quite spectacular; but he had more sense than to rage at a superior officer. Especially one like Chingiz Khuv.

Finally Khuv let go of them, turned abruptly away and clenched his fists. Over his shoulder, without looking at them, he said: "Fetch a trolley. Take him to the mortuary . . . no! Take him to your own quarters. And make sure he's covered up on the way. He can wait there for disposal. But whatever you do, don't let anyone see him like . . . like that! Especially not Viktor Luchov! Do you understand?"

"Oh, yes, Comrade Major Khuv!" Rublev gasped. It seemed he was off the hook.

Still Khuv looked the other way. "Then both of you will prepare and sign the usual accidental death reports and get them in to me. And you'll make sure they're corroborative in every detail."

"Yes, Comrade, of course," the two answered as one man.

"Well, then—*move!*" Khuv shouted.

They collided with each other, then made off down the corridor. Khuv let them go so far before calling after them: "You two!" They skidded to a halt. "Nikolai, for God's sake get out of that *cape!*" Khuv hissed. "And neither one of you is to go near the girl, Kirsecu's daughter. Do you hear me? I'll personally skin whichever one of you so much as *thinks* about her! Now get out of my sight!"

They disappeared in short order.

Khuv was still standing there, trembling with fury, when Vasily Agursky came hurrying from the direction of the laboratories. He saw Khuv and sidled toward him. "I was told you'd be seeing to the prisoners," he said

Khuv nodded. "Seeing to them, yes," he answered. "What can I do for you?"

"I've just been to see Direktor Luchov. He has

returned me to full duty. I'm on my way to see the creature—my first visit in a week! If you would care to accompany me, Major Khuv?"

Right now that was the last thing Khuv would "care" to do. He glanced at his watch. "As it happens I'm headed that way," he said. Anything to get Agursky away from here before Roborov and Rublev returned with their surgical trolley.

"Good!" Agursky beamed. "If we can walk together, perhaps I can ask for your help in a certain matter. In the strictest confidence, you may be able to make a significant contribution to my—to *our*—understanding of that creature from beyond the Gate."

Khuv glanced at the strange little scientist out of the corner of his eye. There seemed something different about him; it was hard to put a finger on it, but some change had occurred in him. "I can make a contribution?" Khuv raised an eyebrow. "In connection with the creature? Vasily—do you mind if I call you Vasily?—I'm here to protect the Prokjekt from, shall we say, outside interference? As a policeman, a spy-catcher, and investigator—as any and all of these things I already make my contribution. As for any other aspect of work at the Projekt: I have no control over the staff as such, no 'official' knowledge of any facet of the scientific work that goes on here. I control my own handful of men, yes, and I protect the specialists from Moscow and Kiev; but outside of these routine duties it is difficult to see how I can be of any assistance to you in your work."

Agursky was not put off; on the contrary, his voice was suddenly eager. "Comrade, there's a certain experiment I would like to try. Now, any theoretical work I perform with the creature is my concern entirely, of course—but there's something I need which is quite beyond everyday requirements."

Again Khuv glanced at him, glanced *down* on him, because beside the tall KGB Major, Agursky seemed almost a dwarf. His bald pate coming through its crown of dirty-grey fluff made him seem very gnome-like. But his red-rimmed eyes, made huge by his spectacles, put him in a much less comical perspective. He was like some strange, devious bottle-imp given the guise of a man.

Devious!—that was the word Khuv had searched for to describe the change in Agursky. There was now something sly about the little man, something furtive.

Khuv put his mental meanderings aside, uttered a none too patient sigh. He had never much cared for the little scientist, and now cared for him even less. "Vasily," he said, "has the Projekt no procurement officer? Is there no quartermaster? A great deal may hinge upon our understanding of that beast. I'm sure that whatever you require for your work can be obtained through the proper channels. Indeed, I would say you have an absolute priority. All you have to do is—"

"The proper channels," Agursky cut in, nodding. "Exactly, exactly! But that is just precisely the problem, Comrade Major. The channels are perhaps *too* proper . . ."

Khuv was taken aback. "Your requirement is improper? Unusual, do you mean? Then why on earth don't you ask Direktor Luchov about it? You've just been to see him, haven't you? I should think Viktor Luchov can lay his hands on just about any—"

"No!" Agursky caught his elbow and drew Khuv to a halt. "That is exactly my problem. He would not—definitely *not*—sanction this requirement.

Khuv stared at him. There were beads of sweat on the man's upper lip. His eyes, unblinking, burned on Khuv through the thick lenses of his spectacles. And the KGB Major thought: *a requirement Luchov wouldn't sanction?* He noticed that Agursky's hand was trembling where it gripped his elbow. It was suddenly very easy to jump to the wrong conclusion. Khuv broke abruptly away from the other, brushed at the sleeve of his jacket, drily said:

"But I thought you were off the bottle, Vasily? The break was a little too sudden for you, was it? And now your supplies have run out and you require a re-stock," he nodded his mock-understanding. "I should have thought that the soldiers could easily fill your needs from the barracks at Ukhta. Or perhaps it's more urgent than that, eh?"

"Major," said Agursky, his expression unchanging, "the *last* thing I need is alcohol. In any case, I assume that you are joking, for I've already made it clear that this has to do with the creature. Indeed, it has to do with fathoming the very *nature* of the creature. Now I repeat: the Projekt cannot legitimately fill my requirement, and certainly Luchov would never sanction it. But you are an officer of the KGB. You have contacts with the local police, authority over them. You handle traitors and criminals. In short you are in a position— the *ideal* position—to assist me. And if my theory works out, you would have the satisfaction of knowing that you were in part responsible for the breakthrough."

Khuv's eyes narrowed. The little man was wily, full of surprises, not his usual self at all. "Just what is this 'theory' of yours, Vasily? And you'd better tell me about your 'requirement,' too."

"As to the first," (for the first time since their conversation began, Khuv saw Agursky blink his eyes, nervously, two or three times in rapid succession,) "I can't tell you. You would probably consider it preposterous, and I'm not even sure of it myself. But as for the second—"

And without further pause he told Khuv what his requirement was . . .

215

Chapter Twelve
Deal with the Devil

WHEN JAZZ SIMMONS REGAINED CONSCIOUSNESS HE SAW that he was where he'd fallen, except now his hands were tied behind him. Zek, who hadn't been trussed, was busy moistening his brow and lips with a water-soaked rag. She sighed in relief as he came to.

Arlek sat close by on a flat stone, watching her at her ministrations. Others of the clan or tribe moved in shadows which had lengthened a little, murmuring with low background voices. As Jazz struggled to sit up, so Arlek came across and stood over him. He fingered a lump under his ear where Jazz had hit him, displayed a right eye rapidly turning black and closing.

"I never saw anyone fight like you," he stiffly complimented his captive. "I didn't even see you strike me!"

Jazz grunted, propped himself against a boulder and brought his knees up a little. "That was the idea," he said. "There's a lot more I could show you, too, like how to fight the Wámphyri. That's what my weapons were for: to keep me alive in a world where things like the Wamphyri rule. Where the hell do men stand in the scale of things on this world, anyway? Why bargain with the Wamphyri, or bow and scrape to them, when you can fight them?"

Despite his painful face, Arlek laughed out loud. Other Travellers heard him, came forward; he quickly repeated what Jazz had said. "Fight the Wamphyri, indeed! We are only lucky they spend so much time fighting with each other! But defy them? *Hah!* You don't know what you're saying. They don't fight with Sunsiders, they just make slaves of them. Have you *seen* a Warrior? Of course not, else you'd not be here! That's why we're Travellers, because to remain in one place is to be at their mercy. You don't 'fight' the Wamphyri, my stupid friend, you just stay out of their way—for as long as you can."

He turned away, walked off with his followers. Over his shoulder he called back: "Talk with the woman. It's high time she told you something about this world you've come to. At least then you'll have some understanding of why I'm giving you—both of you—to Shaithis of the Wamphyri . . ."

Wolf loped out of the shadows, licked Jazz's face. Jazz scowled at the animal. "Where were you when Zek and me were fighting, eh?"

"When *you* were fighting," she corrected him. "Wolf wasn't in it. Why should I risk his life? I told him to be still. He's just back from seeing his brothers. The Travellers have three or four of them, all raised from cubs."

"Funny," Jazz said after a moment, "but you struck me as a woman who'd bite and scratch a lot." He didn't mean it as a reproach, but it was and he regretted it immediately.

"I would," she said, "if there was any point. But I'd look silly trying to bite a dozen Travellers and their wolves, now wouldn't I? My first concern was for you."

Jazz sighed. "I suppose I went off half-cocked, didn't I? But I thought you said we'd be safe?"

"We might have been," she said, "but while you've been lying there Arlek's had word from a runner that Lardis Lidesci is on his way back from the west. Arlek

knows Lardis won't give me to the Wamphyri, and so
he'll do it himself—now! There'll be a price to pay
when Lardis hears about it, but Arlek's got this group
on his side and believes that in the end Lardis will have
to go along with him or split the tribe. In any case, by
the time Lardis gets here it will be too late.''

Jazz said: ''Can you touch me behind my ear just
here? *Ow!* That feels tender!''

''It's soft,'' she said, and he thought he detected a
catch in her voice. ''God, I thought you were dead!''
She squeezed cold water onto the back of his head, let
it soak into the place where his hair was matted with
blood. He looked beyond her to the south, to where the
sun had gone down a little more, crept a little more to
the east.

A stray beam lit her face, let him see her clearly and
really close up for the first time. She was a bit grimy,
but under the dirt she was very beautiful too. She'd be
in her early thirties, only a few years older than Jazz
himself. Maybe five-nine, slim, blonde and blue-eyed,
her hair shone in the beam of sunlight; it looked golden
and bounced on her shoulders when she moved. Her
combat suit, tattered as it was getting to be, fitted her
figure like a glove; it seemed to accentuate her delicate
curves. Right here and now, Jazz supposed any woman
would have looked good to him. But he couldn't think
of one he'd rather have here. Or, (he corrected himself,) rather *not* have here. This was no place for any
woman.

''So what's happening now?'' he asked, when the
cold water had taken some of the sting out of his neck
and head.

''Arlek tracked me using the talents of an old man,
Jasef Karis,'' Zek told him. ''It wasn't too hard. There
was really only one place I could head for: through the
pass to the sphere, to see if I could make it back home.
Anyway, Jasef's like me, a telepath.''

''You told me the wild animals here had a degree of

ESP," Jazz reminded her, "but you didn't say anything about the people. I'd got the impression that only the Wamphyri had these talents."

"Generally, that's true," she answered. "Jasef's father was taken prisoner in a Wamphyri raid; this was a long time ago, you understand. He escaped from them and came back over the mountains. He swore that he hadn't been changed in any way. He'd escaped before the Lord Belath could make a mindless zombie of him. His wife took him back, of course, and they had a child: Jasef. But then it was discovered that Jasef's father had lied. He had been changed by the Lord Belath, but he'd made his escape before the change could commence in him. The truth finally came out when he became uncontrollable—became, in fact, a thing! The Travellers knew how to deal with it; they staked it out, cut it in pieces and burned it. And afterwards they kept a close watch on Jasef and his mother. But they were OK. Jasef's telepathy is something come down to him from his father, or from the thing that Lord Belath put into him.""

Jazz's head swam, partly from the throbbing pain where he'd been clubbed but mainly from trying to take in all that Zek was telling him. "Stop!" he said. "Let's concentrate on the important stuff. Tell me what else I'll need to know about this planet. Draw me a map I can keep in my head. First the planet, then its peoples."

"Very well," she nodded, "but first you'd better know how we stand. Old Jasef and one or two men have gone on into the pass to see if there's a watcher—a guardian creature—in the keep back there. If there is, Jasef will send a telepathic message through it to its master, the Lord Shaithis. The message will be that Arlek holds us captive, and that he'll use us to strike a bargain with Shaithis. In return for us, Shaithis will promise not to raid on Lardis Lidesci's tribe of Travellers. If it's a deal, then we'll be handed over."

"From what Arlek was saying about the Wamphyri,"

Jazz said. "I'm surprised they'll even be interested in making a deal. If they're so much to be feared, they can just take us anyway."

"*If* they could find us," she answered. "And only at night. They can only raid when the sun's down below the rim of the world. Also, there are some eighteen to twenty Wamphyri Lords, and one Lady. They're territorial; they vie with each other. They scheme against each other all the time, and go to war at every opportunity. It's their nature. We'd be ace cards to any one of them—except the Lady Karen. I know for I was hers once, and she let me go."

Jazz tucked that last away for later. "Why are we so important?" he wanted to know.

"Because we are magicians," she said. "We have powers, weapons, skills they don't understand. Even more so than the Travellers, we understand metals and mechanisms."

"What?" Jazz was lost again. "Magicians?"

"I'm a telepath," she shrugged. "To be ESP-endowed and a true man—or a woman—is a rare thing. Also, we're not of this world. We come from the mysterious hell-lands. And when I first arrived here I had awesome weapons. So did you."

"But I'm not ESP-talented," Jazz reminded her. "What use will I be to them?"

She looked away. "Not a lot. Which means you'll have to bluff your way."

"I'll have to what?"

"If in fact we go to the Lord Shaithis, you'll need to tell him you . . . can read the future! Something like that. Something it's hard to disprove."

"Great!" said Jazz, dully. "Like Arlek, you mean? He said he'd read the future of the tribe."

She faced him again, shook her head. "Arlek's a charlatan. A cheap, trick fortune-teller, like many of Earth's Gypsies. Our Earth, I mean. That's why he's so much against me, because he knows my talent's real."

"OK," said Jazz. "Now let's put *our* Earth right out of our minds and tell me some more about *this* Earth. Its topography, for example?"

"So simple you won't believe it," she answered. "I've already described the planet in relation to its sun and moon. Very well, now here's that map you asked for:

"This is a world much the same size as Earth as near as I can make out. This mountain range lies slightly more south than north, points east and west. That's using the compass Earth-style. The Wamphyri can't stand sunlight. Just like the old legends of home say, too much sunlight is fatal to vampires. And they *are* vampires! Sunside of the mountains, that's where the Travellers live. They are human beings, as you've seen. They live close to the mountain range for the water it gives them, and for the forests and game. Sunup they live in easily erected homes, at night they find caves and go as deep as possible! The mountains are riddled with fissures and caverns. Ten miles or so south of the mountains, there are no Travellers. There's nothing there for them to live on. Just desert. There are scattered nomad tribes of aborigines; at high sunup they occasionally trade with the Travellers; I've seen them and they're barely human. Several steps down from Australia's bushmen. I don't know how they live out there but they do. One hundred miles out from the mountains and even they can't live. There's nothing there at all, just scorched earth."

Despite his discomfort, Jazz was finding all of this fascinating. "What about east and west?" he said.

She nodded: "Just coming to it. These mountains are about two and a half thousand miles east to west. This pass lies something like six hundred miles from the western extent of the range. Beyond the mountains west are swamps; likewise to the far east. No one knows their extent."

"Why the hell don't the Travellers live close to the

swamps?'' Jazz was puzzled. "If there are no mountains there, then there's no protection from the sun. Which means there can't be any Wamphyri."

"Right!" she said. "The Wamphyri live only in their castles, right here behind these mountains. But the Travellers can't go too far east or west, because the swamps are vampire breeding grounds. They are the source of vampirism, just as this world is the source of Earth's legends."

Jazz tried to take that in, shook his head. "You've lost me yet again," he admitted. "No Wamphyri there, and yet vampires breed in the swamps?"

"Maybe you weren't listening to me earlier," she said. "I can understand that. It's like Arlek said: you've a lot to learn. And only so much time in which to learn it. I told you that the Wamphyri are what happens when a vampire egg gets into a man or woman. Well, the true vampires live in the swamps. They breed there. Every now and then there's an upsurge; they break out and infest the local animals. And they'd do the same to men, too, if there were any there. The Wamphyri go back to a time when men were infested. Now they do their own infesting." She shuddered. "The Wamphyri *are* men, but changed by the vampires in them."

Jazz took a deep breath, said: "Whoah! Let's get back to topography."

"Nothing more to tell," she answered. "Starside are the Wamphyri castles and the Wamphyri themselves. North of them lie the icelands. One or two polar-type creatures live there, but that's all. They're legendary anyway, for no living Traveller ever saw one. Oh, and at the foot of the mountains on Starside, between the castles and the peaks, that's where the troglodytes live. They're subterranean, sub-human, too. They call themselves Szgany or trogs and hold the Wamphyri as gods. I saw specimens mothballed in the Lady Karen's storehouses. They're almost prehistoric."

She paused for breath, finally said: "That's it, the

planet and its peoples in one. There's only one thing I've left out—that I can think of at the moment, anyway—because I'm not sure of it myself. But you can be certain it's something monstrous.''

"Monstrous?" Jazz repeated her. "Most of what I've heard is that! Let's have it anyway, and then I've got some more questions for you."

"Well," she frowned, "there's supposed to be something called 'Arbiteri Ingertos Westweich.' That's from a Wamphyri phrase and it means—"

"Him in His Western Garden?" Jazz tried it for himself.

She smiled a half-smile, slowly nodded. "Arlek was wrong about you," she said. "And so was I. You do learn fast. It's The-Dweller-in-His-Garden-in-the-West."

"Same difference." Jazz shrugged, and then it was his turn to frown. "But that sounds sort of placid to me. Hardly monstrous!"

"That's as it may be," she answered, "but the Wamphyri fear it or him or whatever mightily. Now, I've told you how they're forever squabbling, warring with each other? Well, in one circumstance—to one extent—they're entirely united. All the Wamphyri. They'd give a lot to be rid of The Dweller. He's legended to be a fabulous magician whose home is said to lie in a green valley somewhere in the central peaks to the west. I say 'legended,' but that might give the wrong impression. In fact it's a very recent legend, maybe as little as a dozen Earth years. That's when the stories started, apparently. Since then he's been said to have lived there, marked out his own territory, guards it jealously and deals ruthlessly with would-be invaders."

"Even the Wamphyri?"

"Especially the Wamphyri, as far as is known. The Wamphyri tell horror stories about him you wouldn't believe. Which, considering *their* nature, is really saying something!"

As she finished speaking, so there was movement

223

northward in the pass. Arlek and his men sprang immediately alert; they called forward their wolves, took up their arms. Jazz saw that they had torches smeared in a black, tarry liquid ready for lighting. Others stood ready with flints.

Arlek hurried over, hauled Jazz to his feet. "This could be Jasef," he said, hoarsely, "and it could be something else. The sun is almost down."

To Zek, Jazz said: "Are those flints of theirs reliable? There's a book of matches in my top pocket. And cigarettes, too. Seems they didn't want them, only the heavy stuff." He'd spoken in Russian and Arlek hadn't caught his meaning. The Gypsy turned his leathery face inquiringly in Zek's direction.

She sneered at him, said something that Jazz didn't catch. Then she unbuttoned Jazz's pocket, took out the matches. She showed them to Arlek, struck one. It flared at once and the Gypsy cursed, gave a great start, struck it aside out of her hand. The look on his face was one of shock, total disbelief.

Zek quickly snarled something at him and this time Jazz caught the word "coward!" He wished she wouldn't be so free with that word, not with Arlek. Then, very slowly and deliberately, as if she talked to a dull child, she hissed: "For the torches, you fool, in case this is not Jasef!"

He gawped at her, blinked his brown eyes nervously, but finally he nodded his understanding.

In any case, it was Jasef. An old man with a staff, assisted by two younger Gypsies, came hobbling gratefully into the last few feeble rays of sunlight. He made his way straight to Arlek, said: "There was a watcher, a trog. But the trog's master, the Lord Shaithis, had given him the power to speak over great distances. He saw the man—this one, Jazz—come through the pass, and he reported it to Shaithis. Shaithis would have come at once, but the sun—"

"Yes, yes—get on with it," Arlek snapped.

Jasef shrugged his frail shoulders. "I did not speak to this Szgany trog face to face, you understand. Worse things might have been lurking in the keep. I stayed outside and spoke to him in my head, in the manner of the Wamphyri."

"Of course, that's understood!" Arlek was almost beside himself.

"I gave the trog your message, and he passed it on to his Wamphyri Lord. Then he told me to return to you."

"What?" Arlek was obviously dumbfounded. "Is that all?"

Again Jasef could only offer his shrug. "He said: 'Tell Arlek of the Travellers that my Lord Shaithis will speak to him in person.' I have no idea what he meant."

"Old fool!" Arlek muttered. He turned away from Jasef—and Zek's radio crackled where its aerial projected an inch or two from her pocket. Its tiny red monitor light began to blink and flicker. Arlek gasped and leaped backwards a full pace, pointed at the radio and stared round-eyed as Zek produced it. "More of your foul magic?" he half-accused. "We should have destroyed all of your things long ago—and you with them—instead of letting Lardis give them back to you!"

Zek had been startled, too, but only for a moment. Now she said: "I got them back because there was no harm in them and they were useless to you. Also because they were mine. Unlike you, Lardis isn't a thief! I've told the Travellers many times that this thing is for communicating over great distances, haven't I? But because there was no one to talk to it wouldn't work. It's a machine, not magic. Well, now there *is* someone to talk to, and he wants to communicate." And to Jazz, in a lower tone: "I think I know what this means."

He nodded, said: "Those ace cards you mentioned?"

"Right," she answered. "I think the Lord Shaithis already has one—or if not an ace, certainly a joker. He's got Karl Vyotsky!" Then she spoke into the radio:

"Unknown call-sign, this is Zek Föener. Send your message, over?"

Her radio crackled again, and a once-familiar voice, shaky, a little urgent and breathless but fairly coherent, said, "You can throw out the radio procedure, Zek. This is Karl Vyotsky. Do you have Arlek of the Travellers with you?" He sounded like he wasn't too sure of what he was saying, as if he simply relayed the requirements of some other.

Jazz said, "Let me speak to him," and Zek held the radio to his face. "Who wants to know, Comrade?" he asked.

And after a moment's silence, in a tone which was suddenly pleading: "Listen, British: we're on different sides, I know, but if you foul me up now it's all over for me. My radio is acting up. Sometimes it receives and other times it doesn't. Right now I have excellent elevation—you wouldn't believe the elevation I have— but still I don't trust this radio. So don't waste any time with games. I can't believe you'd let me live once just to kill me now. So if this Arlek is with you, please put him on. Tell him Shaithis of the Wamphyri wants to talk to him."

Arlek had heard his name spoken twice, and Shaithis's name several times. The conversation obviously concerned himself and the Wamphyri Lord. He held out a hand for the radio, said: "Give it to me."

If Jazz had held the radio he would have thrown it down, stamped on it and wrecked it. No communications, no deal. Zek might well have had the same idea, but she wasn't quick enough. Arlek snatched the radio from her, fumbled with it for a moment and finally, a little awkwardly, said: "I am Arlek."

The radio crackled some more, and in a little while a new male voice said: "Arlek of the Travellers—of the tribe of Lardis Lidesci—it is Shaithis of the Wamphyri who speaks to you. How is it you have the power and not Lardis? Have you replaced him as leader of the tribe?'' The voice was the darkest, most menacing Jazz had ever heard. But at the same time, while there was something inhuman about it, it was definitely the voice of a man. Deep and rumbling with controlled strength, forming each word perfectly and with unswervable authority, the owner of that voice knew that whoever he spoke to, that person was an inferior.

Arlek had quickly mastered the radio. "Lardis is away," he said. "He may return and he may not. Even if he does, still there are Travellers with me who are dissatisfied with his leadership. The futures are not at all clear. Many things are possible."

Shaithis got straight to the point. "My watcher has told me you have the woman who was the Lady Karen's thought-thief, the woman Zekintha from the hell-lands. Also, you have a man from the hell-lands, who is a magician and bears strange weapons."

"These things your watcher tells you are true," Arlek answered, more at ease now.

"And is it also true that you desire to come to some agreement with me in respect of this man and woman?"

"That is also true. Give me your word that in future you will not raid on the so-called tribe of Lardis, and in turn I'll hand over to you these magicians from the hell-lands."

The radio was silent and it appeared that Shaithis was considering Arlek's proposition. At last he said: "And their weapons?"

"Also their belongings, yes," Arlek answered. "All except an axe, which belonged to the man. This I claim for myself. Even so, the benefits for the Wamphyri Lord Shaithis will be great. Strange weapons to aid you in your wars, devices such as this communicator, which you apparently understand well enough, and their magic to use as you will."

Shaithis seemed swayed. "*Hmm!* You know that I am only one Lord and there are others of the Wamphyri? I can only speak for myself."

"But you are greatest of the Wamphyri!" Arlek was sure of himself now. "I do not ask for your protection, merely that if the occasion should arise, then that you'd obstruct the other Lords in their raids. There are many Travellers and we are, after all, only one small tribe. You would not raid upon us, and you would ensure—if it please you—that the raids of your fellow Lords were made that much more difficult to accomplish . . ."

Shaithis's voice sank deeper yet. "I recognize no 'fellow' Lords, Arlek. Only enemies. As for placing obstructions in their way: I do that already. I always will."

"Then you would perhaps do it more diligently," Arlek pressed. And he repeated: "We are a small tribe, Lord Shaithis. I make no request in respect of Travellers of any other ilk."

Zek tried to snatch the radio from him but he turned his back on her. Two of his men grabbed her arms, held her still. "Black-hearted, treacherous—!" She was lost for words.

"Very well," said Shaithis. "Now tell me, how will you give the two to me?"

"I shall bind them securely," Arlek answered, "and leave them here in this place. We are some little way beyond the keep in the pass."

"Their weapons will be left close to hand?"

"Yes," Arlek squared back his shoulders, flared his nostrils. Even in his treachery his dark eyes were bright. It was all going according to plan. The Wamphyri were a curse; but with the curse lifted, even partly lifted . . . it would not be long before Lardis Lidesci would be usurped.

"Then do it now, Arlek of the Travellers. Bind them, leave them there, and begone! Shaithis comes! Let me not find you there upon my arrival. The pass is in any case mine . . . after dark."

*   *   *

They lay there alone, in darkness, with only the sound of their own breathing. To the south Arlek and his band moved off; it appeared that Wolf had gone with them. As the sounds of their hurried departure echoed back, Jazz said: "I still think that beast of yours didn't make much of a guard dog."

"Be quiet," she said. And that was all. She lay very still. Jazz turned his head, stared north up the pass. Only the cold gleam of starlight that way. He strained his ears. Nothing, as yet.

"Why be quiet?" he finally whispered.

"I was trying to get through to Wolf," she answered. "He would have attacked them at any time—and been killed for it. I held him back. He's been a good friend and companion to me, and it wasn't the time. *Now* is the time!"

"For what?"

"You've seen his teeth—they're sharp as chisels! I've called to him. If he heard me, and if he's not too involved with the other wolves, he'll return. We're bound with leather, but given a little time . . . "

Jazz rolled over to face her. "Well, at least we should have plenty of that. I saw the Wamphyri castles on the stacks. They were miles away. And then there's the length of the pass, too."

She shook her head. "Jazz, even now it's almost too late." As she spoke, Wolf came loping, tongue lolling. Behind him the southern gap of the pass was lit with a fast-fading golden haze.

"Too late?" Jazz repeated her. "You mean because the sun's down?"

"That wasn't my meaning," she answered. "And anyway, it isn't down. A mile south of here, the pass rises briefly to a shallow crest, then dips sharply and turns a little toward the east. From there it's a steep, steady slope down to Sunside. The sun's just over our horizon, that's all. On Sunside there are still many

229

hours of light left. But—Shaithis will be here very soon.''

"He has transport?'' Jazz was puzzled, half flippant

"Yes, he has,'' Zek answered . . . ''Jazz, I can't turn face-down. There's a large rock sticking in me. But if you can manage it, then I'll tell Wolf to chew on your bindings.''

"You're crediting old Lupus here with a deal of intelligence,'' Jazz was sceptical.

"A mind-picture is worth a thousand words,'' she said.

"Oh!'' Jazz said. He struggled to turn face-down, but—

"Before you do,'' she said, breathlessly, "will you kiss me?'' She wormed herself fractionally closer.

"What?'' he stopped struggling.

"Only if you want to, of course,'' she said. "But . . . you might never get another chance.''

He craned forward, kissed her as best he could. Out of air, finally they broke apart. "Are you reading my thoughts?'' he said.

"No.''

"Good! But now I know what you taste like, the sooner Wolf gets to work on these bindings the better.'' He rolled over onto his face. Trussed like a chicken, his legs were bent at the knees, feet uppermost. His wrists were tied behind his back, and tied again, to his feet. Wolf at once began tugging at Jazz's leather bindings. "No, dammit!'' Jazz spat out dirt. "Don't pull, chew!'' And in a little while Wolf was doing just that.

Jazz could see his packs, gun, Zek's too, lying only paces away. The weapons had a metallic sheen in the dark. "I notice Arlek took my compo,'' he said.

"Compo?''

"The hard-tack. The food.''

She was silent.

"I mean, he did tell Shaithis he'd leave everything except my hatchet.''

Quietly she said: "But he knew Shaithis would have no use for the food."

Jazz tried to turn his face her way. "Oh? But he eats, doesn't—" And he paused. He could see her eyes, unblinking in the dark shadow of her face. "The Lord Shaithis of the Wamphyri," he grunted. "Of course. He's a vampire, right?"

"Jazz," she said, "hope springs eternal, but—maybe I should tell you something of how it could be. I mean, if we're taken."

"I think maybe you should," he said.

Something small, black, chittering, flitted close by, came closer in dips and swoops, then darted off again. Then another, and more, until the air seemed full of them. Jazz had frozen into stone, stopped breathing, but Zek said: "Bats—but *just* bats. Ordinary bats. Not Wamphyri familiars. The Wamphyri use the real things for that. The big ones. *Desmodus,* the vampire."

A thong parted behind Jazz's back, and very quickly another. Jazz flexed his wrists and felt a little give in his bindings. Wolf carried on chewing. "You were going to tell me about Shaithis's transport," Jazz reminded Zek.

"No," she said. "I wasn't." Her tone of voice told him not to ask any more. But in any case he didn't need to. As the last thong parted and his straining wrists flew apart, he straightened his aching legs, rolled over onto his back and looked up. His eyes were drawn to an ominous stirring overhead. Level with the high walls of the pass, a black blot—several of them—shut out the stars as they began to descend.

"What the hell—?" Jazz whispered.

"They're here!" Zek breathed. "Quickly, Jazz! Oh, be quick!"

Wolf loped anxiously to and fro, whining, while Jazz got his cramped fingers to work on the thongs binding his feet. At last they were free. He turned to Zek, rolled her unceremoniously face-down across his knees, went

frantically to work on her knots. As each one came
undone, he kept glancing up at the heights a little north
of their position.

The descending blots were falling like flat stones
dropped in still water, sliding from side to side, settling
like autumn leaves on a deathly still early September
morning. Three of them, their true outlines were now
distinguishable: huge, diamond-shaped, where opposing
points of the diamonds merged into heads and tails.
They side-slipped this way and that, settling silently
down toward the bed of the pass.

Zek's hands were almost free; Jazz left them and
turned his attention to her feet. It was his thought to
pick her up, throw her over his shoulder and run. But
he faced the truth: his legs were still badly cramped and
the darkness was now almost complete. He'd only be
able to stumble at best, with Wolf bringing up a pitifully inadequate rear guard.

Three dull thumps in close succession announced the
fact that the flying things had settled to earth. Jazz's
fingers were fully alive now, deft where they hastened
to free Zek's feet. She was panting, plainly terrified.
"It's OK," he kept whispering. "Just one more knot to
go." Down the pass, maybe a hundred metres away,
three anomalous shapes lay humped against a horizon
of stars, with spatulate heads swaying at the ends of
long necks. The last knot came loose; and as Zek came
struggling to her feet, staggering a little, so Wolf's tail
went down between his legs. He gave a whining, coughing little bark and began to back off toward the south.

Jazz's arm was round Zek's waist, supporting her.
He said: "Move your arms, stamp your feet and get the
blood pumping." She didn't answer but stared with
saucer eyes beyond him, in the direction of the grounded
flying creatures. He sensed more than felt the shudder
going through her, moving from her head, down through
all her body. An entirely involuntary thing, almost like
a dog shaking off water. Except Jazz suspected that this

was something which wouldn't shake off. And he turned to follow her gaze.

Three figures stood not ten paces away!

They were in silhouette, but that hardly detracted from their awesome aura of presence. It radiated from them in almost tangible waves, a force warning of their near-invulnerability. They had all the advantages: they could see in the dark, were strong beyond the wildest dreams of most Earthly muscle-men, and they were armed. And not only with physical weapons, but also with the powers of the Wamphyri. Jazz didn't yet know about the latter, but Zek did.

"Try to avoid looking at their eyes," she hissed her warning.

The three were, or had been men, so much was plain. But they were big men, and even silhouetted against a backdrop of stars and black, nodding sky-beasts, Jazz could see what sort of men. In his mind a recurring picture of a man like these, dying in an inferno of heat and flame, screamed his fury and his defiance even now: *"Wamphyri!"*

The one in the middle would be Shaithis; Jazz reckoned there'd be close to eighty inches of him, standing almost a full head taller than the two who flanked him. He stood straight, cloaked, with his hair falling onto his shoulders. The proportions of his head were wrong; as he looked with quick, curious glances from side to side and showed his face in profile, Jazz saw the length of his skull and jaws, his convoluted snout, the alert mobility of his conchlike ears. It was a composite face: human-bat-wolf.

The two beside him were near-naked; their bodies were pale in starlight, muscular, easy-flowing as liquid. They wore topknots with tails dangling, and on their right hands . . . those were silhouettes Jazz would know anywhere. The weapon-gloves of the Wamphyri! But so *sure* of themselves: they stood arms akimbo, almost uncaring, staring at Jazz and Zek with their red eyes almost as if they considered the antics of insects.

"Not bound!" Shaithis said in that unmistakable, rumbling voice of his. "So either Arlek is a fool or you are extremely clever. But I see your broken thongs, and so I would say that you are clever. Your magic, of course. *My* magic, now!"

Jazz and Zek backed off a stumbling pace or two. The three moved after them, marginally more rapid but in no great hurry, gradually closing with them. Shaithis's lieutenants moved in the manner of men, with paces swift and sure; but their master seemed to *flow* forward, as if carried on the strength of his own will. His eyes were huge, crimson, seemed to burn with some weird, internal light of their own. It was hard to avoid looking into those eyes, Jazz thought. They might well be the gates of hell—but tell a moth not to investigate the candle's flame.

Zek's elbow struck him sharply in the ribs. "Don't look at their eyes!" she said again. "Run, Jazz, if you can. I'm all cramped, I'll only slow you down."

Wolf came from nowhere, snarling his outrage—and probably his terror, too—as he loped from the shadows under the eastern cliff. He leaped at Shaithis's lieutenant on that flank; the man turned casually toward him, struck him aside left-handed as Jazz might strike aside a small, yapping dog. Wolf backed off, whined, and the man he'd attacked showed him his gauntlet. "Come on then, little wolf," he taunted the animal. "Come, let Gustan pat you on your sleek grey head!"

"Get back, Wolf!" Zek cried.

"*Stand still!*" Shaithis commanded, pointing at Jazz and Zek. "I will not chase what is mine. Come to heel now or be punished. Punished severely!"

Jazz's heel kicked metal. Blued steel. His SMG! His packs were there, too.

He fell to one knee, grabbed up the gun. The three who opposed him saw the weapon in his hand and came to a halt. They stood stock still, glaring with their red eyes. "What?" Shaithis's voice was dangerously low. "Do you threaten your master?"

Jazz faced the three where he knelt; he groped blindly in a pack, then another. He found what he was looking for, slapped home a magazine into its housing. Shaithis came flowing forward. "I said—"

"Threaten you?" Jazz cocked his gun. "Damn right I do!"

But the man on Shaithis's right flank had come swiftly forward in a crouch. His sandalled foot came down on Jazz's right wrist, pinning it to the ground. Jazz deliberately threw himself flat, tried to kick the man away; but this was no novice. Avoiding Jazz's kicks and still pinning his arm and weapon, he came to his knees, caught Jazz's face in a massive left hand, effortlessly bent his head back and showed him his raised gauntlet. He unclenched his fist and hooks, knives, gleaming sickles coldly reflected the starlight. Then the man smiled and raised his eyebrows in mocking query, glancing questioningly at Jazz's hand on the pistol-grip of the SMG. The gun's muzzle was sticking in dirt; Jazz daren't pull the trigger.

He opened his hand and let go of the weapon, and the man who held him lifted him up from the ground by his crushed face. Jazz could do nothing; he felt that if Shaithis's lieutenant wanted to, he could just tear the flesh right off his skull like peeling an orange.

Zek sprang at the man on Shaithis's left, Gustan, where he now stepped forward. "Bullies!" she cried, beating at him with her fists. "Bastards! *Vampires!*"

Gustan swept her up in one arm, grinned at her, ran his free left hand over her body, pinching here and there. "You should let me have this one a little while, Lord Shaithis," he grunted. "Knock some sense into her and teach her the meaning of obedience!"

Shaithis turned on him at once. "She'll be in thrall to me, and no other. Watch your tongue, Gustan! There's room in the pens for another war-beast, if that's your fancy?''

Gustan shrank back. "I meant only—"

"Be *quiet!*" Shaithis cut him short. He came forward, sniffed at Zek and nodded his head. "Yes, there's magic in this one. But remember—she escaped from the bitch Karen. Watch her carefully, Gustan." Now he gazed at Jazz. "As for you—" Again he thrust his convoluted snout forward, seemed to use it like some monstrous bloodhound. And his eyes narrowed to scarlet slits.

"He's a great magician!" Zek cried. She hung dangling in Gustan's arms.

"Indeed!" Shaithis glanced at her. "And what, pray, is his talent? For I sense nothing of magic in him."

"I . . . I read the future," Jazz gasped from a crushed, O-shaped mouth.

Shaithis smiled a terrible smile. "Good, for I have certainly read yours." And he nodded to the man who held Jazz aloft.

"Wait!" Zek cried. "It's true, I tell you! You'll lose a powerful ally if you kill him."

"An ally?" Shaithis seemed amused. "A servant, perhaps." He stroked his chin. "But very well, let us test this talent. Put him down." Jazz was lowered until he stood on straining tip-toes.

Shaithis studied him closely, cocked his head on one side, thought of a suitable test. "Now tell me," he finally said, "what you read in *my* future, hell-lander?"

Jazz knew he was finished, but there was still Zek to consider. "I'll tell you this much," he answered. "Harm this woman in any way—one hair of her head—and you'll burn in hell. The sun shall surely rise on you, Shaithis of the Wamphyri!"

"That is not fortune-telling but wishful thinking!" Shaithis snapped. "Do you think to lay a curse on me? What, I am not to harm a hair of her head? *This* head, do you mean?" He reached out and grasped Zek's

236

blonde hair, bunched it in a knot, tightened his grip until she cried out.

And the sun at once rose in the pass through the mountains, and lit the place with its burning, lancing rays!

Before the man who held Jazz screamed in terror and hurled him away like a rag doll, the Englishman thought an entirely frivolous thought: "Now *that's* what I call magic!"

Chapter Thirteen
Lardis Lidesci

THROWN DOWN, JAZZ AT ONCE SCRAMBLED TOWARD HIS gun, and no one made the least effort to stop him. The reason was simple: Shaithis and his two were moving back toward their mounts, scuttling like upright cockroaches where they threaded their way through scattered rocks and boulders, always seeking shade and refuge from the fatal, blazing light. And where and whenever that light fell upon them, then they screamed aloud as if scalded, covering their heads in their near-blind, blundering panic flight.

But one of them, Gustan, still carried Zek, who writhed like a snake in his grasp, beating at his head with her tiny hands. Gustan was Jazz's first target.

He snatched up his SMG from the hard ground, tilted its barrel downward and shook it. A few tiny pebbles and a trickle of dust fell from the barrel and Jazz prayed there was nothing bigger lodged in there. Then he was down on one knee, seeking out Gustan's fleeting, double-silhouette, finding it and aiming, and at last squeezing the trigger. The gun responded with a chattering diatribe of loud, lead obscenities, all hurled at Gustan's lower legs. Shaithis's lieutenant went down as if pole-axed, raising a cloud of dust where he screamed and flopped in the shadows of a low pile of rocks, and in the next moment Zek came scrambling free of him.

Jazz couldn't fire again for fear of hitting her. "Keep to one side!" he hoarsely yelled. "Give me a clear line of fire!" She heard him, threw herself to one side. A target at once presented itself, moving frantically in a sweeping beam of light. Jazz fixed the vampire in the sights of his mind even as the light swept on, and again he fired. Screams and curses came echoing back. Jazz hoped it was Shaithis himself he'd hit but doubted it: the silhouette hadn't had his bulk. On the other hand, he could still feel the bruises on his face where Shaithis's second man had picked him up. That one would do nicely, thank you. The thing these creatures would have to learn was this: don't mess with magicians from the hell-lands!

Zek came creeping from the shadows at the base of the cliffs. "It's me!" she cried as he jerked his body in her direction. "Don't shoot!" Wolf had met her half-way, was whining and prancing about her like a great puppy.

"Get behind me," Jazz warned, waving the girl and the wolf aside. "Get me another magazine from my packs, quick!"

The searchlight beams from the high wall of cliffs to the south (that's what they were like, Jazz thought: powerful spotlights, seeking out the enemy) continued to play, lancing down and throwing discs of reflected sunlight onto the canyon floor. *Reflected, yes,* Jazz nodded to himself, *from mirrors. And thank God for whoever's aiming them!* And now a pair of beams converged on Shaithis himself where the Wamphyri Lord had almost reached the flank of the nearest flyer.

It was the opportunity Jazz had waited for. He could have taken Zek by the hand and fled south with her, but he'd hoped for a shot at Shaithis. Now his target sprang to the side of his mount and twin beams of light followed him. Beating at the brilliant beams where they fell on him, almost as if he beat at flames, but obviously with no effect whatever, Shaithis leaped to catch his beast's harness and draw himself up into the ornate saddle. And that was where Jazz caught him. He'd held about a third of his magazine in reserve, maybe a dozen rounds, just for this.

He opened up, aiming carefully and squeezing off single shots, praying that at least one would find its target. Shaithis, in the act of climbing into the saddle, suddenly jerked and fell back, but still clung to the harness. Jazz cursed the inaccuracy of his short-range weapon, took still more careful aim. His next shot must have missed Shaithis but hit the flyer in a delicate spot, for the great beast threw back its head and gave a weird cry, then commenced lashing its tail frenziedly. A moment more of this before a nest of hideous worms seemed to uncoil from the creature's belly, thrusting its bulk aloft. And still Shaithis clung there, even managing to haul himself safely into the saddle!

By then the other flyers were airborne, too, and Jazz was astonished to see that they both had riders! Gustan at least should be crippled—or should he? For now Jazz remembered Encounter Five. Bullets hadn't stopped him, either; they'd merely inconvenienced him. Likewise, apparently, with Shaithis and his lieutenants.

Zek came from behind, slapped a fresh magazine into Jazz's waiting hand. He loaded up, looked for his targets; glanced skyward at the wide ribbon of stars riding high over the rearing walls of the pass—*and found all three ''targets'' sweeping down on him!*

"Jazz, get down! Oh, get down!" Zek was screaming. She and Wolf went scrambling on their bellies into a tangle of jagged rocks, but Jazz saw that the aerial beasts would be upon him before he could follow suit. He couldn't dodge them, but he might be able to turn them aside.

Again he went to one knee, and with the three flying creatures and their riders swooping upon him from only thirty metres away, he opened fire in a steady, sleeting arc of lead. Shaithis was in the centre, and that was where Jazz concentrated his fire. He laced the three creatures, and attempted to lace their riders, left to right and then back again to Shaithis. How he could miss at this range—*if* he missed—was beyond his understanding; but when the beasts and their Wamphyri masters were almost on top of him he began to believe he had in fact missed. Until the last moment.

For as the firing-pin on Jazz's weapon slammed home on thin air and the gun fell silent, and even as he made to hurl himself flat behind the nearest boulder, then at last he saw the effect of his fire. The three beasts were bleeding dark red ichor from rows of black holes in the forward parts of their bodies, and their riders rocked to and fro in their saddles, apparently holding themselves upright by willpower alone!

Then—

A great lip of flesh opened in the belly of Shaithis's mount as it swooped on Jazz, a trapdoor gash whose scalloped lower rim scraped across the top of the boulder shielding him and gouged at the dry, pebbly earth behind him. For a moment all was darkness and he smelled the powerful animal stench of the thing, but then its shadow lifted from him. By then, too, the unknown wielders of mirror-weapons had found their targets again and the flying beasts were bathed in lancing beams of searing light. And the light did actually sear them; for wherever the rays struck them, clouds of loathsome evaporation billowed outwards from the shrinking flesh of the beasts, like water boiling on dry-ice in the rarified air of high altitudes.

That was the end of it. Reeling in their saddles, the Wamphyri admitted defeat, dragged their bellowing, straining mounts skyward, wheeled in great arcs and went racing northward to the darkness and the shadows. When the pulsating throb of their leathery wings had faded into distance there was only the silence, and the pounding of Jazz's heart in his chest.

"Zek?" he called out breathlessly in a little while. "Are you OK?"

She came out of hiding, nervously dusting herself down in a spotlight beam of bright light where it found the three, man, woman and wolf, and held steady on them. "I'm all right," she said, but her voice was very trembly. Jazz put his gun down and reached for her where she stumbled into his arms. He held her loosely at first, then fiercely, as much for his own comfort as for hers. The encounter with the Wamphyri had shaken him badly. This was his natural reaction to it. So he told himself, anyway.

Zek clung to him briefly then freed herself and shielded her eyes against the light playing on them from the western heights of the pass. "We're in full view," she said.

Wasting no time, Jazz went to his packs, found another loaded magazine for his gun. He fitted it to his SMG, then seated himself and broke open small cardboard boxes of ammunition to start re-loading the empty magazines. This was his training surfacing. While he worked, he asked: "I take it we've been rescued—by friends?"

As if in answer, there came a shout which echoed down to them from the heights: "Zekintha—is it you? Is all well?" The voice was anxious, taut as the skin on a drumhead.

"Lardis Lidesci!" she breathed. And to Jazz. "Yes, we've been rescued. I've nothing to fear from Lardis—except Lardis himself! He fancies me a little, that's all. But you can be sure he's a good man." Then she cupped her hands to her mouth and called back: "Lardis, we're all right!"

"Come back along the pass," his voice came echoing again in a moment. "You're not safe there."

"He's telling us!" Jazz grunted. He finished loading up his packs, said, "Help me on with this kit."

As they began to make their way south again, they

242

could see several mirrors glinting on the western wall, where the setting sun still turned the crags to the colour of molten gold. The glittering flashes of light were descending, and every so often tiny human figures were glimpsed silhouetted against the sky. From the bed of the pass ahead came the distant jingle of Gypsy movements, and at last the panting of runners where they converged on Jazz, Zek and Wolf. Fleeting shadows became the outlines of men in Traveller garb, their faces anxious. Not men of Arlek's party but faces which were new to Jazz. Zek knew them, however; she breathed her relief and said, "Oh, yes—we're safe enough now."

Oh? thought Jazz. *And am I safe, too? What will your Lardis Lidesci think of me, I wonder?*

From a distance of a mile and more to the south, shrill screams came echoing—cut off as they reached a crescendo of terror. Then silence reigned, the distant flames leaped up, burning orange and yellow.

Tiredly pacing it out beside Zek—with Lardis's runners on the flanks urging them to greater speed, and Wolf loping in the shadows—Jazz said: "Now what do you reckon all that was about?"

Zek's face was very pale. "I would guess Lardis has dealt with Arlek," she quietly answered.

"Dealt with him?"

She nodded. "Arlek was ambitious. That's no crime in itself, but he was also a traitor—and a coward! He sought to make deals with the Wamphyri, at the expense of others—at their total expense. Lardis has warned him before, on several occasions. Now he won't have to warn him again."

"You mean he's killed him," Jazz nodded. "Pretty rough justice around here."

"It's a rough world around here," she said.

Arlek's screams lingered in Jazz's mind. "How would Lardis have done it?"

Zek looked away. "The punishment would fit the

crime," she finally answered. "I think that maybe Arlek died the death of a vampire: a stake through the heart, beheaded, burned."

"Oh?" Jazz took that in, nodded again. "You mean just to be absolutely sure, right?"

Her answer contained no trace of humour. "That's right," she said, "to be absolutely sure. Vampires are hard things to kill, Jazz."

He shook his head, thought: *God, you're a cool one!*

"No, I'm not," she clasped his hand tightly—very tightly—in her own. "It's just that I've been here longer than you, that's all . . ."

Lardis Lidesci wasn't what Jazz had expected. He was maybe five-eight tall, long-haired, gangling in the arm as Jazz himself but built like a rhino as opposed to Jazz's cat. He was young, too—younger by three or four years than Jazz—and, in sharp contrast to his squat shape, he seemed surprisingly agile. This agility of Lardis's wasn't only physical; his intelligence was patent in every brown wrinkle of his face, which was expressive and had more than its share of laughter-lines. Open and frank, Lardis's round face framed in dark, flowing hair had slanted, bushy eyebrows, a flattened nose, and a wide mouth full of strong if uneven teeth. His brown eyes held nothing of malice; indeed, they were usually smiling, but they could also turn very thoughtful. On the Earth Jazz and Zek had left behind he'd have made a professional wrestler; certainly he looked like one. Among his people here in this vampire-ruled environment beyond the Gate he was a natural leader, and the great majority of his five-hundred strong "tribe" rallied behind him all the way. Arlek had been a rare exception which proved the value of Lardis's rule, and Arlek was no more.

Since taking on the job of leader from his father five years ago when the elder Lidesci had grown crippled with some arthritic disease, Lardis had succeeded in keeping his Travellers free and secure from the ever-present Wamphyri threat; so that the tribe had grown and expanded, absorbing other smaller Gypsy groups into itself. Not nearly as large or strong as many of the eastern tribes, still Lardis's people had a record for safety which was the envy of all the Travellers: namely that since he became leader, the Wamphyri had not once ravaged successfully amongst them. There were several reasons for this.

One of these stemmed from that fundamental difference between Lardis and Arlek, which was so strong that it had now resulted in the latter's permanent removal. Lardis did *not* believe that the Wamphyri were the natural Lords and Masters of this sphere, or that the time must come when a devastating raid would decimate his tribe. He would *not* give in to the Wamphyri, would not placate them in any way. Other Traveller tribes had tried this in the past, were trying it even now, and it had never worked. Gorgan Lidesci, Lardis's father, still talked of the fate of his first tribe, when he himself had been a mere boy.

In those days, for a time, there had been a measure of peace among the Wamphyri; this had enabled the vampire Lords to consolidate their forces and commence raiding far more effectively and in overwhelming numbers. Gorgan's tribe; a large one and governed by a Council of Elders, had attempted to make a deal with the Wamphyri, to come to a mutually satisfactory "arrangement" with them. Before each sundown a raiding party would go out from Gorgan's people to make captives of men and women of lesser Traveller groups. Since such minor groups might be as small as two- or three-family units, ranging up to the strength of small tribes of perhaps forty adults, and since they were scattered all along the Sunside flank of the mountains, there was little difficulty in obtaining before each sundown, a "tithe" of about a hundred people. These were kept prisoned through the long nights, so that in the event of a Wamphyri raid they could be offered in appeasement. The belief among the elderly leaders of Gorgan's tribe was simply this: that so long as the Wamphyri could find ready-made tribute, they would not have need to glut themselves on the tithe-paying people of the tribe; they would not bite, as it were, the hands that fed them.

For some years and through many nights this scenario held true. There were times when the Wamphyri came and others when they failed to find Gorgan's tribe, (for the Travellers were never sedentary but constantly on the move, a restlessness bred into them through hundreds of years of Wamphyri rapaciousness), on which fortunate occasions at sunup the prisoners would be set free to fend for and feed themselves, and continue their lives as of old or until the next time they were taken prisoner, perhaps before the next sundown.

And when the Wamphyri did come, why, then there were offerings to be made, and the Wamphyri Lords, their warriors and undead soldiers would collect their tithe of one hundred Travellers and depart. In short, the Wamphyri became like tax-collectors; and true to the scenario, they did no harm to those who paid this regular human tribute.

With the result that the people of Gorgan's tribe grew weak, fat and increasingly careless. They lost their urge to travel and so avoid Wamphyri incursions; they used regular routes, watering-holes and harbouring areas, and their treks along the Sunside flank of the mountains fell into ever more foreseeable patterns; contrary to the very nature of Travellers, there was no longer any mystery to their movements. In short, they no longer bothered to hide themselves and thus were easily found. Now there were far fewer nights of peace and rest, when more and more often the Wamphyri would come and carry off their human tribute; but what did that matter? The tribe itself was safe, wasn't it?

Safe, yes—until the brief alliance of a handful of

Wamphyri Lords had fallen apart, until they had quarreled and split up, and each faction of the former alliance determined to build up its individual forces, refill its storehouses, define once more its old territorial boundaries and become strong again in the former Wamphyri traditions! For when armies build for war— and in the case of the Wamphyri not against a mutual enemy but internecine, each vampire Lord against his neighbours—then they take and use whatever resources are available, with never a thought for conservation. And the natural resources of the Wamphyri had ever been the flesh and blood of Travellers!

In a single night of terror and madness—one sundown, the space of time between the sun's setting and its rising again, a matter of only forty hours—Gorgan's tribe was decimated! The Wamphyri had come, first Shaithis to demand the usual tribute, which he took; then Lesk the Glut; finally Lascula Longtooth. More might have come, Belath and Volse and the others, except that by then there was nothing left to take; or if they *did* come, then the survivors of Gorgan's tribe were no longer in their customary holes waiting for them. For after Shaithis, when the Lords Lesk and Lascula found no tribute, they had simply killed the Council of Elders out of hand and proceeded to herd off the flower of the tribe itself! At which the handful of survivors, maybe fifty old ones and a hundred children, had fled for whichever sanctuaries they could discover. And not many of those in a land where the people of Gorgan's tribe were universally loathed! From which time forward the tribe had been no more, and the youth Gorgan had vowed never to put his faith in any "deals" with the treacherous Wamphyri. Lardis, in his turn, was of the same mind: let other tribal leaders do what they would, go their own ways and good luck to them, his people would never submit to the Wamphyri, nor would they prey on brother and sister Travellers for dubious personal benefits and the well-being of vile, inhuman Starside overloads.

As to how Lardis's convictions worked in his favour:

There were still tribes who operated one tithe system or another, using either captive Travellers stolen from other groups to placate the Wamphyri, or even drawing lots and sacrificing members of their own nomad communities. Such Travellers who had adopted or accepted this servile existence were generally of large eastern-flank tribes numbering more than a thousand strong. Their size protected them from any retaliatory attacks which previous victims might possibly dream up, and/or allowed them to make the required periodic sacrificial cull without appreciably diminishing the strength of the tribe.

They dwelled east of the pass because the game was more plentiful there and survival, in one sense, that much easier. Lardis knew this and kept his people west of the pass; it was a little harder to make a living but it was also that much safer. When it was sunup he kept lookouts in the southern extremes of the pass, to warn of Travellers moving west and supply intelligence reports of their strengths, persuasions, and any possible dangers to his own people springing from their presence or route of passage.

Lardis did not as a matter of course make war on Travellers who kowtowed to the Wamphyri but preferred to keep out of their way. In the event that they should war on him, however, he was always ready. His men—even many of his younger women—were well-trained, formidable fighters; they were skilled in ambush, entrapment, hand-to-hand combat, and in the use of all manner of weaponry. On the few occasions when outsiders had attempted to raid on him, then they'd been severely chastised; so that in the five years of his leadership the legend had spread abroad that he was not a man to fool with. He would accept small groups into the tribe for its own good, but would not amalgamate

248

with larger bodies. His motto was this: to be medium-sized is to be safe. Not large enough to stir too much Wamphyri interest, mobile enough to confuse them, and just a trifle too vicious to tempt raiding parties from Wamphyri-supplicants. Up until now, at least, these integers had made for a remarkably effective equation.

But Lardis's scepticism (if not scorn) with regard to Wamphyri superiority, and his disgust at the mere thought of appeasement, were not the only reasons for his success. Oh, he knew well enough the purely *physical* and *tactical* superiority of the vampire Lords—their strengths and cruelties, the awesome horror of their war-beasts, the silent, speedy efficiency of their familiar spies the great bats, and the mobility of their flying creatures—but he also knew and made use of their weaknesses.

They could only raid at night, usually in the lull before (or in the wake of) one or other of the interminable vampire wars—to supply their war effort or replenish a depleted capability as the case may be—and they invariably completed their raids with dispatch. They didn't like to spend too much time Sunside, for while they were away they could never be sure what their Starside enemies were up to; aeries were wont to become occupied while their rightful masters were raiding abroad! Lardis knew, too, that the Wamphyri rarely raided west of the pass: most of the tribes, and especially those which were Wamphyri-supplicant, dwelled east; so why should the Wamphyri waste time chasing their prey in the west when it was openly on offer in the east? For the fact of it was that for all their much-vaunted pride and arrogance, the Wamphyri tended toward laziness. If they weren't warring with each other or raiding, then they were scheming for war, indulging themselves, or asleep! That was a weakness, too. For the great part, Lardis Lidesci went without sleep. And at sundown he took his rest in the briefest snatches.

Another Wamphyri weakness was this: that while it was hard to kill them, they *could* and *did* die eventually—

and Lardis knew how to do it. But there was death and there was death. At the hands of another vampire, that was thinkable; Wamphyri pride would allow, however grudgingly, for that possibility. But at the hands of some lowly Traveller? Never! Where was the glory in *that*? What sort of way was *that* for a life to blink out? Lardis had killed no actual Lord, but he had twice dealt with aspirants to that final level of vampire power. They had been the sons and lieutenants of Lesk the Glut, who'd thought to come against him in the hour immediately before sunup, when he'd be unwary and emerging from his cave sanctuary; except Lardis didn't know the meaning of the word "unwary."

Put a hardwood bolt through a vampire, behead him, burn his corpse . . . he was dead. But Lardis had made an example of Lesk's lads. Staked out, the sun had found them and steamed them away slowly and with a great deal of shrieking. Aye, let other Traveller leaders balk at the difficulties involved in the slaying of vampires, but not Lardis. The Wamphyri had come to know his name, perhaps even to respect it. Being able to live for centuries, near-immortal, it was generally deemed unwise to go up against Travellers like Lardis, who could—and would, given the chance—so rapidly and cruelly shorten one's span to nothing!

Then there was the Wamphyri fear of silver, which metal was a poison to their systems, acting upon them like lead acts on men. Lardis had discovered a small mine of that rare metal in the western foothills, and now his arrows were tipped with it. Also, he smeared his weapons in the juice of the kneblasch root, whose garlic stink would bring about a partial paralysis in any vampire, causing endless vomiting and a general nervous disorder lasting for days. If a kneblasch-treated blade cut Wamphyri flesh, then the infected member must be shed and another grown in its place.

It wasn't so much that these things were secret or known only in the tribe of Lardis—indeed, all Travellers had been aware of these facts immemorially—but rather that Lardis dared *use* them in the defense of his people. The Wamphyri had forbidden to all Travellers the use of bronze mirrors, silver and kneblasch, on penalty of dire torture and death; but Lardis cared not a jot. He was already a marked man, and a man can die only once . . .

These were some of the things, then, that influenced Lardis in the way he ruled his tribe and did his best to keep them secure west of the pass through the mountains; but there was one other element beyond Lardis's control, which nevertheless figured high in his favour, confirming his commonsense measures. It was this: that somewhere in those western peaks, in a small, fertile valley, lived the one whom the Wamphyri feared and had named The-Dweller-in-His-Garden-in-the-West. The Dweller legend was the main reason Lardis had been away this time. Ostensibly he had been seeking new routes and harbour areas for the tribe (and in fact he'd discovered several) but in reality he had been trying to locate The Dweller. He'd reasoned that what was bad for the Wamphyri must be good for the tribe of Lardis the Traveller. Also, rumours had been spreading for some years now that The Dweller offered sanctuary to anyone with spit enough to dare seek him out. For Lardis himself, sanctuary wasn't the hook, though certainly it would be a wonderful thing to find a safe, permanent home for the tribe; but if The Dweller had power to defy the Wamphyri . . . that in itself were sufficient reason to seek him out. Lardis would learn from him and with his new knowledge carry the fight right back to the very keeps of his vampire enemies.

He had sought for him—and found him!

Now he was back from that quest, and back barely in time to save the hell-lander woman Zekintha from Arlek's treachery; Zekintha . . . and the newcomer, whose fighting skills Arlek's dupes had mentioned in something approaching awe. On a one-to-one basis and without the intervention of his followers, Arlek hadn't stood a chance against Jazz. Well, if there was one thing Lardis Lidesci liked, it was a good fair fighter. Or even a good dirty one!

Lardis saw them coming across the canyon's floor, stepped forward to meet them. He clasped Zek in his great arms, kissed her right ear. "Tear down the mountains!" he greeted her. And: "I'm glad you're safe, Zekintha."

"Only just," she answered, breathlessly. "All credit to this one," and she nodded at Jazz.

Weary now, and climbing out of his gear as if he unhitched an anchor, Jazz returned her nod, then looked all about in the canyon's hushed twilight. Men and wolves moved here and there in the shadows of the cliffs, their jingling and low talk seeming very normal and pleasant to Jazz's ears. But central in a jumble of boulders which lay towards the western wall burned a great fire, emitting roiling black smoke which climbed into a near perpendicular column in the still air. Arlek's funeral pyre, he supposed.

Some hundred or more yards to the south, the pass turned a little eastward and there commenced a steady descent toward the unseen foothills of Sunside. The rays of the slowly declining sun, blazing full through that last stretch of pass, beat on the western wall of the canyon and lit its crags and outcrops. Coming down from those heights, agile as goats, a half-dozen male Travellers bore mirrors like shields in their capable hands, always directing the sun's beams into those gloomy deeps of the gorge which lay to the north. Jazz frowned as the first of the mirror-bearers came closer. The man's great oval mirror was of glass, surely? Did the Travellers have that sort of technology at their disposal?

Lardis watched Jazz strip down to his combat suit, then approached him smilingly with outstretched right hand. Jazz tried to take his hand, found himself clasp-

ing his forearm instead; Lardis likewise clasped his. It
was a Traveller greeting. "A hell-lander," Lardis nodded. "How are you called?"

"Michael Simmons," Jazz answered. "Jazz to my
friends."

Again Lardis's nod. "Then I'll call you Jazz—for
now. But I need time to make up my mind about you.
I've heard rumours about hell-landers like yourself;
some take sides with the Wamphyri, working for them
as wizards."

"As you've seen," Jazz told him, "I'm not one of
them. And in any case, I don't think any, er, hell-
lander, would side with the Wamphyri of his own free
will."

Lardis took Jazz aside, guided him toward a spot
where a party of men sat forlornly on broken boulders,
heads hanging low. Around them stood a guard composed of Lardis's men. The ones who were seated had
been Arlek's followers; Jazz recognized several faces.
As Jazz and Lardis approached, the captives hung their
heads lower still. Lardis scowled at them, said: "Arlek
would have given you to the Wamphyri Lord Shaithis.
But he was a great coward, and he coveted the leadership of the tribe. You've seen the fire burning there?"

Jazz nodded. "Zek told me what you'd do," he said.

"Zek?" Lardis's smile faded a little. "Did you know
her before? Did you come to seek her out and take her
back?"

"I came because I had no choice," Jazz answered,
"not because of Zek. I had heard something of her;
we'd never met, not until now. Back in our own world,
our people are . . . not friends."

"But here you're both hell-landers, strangers in a
strange world. It draws you together." Lardis's assess-
ment was fairly accurate.

Jazz shrugged. "I suppose it does." He looked straight
into Lardis's face. "Will you make Zek an issue?"

Lardis's expression didn't change. "No," he said.

"She's a free woman. I have no time for small things. The tribe is my main concern. I have had thoughts about Zekintha, but . . . she would be too much of a distraction. Anyway, I fancy she'd rather be friend and adviser than wife. Also, she's a hell-lander. A man shouldn't get too close to something he doesn't understand."

Jazz smiled. "The place you call the hell-lands is very large, with many people of diverse cultures. It's a strange place, but hardly the hell you seem to imagine it to be."

Lardis raised his eyebrows, thought about what Jazz had said. "Zekintha says much the same thing," he said. "She's told me a great deal about it: weapons greater than all the Wamphyri's war-beasts put together; a continent of black people dying in their thousands, of disease and starvation; wars in every corner of your world, men against men; machines that think and run and fly, all filled with fire and smoke and a terrible roaring. It sounds close enough to hell to me!"

Jazz laughed out loud. "Put it that way and you could be right!" he said. He had kept his SMG, whose strap he now adjusted where it crossed his shoulder. Lardis glanced at the weapon, said:

"Your . . . gun? The same as Zekintha's. I saw her kill a bear with it. The bear had more holes than a fishing net! Now it is broken, but she still carries it."

"It can be repaired," Jazz told him. "I'll do it as soon as I have the time. But your people understand metal. It surprises me no one has tried to fix it."

"Because they're afraid of it," Lardis admitted. "Me too! They're noisy things, these guns . . ."

Jazz nodded his agreement. "But noise doesn't kill the Wamphyri," he said.

Lardis grasped upon that, became excited as a child. "I heard the chattering of it, echoing up the pass! Did you really strike at Shaithis?"

"At close range, too." Jazz smiled wryly. "—for all

the good it did! I put a good many holes in their flyers, and a few in them, too, I think—but it didn't stop them.''

"Better than nothing!" Lardis slapped his shoulder. "Their wounds will take time to heal. Give the vampires in them something to do. Keep them out of mischief a while!" Then he grew thoughtful again. "These men," he scowled at the seated group of unfortunates, "were Arlek's followers. If they'd had their way you'd be vampire-fodder by now. With your gun, you could kill them all as easy as that!" He snapped his fingers.

Zek had followed on behind; she heard what Lardis said and her eyes went very wide. The men Lardis had been speaking about had also heard him (he'd ensured that they had); they straightened up where they sat, their faces suddenly gaunt and full of apprehension.

Jazz looked at them, remembered how a few of them had seemed ill at ease with some of Arlek's ideas and actions. "Arlek made fools of them," he answered Lardis. "Great fools. And you weren't here to set it right. He was a coward, as you've said; he needed others to lend his opinions strength. These are the ones who were foolish enough to listen to them. Obviously they wish they hadn't. But you punish traitors, not fools.''

Lardis glanced at Zek, grinned. "It might have been me speaking," he said; and she relaxed and took a deep breath. "On the other hand," Lardis continued, "one of these men struck you from behind. Don't you feel any anger toward that one?"

Jazz touched the tender bump behind his ear. "Some," he admitted. "But not enough to want to kill him. I could teach him a lesson, perhaps?" He wondered what Lardis was after. Obviously he'd heard how Jazz had dispatched Arlek. Maybe he wanted to see his fighting skills at first hand. It would be a bonus for the tribe to have a man who could teach them or at least introduce superior fighting skills.

"You want to teach him a lesson?" Lardis grinned. Jazz had guessed right. Now Lardis walked among the seated men, pushing them left and right off their boulder seats, roughly away from him as he poured his silent scorn on them. "Which one of you struck him?" he demanded.

A young man, muscular, nervous-looking, slowly stood up. Lardis pointed to an area of flat ground fairly clear of rocks. "Over there," he growled.

"Wait!" Jazz came forward. "Let's at least make it a match. He doesn't stand a chance on his own. Does he have a friend? A close friend?"

Lardis raised his expressive eyebrows, shrugged. He scowled at the youth. "Well, do you? Unlikely, I should think."

Another young man, burlier, craggier, less apprehensive, got to his feet. As he joined the first on the open ground, Jazz thought: *I deal with you first!* Out loud he said: "That should do it." He made sure his SMG was on safe and handed it to Lardis—who accepted it gingerly and held it awkwardly.

Jazz approached his two opponents. "Whenever you're ready," he said casually. "Unless you haven't the guts for it, in which case you can get down on your knees and kiss my boots!" The last was a deliberate ploy—to goad them into speedy action, cause them to lose their self-control.

Which it did!

They looked at each other, their chests filled out, and they charged like young bulls. And almost as wildly.

Jazz had determined to put on a show for Lardis. He avoided the rush of the man who'd clubbed him, delivered a slicing rabbit punch to his neck as he flew past. Not sufficient to put him out of the fight—not yet—but just hard enough to send him dazed and sprawling to the hard ground. The second man, sturdier and a shade more wary, swerved his body and threw himself into a dive, rolling to knock Jazz's feet out from under him.

The plan failed as Jazz leaped high, avoiding his tumbling body, then stepped in close as the clever one sprang to his feet. He offered a feint, telegraphing a blow to his opponent's face. The other saw it coming, snatched the top half of his body back out of harm's way—which left his lower half not only exposed but proffered. Jazz kicked him smartly in the groin; but again, not hard enough to cripple him, sufficient only to make him curl up and drop like a stone.

The first one, groggy but game, was back on his feet. He'd picked up a jagged rock, now commenced circling Jazz while looking for an opening. Jazz was long-legged and knew that in certain circumstances the reach of his legs was greater than that of his arms—and in any case this was no boxing match He half-turned from the man with the rock, who at once stepped forward. But as Jazz turned away, so he bent his body sharply forward and downward from the waist, lifting and lashing out with his right foot. The move was so fast and so alien to any of the other's previous fighting experience that he seemed hardly aware of its offensive character at all! But suddenly his arm was numb and the rock had been kicked from his grasp. Still in fluid motion, Jazz straightened up, continued his turn through its natural circle, and sliced the other stiff-fingered across the Adam's apple. And again he pulled his punch.

Then he fell into a defensive crouch, looking to see what damage he'd done. And finally he relaxed, straightened up, stepped back and folded his arms.

Both opponents were on the ground, one clutching his groin and groaning, rocking himself to and fro, and the other choking, sucking at the air, massaging his throat. They'd recover soon enough, but it would be a long time before they'd forget.

For a moment there was a stunned silence, then Lardis began clapping his hands in spontaneous applause. Many of the men with him followed suit, but not Arlek's ex-gang. They sat very quietly, looking anywhere except at Jazz. To them he offered: "Well, is there anyone else would like to try me?" But there were no takers.

"I leave their punishment to you, Jazz." Lardis shouted. "What shall be done with them?"

"You've shamed them enough," Jazz answered. "Arlek had his warnings, which he failed to heed. He's paid for that. Now these men have been warned. If it's my choice, then I say leave it at that."

"Good!" Lardis barked his agreement.

Men at once stepped forward to help their two fallen colleagues to their feet. One of them was a mirror-bearer; he carefully laid his mirror down as he stooped to assist the man with the bruised throat. Jazz glanced at the large oval mirror where it lay face-down, then looked again—then pounced on it. *"What?"* he gasped. "What in all the—?"

Zek had been moving toward him. Now she came flying. "Jazz, what is it?"

"Lardis," he called out, ignoring her for the moment. "Lardis, where did you get these mirrors?" And suddenly, quite out of character, his voice had a breathless, unbelieving quality.

Lardis came over. He was grinning ear to ear. "My new weapons!" he answered, with something of pride. "I went to seek out The Dweller—and found him! As a sign of our friendship, he gave me these. Fortunate for you that he did . . ."

Jazz picked up the mirror, stared incredulously at its backing. "Fortunate indeed!" he finally got the words out. "Maybe in more ways than you know." He licked his lips, looked at Zek for her confirmation that his eyes weren't playing games with him.

She looked at what he held in his suddenly trembling hands and her jaw dropped. *"My God!"* she said, very faintly.

For the mirror was unmistakably backed with chip-board, to which some Traveller had attached leather straps. What was more, it bore a manufacturer's label, carrying the embossed legend:

MADE IN THE DDR.
KURT GEMMLER UND SOHN,
GUMMER STR.,
EAST BERLIN.

Chapter Fourteen
Taschenka—Harry's Quest— The Trek Begins

TASCHENKA "TASSI" KIRESCU WAS NINETEEN, SMALL AND slim, completely unpolitical and very frightened.

Her skin was a little darker than that of the rest of her family; her eyes were large and very slightly tilted in an oval face; her hair was black and shiny to match her eyes, and she wore it in braids. Tassi's father, Kazimir, whom she hadn't seen since the night they were arrested, had used to explain jokingly that she was a throwback. "There's Mongol blood in you, girl," he'd told her, his eyes sparkling. "Blood of the great Khans who came this way all of those hundreds of years ago. Either that . . . or I don't know your mother as well as I think I do!" Following which Anna, Tassi's mother, would invariably sputter furiously and chase him with whatever she could lay her hands on.

That, of course, had been in the good times, all of a few weeks ago, which now felt like several centuries.

Tassi had known nothing of Mikhail Simonov's real reason for coming to Yelizinka in the Ural foothills; the story she'd heard was that he was a city boy who'd been something of a wild one, that he'd always been getting himself into one sort of trouble or another, until finally he'd been sent logging as a punishment, a penance guaranteed to cool him off. Well, places didn't

260

come much cooler than Yelizinka, not in the winter, anyway; but Tassi wasn't at all sure that Mikhail's blood had been cooled by it. In fact they'd very quickly become lovers, in a strange sort of way. Strange because he'd always been quick to warn her that it couldn't last, and that therefore she mustn't *fall* in love with him; strange, too, in that she'd felt exactly the same way about it: he'd serve his time here and wipe his record clean, and then he'd move on, probably back to the city, Moscow, and she would find herself a husband from the logging communities around.

The attraction had been the loneliness she'd felt in him, and a contradictory bowstring tension lying just beneath the surface of him. For his part: once, in a dreamy, faraway moment, he'd told her that she was the only real thing in his life right now, that sometimes he felt the entire world and his place in it were just an enormous fantasy. And now she'd been told that he was a foreign spy, which to Tassi had seemed like the greatest possible fantasy—at first. But that had been before they took her down into the Perchorsk Projekt.

Since then . . . everything had turned into a real fantasy, a horror story, a living nightmare.

Her father had been incarcerated in the cell next door to hers and she knew he had been tortured on a number of occasions. She'd heard it all coming right through the sheet steel walls. The hoarse, terrified panting, the sharp slapping sounds, his anguished cries for mercy. But there'd been precious little of that last. Then, three days ago, there'd been one especially bad session; in the middle of it, at its height, the old man had screamed . . . and then, he'd stopped screaming—abruptly. Since when Tassi had heard nothing from him at all.

She couldn't even bear to think what might have happened; she hoped the silence meant that her father was now in a hospital somewhere, recovering; she *prayed* that's what it meant, anyway.

Almost as bad had been Major Khuv's questioning.

261

The KGB Major had not once laid a hand on her, but she'd had the suspicion that if he did he would hurt her terribly. The awful thing was that she didn't have— didn't know—anything to tell him. If she had then fear on its own would have obliged her to tell it, or if not fear certainly the desire to stop them hurting her father.

And then there had been the beast Vyotsky. Tassi hadn't stood so much in fear of that one as in horror of him. And she had sensed—had known instinctively— that he *enjoyed* her horror, feeding upon it like a ghoul on rotting flesh! There had been little or nothing sexual about his treatment of her that time when he'd had her photographed naked with him. It had all been done for effect: partly to shame her, underline her vulnerability and make her feel the lowest of the low; partly to show her the power of her tormentor—that he could strip her naked, leer at her and paw her body, while she was incapable of lifting a finger to stop him—but mainly to aid him in the mental torture of someone else. The sadist Vyotsky had told her that the photographs were for the "benefit" of the British spy, Michael Simmons, whom she had known as Mikhail Simonov: "to drive the poor bastard out of his mind!" Plainly the idea had delighted Vyotsky. "He thinks he's so cool—*hah!*" he'd said. "If this doesn't get him boiling, then nothing will!"

The KGB bully was quite mad, Tassi was sure. Even though he hadn't been back to torment her for quite some time now, still she would freeze whenever she heard someone approaching the door of her cell; and if the footsteps should pause . . . then her breathing would go ragged at once, and her poor heart begin beating that much faster.

It had started to beat that way just a little while ago, but on this occasion her visitor was only Vyotsky's superior officer, Major Khuv.

Only Major Khuv! Tassi thought, as the suave KGB officer entered her cell. *That was a laugh!* But she wasn't even close to laughing as he cuffed her wrist to his own, then told her:

"Taschenka, my dear. I want to show you something. It's something I feel you really ought to see before I question you again at any great length. You'll understand why soon enough."

Stumbling along behind him, she made no effort to even guess where he was taking her. Essentially a peasant girl, to her the Projekt was a maze, a nightmare labyrinth of steel and concrete. Her claustrophobia had so disoriented her that she was lost from the first step she took across the threshold of her cell.

"Tassi," Khuv murmured, leading her on through the almost deserted, dimly lit night corridors, "I want you to think very carefully. Much more carefully than you've been thinking so far. And if there's anything at all you can tell me about the subversive activities of your brother, your father, the people of Yelizinka in general— and in particular about the underground, anti-Soviet organization to which any or all of them belonged . . . I mean, this really is going to be your last chance, Tassi."

"Major," she gasped the word out, "sir, I know nothing of any of these things. If my father was what you say he was—"

"Oh, he was," Khuv glanced at her and nodded gravely. "You may be sure that . . . he *was!*"

It was the way he said the last word, its ominous emphasis. And in a moment it had Tassi's free hand flying to her mouth. "What . . . what have you done to him?" her question was the merest whisper.

They had arrived at a door bearing a legend familiar to Khuv but one which Tassi had never seen before. She only glanced at it; it said something about a keeper and security classified persons only. Using his plastic ID tag, and as the door's mechanisms were activated, Khuv turned to Tassi and answered her question:

"Done to him? To your father? Me? *I* have done nothing! He did it all himself—with his refusal to cooperate. A very stubborn man, Kazimir Kirescu . . .''

The door opened with a click. Khuv held it open a crack, called out: ''Vasily, is all in order?''

''Oh, yes, Major,'' came back an unctuous reply. ''All ready.''

Khuv smiled at Tassi. The smile of a shark on its attack run. ''My dear,'' he said, shoving the door open wide and leading her into the room of the creature, ''I'm going to show you something unpleasant, and tell you something even more unpleasant, and finally suggest the most unpleasant thing of all. Following which you shall have the rest of the night and all day tomorrow to think about where you stand. But no more time than that.''

The room was in near-darkness, to which the ceiling lights added only an eerie red glow. Tassi could make out the figure of a small man in a white smock, and the shape of a large oblong box or tank covered with a white sheet. The tank must be of glass, for a small white light in the wall behind it shone right through, casting on the sheet a milky, ghostly outline, the silhouette of something that flopped sluggishly inside the tank.

''Come closer,'' Khuv drew Tassi toward the tank. ''Don't be afraid, it's perfectly safe. It can't hurt you— not yet.''

Standing beside the KGB Major, unconsciously clutching his arm in her innocence as she stared wide-eyed at the weird silhouette on the sheet, Tassi heard him say to the scientist in the white smock: ''Very well, Vasily, let's see what we have here.''

Vasily Agursky tugged at one corner of the sheet and it began to slide slowly from the tank, letting a little more of the subdued light shine through. Then the slide accelerated and the sheet whispered to the floor. The thing in the tank had its back to the three; feeling their eyes upon it, it glanced over one hunched shoulder. Tassi looked at it, stared at it in disbelief, shuddered and clung to Khuv that much more fiercely. He patted her hand almost absent-mindedly, in a fashion which in other circumstances might almost have seemed fatherly. Except this was not her father but the man who had let Karl Vyotsky terrorize her.

"Well, Tassi," he said, his voice very low, very sinister, "and what do you think of that?"

She didn't know what to think of it, and later she would give anything to be able to forget it entirely. But for now: the shape of the thing was vaguely manlike, though even in this poor light it was quite obviously not a man. It appeared to be feeding, using taloned hands to tear its food and stuff strips of raw red meat into its mouth. Its face was mainly hidden, but Tassi could see the way its jaws worked, and the baleful glare of the very human eye that peered back over its shoulder.

Hunched down, crouching or squatting there on the sandy floor of its tank, the thing might have been an ape; but its leprous skin was corrugated and its feet gripped the floor with too many hooked, skeletal digits. An appendage like a tail—which was *not* a tail—lay coiled behind it; Tassi gasped as she saw that this extraneous *member,* too, was equipped with a rudimentary, lidless, almost vacant eye.

The thing was entirely freakish, and as for what it fed upon . . .

Tassi gave a massive start, jumped back from the tank. The creature had snatched up more food from the floor of its glass cell—and a *human arm* had suddenly flopped into view, dangling from its terrible hands! As Tassi's eyes bulged in horror, so the thing commenced munching on the dismembered arm's hand and fingers.

"Steady, my dear," said Khuv quietly, as the girl moaned and reeled beside him.

"But . . . but . . . it's eating a . . . a—"

"A man?" Khuv finished it for her. "Or what's left of one? Indeed it is. Oh, it will eat any sort of meat, but it appears to like human flesh the best.'' And to Agursky: ''Vasily, do you have something for Tassi?''

The strange little scientist came forward, pressed something—several somethings—into her hand. A wallet? A ring? An ID card? And however familiar these things were, for a long moment her mind wouldn't recognize them, refusing to make the final, terrible connection. Then—

She felt dizzy and put her free hand on the glass wall of the tank to steady herself, and her eyes went from the items in her hand to the thing where it crouched. Horrified but at the same time fascinated, she stared and stared at it. Were these men trying to tell her that . . . that this creature was *eating her father?!*

Agursky had gone to one side of the room, where suddenly he switched up the lighting. Everything sprang into sharp, almost dazzling definition. The creature threw its food to one side and turned snarling toward Khuv and Tassi where they *both* shrank instinctively back.

And that was when she fainted and would have fallen to the floor if her wrist hadn't been cuffed to the Major's, and if he hadn't turned quickly to catch up her sagging body in his arms.

For the thing in the glass tank was . . . oh, it was something hellish, yes, nightmarish. But the greater nightmare was this: that however monstrous and warped, however altered and alien that thing's caricature of a face was when it had snarled at her, *still she'd recognized it as the face of her father!*

Jazz Simmons's Georgian terrace bachelor flat in Hampstead was colourful, cluttered, and when Harry Keogh had first moved in a little over twenty-four hours ago it had been bitterly cold and the telephone was off. He'd had E-Branch clear it for him to use the place as his base, and he'd warned them not to come bothering him. He had Darcy Clarke's word that he could play the entire game his way, without interference.

His way had been to attempt to absorb something of the atmosphere of the place first. Maybe he could get to know Simmons by understanding how he'd lived: his tastes, likes and dislikes, and his routine. Not his work routine, his private routine. Harry didn't believe that a man was what he did professionally; he believed a man was what he thought privately.

The first thing that had impressed itself upon him was the clutter. Privately, Jazz Simmons had been a very untidy man. Maybe it was his way of relaxing. When you're trained to a knife-edge you have to have a place where you can sheathe yourself now and then, or else you might cut yourself. This had been Jazz's unwinding place.

The "clutter" consisted of books and magazines dropped any and everywhere, more off the bookshelves than on them. Spy-thrillers (not unnaturally, Harry supposed) lay alongside piles of foreign language publications, most of the latter being Russian. There was also, beside Jazz's bed, a dusty, foot-thick stack of *Pravdas*—topped by a copy of the latest *Playboy*. Harry had had to smile: hardly the most compatible meeting of ideologies!

Also in the bedroom were dust-free framed photographs of Jazz's father and mother; on the wall a lifesize Marilyn Monroe poster; a cabinet standing close to the window, containing cups won in various ski events; and again affixed to the wall a battered pair of bright yellow skis and sticks which must be of some special significance. A recessed cupboard in a narrow passageway had showered Harry with an accumulation of skiing requisites, and beside Jazz's video cassette recorder were haphazardly stacked films of all the main winter athletics for the last five years. While Jazz hadn't been available to participate, still he hadn't been willing to miss out entirely.

There were photographs of girls, too, quite a pile of them, in one corner of a bedroom drawer; a scrap-book continued a photographic record of Jazz's military term; perhaps significantly, a second album carefully wrapped in an old pullover consisted of faded letters to Jazz from his father.

Harry had let the feel of all of these things sink in. He'd slept in Jazz's bed, used his kitchen and bathroom, even his dressing gown. He discovered several phone numbers of old girlfriends, called them and asked about Jazz, discovered them to be a mixed bunch with little in common except their obvious intelligence, and the fact that one and all they thought Jazz was "a very nice guy." Harry was starting to think so, too; and where before Michael J. Simmons had been merely a means to an end—hopefully to the discovery of Harry's family—now he had become something of an issue in his own right. In short, the horizon of Harry's obsession was expanding beyond purely personal interests.

At this stage, too, Harry had felt that he now must get a little closer to Simmons himself. Or if not the real man, then at least his metaphysical echo. Simmons no longer existed in this universe, but he had once existed in the past . . .

In Harry's incorporeal days he had been able to travel into the past and "immaterialize" there: he'd been able to manifest a ghostly semblance of himself on the bygone event screen. Now, embodied and fully corporeal once more, this was no longer possible; it would create unthinkable paradoxes, perhaps even damage the structure of time itself. He could still travel *in* time, but while doing so he must never attempt to leave the metaphysical Möbius Continuum for the real world.

Not that this was a necessity; to achieve his aim on this occasion, time-*travel* itself should suffice. And so he entered the Möbius Continuum, found a past-time door and journeyed back a little way, less than two years into the past. In doing so Harry had altered his position in time but not in space; he still "occupied" Jazz Simmons's flat. And so, when as he judged it he had journeyed far enough and reversed his direction to head once more for "the future," he knew beyond a reasonable doubt that the strong blue life-thread which travelled parallel to his own must be that of Simmons. For after all, he'd picked it up in Simmons's flat. And following that life-thread into the future, he also knew that he was now about to prove one way or the other any similarity between Simmons's— transference?—and those of his wife and son.

The proof wasn't long in coming, and temporaneously it agreed exactly with the time Darcy Clarke had specified in defining Simmons's exit point. Although he expected it, still Harry didn't see it coming, just an eyeball-searing blaze of white light; following which . . . he journeyed on alone. Jazz Simmons had gone— elsewhere! The same elsewhere, presumably, as Harry Jr. and Brenda before him.

Harry didn't need to go back and play it all over again; he'd seen the same thing plenty of times before, and it was always the same. There was nothing new here, the only difference being that Simmons had gone in a single white instantaneous blaze, while the departure of Harry Jr. and his mother had been accompanied by twin bomb-bursts. As for what those terminal flares signified, Harry was at a complete loss. He only knew that before the white dazzle blue life-threads raced for the future, and that after it those life-threads no longer existed. Not in this universe anyway.

Which led to his next line of inquiry: Möbius himself.

August Ferdinand Möbius (1790–1868), a German mathematician and astronomer, lay in his grave in a Leipzig cemetery. His dust was there, anyway, which to Harry Keogh, Necroscope, was one and the same thing. Harry had been to see Möbius before, to discover the secret of the Möbius Continuum. In life Möbius had invented it (though he personally had denied that, telling Harry that in fact he'd merely "noticed" it) and in death he'd gone on to develop his theories into precise sciences, albeit sciences no living person would ever comprehend. None, that is, except Harry Keogh himself. And Harry's son, of course.

The last time Harry was here he'd come by rather more conventional means: by air to Berlin, then through Check-Point Charlie to the east—as a tourist! But mundane as his arrival had been, his exit from Leipzig had been along an entirely different route—through a Möbius door. That had been Harry's first experience of the Möbius Continuum, since when he'd become an expert in his own right.

But there had been far more than that to Harry's visit, and even now he might not have discovered the correct mental formulae but for the spur he'd received at that time. Harry had been on the "wanted" list of the Soviet E-Branch. The emerging vampire Boris Dragosani, a member of that branch, had wanted to take Harry— alive if possible—and draw from him the secret of his weird talents. Dragosani was a necromancer who ripped the private thoughts of the dead out of their ravaged bodies, who read their secrets in brain fluids and torn ligaments, in ruptured organs and eviscerated guts. It would be so much easier if he could simply talk to the dead, like Harry. They might not respect him as they did Harry, but the threat of defilement should suffice to open them up. If not . . . well, there was always the other way.

Dragosani had issued a detention warrant, ordering the East German Grenzpolizei to pick Harry up on trumped-up charges. They had tried, and out of necessity Harry had solved the final equation of Möbius's metaphysical space-time dimension, with which he could summon "doors" on the entire space-time universe. Barely in time, Harry had used one of these doors. Ironically, perhaps, it had floated into view (but only Harry's view) across the face of Möbius's headstone!

From then on Harry's invasion of the Soviet E-Branch and the destruction of Dragosani had been an inexorable process, in the course of which his own body had been destroyed and abandoned as once more he escaped to the Möbius Continuum. There, as an incorporeal being, a bodiless mind and soul, eventually he had discovered and entered into the drained shell of Alec Kyle. This had been an almost involuntary event—Kyle's body, a living vacuum, had seemed to reach out and suck Harry in—but it had given him a place among men again and ended what was otherwise an interminable existence in the matterless Möbius Continuum.

And now Harry was back in Leipzig, standing by Möbius's grave as before. Almost nine years had passed since last he was here, but he hadn't forgotten those events which terminated his first visit. And so on this occasion he'd come by night.

A moon hung low over the city's skyline, and the stars were very bright between streamers of fast-fleeing cloud. The night wind, moaning through the headstones, sent wrinkled leaves scurrying like mice, and Harry felt a chill in his bones which was born partly of the natural cold of a November night, and partly of his feeling of alienation here in this place. But the cemetery gates were closed for the night, the lights in the city subdued, and apart from the scrape of leaves all was silence.

He sought Möbius out and found him, and as before the great mathematician was busy with his formulae and his calculations. Tables of planetary mass and motion, the "weights" of the sun and her satellite worlds in their careening round, were balanced against orbital velocities and gravitic forces; formulae so complex that even Harry's intuitive grasp found their purpose elusive, together with simultaneous equations whose answers filled themselves in even as he watched; all of these figures and configurations beat on Harry's awareness like the ever-changing results of an on-going process on the screen of some vast computer. And Harry saw that the problem was so complex and so close to

271

completion that he let it go on undisturbed by his presence to the end. At which time the screen went blank and Möbius sighed. It was a strange thing, even now, to hear the ''sigh'' of a dead man.

''Sir?'' said Harry. ''Are you available now?''

''Eh?'' said Möbius, in that moment before he recognized Harry's thoughts. Then: ''Is that you, Harry?'' he continued eagerly. ''I *thought* there was someone here. You very nearly put me off just then, and I was working on something which is *very* important!''

''I know,'' Harry nodded. ''I saw it, but I didn't want to disturb you. Those are very wonderful discoveries!''

''Oh?'' Möbius seemed surprised. ''You could understand my working, then? Very well, and what have I discovered?''

Harry drew back a little, hesitating. He was in the presence of genius and he knew it. Möbius had been a great mathematician all his life, and after that life he had continued his work unabated. Where Harry's mathematical skills were intuitive, Möbius had worked hard to achieve his results. No quantum leaps for him but dogged trial and error and an unwavering, all-consuming passion for his subject. It seemed somehow improper for Harry to have come here at this time, spying on the man in his triumph.

''Not at all,'' Möbius tut-tutted him. ''What?—a man who can impose his physical being on the metaphysical universe, and use it at will? Spying on me? I consider you a colleague, Harry, an equal! And truth be told, you couldn't have come visiting at a more opportune time. Now come on, tell me what I've been doing. What is it that I've proved with my numbers, eh?''

Harry shrugged. ''Very well,'' he said. ''You've shown that instead of the nine planets we believed to exist in the solar system, there are in fact eleven. Both of the new worlds are small, but true planets for all that. One occupies a position exactly behind Jupiter, with the same rotation period, so that it's always occluded, and the other's a non-reflector and lies about as far out again as Pluto from the sun.''

''Good!'' Möbius applauded him. ''And their moons?''

''Eh?'' Harry was taken by surprise. ''I read only the problem you'd set yourself and the answers to the problem as you arrived at them! There *were* slight deviations—percentages of error, I suppose—but . . .'' He paused.

''But? But?'' Harry could almost picture Möbius raising his eyebrows. ''All the clues were there in the equations, Harry. No? Very well. I'll tell you:

''The inner world has no moon, but the 'percentage of error,' as you call it, for the outer world was just too big to be ignored. I have checked it and it indicates an almost spherical nickel-iron moon three kilometres in diameter orbiting the parent at a distance of twenty-four thousand planetary circumferences. Now *that* is what we call a calculation! Of course, I shall prove it by going there and seeing it for myself.''

Harry shook his head in defeat, offered a wry grimace. ''You're too good for me,'' he said. ''You always will be.'' And after a moment: ''Do you want me to let this 'leak out,' as it were? I could do that easily enough, with just sufficient information to set the entire astronomical fraternity jumping! It could be done anonymously, by an 'amateur,' you understand, on the solemn promise that when the calculations are shown to be correct, then that one of the two worlds should be named Möbius!''

Möbius was stunned. ''Could you really *do* that, Harry?''

''I'm sure I could find a way.''

''My boy . . . *God!*'' Möbius was overjoyed at the prospect. ''Harry, how I *wish* I could shake your hand!''

''You can do rather more than that.'' Harry told him, growing serious in a moment. ''You remember the last time I came to see you I had a problem? Well, now I have an even bigger one.''

"Let's have it, then," said the other at once, and Harry told him of his quest for his wife and son. He finished by explaining:

"And so you see, it's no longer simply a question of my family, but I also have the British agent Michael Simmons to consider.''

Möbius seemed nonplussed. "And you've come to me for help? Well, obviously you have—but for the life of me I can't see what I can do! I mean, if they're not *here*, these three people—if they have physically ceased to exist in this universe—then how can I or anyone else suggest where or how to find them? The universe is The Universe, Harry. Its very name defines it. It is THE All. If they're not in it, then they're not anywhere.''

"That was my line of reasoning, too." Harry admitted, "—until recently. But you and me, why, don't we both contradict that very fact?''

"Eh? How's that?''

"The Möbius Continuum," Harry answered, by way of explanation. "You yourself admit that it's a purely metaphysical plane, not of this universe. Step into the Möbius Continuum and you step out of the three mundane dimensions. The Möbius Continuum not only transcends the three dimensions of mundane space but time also, and runs parallel to all of them! And what of a black hole?''

"What of it?" (Möbius's mental shrug).

"Well, isn't a black hole an exit from this universe? That's how they've always been explained to me: a focus of gravity so great that space and time themselves are drawn into the whorl. And if they *are* exits from the here and now, *then where the hell do they lead?*''

"To another part of the universe," Möbius answered. "That seems the only likely explanation to me. Mind you, I haven't really looked at black holes yet. I have them scheduled, though.''

"Are you missing the point or deliberately avoiding it?" Harry wanted to know. "This is my question: if a black hole goes somewhere, emerging maybe light-years away, what of the space in between? Where *is* the material which is drawn into the hole, between its disappearing and its reappearing? You see, to me this all seems very much like our Möbius Continuum."

"Go on," Möbius was fascinated.

"OK," said Harry, "let's look at it this way. First we have the . . . let's call it the mundane universe. And we'll say it looks like this."

He showed Möbius a mental diagram.

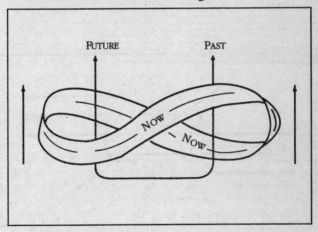

"Why the bends?" the mathematician was immediately curious.

"Because without them it would just be a pair of straight lines," Harry told him. "The bends give it definition, make it look like something."

"Like a ribbon?"

"For the purpose of the exercise, why not? For all I know it could be a circle, or maybe a sphere. But this way we can envisage a past and a future, too."

"Very well," Möbius conceded.

"Now in this diagram of the universe," Harry went on, "we can't go from 'A' to 'B' without crossing the edge. We can go up the ribbon from 'A' to the edge, then down to 'B.' Or down to the edge and up, it makes no difference. The edge represents the distance between 'A' and 'B,' right?"

"Agreed," said the other.

"Now this is how I see the Möbius Continuum," said Harry:

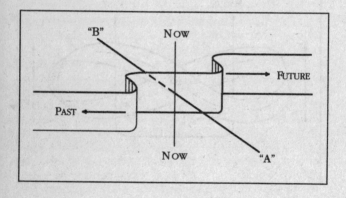

And he continued: "It's the ribbon universe we know with the half-twist of your Möbius strip. 'Now' has turned through ninety degrees to become 'forever.' Which means that 'A' and 'B' are now on the same plane. We no longer have to cross the edge. We can go from one to the other instantaneously—'now!' "

"Go on," said Möbius again, but much more thoughtfully.

"Previously we've thought of it like this:" said Harry. "Like . . . like putting on a pair of seven-league boots and striding to our destinations in seconds. Covering distances that should take hours in minutes. But I've checked it out and it's not like that. In fact we go there *instantaneously*—accordingly to Earth-time, anyway. It's not simply that we go there faster, but that the space in between actually disappears!"

After a while Möbius said, "I think I understand. What you want to know is this: if for us the space between 'A' and 'B' reduces to zero—if it disappears—"

"Exactly!" Harry cut in. *"Where does it go to?"*

"But it's an illusion" Möbius cried. "It's still there. It's we who have disappeared—into the Möbius Continuum, as you insist upon calling it!"

"Now we're getting somewhere," Harry took a deep breath. "You see, the way I see it, the Möbius Continuum is no-man's-land, it's limbo, it's the middle ground *between* universes. 'Universes'—plural! It has doors to the past, the future, and to every point in present time. Using it, we can go everywhere and -when—or at least I can, because I still have a life-thread to follow. But the point I'm trying to make is this: I believe there may be other doors which we haven't found yet. We don't have the equations for them. And I believe that one of those doors, when I find it, will—"

"—Lead you to your wife and son, and to Michael J. Simmons?"

"Yes!"

Möbius nodded (in his fashion) and gave it some thought. "Other doors," he mused. Then: "Grant me this—that I know more about the Möbius dimension than you do. That I have had one hundred and twenty years to examine it more thoroughly than you could ever hope to. That I *discovered* it, and have used it to go places you can *never* go, not in your lifetime."

"Oh?" said Harry.

"Oh?" Möbius raised his eyebrows again. *"Oh? And can you go to the centre of a star in Betelgeuse to measure its temperature? Can you visit the moons of Jupiter or sit in the middle of that planet's monumental tornado which we call the Red Spot? Can you journey to the bottom of the Marianas Trench and every other deep on Earth to calculate the mass of water in this world? No, you can't. But I can—and have! Now grant me this: that I know the Möbius Continuum better than you do!"*

When the point was made like that, there seemed little use in arguing it. Harry could only agree, but: "I think you're going to tell me something I don't want to hear," he said.

"You know I am!" Möbius told him. "There are no other doors we haven't discovered, Harry. Not in the Möbius Continuum. Other universes?—which seems to me something of a contradiction in itself—I can't say. And in any case you're talking to the wrong man, for I only deal in the three-dimensional worlds we know. But of one thing I'm sure: you won't find your way into any parallel world through the Möbius Continuum . . ." He fell silent as Harry's disappointment swelled like a physical thing, until it hung heavy over Möbius's grave like a blanket of fog.

"Sir," Harry finally said, "I thank you for your time; I've already wasted far too much of it."

"Not at all," Möbius answered. "Time is only important to the living. I have more than enough time! I just wish I was able to help."

"You've helped," Harry was grateful, "if only to settle a point I've argued with myself time and time again. You see, I know Harry Jr. and his mother are alive, and I know that he can use the Möbius Continuum maybe even better than we can. He's alive but not in this universe, so he must be in some other. There's no way round that. I thought he'd gone there, wherever, along the strip. You've assured me that he hasn't. So . . . there has to be some other route. I already have a clue where to start looking for it, except . . . from here on in my work becomes that much more dangerous, that's all. And now—''

"Wait!" said Möbius. "I've been considering your diagrams. Can I show you one for a change?"

"By all means."

"Very well: here's your ribbon universe again—*and* a parallel universe of a similar construction:''

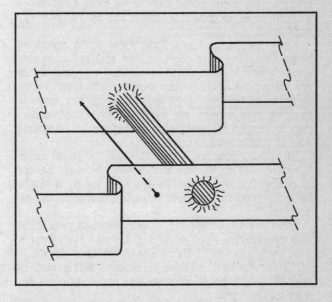

"As you can see, Möbius continued, "I've joined them by use of—''

"A black hole?" Harry guessed.

"No, for we're talking about survivability. Nothing of solid matter and shape can enter that sort of awful maw and retain any sort of integrity. No matter what you are when you enter a black hole, you come out—*if* you come out—gaseous, atomic, pure energy!"

"Which cancels out white holes, too." Harry was growing gloomier by the minute.

"But not grey ones," said Möbius.

"Grey holes?" Harry frowned.

". . . Yes, I see it now," Möbius mused, almost to himself. "Grey holes, without the disruptive gravity of black holes. Gateways pure and simple, between universes. Entropy radiators, perhaps? Inescapable once entered into, there would have to be more than one— if a traveller intended to make the return journey, anyway . . ."

Harry waited, and in a little while weird equations began flickering once more on that amazing computer screen which Möbius called his mind. They came faster and faster, calculi in endless streams, which left Harry dizzy as he tried to grasp their meaning. For seconds merging into minutes the mental display continued— only to be shut off, suddenly, leaving the screen blank. And in a little while longer:

"It is . . . possible," said Möbius. "It could occur in nature, and might even be duplicated by man. Except of course that men would have no use for it. It would be a by-product of some other experimentation, an accident."

"But if I knew how—if I could translate your math into engineering—you're saying I could manufacture this, well, gateway?" Harry was clutching at straws.

"You? Hardly!" Möbius chuckled. "But a team of scientists, with enormous resources and a limitless energy supply—yes!"

Harry thought of the experiments at Perchorsk, and his excitement was now obvious. "That's the confirmation I needed," he said. "And now I have to be on my way."

"It was good to talk to you again," Möbius told him. "Take care, Harry."

"I will," Harry promised. And hugging his overcoat close to him (or if not "his" overcoat, one which he'd borrowed from Jazz Simmons's wardrobe) Harry conjured a Möbius door and took his departure.

Leaves blew skitteringly between the graves and along the pathways. One such leaf, taken by surprise as it leaned against Harry's shoe, suddenly went tumbling across the empty flags where a moment ago he'd been standing. But now, under the high-flying moon and cold, glittering stars, the Leipzig graveyard was quite, quite empty . . .

Some three days prior to (and an entire dimension away from) Harry's visit to Möbius:

Jazz Simmons journeyed west with Zek, Lardis and his Travellers, journeyed in the golden glow of the slowly setting sun. He'd been pleased to be relieved of his kit, all except his gun and two full magazines, and knew that even though he was dog-tired he could now hold out until the Travellers made camp.

By this time, too, he'd had the opportunity to get a good close look at Zek in the extended evening light of Sunside, and he hadn't been disappointed. She had somehow found the time to snatch a wash in a fast-flowing stream, which had served to greatly enhance her fresh, natural beauty. Now she looked good enough to eat, and Jazz felt hungry enough, too, except that would be one hell of a waste.

Zek had wrapped her sore feet in soft rags and now walked on grass and loamy earth instead of stone, and for all that she too was tired her step seemed lighter and most of the worry lines had lifted from her face. While she'd cleaned herself up, Jazz had used the time to study the Travellers.

His original opinion seemed confirmed: they were Gypsies, Romany, and speaking in an antique "Romance" tongue, too. It was hard not to deduce connections with the world he had left behind; maybe Zek would be able to explain some of the similarities. He determined to ask her some time, yet another question to add to a lengthening list. He was surprised how quickly he'd come to rely on her. And he was annoyed to find himself thinking about her when he should be concentrating on his education.

Many of the male Travellers wore rings in the lobes of their left ears, gold by the look of it, to match the bands on their fingers. No lack of that previous metal here, apparently; it decorated in yellow bands the hauling poles of their travois, studded their leather jackets and stitched the seams of their coarse-weave trousers, was even used to stud the leather soles of their sandals! But silver was far less in evidence. Jazz had seen arrows and the bolts of crossbrows tipped with it, but never a sign of the stuff used for decoration. In this world, he would in time discover, it was far more precious than gold. Not least for its effect on vampires.

But the Travellers puzzled Jazz. He found strange, basic anomalies in them beyond his understanding. For example: it seemed to him that in many ways their world was very nearly primal, and yet the Travellers themselves were anything but primitive. Though he'd not yet seen an actual Gypsy caravan here, he knew that they existed: he'd observed a small boy of four or five years, sitting on a loaded, bouncing travois, playing with a rough wooden model. Between its shafts a pair of creatures like overgrown, shaggy sheep, also carved of wood, strained in their tiny harnesses of leather. So they had the wheel, these people, and beasts of burden; even though none were in evidence here. They could work metals, and with their use of the crossbow their weaponry could hardly be considered crude. Indeed, in almost every respect it was seen that theirs was a sophisticated culture. But on the other hand it was hard to see how, in this environment, they'd achieved any degree of culture at all!

As for the "tribe" Jazz had expected to see, so far there were no more than sixty Travellers in all: Arlek's party (now fully accepted back into the common body), and Lardis's companions, plus a handful of family groups which had been waiting in a stand of trees to join up with Lardis at the Sunside exit from the pass and head west with him through the foothills. And all of these people going on foot, with the exception of one old woman who lay in a pile of furs upon a travois, and two or three young children who travelled in a similar fashion.

Jazz had studied their faces, taking note of the way they'd every so often turn their heads and stare suspiciously at the sun floating over the southern horizon. Zek had told Jazz that true night was a good forty-five hours away; but still there was an unspoken anxiety, a straining, in the faces of the Travellers, and Jazz believed he knew why. It was that they silently willed themselves westward, desiring only to put distance between themselves and the pass before sundown. And because they knew this world, while Jazz was a newcomer, he found himself growing anxious along with them, and adding his will to theirs.

Keeping his fear to himself, he'd asked Zek: "Where is everyone? I mean, don't tell me this is the entire tribe!"

"No," she'd told him, shaking her damp hair about her shoulders, "only a fraction of it. Traveller tribes don't go about en masse. It's what Lardis calls 'survival.' There are two more large encampments up ahead. One about forty miles from here, the other twenty-five miles beyond that at the first sanctuary. The sanctuary is a cavern system in a huge outcrop of rock. The entire tribe can disappear inside it, spread out, make themselves thin on the ground. Hard for the

Wamphyri to winkle them out. That's where we're heading. We hole up there for the long night."

"Seventy miles?" he frowned at her. "Before dark?" He glanced at the sun again, so low in the sky. "You're joking!"

"Sundown is still a long way off," she reminded him yet again. "You can stare at the sun till you go blind, but you won't see it dip much. It's a slow process."

"Well, thank goodness for that," he said, nodding his relief.

"Lardis intends to cover fifteen miles between breaks," she went on, "but he's tired, too, probably more than we are. The first break will be soon, for he knows we all need to get some sleep. The wolves will watch. The break will be of three hours' duration—no more than that. So for every six hours' travel we get a three-hour break. Nine hours to cover fifteen miles. It sounds easy but in fact it's back-breaking. They're used to it but it will probably cripple you. Until you're into the swing of it, anyway."

Even as she finished speaking Lardis called a halt. He was up front but his bull voice carried back to them: "Eat, drink," he advised, "then sleep."

The Travellers trudged to a halt, Zek and Jazz with them. She unrolled her sleeping-bag, told Jazz: "Get yourself a blanket of furs from one of the travois. They carry spares. Someone will come round with bread, water, a little meat." Then she flattened a patch of bracken, shook out her bed on top of it and climbed in. She pulled the zipper half-way shut from bottom to top. Jazz lit her a cigarette and went to find himself a blanket.

When he too lay down close by, food had already been brought for them. While they ate he admitted: "I'm excited as a kid! I'll never get to sleep. My brain's far too active. There's so much to take in."

"You'll sleep," she answered.

"Maybe you should tell me a story," he said, lying back. "Your story?"

"The story of my life?" she gave him a wan smile.

"No, just the bit you've lived since you came here. Not very romantic, I know, but the more I learn about this place the better. As Lardis might say, it's a matter of survival. Now that we know about this Dweller—who apparently has a season ticket to Berlin—survival seems so much more desirable. Or more correctly, more feasible!"

"You're right," she said, making herself more comfortable. "There have been times when I've just about given up hope, but now I'm glad I didn't. You want to hear my story? All right then, Jazz, this is how it was for me . . ."

She began to talk, low, even-voiced, and as she got into the story so she fell into the dramatic, colourful style of the Travellers—and of the Wamphyri themselves, for that matter. Being a telepath, their manner and modes of expression had impressed themselves upon her that much more quickly, until now they were second nature. Jazz listened, let her words flow, conjured from them the feel and the fear of her story . . .

Chapter Fifteen
Zek's Story

"I CAME THROUGH THE GATE KITTED-UP JUST LIKE YOU," Zek commenced her tale, "but I wasn't as big or as strong as you are. I couldn't carry as much. And I was dog-tired . . .

"It was night on Starside when I arrived—which is to say I didn't stand a chance! But of course I didn't know what my chances were, not then—or I might simply have put a bullet through my brain and that would have been the end of that.

"I came through the Gate, climbed down from the crater rim, saw what was waiting for me. And nothing I could do but face it, for there was no way back. Oh, you can believe that before I climbed down I threw myself at the sphere in a last desperate attempt to escape; but it just stood there, pouring out its white light, implacable and impenetrable as a dome of luminous rock.

"But if the sight of *Them* waiting there had scared me, my exit from the Gate had not been without its own effect upon them. They didn't know what to make of me. In fact they weren't 'waiting for me' at all—they were there, at the Gate, on business of their own—but I didn't find that out until later. The whole thing is a blur in my mind now, like a bad dream gradually fading.

It's hard to describe how it was, how it felt. But I'll try.

"You've seen the flying beasts that the Wamphyri use, but you haven't seen the warrior creatures—or if you have, then you haven't seen them up close. Now I'm not talking about such as Shaithis's lieutenants, Gustan and that other one; they were ex-Travellers, vampirized by Shaithis and given a little rank and authority. They had not received eggs, as far as I'm aware, and could never aspire to anything greater than service to their Lord. They *were* vampires, of course—of a sort. All the changelings of the Wamphyri are, but Gustan and the others are still men, too . . ." She paused and sighed.

"Jazz, this will be difficult. Vampires are . . . their life-cycles are fantastically complex. Maybe I'd better try to clarify what I know of their systems before I carry on. Their biological systems, I mean.

"Vampires, the basic creatures, are born in the swamps east and west of the mountains. Their source, their genesis, is conjectural; there are perhaps parent creatures, mother-things, buried there in the quag, never seeing the light of day. These mothers would be pure and simple egg-layers. Now I've talked to the Travellers, and to the Lady Karen—Wamphyri herself—and no one knows any more than I've told you about the basic vampire. One thing you can guarantee, though: they don't emerge from their swamps during sunup.

"When they do spawn, then the first task of each and every one of them is find a host, which they pursue with the same instinct as a duck taking to water. It isn't in their nature to live by themselves, indeed if they can't find a host they quickly dessicate and die. You could say they're like cuckoos, who . . . but no, that's a poor analogy. Like tapeworms, maybe—or better still, like liver flukes. So they're parasitic, yes, but that's where any similarity ends . . .

"Anyway, I said their life-cycle was complex. Well, so it is, but when you think about it so are many of the

life-cycles of the creatures in our own world. The liver
fluke is a good example. Living in the intestines of
cows, pigs and sheep, dropping their eggs in the animal's dung, to be picked up on the feet and in the sores
or openings of other animals—including men! And once
they take hold on the liver—then the animal is finished.
The organ is reduced to so much gorgonzola! And if the
beast dies in a field, to be eaten by pigs . . . or if it is
slaughtered and eaten by ignorant men . . . you can see
how the cycle is continued. So, the vampire is something like that. It's a parasite, anyway. But as I said,
that's the only similarity.

"The big difference is this:

"The tapeworm and liver fluke gradually destroy
their hosts, reduce them to nothing, kill them off. In so
doing they kill themselves off, too, because without a
living host they themselves can't live. But the vampire's instinct is different. It doesn't kill its host but
grows with him, makes him more powerful, changes
his nature. It learns from him, relieves him of physical
weaknesses, increases his strength. It encompasses his
mind and character and subverts them. Sexless in itself,
the vampire adopts the sex of its host, adopts all of his
vices, his passions. Men *are* passionate creatures, Jazz,
but with a vampire in them there's nothing to temper
them. Men *are* warlike, and as Wamphyri they bathe
estatically in the blood of their enemies. Men *are* devious, which makes the Wamphyri the most devious creatures of all!

"But all of that is only one part of the cycle, one
facet . . .

"Now, I've explained how with a vampire in him a
man is mentally corrupted. But then there's the purely
physical side. Vampire flesh is different. It is a protoplasm, compatible with *all* flesh! With the flesh of men
and beasts and almost anything which lives. And as the
vampire grows in its host, so it is able to change that
host to its own ends—*physically* change him! And the

Wamphyri are masters of metamorphosis. I will explain:

"Suppose a freshly emerged swamp vampire was fortunate enough to take a wolf as its host. It would gain the wolf's cunning, its fierceness, all its predator instincts. And it would amplify them. There are legends of wolves like that here on Sunside. It's the same legend as the one we knew back on our Earth, which we called the legend of the werewolf! The silver bullet, Jazz, and the full moon!

"To seduce men—for food—the vampire-ridden wolf will *imitate* men! It will go upon two legs, contort its features into manlike features, stalk its prey by night. And when it bites . . .

"The vampire's bite is virulent! It is an absolute contamination, more certain than rabies. Ah, but where rabies kills, the vampire's bite does not. It *might,* if the vampire desires to kill, but on occasion the victim lives. And if at the time of the attack the vampire *puts into* the victim part of its own being, its own protoplasmic flesh, then that victim is vampirized. But let's say that the attack is fatal, that the vampire drinks the victim's blood, drains him dry (which is often the case) and leaves him a corpse. Again, in this case, *even though the victim is dead,* that which was inserted—which was traded for his blood—is *not* dead! In about seventy hours, occasionally less, the transformation is made, the metamorphosis complete. Again, as in the myths of Earth, after three days the vampire emerges, undead, to spread its contamination abroad.

"Anyway, I've strayed from the point. I was trying to explain what a Wamphyri warrior creature is. Well, picture one of their flying beasts magnified in bulk by a factor of ten. Imagine such a creature with a dozen armoured necks and heads, all equipped with mouths full of unbelieveable teeth—teeth like rows of scythes! Imagine these *things* having a like number of arms or tentacles, all terminating in murderous claws and pincers or fitted with huge versions of the Wamphyri battle-gauntlets. Get all of that formed in your mind's eye, and you are looking at the warrior creature. They are vampires, but utterly mindless, with one and *only* one loyalty—to whichever Lord created them.

"Ah!—but I see the question in your eyes, Jazz. You're thinking: whichever Lord created them from what? But haven't I told you that they are masters of metamorphosis? Their creatures—*all* of their creatures, which take the place of machines in their society—*were once men!*

"Don't ask me the hows of it; I don't have all the answers, and I don't think I could bear to know them. What I do know I'll pass on to you, as time allows. But right now you've asked me what it was like for me when I first came here, and I'm telling you that the first things I saw—two of them—were Wamphyri warrior creatures. I saw them first, before anything else, in the same way you would notice a pair of cockroaches among ants. One: because ants are tolerable, while cockroaches are not. And two: because cockroaches are that much bigger, and so much more ugly!

"Two of them, out there on that rock-strewn plain under the moon and stars. And I couldn't believe their size! That they were fighting things was obvious: take a look at a picture of Tyrannosaurus Rex in a book of prehistoric animals and you don't need to be told he was a warrior. These creatures were like that: with their weaponry, armour-plated, in all their utter hideousness, they couldn't be anything else. It was only when I saw that they were quiescent, controlled, that I dared to take my eyes off them. Then, having observed the 'cockroaches,' as it were, I looked at the 'ants.' Seen in contrast, beside the warrior creatures and flying beasts, that's what the Wamphyri looked like: ants. But they were the masters, and the monstrous giants their obedient slaves.

"Try to picture it:

"Out on the boulder plain, these two mountains of

armour-clad flesh. Closer, a half-dozen flyers, all craning their necks and swaying their heads to and fro. And
closer still, a few paces away from the shining dome of
the Gate, the Wamphyri themselves come here to punish one of their own, a transgressor against the Lady
Karen's laws. I saw them, stared at them in a mixture
of awe and morbid fascination, and they stared back at
me. For they were here to thrust someone *into* the Gate,
and the last thing they'd expected was that some other
should come *out* of it!

"There was Karen herself, and four subordinates—
'lieutenants' if you like—and one other who was ugly
as sin and draped in chains of gold. Now gold is a soft
metal, as you know, Jazz, and easily broken. But not
when its links are thick as your fingers! There was more
gold in those chains than I've ever seen in my life in any
one place, in one mass, and yet this Corlis who was
decked in them wore them like tinsel! Corlis, that was
his name; he was huge, a brute, and stark naked except
for the gold. No gauntlet on this one's hand, for he was
in shame. But though he stood there naked, unweaponed,
still his red eyes burned furiously and unrepentant!

"The four who surrounded him were big men, too,
but smaller by a head than their prisoner; they carried
long sheaths of leather strapped to their backs, and in
their hands slender swords. The sword, as I'd learn
later, is a shameful weapon; only their evil gauntlets are
considered honorable and fitting tools for hand-to-hand
combat. Also, *these* swords were tipped in silver. And
all four of them were pointed at Corlis, who stood there
panting, his head lifted high, engorged with rage.

"Behind their prisoner, and shielded from him by the
four who guarded him, stood the Lady Karen trans-
fixed. Sighting me, her red mouth had fallen open.
Now, I'll tell you something, Jazz—something which
no woman should ever admit, which I hadn't admitted,
not even to myself, until that moment. Women are
envious creatures. And the good-looking ones more so

than others. But *now* I admit it because I know it's true. Except I didn't know how true until I saw this Karen.

"Her hair was copper, burnished, almost ablaze; it reflected the white light of the dome like a halo over her head, bounced like fine spun gold on her shoulders, competed with the polished bangles she wore on her arms. Gold rings on a slender golden chain around her neck supported the sheath of soft white leather which she wore like a glove, and on her feet sandals of pale leather stitched in gold. Over her shoulders a long cloak of black fur, skilfully shorn from the wings of great bats, shimmering with a weave of fine golden stitches, and about her waist a wide black leather belt, buckled with her crest—a snarling wolf's head—and supporting, on one rounded hip, her gauntlet.

"A woman, an incredibly beautiful woman; or she would have been, if not for her scarlet eyes. Who or whatever these people were, she was one of them; indeed she was the mistress of this group, their Lady. And before too long I'd know what they called themselves—Wamphyri!

"She came forward, around the group standing there, and approached me where I crouched by the crater wall, with the half-space of the Gate at my back. Close-up she was even more beautiful; her body had the sinuous motion of a Gypsy dancer, and yet seemed so unaffected as to be innocent! Her face, heart-shaped, with a lock of fiery hair coiled on her brow, could have been angelic—but her red eyes made it the face of a demon. Her mouth was full, curved in a perfect bow; the colour of her lips, like blood, was accentuated by her pale, slightly hollow cheeks. Only her nose marred looks which were otherwise entirely other-worldly: it was a fraction tilted, stubby, with nostrils just a little too round and dark. And perhaps her ears, half-hidden in her hair, which showed whorls like pale, exotic conches. But golden rings dangled from their lobes, and all in all, and for all her weirdness and contrasting colours, still there was the look of the Gypsy about her. I could hear the jingle of her movements, even when there was none to hear . . .

" 'Hell-lander,' she said, in a tongue I wouldn't have known without my talent to rely on. Languages are easy when you're a telepath. But what I couldn't recognize in her spoken words, I read in her mind—and she knew it at once! Her pale hand, crimson-nailed, flickered toward me, pointed, accused: 'Thought-stealer!'

"Then she narrowed those blood-hued eyes of hers, and when next she spoke her tone was thoughtful. 'A woman, from the hell-lands. I have heard of men, wizards, coming through the portal, but never a woman. Perhaps it is an omen. I could make good use of a thought-stealer.' She nodded, came to a sudden decision. 'Give yourself up to me, and all your secrets, and I'll protect you,' she said. 'Refuse me, and . . . go your own way, *without* my protection.' But behind her as she spoke I could see the leers and the lusting stamped clearly on the faces of her henchmen. I thought quickly—for my life! If I didn't go with her, wherever, then where could I go? Was there anywhere to go? Or . . . if I didn't go with her, then where would I be taken?

" 'I'm Zekintha,' I told her. 'And I accept your protection.'

" 'Then you may call me the Lady Karen,' she tossed her head, setting her hair ablaze where it bounced. 'Now stand aside a little way. We've business here.' And to her aides: 'Bring the dog Corlis forward!'

"Karen's men shoved their prisoner to the fore; even chained, he might have turned on them, but their silver-tipped weapons pressed him close. They took off his chains, and as the last of these was being removed—

"It was the moment he'd been waiting for!

"Knotting that last length of chain about one great fist, Corlis whirled, flailed, sent his warders dancing back. Before they could gather their thoughts he'd released the heavy chain, sent it crashing into them. In another moment he laughed—a mad, reckless laugh— and leaped for the Lady Karen to snatch her up. 'If I'm to be a victim of the portal, Karen, then so are you!' he cried.

"So, in the same way you brought Karl Vyotsky here, Jazz, Corlis had determined to take the Lady Karen *out* of here.

"Now, clutching Karen to him, Corlis had almost reached the shallow crater wall. Here men were after him like hounds, but he had the advantage. It seemed that my one hope in this strange world was about to be removed from it. But Corlis hadn't reckoned with me. As he dodged Karen's retainers and the mouths of magmass holes, so he came close to where I crouched. Karen was kicking and biting him, but it made little difference. She was Wamphyri, but she was a woman, too. Finally, with the Lady tucked under one arm, Corlis saw his chance and bounded straight for natural steps of stone where they climbed the crater wall. He was now within three or four short paces of the Gate. But as he lumbered past me, so I reached out my leg, and braced it . . . it was a simple as that.

"He tripped; Karen went flying free, almost fell into one of the gaping magmass wormholes. Corlis got up on one knee, glaring his hatred and frustration at me. I was almost within reach of him. His arms reached for me and I backed away—but, *God,* Jazz, those hellish arms kept reaching! They stretched like rubber, straining after me, and I could hear the tearing of muscles and ligaments! His face—God, his *face*—it opened like a hinged steel trap, with rows of needle teeth that were visibly growing and curving out of his jaws! I don't know what he was becoming—something utterly invincible, I'm sure—but I wasn't about to give in to him. Not to that.

"My SMG was in my hands, had been there all the time. But I'm not a soldier, Jazz, and I had never killed. Against *this*, however, I had no other choice. I cocked the gun, (don't ask me where I found the strength, for my muscles were jelly) and squeezed the trigger.

"Well, as you know, bullets don't kill them—but they do make a mess of them. The stream of fire I turned on Corlis was almost a solid wall of lead. It turned his trunk scarlet, punched holes in his chest and hideous face, blew him back away from me and sent him sprawling, flopping like a wet rag. And admidst the chattering madness of my weapon, everything else seemed frozen. In the relative quiet of Starside, that gunfire must have sounded like the laughter of hell! And only when the magazine was empty did the noise abate, allowing its echoes to come thundering back from the hills.

"Stunning, the effect—but then the tableau unfroze. Urged on by Karen where she came to her feet, her men leaped toward Corlis. He sat up!—I couldn't believe it, but he did. Already the holes were healing in his body, his bloody face sealing itself. He saw them bearing down on him with their silver-tipped swords and looked wildly all about. There!—a magmass hole; he stood up, all lopsided, crouched, sprang, went sprawling towards its dark mouth. In mid-air one of Karen's retainers caught him; a sword flashed silver; Corlis's head sprang free! His trunk crashed forward, spurting blood from its severed neck. Corlis's dive took his twitching body down the magmass wormhole and out of sight. But his head lay grimacing, gnashing its evil teeth, where it had fallen.

"Karen gave a cry of disgust, stepped forward and kicked the vomiting thing into another hole. Whatever Corlis had done, it must have been very bad. Scarlet stains were all that remained of him . . .

"Karen looked at me, looked at the smoking gun in my hands. Her red eyes were wide now, making her face seem paler still. As well as the gun, she was aware of the rest of my kit; she couldn't keep her gaze from straying to my packs, the nozzle of the flamethrower hooked to my belt, the sigil on the left-hand breast pocket of my combat suit. The latter finally impressed itself upon her and she stepped closer, peering at the crest. It was a hammer and sickle, of course, crossed with the bayonet of an infantry unit. Some small soldier had sacrificed his suit for me.

"But it signified much more than that to the Lady. She pointed, stretched herself tall—perhaps in outrage— and spat words in my face. They came much too fast to be anything but a gabble; I read them in her mind:

" 'Is that your banner? The curved knife, the hammer and the stake? *Do you mock me?*'

" 'I mock no one,' I answered. 'This badge is merely—'

" 'Be quiet!' she added: 'Also beware, for if your weapon so much as snaps at me, then I'll feed you as a tidbit to my warrior creatures!'

"My gun was empty and I didn't dare try to reload. In a moment of inspiration I held it out, offering it to Karen; she at once shrank a little back from it. Then she scowled, knocked the gun aside, reached out and hooked her scarlet fingernails into the stitching of my pocket. She tore the offending blazon from me and tossed it away. 'There!' she said, and: 'Do you denounce these signs?'

" 'I do,' " I answered.

"She nodded, became calm. 'Very well,' she said, —'but be thankful I'm in your debt. You can tell me why you wore that—that *insult*—later.' And she turned from me and made a motion to her men, who hurried down onto the plain and mounted-up on their flyers.

"Karen made to move after them but I stood still, uncertain of what I should do. She saw my indecision, said: 'Come, they're waiting for us.'

"She took me to one of the nodding, lolling creatures. It had been Corlis's, I thought, for upon its back, where the neck stuck out, a cage of metal was bound in position. 'Climb up and get in,' Karen told me, but I couldn't. I backed away, shook my head. My fear seemed to give her a lot more confidence—not that I thought she needed any!

"She laughed: 'Then ride with me.'

"We went to the next unoccupied beast. Beneath its harness it wore a purple blanket huge as a carpet; the harness itself was of black leather with golden trappings, and the saddle at the base of the flyer's neck was huge, soft and sumptuous. The thing lowered its neck and Karen grasped nodules and harness, drew herself easily aloft and into the saddle. I could scarcely bring myself to touch that alien flesh. She reached down, grasped my fevered hand in her own cool one, and with her help I mounted-up behind her.

" 'If you get dizzy, cling to me,' she said. And then we flew to her aerie. I can't say more than that about the flight for my eyes were closed most of the way. And I did cling to her, for there was nothing else to cling to.

"The aerie was a horrible place. It . . . Jazz?" Zek leaned across and looked at him. In his mouth, the cork tip of a cigarette stuck straight up in the air. Even as she smiled her soft, slow smile, a puff of wind blew half an inch of cold ash loose onto his chest, which began to rise and fall in a steady rhythm. And he had said he wouldn't be able to sleep! Well, it was better that he get his rest. Better that she get some, too.

But she wondered how much of what she'd said had gone in.

As it happened, most of it had. And Jazz's opinion of her hadn't changed. She was a hell of a woman . . .

The next fifteen miles weren't so easy and Jazz began to understand what Zek had meant by "backbreaking." After what he'd been through prior to and since leaving Perchorsk (and his own world) far behind, something a little less than three hours of sleep hadn't seemed a great deal. Not in the way of preparation for this, anyway. The trail had been rough, winding up into higher foothills where tumbled scree made the going a veritable obstacle course; it had soon started to rain, a deluge which eventually petered out just as Lardis called for the second break. Here there were dry, shallow caves under broken ledges of rock, into which most of the Travellers dispersed themselves. Jazz and Zek likewise, peering out from their cramped refuge while the sky cleared and the low, unshakable sun began to aim its wan but still warming rays into their faces again.

From this vantage point, as the air cleared and the sun sucked up and steamed away a swirling ground mist, Jazz was able to see why Lardis had chosen such a difficult route. Down below a forest stretched deep and wide, away out onto the Sunside plain. Crisscrossed with rivers tumbling from the mountains, the deep, dark green of the woods told of an almost impenetrable rankness. Up here the rivers were still streams, easily forded, but down below they tumbled through gulleys, joined up, finally broadened into wide watercourses winding through the forest. Good for hunting and fishing, certainly, but no good at all for trekking. The choice had been as easy as that: a difficult route or an impossible one. And of course the foothills did command a view of all the land around, a factor much to Lardis's liking.

"This time," Jazz told Zek, "I believe I'll sleep."

"You did last time," she reminded him. "Are you beginning to feel the strain?"

"Beginning to feel it?" He managed a grin. "I'm looking for a muscle that doesn't ache! And yet the Travellers have these damned cumbersome travois to lug around, and I don't hear them complaining. I suppose it's like you said: I'll get used to it. But I'd hate to think what it would be like for anyone who was unfit, or maybe an older person, stranded here."

"I wasn't so fit," she reflected. "But I've had more time to get myself broken in. I suppose in a way I was lucky that the Lady Karen got me first. And then that she *was* . . . well, a 'Lady', or as much of a one as her condition would allow her to be.''

''Her condition?''

''She has Dramal Doombody's egg,'' Zek nodded. ''The Wamphyri Lord Dramal was doomed from the day he took a leper—which was how he came to be named that way. I'll explain:

''Leprosy is also part of the Travellers' lot. They are prone to it. Passed on, inherited or simply contracted from another leper—don't ask me. I don't know anything about the disease. But when its symptoms start to show in a Traveller, then he's kicked out. It happens now and then: his tribe simply abandons him. Or her. Dramal, in his youth five hundred years ago, took a female leper. She had the disease but it hadn't started to show yet. The vampire Lord found her comely; he cohabited with her in his aerie; too late he discovered her curse.''

Jazz was puzzled yet again. ''You mean she passed it on to him? But I'm amazed that *any* of these terrible creatures have survived at all! Quite apart from the fact that they continually war with each other, they drink the blood of Travellers, have sex with Traveller women, generally leave themselves wide open to all sorts of diseases.''

''And yet,'' Zek answered, ''in their own way they're scrupulous. The true Wamphyri Lord or Lady is, anyway.''

''Scrupulous?'' Jazz was taken aback. ''Are you serious?''

She looked at him, stared unblinking into his eyes. ''Cockroaches are also scrupulous, in their way. But all in all, the Wamphyri are . . . choosy, yes. Their retainers, their henchmen—generally Travellers who've been changed, vampirized but not given an egg, like those two you saw with Shaithis—they're not so fussy. But as for 'leaving themselves wide open to disease': that might be true if they were wholly human. But as you've seen, they're not. Once a man is vampirized his body becomes invulnerable to disease. That's why they live so long. Even the aging process is defeated.''

''But not invulnerable to leprosy? Is that what you're saying?''

''Apparently. Anyway, this woman of Dramal's died in the tower where he locked her. Then the disease came out in him. Of course, his vampire flesh fought it. When limbs withered down they were regenerated, and when flesh wasted away it was replenished. But Dramal couldn't win. The vampire in him was itself infected. As the disease got a hold, all of Dramal's energies went into combatting it, holding it at bay. His aerie was shunned by the Wamphyri, and even in times of truce he had no visitors. He held his own people in thrall, of course, but as he weakened even they began to whisper and plot against him. They were afraid of catching the disease.

''Now all of this took time, almost five hundred years of gradual deterioration, but just a few years ago Dramal began to fear that the end was in sight, that one of the Great Undead was about to die—or that he would soon become so weak that his retainers would rise up against him, stake and behead him, and burn his remains to ashes. Then they would flee the aerie, which was now generally considered a pesthole. He determined that before they could do that he must deposit his egg—but not with one of the treacherous gang who now surrounded him. With the egg would go his power, of course, and the aerie would pass into the hands of his successor. So he took Karen Sisclu from an eastern Traveller tribe and made her one of the Wamphyri, and before he died transferred all of his power to her. In better times he would most certainly have passed on his egg through the sex act, but he no longer had the strength for that. He had expended all in teaching Karen the ways of the Wamphyri, the secrets of the aerie, and in passing on his sigils and the loyalty of his various beasts. And so he merely kissed her; that was sufficient; during that monstrous kiss his egg passed into her.''

Jazz couldn't suppress a small shiver. He grimaced and said: ''God, what a world this is! But tell me: by 'her condition' do you mean the fact that she's now Wamphyri, or is it worse than that? I mean, does she have Dramal's leprosy, too?''

''No, not that,'' Zek answered, ''but it's possible she's in an even worse fix, if you can imagine that. You see, Wamphyri legends have it that the first true Mother was a human female whose vampire produced more than the normal single egg. Indeed, the eggs were produced almost endlessly, until the vampire itself and its female host were drained—until there was nothing left of them! They gave birth to vampires until the effort withered them to lifeless husks. And this was how Dramal had determined to repay the others of the Wamphyri for their scorn, their naming him Doombody and for his isolation: but mainly for the sheer evil of it. He would cause to be brought into this world a hundred vampire eggs, all of which would find hosts in the denizens of his aerie. Why, even the flying beasts and warrior creatures would *be* Wamphyri! Which would mean the debasement of the entire hag-ridden race! Do you understand?''

Jazz nodded, but a little uncertainly. ''I think so. He hoped that Karen would become a Mother, that her vampire would produce the same endlesss stream of eggs. But how could he be sure?''

''Maybe he couldn't,'' she shrugged. ''Maybe he merely hoped it would be so—but he told Karen it *would* be. And she, poor, damned, doomed creature that she is, she believes it. And the Wamphyri do have strange powers. Perhaps in some way he has engineered it. Anyway, he's gone now into corruption and so she waits, and the vampire in her slowly matures. Except . . . some mature more quickly than others. In some it is a matter of days, in others many years. If her vampire *is* a Mother, then she'll suffer the same fate as that first Mother of legend . . . ."

Zek paused, and on impulse reached across and touched Jazz's face. Before she could withdraw her hand, he kissed her fingers. This, too, was on impulse. She smiled at him and shook her head.

"I know what you're thinking," she said. "And I certainly don't have to read your mind. It's a grasshopper mind anyway; from such a very dire subject to—dalliance?—in one move." Then she grew serious again. "But you're right, Jazz, this is a very terrible world. And we're not out of it yet by a long shot. We should both save our strength."

"I've noticed," he told her, "that you've been sticking pretty close to me. Maybe it's as well I can't read *your* mind."

She laughed. "There are a lot of unattached male Travellers, Jazz," she said. "Now to them, and to Lardis too, it will seem I've made up my mind—whether I have or not. This way I won't have to keep fending them off. But don't make me keep fending you off, too, for I'm not sure how well I'd succeed."

He gave a mock sigh, grunted, "Promises, promises!" Then he grinned. "OK, you win. And anyway, I ache enough already."

At the end of the next leg of their journey, the sun appeared to have moved some degrees eastward, at the same time sinking appreciably lower in the sky; or maybe it was just that the Travellers had come down out of the foothills, so lowering their horizon. Whichever, Jazz noticed a definite urgency—a heightened awareness—in Lardis and his people; the pass through the mountains was still only a few miles to the east, and the sun's descent seemed that much more obvious. Yes, and Shaithis of the Wamphyri had a score to settle, so the sooner the tribe reached its cavern sanctuary the better.

Following a fairly well-defined trail down out of the foothills, the going had been quick and surprisingly easy. A little less than twenty miles had been covered in the time allowed for only half of that, and Lardis was well pleased. He called camp on the westward bank of a river at the edge of the great forested region, told his people they could have four hours of rest. He sent out hunters, too, into the thigh-length savanna grass after whichever birds and animals lived there. Then he found himself a spot on the riverbank and cast a line there, and sat in the long twilight with his back to the bank fishing and making his plans.

Meanwhile his men had found signs left by runners, (free- and far-ranging members of the tribe who acted as Lardis's intelligence agents) which corroborated previously arranged liaison points for both the next Traveller group, only five miles ahead, and the primary encampment some twenty to twenty-five miles beyond that. As Lardis got his hook into a large catfish and hauled it ashore, he was well satisfied. Things seemed to be working out exactly to schedule.

As for Jazz and Zek: while she bathed in the river he worked on her SMG, clearing the blockage and oiling the parts, getting the weapon back into serviceable order. In the event of another confrontation, two guns would be better than one. Also, Jazz had called for the rest of his equipment to be brought to him; he wanted at least one member of this Gypsy band he travelled with, preferably Lardis himself, to understand the workings of various items—specifically the flamethrower. When his gear arrived, Jazz found to his surprise that no one seemed to have tampered with his packs since he'd re-packed them. And maybe that was just as well. In the bottom of one pack there was a small nest of six deadly Russian fragmentation grenades. About the same size as hen eggs, they reminded Jazz of foil-covered chocolate Easter eggs in the compartmented, sawdust-packed tray of their wooden box. If anyone had tampered with *those* . . . Jazz supposed he'd have heard about it long before now.

Lardis, on his way to the campfire with the huge catfish jerking spasmodically where it lay across his shoulder, nodded to Zek and Jazz on the riverbank and called out: "Let me just rid myself of this, then I'll be back to see these tricks of yours."

They watched his burly figure out of sight over the rim of the bank, then turned back to what they were doing. While Zek finished drying her hair, Jazz tested her gun one last time; he drew back its cocking piece sharply and was rewarded by the clean, clear, very familiar ch-*ching* of metal parts engaging. Then he squeezed the trigger and the breach-block flew forward, slapped firmly home. Jazz nodded his satisfaction, put the gun on safe and slotted a full magazine into its housing. He handed the weapon to Zek and said: "There, and now you're a power in the world again. I still have six full mags and ammo to refill four of them. That's five apiece. Hardly an armory, but a sight better than nothing."

He picked up a grenade and weighed it in his hand. It had a twist-action, ring-pull pin. Packed with high explosive, on detonating the shell would break down into two hundred curved metal splinters, each one scything outwards from the blast at the speed of a bullet. Devastating! Even the most powerful vampire Lord wouldn't stand a chance against one of these. At the very least he'd be maimed, and at best decapitated. Jazz would have used them back in the pass that time, except he hadn't been sure what Arlek's lot had done with the grenades, and anyway his SMG had been more immediate.

Zek dragged his thoughts back to the here and now with: "Do you want me to tell you about the Lady Karen's aerie?"

Jazz stood up, said: "Yes, while I bathe. I'm starting to smell like you did the first time we met! Shouldn't look if I were you—it's gruesome in here." He stripped down to his shorts, took a dive into the water. Then he swam back close to the bank and started washing himself. "OK," he said, "let's hear about these vampire castles. I've a feeling it won't be pleasant, but whatever you consider to be worth the telling . . ."

And so she continued with her story . . .

Chapter Sixteen
Karen's Aerie—Harry at Perchorsk

"FIRST OF ALL, LET ME EXPLAIN THAT NO HUMAN BEING could ever adequately describe an aerie of the Wamphyri. I don't think our language, or any language of the old world, has the right words for it. Or if there are such words, then the description would become so repetitious—so laced with grisly-sounding adjectives—that the entire exercise would soon become a bore.

"That's why I'll tell it as I saw it, like describing a picture or series of pictures, without putting too much emphasis on the grotesque anomalies and abnormalities of the . . . but there!—do you see what I mean?

"The Lady Karen's aerie had belonged to Dramal Doombody, and so it has to be fairly representative of all the aeries, or castles if you wish, where they sit atop those fantastic stacks. So let's begin with the stacks themselves:

"As far as I was able to tell they're natural, weathered out from the mountains in their slow retreat. Why the stacks should remain while the earth around them crumbled . . . I'm no geologist. Maybe they were once the cores of a series of volcanoes, choked with a basalt magma which was tougher than the surrounding cones. The craters have long gone but these titan plugs remain. That's theory, of course, and anyway it doesn't matter.

The stacks are real, and since time immemorial the Wamphyri have built their aeries on them.

"But just looking at a stack from a distance, you don't see the entire picture. By that I mean that you don't see the actual stack. It's there, inside the shell, but what you see *is* that shell, which through the ages the Wamphyri have built around the inner core. So . . . the next question has to be: what is this artificial 'skin' made of?

"Well, I think the best way to answer that would be to liken a stack to coral on a submarine shelf. The stone is there, and the living coral forms a skin on it, and the skin dies and itself becomes stone. So on the submarine shelf the 'skin' is dead coral. And on the stacks . . . it's dead flesh.

"When an aerie requires repairs or extensions, the Wamphyri breed cartilage creatures whose sole function is to bridge a gap, form a section of wall, roof over a new hall or causeway. Which is to say, *their living bodies* form the building or repair materials. Except I said 'breed' and that's the wrong word. They don't really breed anything, they merely *change* what already is. They take out of storage a troglodyte, perhaps, or punish a vampirized henchman who has been remiss in some way, or maybe steal a Traveller or two from Sunside. All human or sub-human flesh is the same to the Wamphyri. They can take it, change it, mould it to their individual needs. These cartilage things lock themselves in position wherever they're required, die and eventually fossilize there. Being of vampire origin—having been vampirized—they take a long time to die; maybe they don't die as we understand it, but simply age and become . . . fixed.

"So what I'm saying is this: when you walk through an aerie, as often as not you're surrounded by the fused, polished bones and the hard, leathery hides of what were once men. And if you look closely enough—which is something you very quickly learn *not* to do—

then you start to recognize the shapes of altered rib-cages, thigh bones, spinal columns and even . . . but I think you get the picture.

"The Wamphyri can stand extremes of cold. That's not to say they prefer it, simply that they seem inured. Except when under siege, they do heat their stacks with a complicated sort of central heating. Gasses are burned in the base of the stack and the hot air is channelled through pipes—great, hollow bones, usually—to every level. Other pipes carry the gas itself, which may then be burned as required. There are two sources for these gasses.

"Each aerie has its refuse pit. 'Refuse' to a Wamphyri Lord can be anything from bodily wastes to wasted bodies. You know what vampires feed on. Well, they're not obliged to (indeed they can go without blood, without sustenance generally, indefinitely) and they do vary their diets with vegetable fibers, various oils, even fruits which are gathered during sundown on Sunside. They have vast storehouses of foods such as these, not to mention larders of suspended troglodytes and Travellers. In this instance, let's consider their 'usual' fare.

"If a person is eaten and it is not desired that he or she becomes a vampire, then the remains of the meal go to the refuse pit along with all other garbage. Consider that a stack or aerie may house a thousand or more—creatures—and you get something or an idea of the *contents* of a refuse pit. Gasses are of course generated in large volumes. These are the gasses which are usually burned close to their source, in the bowels of the stack. Wamphyri conduits are leaky systems at best, and if gasses such as these are allowed to escape . . . the atmosphere in the rest of the aerie would be quite intolerable.

"Also to be found in the lower levels are the stables of the gas-beasts. These are what their name describes them to be: living gas bladders, as mindless as the cartilage creatures. Their single function is the production of gas. They are fed on coarse grasses and a little grain; obviously, the gas these beasts produce is close to methane; I don't think I need to explain further than that . . .

."Water:

"Now, I said that in their way the Wamphyri are scrupulous. The Lady Karen bathed frequently, as often as I myself. I watched her bathing and it was as if she tried to scrub the taint out of herself, which of course she never could. But she didn't stop trying. Oh, she talked hard to her retainers, but what was she inside but a poor frightened girl? At least, she had been.

"Anyway, you'll appreciate that water does not rise as readily as gas. In our world it has to be pumped uphill, or 'rammed' under pressure, or else it arrives by aquaduct from a source higher still. The aeries have their catchment areas, inward-sloping skins on all levels, channelling rain water into great barrels with overflow systems into other barrels. In the event of a great downpour, wells at the foot of the stacks are filled to brimming. When all reservoirs are filled, then the skins are allowed to hang loose like flags. In fact they're woven with the various Wamphyri sigils and so act as their banners as well. But the rains are infrequent and if an aerie were under siege this system alone would be unreliable. That's why there's a back-up.

"You'll understand the meaning of 'capillary attraction'? The way sap rises through a stem, or water between sheets of glass? The Wamphyri use capillary attraction to lift water from their wells to the top of the aeries. The tubes through which the water passes are quite literally capillaries—those same narrow tubes which connect veins and arteries. *Real* capillaries, Jazz, whose owners lie in placid heaps of pseudolife in secret rooms high in the aeries. Secret because the Wamphyri will not tolerate their creatures except in their proper places. They know the difference between acceptable and unacceptable, you see. And the proper place for the thing whose veins hang down inside pipes through half a mile or more of stack is, obviously, at the top of such a stack. And so, because they're unseemly, the Wamphyri hide them away.

"I stumbled across just such a room and its inhabitants in the Lady Karen's aerie. That's all I can remember of it: that I found it, and then that someone found me and took me out of there. I had fainted. My mind hasn't retained anything of the episode except the fact that it happened. And this was only retained—as a warning, I suppose—in case I should forget totally and wander back that way again.

"Also to be found in the lower regions: the pens of the warriors. The warrior creatures are kept, like lions in a Roman amphitheatre, close to starvation. Or they would be except for one thing: like the Wamphyri, they don't need to eat. When they do eat, their food is invariably meat, preferably living. They are pure carnivores, created to tear, maim, kill—and devour. Their reward in battle is to be allowed to glut themselves. They fly into battle, launching themselves from the stacks and squirting through the sky like giant squids; but if they're victorious, they soon become far too bulky to fly back again to their aerie and so return across the boulder plains as best they can. Apart from battle proper, the Wamphyri also use them during sundown for the rounding up of Travellers. Then, too, if they are successful, they're allowed the occasional tidbit.

"But enough about them. Just pray God, if you're a believer, that you never see one. And especially that you never see one in battle . . .

"Flying beasts are stationed in various levels. You've seen *them* and know what they look like. They aren't especially dangerous, not on their own. Grounded they're clumsy, stupid; aloft they are graceful in their own alien sort of way. For control they are linked closely with their masters—by telepathy. It has to be that way when

310

the Wamphyri ride them to battle. They are the sky-floating command-posts of their masters.

"One other thing about the Wamphyri in battle: they have their own codes of combat, their own warped 'values' and ideas about valour, chivalry and such! Can you imagine that? But each one of them changes these values to suit himself, to his own advantage. If ever it gets down to hand-to-hand combat, one against one, the single weapon deemed allowable by high-ranking aerie masters—the Lords and their aides or lieutenants—is the war-gauntlet. Somewhere in the east, in a small Gypsy settlement, those hideous weapons are made to order for the Wamphyri. All metal things are made for them; they have no understanding of metalworking, or more correctly, they have a general dislike for metals. Silver is a poison, iron despised, only gold is relatively acceptable.

"So, I've covered a few points, helped to give you something of a picture of Wamphyri life and how their aeries operate. It's all too complicated for me to be more specific than that. Now, if you still want to hear it, I'll go on and tell you about my own experiences in the Lady Karen's aerie . . ."

Jazz had finished bathing and now climbed out of the river. He felt a lot easier, relaxed; the water had washed away most of his coiled-spring tension. He squeegeed the water from his body with the hard edges of his hands, shivered a little in the oh-so-gradually fading rays of the sun where it sat over the horizon's edge. As he began to dress and before Zek could continue her story, they spotted Lardis returning across the rim of the riverbank.

Jazz had dissembled most of his combat-suit harness, leaving only the belt and upper cross-straps with their various attachments. As Lardis arrived and cast a speculative eye over the several items of gear where they lay spread out, so Zek gave Jazz a helping hand to get

311

himself kitted-up again. He preferred to sleep fully-rigged, or at the very least in "skeleton order," so that he could wake up ready for any eventuality.

Finally, taking out a cigarette and lighting it, Jazz turned to the Gypsy leader—in time to see him twist and yank the pin from a fragmentation grenade!

Jazz drew air in a gasp, threw Zek aside and down, leaped toward Lardis. The other had not yet seen the consternation on Jazz's face. He frowned at the grenade in his left hand and the pin in his right. Jazz snatched the grenade away from him. He'd been counting in his head: *one, two, three*—

He hurled the grenade out over the river. *Four, five*—

It made a small splash—and immediately made a much larger one!

The detonation thundered, but most of the razor-sharp shrapnel was lost in the river. Some fragments whistled where they slashed the air overhead; a fountain of water rose up, sprayed out, fell back; the echoes of the detonation came back from the foothills and the water of the river in wavelets against the bank. Dozens of stunned or dead fish were already floating to the surface.

Lardis closed his mouth, looked at the firing-pin in his hand—hurled it violently away. "Eh?" he said then. "What—?"

Jazz scowled at him, said: "Pretty effective fishing!"

His sarcasm was lost on Lardis. "Eh? Oh, yes, I suppose it is!" The squat, bemused man turned away, went to climb the riverbank and calm his people where they came running. "*Indeed* it is!" he finally, emphatically agreed. "But I think I prefer to do it my way." He glanced at Jazz's weaponry laid out on the river-bank. "Er, show me these interesting things of yours some other time. Right now I've much to do."

Jazz and Zek watched him walk away . . .

* * *

312

As Jazz packed his kit again and settled down comfortably where he intended to sleep, Zek continued her story:

"I had my own room in Karen's aerie. She and I shared the topmost level—literally acres of room, all of them enormous—where we were the only human creatures. Remember, the Wamphyri *are* human; it's the vampire in each one of them which makes him alien, and Karen's vampire had yet to gain total ascendancy. So we were the only *people* up there, but there was a warrior. It was a small one of its sort, which is to say it was about as big as an armoured personnel carrier and just as deadly! It guarded the stairwell to the next lower level. That was how well Karen trusted her aides.

"Then there were the water-drawing creatures, which I've already mentioned. And that was all, nothing and no one else.

"Every so often (I calculated at the time that it was about every twenty-four hours), Karen would hold audience. She'd call her lieutenants up from below, all seven of them, none of them having an egg, and apportion the aerie's duties or check on orders already issued. Then they'd make their reports, warn of any deviations in the balance which the aerie maintained, detail their recommendations, and so forth. It was like a military 'O'-group, in a way, with Karen as the C-in-C. And she carried it off very well. These were the only occasions when I saw Karen's men without their gauntlets. Her warrior had orders—direct from her mind—to savage anyone who attempted to enter her level wearing a gauntlet.

"But don't be misled by anything I've said about her. Don't in any way make the error of believing she was vulnerable. For she wasn't; not physically, anyway. She was Wamphyri!—the real thing—and her lieutenants knew it. She looked, and for the moment perhaps still thought like a young woman, yes, but that was only the shell.

"Within her she had a vampire and its strengths were

313

hers, growing stronger every day. If she appeared weak it was simply that she didn't want her underlings to test her, didn't want to have to punish them as she'd been obliged to punish Corlis, for that might mean calling again upon the monster within her for its assistance. And she was dedicated to her stance, which was to hold it at bay. Let it gain true ascendancy just once . . . she believed it would dominate her always. And eventually it will, of course, for that is the nature of the vampire. Karen *is* doomed to change, to metamorphosis, to the gradual deterioration of what she was into what she must become . . .

"I remember that toward the end of my captivity there in her aerie, I asked her what Corlis could have done that she'd wished to banish him to the hell-lands. Perhaps because I was the only one she could talk to without worrying about their motives, she told me all about it.

"Corlis had been the biggest of Karen's men, both in size and in the aerie's pecking-order. He was also surly, a trouble-maker, the Wamphyri equivalent of a male chauvinist whatever—in spades! Even as a Traveller he'd been a brute, but that had been forty years ago. Then he had been taken in a raid; since then he'd served Dramal Doombody—if 'served' is the right word for it. God knows why Dramal suffered him, but the ways of the Wamphyri are never easy to figure out. Maybe at one time Dramal intended that Corlis should have his egg. But that's pure guesswork, of course.

"Let me explain Corlis like this: he wasn't true Wamphyri, but if ever a man should have been then he was that man. And he knew it.

"Most men would shrink from the idea, but not Corlis. He *wanted* an egg—and the power it would bring. He wanted to be master of the aerie, a Wamphyri Lord. He would like nothing better than to ride to war on the back of a flying beast, and command his warriors in their terrifying aerial battles. But while he and the others called themselves Wamphyri, they knew that in fact they were merely the undead servants of their true vampire mistress. And that was the great thorn in Corlis's side.

"He had asked the Lady Karen that she make him the aerie's warlord. To which she'd replied that she had no need of a warlord, for there was no war. He had demanded rank and position above his fellows, only to be told he had no right to such honours. There was room for only one master (or mistress) in an aerie, and in this aerie that one was the Lady Karen herself. Then Corlis had offered himself as Karen's consort and protector—at which she'd lost her temper and told him she'd rather sleep with a warrior! As for his protection: he should worry about protecting himself, especially if he intended to continue his current campaign of mischief and annoyance.

"But Corlis wasn't to be put off lightly. He'd argued heatedly that the other Wamphyri Lords were plotting for war, that now that Dramal was dead the aerie was vulnerable, and that Karen, a mere woman, could never hope to achieve any sort of effective command of her army in battle. She should choose her champion now, without delay, and the champion she chose had better be him!

"At that Karen ordered him out of her presence, Corlis and the other six with him. Four of them had made to obey her, but the others . . .

"They had sided with Corlis. And warning off the four who remained half-loyal to her, Corlis and his two (for surely he'd suborned them) had surrounded her where she sat upon her throne of office, which had once been Dramal Doombody's 'bone-throne', made of the curved, fossilized jaw of a vast cartilage creature. From under his jacket, one of these traitors produced a stake of wood, forbidden in every aerie since time immemorial, and sprang at her. The second produced chains of iron, to bind her. As for Corlis:

"He stood, arms akimbo, and watched. His plan was this: to stake Karen through her vampire heart and then, when she lay helpless, to threaten her with decapitation and fire. This threat, he hoped, would drive her vampire to produce its egg, for even immature vampires will do this when true death seems imminent. The egg would be his, for he intended to be in such a position as to leave no alternative host. Namely: fused sexually with his victim!

"But Karen had divined his purpose. Being Wamphyri, she'd been gifted with an element of telepathic talent. Now, in her hour of need, that talent worked for her not only in reading Corlis's intentions, but also to call her warrior creature from its vigil at the top of the stairwell. The creature came—and swiftly!

"Corlis and his two now held Karen down. She was not wearing her gauntlet, but still she put up a fight. She wouldn't lie still long enough for the one with the chains to bind her; her nails opened up Corlis's face; she kicked the one with the stake repeatedly in the groin! And the four who were half-faithful were torn two ways: they danced here and there, undecided, not knowing what to do for best. But then, when they saw Karen's warrior coming—ah!—but *then* they knew what to do for best!

"Two of them leaped on the one with the stake and dragged him away. The enraged warrior took him from them and that was the end of him. He had no egg; he was just flesh, however vampirized; the warriors know how to deal with mere flesh. The other two more-or-less faithful ones fell on Corlis where he tried in vain to rape Karen, and finally they pinned him down. That left the Lady herself to deal with the one who had tried to chain her. Unlike Corlis this one was small, and Karen's full vampire fury had been roused!

"She dragged him screaming to her throne and drove his face down on the jagged cartilage finial which formed the grip at the end of an arm rest. The finial was the eye-tooth of the creature whose massive jaw formed the throne; it entered the traitor's mouth and came out at the base of his skull, so that he kneeled there and flopped about like a speared fish. He was taken to the refuse pit.

"And Corlis, of course, was taken to the Gate . . ."

Zek looked at Jazz where he lay awake and listening. But she saw that he was bleary-eyed and close to the edge of sleep. "I'm tired, too," she said. "Let's sleep now, and I'll finish up on the next leg of our journey. We'll be spending the long night in the caves, I should think. You can ask me any questions then. And by then, too, you'll know just about as much as I do."

Jazz nodded. "You're doing a great job," he said, watching her lie back in her sleeping-bag. Then he stifled a yawn, said: "Zek?"

"Yes?" she turned her head and looked at him, her face a strange mixture of mystique and ingenue.

"If and when this is ever finished, I think maybe you and I—"

She shook her head, cutting him short. "We're drawn to each other because we're all we have," she said. "In the caves we can be together, if that's what you want. But don't think I'm being generous, for I want it too. Just don't make me any promises about if and when, OK? We don't know 'if'—and we certainly don't known 'when'! Going home, should we ever be so fortunate, will be like stepping out of darkness into light. We might see each other very differently. Let's leave it at that."

He smiled, yawned again and nodded. *A hell of a woman!* "OK, but I've always been an optimist, Zek. Take my word for it: we'll make it!"

She lay back, closed her eyes, said: "Well, here's to optimism, and to the conclusion of a trouble-free trek—and to The Dweller, and, oh—"

"The future?"

"The future, yes," she agreed. "I'll drink to that. God knows it has to be better than the past . . ."

From Leipzig, Harry Keogh returned direct to E-Branch HQ in London. He materialized in the armoury, a room not much bigger than a cupboard, took a 9mm. Browning automatic and three full magazines (and signed for them) and was out of the place almost before the alarms could start up.

Then back to Jazz Simmons's flat where he donned a black shirt, pullover and slacks, and finally to Bonnyrigg near Edinburgh to visit his mother. This last wasn't absolutely necessary, for once Harry had communicated with a dead person he could usually speak to that person again even over great distances, but whenever possible it seemed only polite and much more private and personal to go to them in their final resting places or the places where they had died.

"Ma," he said, the moment after emerging onto the riverbank above the place where the water gurgled dark and deep. "Ma, it's Harry."

Harry! she answered at once. *I'm so glad you've come. I was just about to start looking for you.*

"Oh? Is there something, Ma?"

You asked about people dying in the Upper Urals.

"Jazz Simmons?" For a moment Harry felt like the ground had been ripped out from under him. If Simmons was dead after all, here in this world, it rubbished all of Harry's and Möbius's theories. And it left Brenda and Harry Jr. stranded . . . wherever.

But: *Who?* his mother seemed taken by surprise. But only for a moment. *Oh! No, not him. We couldn't find him. This is someone else. Someone who knew him.*

"Someone who knew Jazz Simmons? At Perchorsk?" Relief flooded through Harry. "Who are you talking about, Ma?"

A different voice spoke in Harry's head. A voice that was new to him. *She means me, Harry. Kazimir Kirescu.*

I knew Jazz, yes, and now I'm paying for it. Oh, I don't blame him, but someone is to blame. Several people. So . . . if you can help me, son, then I'll be very glad indeed to help you.

"Help you?" Harry stood on a riverbank in Scotland and talked to a dead person two and a half thousand miles away, and it seemed perfectly natural to him. "But how can I help you, Kazimir? You're dead, after all."

Ah! But it's how I died, and it's where I am now.

"You want revenge, through me?"

That's part of it, yes, but mainly I want . . . to be still!

Harry frowned. Often the dead were more vague than the living. "Maybe I'd better come and see you. I mean, this is sort of impersonal. Is it safe where you are?"

It's never safe here, Harry, Kazimir told him. *And where I am it's always horrible. I can tell you this much: I'm in a room at the Perchorsk Projekt, and at the moment I'm alone. At least there are no people with me. But . . . do you have a strong stomach, Harry? How are your nerves?*

Harry smiled briefly. "Oh, my stomach's strong enough, Kazimir. And I think my nerves will hold up." Then the smile slipped from his face. What was the other's situation, he wondered?

Then come, by all means, said the old man. *Only don't say I didn't warn you!*

Harry grew cautious. It had been his intention to visit Perchorsk anyway. That was why he had come to see his mother; so that with the aid of her friends she could guide him there. But now . . . "Just tell me this," he said. "If I come, right now, will my life be endangered?"

No, nothing like that. I've been told you can come and go as you wish, and in any case we're not likely to be disturbed—though there is always that possibility.

319

But . . . I'm with something that isn't pleasant. The old man's mental voice was full of shudders.

"I'll come," said Harry. "Just keep talking to me and I'll home in on you." He conjured a Möbius door and followed Kazimir's thoughts to their source . . .

At Perchorsk it was an hour after midnight. The room of the thing was in darkness, where only the red ceiling lights gave any illumination. Harry emerged from the Möbius Continuum there, stared all about in the red-tinged gloom and felt the sinister heart of the place throbbing through the floor under his feet. Then he saw the tank, and the shape inside it, but for the moment he couldn't quite see what that shape was.

Me! said Kazimir Kirescu. *My resting place. Except it doesn't rest.*

"Doesn't rest?" Harry repeated him, but softly. There were dimmer switches on the wall, a nest of them. Harry reached for them, went to turn up the lights. They came up slowly. "Oh, my God!" said Harry in a shaky whisper. "Kazimir?"

That's what ate me! the other answered, in a voice horrified as Harry's own. *That's where I am. I don't mind being dead so much, Harry, but I would like to lie still.*

Harry moved uncertainly across the room toward the creature in the tank. It seemed slug- or snail-like; its corrugated "foot" or lower body pulsated where it adhered to the glass wall; atop its lolling neck sat an almost human head with the face of an old man. Flaccid "arms" hung down bonelessly from rubbery "shoulders," and several rudimentary eyes gazed wetly, vacantly from where they opened like suckers in the thing's dark skin. Its normal eyes—those in the old man's face—moved to compensate for the languid lolling of the head, remained firmly fixed upon Harry. But they were only normal in that they occupied a face. Other than that, they were uniformly scarlet.

My face, said Kazimir with a sob. *But not my eyes,*

Harry. And dead or alive, no man should be part of this thing.

And then, while Harry continued to stare at the monstrosity, Kazimir told him all he knew about the Perchorsk Projekt, and of the events leading to his current predicament . . .

Fifteen minutes later and a mere fifty yards away:

Major Chingiz Khuv, KGB, came awake, sat up jerkily in his bed. He was hot, feverish. He'd been dreaming, nightmaring, but the dreams were quickly receding in the face of reality. Reality, as Khuv was well aware, was often far more nightmarish than any dream. Especially here in Perchorsk. But it was as if the unremembered dreams were premonitory; Khuv's nerves were already jangling to the buzzing of his doorbell. He got up, threw on a dressing-gown and went to the door.

It was Paul Savinkov, puffing and panting from his exertions, his fat hands fluttering.

"What is it, Paul?" Khuv brushed sleep from the corners of his eyes.

"We're not sure, Major. But . . . Nik Slepak and I—"

Khuv came fully awake on the instant. Savinkov and Slepak were both ESP sensitives; they could detect and recognize foreign telepathic sendings, psychic emanations, anything of a paranormal nature. And in the event of ESPionage, they were adept at intercepting and scrambling alien probes.

"What *is* it, Paul?" Khuv demanded this time. "Are they spying on us again?"

Savinkov gulped. "It could be worse than that," he said. "We think . . . we think something is here!"

Khuv's jaw dropped. "You think something is—?" he grabbed the other's arm. "Something from the Gate, do you mean?"

Savinkov shook his head. His fat face was shiny,

eyes very bright. "No, not from the Gate. Those things that come through the Gate, they leave a slimy trail in the mind. They're alien—to this world, I mean. This thing we can sense here, it isn't that sort of alien. It might even be a man; Nik Slepak thinks so. But it—he, whatever—has no right to be here. Two things we're sure of: whatever it is, it's powerful! And it *is* here."

"Where?" Khuv threw back the top half of his dressing-gown, thrust his left arm through the leather loop of a shoulder holster hanging from a peg inside the door. The holster contained Khuv's KGB issue automatic. Belting his dressing-gown savagely about his waist, he shoved Savinkov ahead of him down the exterior corridor. *"Where?"* he shouted now. "What, are you deaf as well as queer? Has Slepak also been struck dumb?"

"We don't know where, Major," the fat esper gasped. "We've got our locator on it, Leo Grenzel." As he stuttered his apologies, so Slepak and Grenzel came hurrying round the bend of the corridor. They saw Khuv and Savinkov, hurried to meet them.

"Well?" said Khuv to Grenzel, a small, sharp-featured East German.

"Encounter Three," Grenzel whispered. His eyes were an incredibly deep grey and very large in his small face. Never larger than right now.

Khuv frowned at him. "The thing in the glass tank? What about it?"

"That's where he is," Grenzel nodded. His face was pale, strangely serene, like the mask of a sleep-walker. His talent affected him that way.

Khuv turned sharply to Savinkov. "You—hurry, get Vasily Agursky." Savinkov made off down the corridor. "I said *hurry!*" Khuv called after him. "Meet us in the room of the creature, and make sure you're both armed!"

*   *   *

Harry had listened to Kazimir's grim tale. He now knew about the fate of the old man's family, especially Tassi. He knew a little about Chingiz Khuv, too, about his espers and handful of KGB thugs; but he still didn't know the Projekt's secret, which lay in the heart of the place. Kazimir had not been privy to that, had no knowledge of it.

"This . . . thing," said Harry. "Do you know what it is?"

No, only that it's horrible! Kazimir answered in Harry's mind.

"It's a vampire," Harry told him. "At least, I think it is. And you don't know how it got here? Was it perhaps made here?"

I know nothing about it.

Harry nodded, chewed his lip. "About your daughter: do you know where she is? Show me a plan of this place in your mind. Or as much as you know of it."

Kazimir was glad to co-operate, said: *She was in the cell next to mine.*

Again Harry's nod, and: "Kazimir, you have my word that if I can find her, I'll take her out of this. More than that, if I can find her mother I'll reunite them in a safe place."

The old man's mental sigh of relief was almost audible. *If you can do that, then it's enough. Don't worry about me.*

"But I do. Kazimir, this thing isn't you. You were dead when it . . . when you . . . you were already dead."

I feel part of it. I'm being absorbed by it.

Harry chewed harder on his lip. He'd seen the room's equipment. He had a plan but wasn't sure if it would work. "What if I could kill this thing? You can't die twice, Kazimir."

Destroy it and I'll be free, I'm sure! Renewed hope rang in the old man's mental voice. *But . . . how can you destroy it?*

323

Harry knew how: the stake, the sword and the fire. If this creature had a vampire in it, then these things would kill it. So . . . why not skip the first two steps and go straight to the third?

Outside, ringing faintly, running footsteps sounded. And somewhere an alarm bell had started to gong its raucous warning through the bowels of the subterranean complex.

"They know I'm here," Harry said. "This has to be quick."

He wheeled Agursky's shock-box over to the tank. It was an electrical transformer on wheels, with a flexible heavy-duty cable to a wall socket. It had a pair of clamps on coiled extension leads, which Harry quickly made fast to terminals on the side of the tank. Watching him, the creature came to life, changing colour and shape as it began to work through several rapid metamorphoses. It knew what the shock-box was, knew what was coming. Or it thought it did.

Harry didn't have time to watch its contortions, and in any case he didn't want to. Feeling slightly sick he turned on the current—and the thing at once went beserk!

Harry wasted no time but turned the current up all the way. The clamps spluttered and issued blue sparks, smoke and a heavy ozone reek. The room's lights flickered momentarily, then steadied and brightened again. High voltage current flowed through electrical cables in the glass walls of the tank, and the creature took the full charge. It became a writhing puppet of a man, small, with one tiny arm and hand and one huge one. It balled a massive fist, a fist almost as big as Harry's head, and slammed it again and again at the glass wall of its prison—the wall of its incinerator.

The thing was melting, mewling and melting. Steam poured off it as its liquids boiled. Its corrugated skin blistered, cracked open, blackened. Gusts of vile vapour escaped in jets from its rupturing pores. It screamed and screamed with old Kazimir's face, through his mouth, but its voice wasn't human. Then the glass shattered and its great black steaming fist came through— at which the thing curled up on itself and gave up the ghost.

It collapsed, half-in, half-out of the shattered tank, became still. Then—

The blackened, smoking flesh of its head split open like an overripe pomegranite. *A cobra's head writhed in the mush of boiling, steaming brains!* The vampire! And it too died even as Harry watched.

Free! said Kazimir. *Free!!!*

Behind Harry the room's great door sighed open. He conjured a door of his own and stepped through it . . .

Chapter Seventeen
Intruder

KHUV, AGURSKY AND THE OTHERS REELED AS THEY ENtered the room of the thing. In the swirl and reek of the dead, frying creature in the tank, they failed to see that man-shaped space where the smoke rushed in to fill a sudden gap. Harry had made his exit just in time.

Agursky recovered first, leaped across the room and switched off the power. "Who has *done* this?" he demanded of no one in particular. "Who is responsible?" He clapped a hand to his brow, staggered toward the sputtering, smoking tank, where even now shards of glass were beginning to melt in the intense heat. Then, as the smoke began to clear, he saw the creature's blackened remains hanging out through the shattered glass wall; saw, too, something else—something which he didn't want anyone else to see. He ripped off his smock, quickly threw it over the monstrous remains.

Khuv had meanwhile turned to Leo Grenzel, the locator. "You said he was here, an intruder. Well, someone has certainly been here—though I'm damned if I can see how! The door was locked, and there's a guard outside. Oh, a half-asleep stupid guard, that's true, but he's not a complete idiot! So . . . just getting in here would be hard enough if not impossible—but as for getting out . . . ?" Then Khuv grasped Grenzel by the shoulders, stared hard at him. "Leo? Is there something else?"

Grenzel's face was pale again; his grey eyes were deep as deep space; he swayed where Khuv held him upright. "Still here," he finally said. "He's still here!"

Khuv stared all about the room, as did the others. Black smoke boiling from the mess under Agursky's smock, and the crackle of cooked, alien flesh starting to cool; but no sign of any intruder. "Here? Where, here?"

"The girl," Grenzel swayed. "The prisoner . . ."

"Taschenka Kirescu?"

"Yes," Grenzel's nod.

Khuv whirled on Savinkov and Slepak. "How can this be?" he asked. But already his mind was working; memories of reports he'd read flashed before his mind's eye; it was something from before his time, but weren't the British supposed to have a man who could do this sort of thing? Harry Keogh was said to have been one such, and after him Alec Kyle. Keogh was dead but— but they never had found Kyle's body after the mess at the Château Bronnitsy.

"How can it be?" Savinkov repeated his KGB master. "It *can't* be!" He was definite. But:

"Oh, it can," Grenzel's far-away voice contradicted him. "It *is!*"

"Quickly!" Khuv rasped. "The cells. I want to know what the hell is happening here!"

They ran out of the room, left Grenzel swaying there, his face slack and vacant, but his eyes seeing, seeing. And Agursky, bundling up the dead creature and its dead parasite in his smock, trembling in his eagerness to get it back to his private quarters and away from any threat of inspection by others. For he now knew what had controlled this nameless thing, and he wanted to examine that controller most minutely.

Indeed, to Vasily Agursky there was *nothing* more important in the entire world but that he examine the thing's parasite—whose egg had been deposited and was even now maturing inside Agursky himself!

Tassi's nightmare—of the key grating in the lock on her cell door, and of Khuv entering, dark-eyed and evil—had kept her awake. It was that sort of nightmare, the sort you suffer when you're awake. It was doubtful if she would have slept anyway; she hadn't since . . . since the horror Khuv had shown her in the room of the thing. She couldn't sleep, for the face of her father kept smiling at her from the darkness behind her eyelids whenever she closed her eyes; her father's face—on the body of a beast.

She kept her cell light on, and lay warm on her cot but shivering, drained of energy, waiting for Khuv. For her time was up, and she knew he would soon be coming for her. That had been his threat, and Major Chingiz Khuv didn't make idle threats. If only there was something she could tell him, but she didn't know anything. Only that she was the most wretched, unhappiest girl in the world.

When Harry stepped out of the Möbius Continuum, Tassi had just turned on her side, turned her face away from his re-entry point into this universe. A quick glance about the cell told Harry they were alone; he took a single pace to the metal bed, put a hand round Tassi's face and over her mouth, cautioned her in Russian: "*Shhh!* Be quiet. Don't shout or do anything stupid. I'm going to get you out of here."

He kept his hand clamped to her face but let her turn her head to look at him. And with his hand still in place, he helped her to sit up. Then: "OK?" he asked.

Tassi nodded, but she was trembling in every limb. Her eyes looked like saucers above her nose and the bands of Harry's fingers. He slowly took his hand away, gently urged her to her feet. She looked at the door, then at Harry, said: "Who?—How?—I don't . . ."

"It's OK," Harry put a finger to his lips.

"But how did you get in here? I didn't hear you come. Was I asleep?" Then her hand flew to her mouth. "Did the Major send you? But I've told him: I don't *know* anything! Oh, please don't hurt me!"

"No one's going to hurt you, Tassi," Harry told her. And then he made his mistake: "Your father sent me." Seeing her expression, he could have bitten his tongue through.

She shook her head and backed away from him. There were tears in her eyes now. "My father's dead," she wept. "He's dead! He *couldn't* have sent you . . ." And accusingly: "What are you going to do to me?"

"I've told you," Harry answered, an edge of desperation in his tone, "I'm going to take you out of this place. Do you hear those alarms?"

She listened, and indeed she could hear the klaxons, sounding from deep down in the heart of the place. "Well," Harry continued, "I'm what those alarms are all about. They're looking for me, and pretty soon they'll be looking in here. So now I'm asking you to trust me."

What he was saying was impossible. It was either a trick of Khuv's or else this man was insane. No one could get out of this place, Tassi was sure. But on the other hand, how had he got in? "Do you have keys?" she asked.

Harry could see he was making an impression. "Keys?" he grinned, however tightly. "I have an entire door! Lots of doors!"

He was mad, surely. But he was different from the others here, totally different. "I don't understand," she said, still backing away. Her legs struck the edge of her bed and she flopped down on it again.

Running footsteps sounded, and the tight grin slipped from Harry's face. "They're coming," he said. "Get up." The sudden authority in his voice had her on her feet again in a moment.

329

There was shouting outside, the jangle of keys, Khuv's voice hoarsely commanding: "Open it! Open it!"

Harry grabbed Tassi by the waist. "Put your arms round my neck," he said. "Quickly, girl. No arguments, now!" She did it. She had no reason to trust him, but she had no reason not to. "Close your eyes," he said. "And keep them closed." Tightening one arm around her narrow waist, he grunted as he lifted her feet from the floor.

She heard the cell door grating open, then silence—but such *absolute* silence.

"Wha—?" she commenced a question she couldn't finish, and shrank from the booming of her own voice. Startled, she opened her eyes for a moment—but only for a moment. Then she snapped them tightly shut again.

"There," said Harry, and he lowered her feet on a solid floor. "You can open your eyes now."

She did, the merest slit . . . then opened them wide, wider—and sagged against him. Her eyes rolled up and she began to slide down his body.

Harry caught her up, lifted her, laid her on the Duty Officer's desk. Behind his newspaper, the D.O. had just this moment realized that he had visitors. Then the girl's arm and hand flopped into view under his open newspaper and he reared up and back with an inarticulate cry: *"G-yahhh!"*

"It's OK," said Harry, who was growing accustomed to excusing himself. "It's only me, and the friend of a friend of mine."

"Jesus! Jesus!—oh, sweet Jesus!" the D.O. clutched at his desk for support. Of all people, it was Darcy Clarke. Harry nodded the very briefest of greetings, began to massage the unconscious girl's hands . . .

It had been 1:15 A.M. when Harry arrived at E-Branch HQ, and it was almost an hour later when he left. In between times he passed on some information, told

330

Clarke all he had learned, and in return received a little information from the other. His instructions for the welfare of Tassi Kirescu were these:

She was to be given refuge, comforted as best the staff of E-Branch knew how, offered permanent political asylum. A Russian interpreter was to be provided for her, and she should be de-briefed (but with a great deal of care and sensitivity) with regard to the Perchorsk Projekt. For the present she was to keep a low profile: her presence here in the West should be kept secret, and when she was released it must be with a new identity. Lastly, E-Branch was to use such usual and paranormal means as were required to discover the whereabouts in the USSR of her mother. Harry had made Kazimir Kirescu a promise and it was one he intended to keep—eventually.

As for the information Darcy Clarke had for Harry:

"It's Zek Föener," he had told the Necroscope.

"Zek? What about her?" The last time Harry had seen Zek was eight years ago. She had been a telepath at the Château Bronnitsy, the USSR's equivalent of E-Branch HQ, which had made her an enemy, but a reluctant one. Harry could have destroyed her, but he'd sensed a deep-rooted decency in her, a desire to be free of her KGB masters. All she had wanted was to return to Greece. He had suspected she would. But . . . he had warned her not to come up against him again.

"She may be part of this," Clarke had told him.

"How do you mean? Part of Perchorsk?" Was Zek the one who'd betrayed his presence there? She would have known his mind at once, as soon as he materialized in the place. Of course, there was also Khuv's detachment of espers; they could have picked him up just as easily. For the moment Harry preferred to believe the latter. At least he hoped so.

"Part of Perchorsk, yes. A cog in the wheel of the place. We've kept an eye on her ever since the Bodescu affair. She was doing time at a forced labour camp; not especially hard stuff, but not pleasant either. Then they sent her to Perchorsk. This was some months ago and we've just had news of it. We can only assume she's working for Soviet E-Branch again. And for the KGB . . ."

Harry's face soured. "Again," he said. "I warned her not to. Well, if I have to mix it with them again . . ." He let the threat hang there.

Clarke stared hard at him. "But isn't it more serious than that, Harry? At the end of the Bodescu affair, Zek Föener was working with Ivan Gerenko—"

"*Had been* working with him," Harry cut in, correcting him. "But she'd quit. I thought so, anyway."

"But you know what I mean," Clarke insisted. "Gerenko had some crazy idea about using vampires. That's why he and Theo Dolgikh—*and* Zek—went back to that mountain pass east of the Carpathians: to see if, after all those centuries, anything remained of Faethor Ferenczy's buried creatures. Zek *knows* about vampires! It makes it that much more definite that the Russians have discovered a way to make the damned things, and that they're doing it there at Perchorsk!"

"So you're saying . . . ?"

"Harry, you remember how you dealt with the Château Bronnitsy?"

After a moment, Harry had nodded. Oh, yes, he remembered it well enough. Using the Möbius Continuum, he'd laid plastic explosive charges there. Gouting, shattering fire and lashing heat, and the Château reduced to smouldering rubble. And the Soviet E-Branch reduced along with it, for their sins. In the space of less than a minute, enough sheer destructive savagery to last any man a lifetime. "I remember," he had finally answered. "Except—"

"Yes?"

"Darcy, *if* you're right, well, obviously the place has to go. But not until we're sure one way or the other, and not yet. I have this feeling that the answer to my one big problem is right there. It may be risky—I mean, I know what has escaped from that place, and what could presumably escape from it in future; indeed, I've seen and dealt with an example—but for the moment I can't, *daren't*, try to close it down. Not if I want to see Brenda and Harry Jr. again.''

For a moment it had seemed that Clarke understood, but then he'd said, "Harry, it's not just a case of 'risky'—it's deadly! Unthinkable! You must see that?''

And then it had been Harry's turn. Coldly he had answered: "There are a couple of things you have to see, too, Darcy. Like old man Kirescu being dead—his death probably precipitated by your sending Jazz Simmons in there. And that poor girl having lost both her father and her brother. And her mother, probably in a forced labour camp by now, half out of her mind with grief and worry, no doubt. These are things you can't write off, Darcy, and you're certainly not going to write off Brenda and Harry Jr. So for now we'll continue to play this my way.''

White-faced, Clarke could only agree. "So . . . what's your way going to be? What's your next step, Harry?''

"Well, there are questions I need answered. It looks like I'll have to go right to the top to get them answered.''

"The top?''

Harry had nodded. "The Perchorsk Projekt. If I'm right and it's not about breeding vampires, then what is it about? Someone in that place knows and is going to tell me. There has to be a boss, a controller. Not Khuv but someone above him.''

"Of course there is,'' Clarke had answered at once. "Khuv's in charge of security, that's all. The man you want is Viktor Luchov.'' And he'd gone on to fill Harry in on Luchov's background.

When he was done Harry had nodded grimly. "Then he's the man I need to talk to. If anyone has the answers, Viktor Luchov has to be the one.''

"When will you try to see him?''

"Now."

"Now?" Clarke had been taken aback. "But the place will still be on top alert!"

"I know. I'll create a smoke screen."

"A what?"

"A diversion. Let me worry about it. You just look after that girl."

Clarke had nodded, stuck out his hand. "Best of luck, Harry."

The Necroscope wasn't one for holding grudges. He shook hands, conjured a Möbius door. Clarke watched him take his departure, thought: *I was there once!* Pray God he'd never be there again . . .

Viktor Luchov was back in his own executive quarters (which meant that they were slightly less austere than anyone else's at Perchorsk) and he was furious. Quite apart from this latest incident—this "intrusion," if such it had been—the Projekt Direktor had chosen the period of the alert to approach and challenge Khuv in respect of certain rumors which were beginning to circulate through the Projekt, rumors alleging brutality and murder. They concerned the KGB officer's prisoners, Kazimir and Taschenka Kirescu.

Perhaps Luchov's approach had been a little too liverish (he had after all been shocked awake in the middle of the night, with klaxons sounding all around like wailing demons out of hell) but that could not excuse Khuv's response, which had been brusque to put it mildly. Namely, he had told Luchov that he should get off his back and let him attend to the Projekt's security with a minimum of interference. Or better still, with no interference at all. This confrontation had taken place not in private but in the detention area, where Khuv's espers had been crowding one of the cells in their search for something or other. "Sniffing the aether!" as one of them had put it.

Appalled at the apparent chaos and confusion, Luchov

had demanded to see the prisoners, which was when Khuv had rounded on him.

"Listen, Comrade Direktor," the KGB Major had hissed. "I would be *delighted* if I could show you the girl Tassi Kirescu. This was her cell. A little over one hour ago she was here, and a guard on duty in the corridor outside. Then—" he had thrown up his hands. "—she was no longer here, and the door still locked! Now, I know you hold E-Branch in small regard, and the KGB in no regard at all, but surely it must be amply apparent even to your oh-so-scientific mind that something quite exceptional—something, indeed, entirely metaphysical—has occurred here? My espers are attempting to discover what that something was. And I, who have no ESP talent of my own, am trying to make sense of what they're telling me. So . . . now is *not* the ideal moment for you to come interfering!"

"You go too far, Major!" Luchov had shouted.

"And I shall go further," Khuv had shouted back. "If you do not get out of my way I shall have you escorted back to your quarters and locked in!"

"What? You *dare*. . . !"

"Listen, you damned *scientist!*" Khuv had then snarled at him. "In my capacity as the Projekt's security supervisor I dare almost *anything!* Now I'll tell you one more time: the creature from the Gate is dead, destroyed by some unknown person or thing; the Kirescu girl, formerly my prisoner is missing; her father is . . . dead: an unfortunate accident. I shall ensure that you get a copy of the report. And finally, the Projekt has had an intruder. Our security has been breached in the worst possible way. I repeat: our security. My sphere of work, Direktor, not yours. So go back to bed. Go back to your mathematics and your physics and what all. Go study your magmass and your grey holes and your particle beam acceleration—*only leave me alone!*"

And Luchov, shouted down, had returned to his rooms and commenced to write a furious, comprehensive report on Khuv's suspected activities and his rank insubordination.

Meanwhile:

For the last five minutes Harry Keogh had been making a nuisance of himself. First he'd appeared outside the Projekt, on the patrolled ramp cut into the Perchorsk ravine's wall, where he'd taken a half-hearted pot shot at a guard. He hadn't attempted to hit the man, for he'd need serious reason before sending yet another human being to join the Great Majority. Before the soldier could fire back at him, Harry had ducked into the cover of darkly swirling snow—and through a Möbius door.

From there he'd returned to the room of the thing. Emerging there, he'd been ready on the instant to return into the Möbius Continuum. But the room was empty and so he'd simply gone to the locked door and banged on it, shouting to be let out. The guard outside the room had responded to this, of course, and moments later so had the alarm system.

Tassi Kirescu's cell had been next; Harry emerged amidst a handful of baffled espers, struck two of them rapid, stunning blows, retreated to the Möbius Continuum. Behind him he left Leo Grenzel and Nik Slepak groaning on the floor, and others white-faced and wide-eyed, astonished by what they'd seen and felt. Grenzel was still feeling it, and not just the two front teeth Harry had loosened.

"That's him!" he gurgled, sitting up and spitting blood. "That's *him!*"

Khuv was heading for KGB accommodation when the klaxons began to sound again. He cursed, put on speed. Coming through a door between sections of the corridor, he ran into Harry Keogh. He knew him at once—or thought he did. Khuv had a good memory; he'd seen photographs of this man: a one-time head of British E-Branch—Alec Kyle!

Harry pressed his Browning up under Khuv's chin, said: "I can see by the look on your face that you know me. Which puts me at a disadvantage—but let me guess anyway. Major Chingiz Khuv?''

Khuv gulped, nodded, shoved his hands high in the air.

"Major, you're in the wrong business,'' Harry pressed harder with his gun. "Take some good advice and get out while the going's good. And pray you never see me again.'' He stepped back away from Khuv, looked for a door.

In the moment of Harry's distraction, Khuv snatched his own gun from its holster, triggered off a shot. Harry felt the bullet buzz past his face like an angry wasp to speed forever through the Möbius Continuum. Then Khuv and the corridor blinked out of existence and he headed for somewhere else.

He emerged in a military Duty Room situated just inside the Projekt's service bays, put the muzzle of his pistol in the Orderly Sergeant's ear where he sat at his desk and ordered him to tell him the way to Direktor Luchov's quarters. The terrified Sergeant showed him what he wanted to know on a wall chart, a diagram of the Perchorsk complex, and Harry rewarded him with a chop to the neck that would keep him out of things for at least half an hour. Then he was on the move again.

Harry's "smoke screen'' was now established. It was 5:22 A.M. precisely, local time, when he materialized in Viktor Luchov's claustrophobic suite of rooms. Luchov was on the phone, demanding to know what this fresh spate of clamouring alarms was all about, when Harry arrived. His back was to Harry, who let him finish his conversation and slam the telephone down before he spoke:

"Direktor Luchov? I'm what those alarms are all about.'' He pointed his automatic at Luchov's heart, said: "Better sit down.''

Luchov, whirling from the telephone, saw Harry, his gun and where it was pointed, in that order. He staggered as if he'd been struck in the temple. "What—? Who—?"

"Who doesn't matter," Harry told him. "And what is what I'm here to find out."

"Khuv's intruder!" Luchov finally gasped. "I thought it was all part of some elaborate scheme of his."

"Sit," Harry said again, waving his gun toward a chair.

Luchov did as Harry ordered, the yellow veins pulsing rapidly under the scar-tissue skin of his seared skull. Harry looked at Luchov's disfigurement, saw that the damage was fairly recent. "An accident?"

Tight-lipped, breathing just a fraction too quickly, Luchov said nothing. Both he and Harry jumped as the telephone came janglingly alive, ringing repeatedly. Then Harry scowled. They must have some clever people working here; it seemed they'd already located him; he wouldn't have time to interrogate Luchov—not here, anyway. "Get up," he said, reaching out and jerking Luchov to his feet.

And still holding him, he conjured a door and dragged the other through it.

In a moment, for the moment, they were out on the ramp in the ravine, snow stinging their eyes and a cold wind rushing down the length of the canyon. Harry looked up at the bleak mountains showing their fangs through the snow. Luchov, seeing where he was—where according to all the laws of science he had no right to be—had barely sufficient time to voice some inarticulate query before—

—Harry dragged him squalling through another door, passed through the Möbius Continuum and exited on a ledge high over the Perchorsk ravine. Luchov saw the sheer drop under his feet and almost fainted. He let out a wild shriek and pressed himself back into the face of the cliff behind him. And again Harry commanded: "Sit—before you fall."

Luchov carefully sat down, hugged his dressing-gown

to him, shivered partly from the cold and partly from the terror of this totally unbelievable and yet entirely inescapable experience. Harry went down on one knee before him and put his gun away. "Now," he said. "I should think that dressed as we are, we've about ten to fifteen minutes before we freeze to death. So you'd better talk fast. There are things I want to know—about the Perchorsk Projekt. And I have it on good authority that you'd be the one to tell me. So I'll ask the questions and you'll answer them."

Luchov collected his whirling senses as best he could, recovered something of his dignity. "If . . . if I have only fifteen minutes left, then so do you. We both freeze."

Harry grinned wolfishly. "You don't catch on too quickly, do you? I don't have to stay here. I can leave you right now. Like this—" And he was no longer there. Snow swirled in the space where he had kneeled. He returned, said: "So what's it going to be? Do you talk to me or do I simply leave you here?"

"You're an enemy of my country!" Luchov blurted, feeling the cold start to bite.

"That place of yours," Harry nodded toward the grey sheen of lead far below, "appears to be an enemy of the world— potentially, anyway."

"If I tell you anything—*anything*—about the Projekt, then I'm a traitor!" Luchov protested.

This wasn't getting Harry anywhere, and now he was cold, too. "Listen," he said. "You've seen what I can do—but you haven't seen everything. I'm also a Necroscope: I can talk to the dead. So I can talk to you alive, or I can talk to you dead. If you were dead you'd be only too glad to talk to me, Viktor, for then I'd be your only real contact with the world."

"Talk to the dead?" Luchov shrank even further down into himself. "You're a madman!"

Harry shrugged. "Obviously you don't know much

about espers. I take it you and Khuv don't get on too well?''

Luchov's teeth had started to chatter. ''ESP? Is this something to do with ESP?''

Harry had run out of time and patience. ''OK,'' he said, straightening up, ''I can see you need convincing. So I'm going to leave you now. I'm going somewhere else, somewhere warm. I'll come back in about five minutes, or maybe ten. Meanwhile you can make up your mind; to talk to me or to attempt to climb down from here. Personally I don't think you'd make it. I think you'd fall, and then that we would talk again when I found your body at the bottom of the ravine.''

Luchov grasped his ankle. It was all a nightmare—had to be a nightmare, surely—but it felt horribly real, as real as the flesh-and-blood ankle he was grasping. ''Wait! Wait! What . . . what is it you want to know?''

''That's better,'' said Harry. He drew Luchov to his feet, took him somewhere more comfortable: an evening beach in Australia. Luchov felt the hot sand under his feet, saw a shimmering ocean with its endless lines of whitecaps, sat down abruptly as his legs gave way. He sat there in the sand, wide-eyed, shivering and very nearly exhausted.

The beach was deserted. Harry looked down at Luchov and nodded. Then he stripped down to his underpants, went for a swim. When he came out of the sea, Luchov was ready to talk . . .

When Luchov was finished (which is to say when Harry had run out of questions) it was getting dark. A handful of cars had come roaring down to the beach a quarter of a mile away, spilled young people with blankets and barbecue gear. Laughter and rock music came wafting on a crosswind.

''Back at Perchorsk it'll be morning, daylight,'' said Harry. ''But they'll still be running around in circles looking for you. If Khuv has a locator, they'll know approximately where you are. To be absolutely sure, though, they'll go over the Projekt with a fine-toothed comb. And by now everyone involved will be very tired. One thing is certain: Khuv now knows something of what he's up against.

"Now listen: you've co-operated with me and so I'll give you fair warning. It may be that I have to destroy Perchorsk. Not for my sake or in the interest of any nation or specific group of people, but for the sake of the world. But in any case, even if anything should happen to me, eventually Perchorsk *will* be destroyed. The USA won't sit still for any more monsters coming out of that place."

"Of course," Luchov answered. "I had foreseen that eventuality. Some months ago I passed on my warning to people in authority, made my recommendations. The warning was heeded and the recommendations accepted. Within the week, possibly as soon as tomorrow—today— trucks will start to arrive at Perchorsk from Sverdlovsk. They will deliver a new failsafe. So you see, on this one point if on no other, we are in agreement. Nothing— alien—must ever again get out of Perchorsk . . ."

Harry nodded. "Before I take you back there," he said, "I'd like to ask you one more thing. With that space-time Gate down there in Perchorsk's guts, how come you found me so incredible? I mean, surely the two principles come pretty close? In Perchorsk you have . . . a grey hole? And I make use of a dimension or space-time place other than my own."

Luchov stood up, stiffly brushed sand from his clothes. "The difference is this," he said. "I know how the Perchorsk Gate came into being. I've worked out most of the mathematics. The Gate is a physical reality, with nothing transient or insubstantial about it. It *is* physical, not metaphysical. The result of an accident, yes, but at least I know how that accident happened. You, on the other hand—you're just a man! I *can't* understand how you could ever possibly have happened."

341

Harry thought about his answer, eventually nodded. "Actually, I believe I was an accident, too," he said. "The product of a one-in-a-million combination of events. Anyway, I've warned you about Perchorsk. You risk your life staying there."

"Do you think I don't know that?" Luchov shrugged. "Still, it's my job. I'll see it through. And you. What will you do now?"

"After I've taken you back? I have to know what's on the other side of that Gate. There has to be more there than the nightmares you've described." There *had* to be, for how else could little Harry and his mother exist there? *If they exist there. But what if there are other dimensions beyond that one? What if Harry Jr. has taken his mother even further afield?*

Harry dropped Luchov off outside the great sliding doors of the service bays, left him in the grey morning light and the sullen snow, hammering at the wicket-gate and bellowing to be let in. Then Harry went to Luchov's quarters, (which he found empty and locked from the outside) where he donned a white smock which on his last visit he'd seen hanging there. The smock was the insignia of a Projekt scientist or technician. In the garment's pocket he found tinted spectacles and put them on.

And without more ado he went straight to the magmass heart of the place, materializing on the Saturn's-rings circumference midway between two sets of manned Katushev cannons. He stayed perfectly still, held a Möbius door fixed in his mind, ready to take cover—but all seemed well. A soldier lounging against the smooth magmass wall saw him, looked a little startled, straightened up and gave a half-hearted salute. Harry stared hard at him, much to the man's discomfort, then turned and scanned the great unnatural cavern in which he found himself. Especially he stared at the blinding white sphere which was the Gate . . .

* * *

There were other technicians about. Everyone looked tired following their night-shift, even the gunners in their padded bucket-seats where they sighted their weapons on the Gate. Two scientists walked past Harry, talking, moving in the direction of the walkway to the sphere. One of them glanced his way as they passed, smiled and nodded in a familiar manner. Harry wondered who the man thought he was. He nodded back, began to follow the pair, and as he drew level with the walkway turned off and moved toward the centre, heading directly for the sphere of light.

Behind him a soldier shouted: "Hey!—not in our line of fire, sir! Regulations!"

Harry glanced back casually over his shoulder and kept going. He left the outer platform and moved onto the walkway. Even as the gate in the electrified fence began to close, he passed through it, reached the spot where the boards were scorched. Behind him the gates opened again; footsteps came hurrying; Harry was aware of a low, angry muttering. But he was more aware of the Katushevs aimed directly at him; or rather not trained on him but on the Gate, which amounted to the same thing. "Sir!" a voice shouted in his ear, from directly behind him.

Harry conjured a Möbius door—*and with a tremor of unaccustomed panic saw that it was all wrong!*

The outline of the door wasn't clear-cut in Harry's mind. Its edges shimmered like a heat-haze mirage. It floated up alongside him, drifted toward the sphere as if attracted by it, and was held there, gradually fading where it trembled above the wooden walkway. Harry had seen nothing like this before. He conjured a second door with the same result: the sphere both attracted and repelled the doors; it made them less substantial, pinned them down and broke them up. It *cancelled* them!

A hand fell on Harry's shoulder, and at the same time he heard shouts from the wide wooden staircase where it emerged from the magmass shaft. Someone with a high-pitched voice was screaming: "He's here! He's here!" As the Sergeant who'd grabbed Harry's shoulder turned him about face, he glanced toward the stairs, saw Chingiz Khuv and a second man coming down from the shaft. Harry thought; *God! Doesn't that bastard ever sleep?*

Khuv seemed to be holding his companion up, keeping him from toppling headlong. The man he helped was one of the espers Harry had struck while he was laying his smoke screen. And he was the one who was doing all the shouting. Then he pointed directly *at* Harry—screamed one last time, "That's him!"—and Khuv's dark gaze followed his shaking hand.

Khuv's eyes blazed in a moment. "Open fire!" he shouted at once. He too pointed at Harry, shouting, "Shoot him! Kill him! He's an intruder!"

The Sergeant who had taken hold of Harry let go of him, stepped back, went to draw the pistol at his hip. Harry moved quickly after him, drop-kicked him and sent him flying off the walkway. Falling to the boards, Harry stayed low, out of the line of fire of the Katushevs. He conjured a Möbius door level with the walkway, hanging over empty space. It was his notion to dive headlong through it—*but the door shimmered and warped, was drawn up and toward the sphere of light!*

Harry could hear the Katushev commander yelling: "Target to the front—take aim—" and knew that the next command would be "fire!" He mustn't be here when that order was given. Before the shimmering, disintegrating door could disappear entirely, he sprang for it. Even though it appeared printed on the very face of the sphere itself, still it was his one chance.

He passed through the door—*into a hell of physical and mental agony!*

When Harry regained consciousness he was adrift in the Möbius Continuum, apparently in motion through a region of the Continuum which was new to him. His body and his psyche both felt badly battered, and that sixth sense of Harry's which was usually sharp as a razor felt tarnished and dull. Not without a deal of effort, he formed the mental equations and conjured a door; it opened on deep voids of space shot with stars in alien constellations. He closed the door at once and groped for others.

He found a door on future-time and peered through it. No blue life-threads raced into the future here, only his own, which bent violently aside beyond the door to disappear at right-angles to Harry's viewpoint. The past was equally hostile: indeed there seemed to be no past in this place, just an ocean of interminable, impersonal stars. The lack of human activity, of even traces of activity, reinforced Harry's opinion that he had been blown off-track and had left the mundane world of men far behind.

Beginning to panic, he tried one last door—and gazed out on the surface of a roaring furnace star! He closed that door, too, then forced himself into a state of calm, a condition in which he might at least apply a little reason to the problem. He was lost, yes, but what is lost can be found again. He didn't know where he was or how he had got here, true, but, since he *had* come here there must be a way back. Except . . . space is a big place and Harry Keogh felt like an exceedingly tiny mote in the eye of the infinite.

Then . . .

Harry? whispered a familiar, distant voice in his mind. *I thought I recognized you!* The voice sped closer, rapidly grew stronger. *But what's this? Are you trespassing?*

"Möbius! Thank God!" said Harry.

God? That's outside my line of research, Harry, Möbius told him. *I prefer to thank my equations, if it's all the same to you. Though I suppose it could be argued that they* are *one and the same!*

345

"How come you're out here?" Harry was calmer now. "Wherever 'here' is."

Here is in the constellation of Orion, Möbius answered. *And the point is, what are you doing out here?*

Harry explained.

Hmm! Möbius mused. *Well, first let's get you home again, and then we'll see if we can find an explanation for what's happened. If you'll just follow me . . .*

Harry stayed with Möbius, sped with him homeward, materialized in the Leipzig graveyard. It was evening, which told him he'd spent an entire day (or possibly two?) in the Möbius Continuum. In the grey, wintry light of the graveyard, Harry blinked, staggered; his legs wouldn't hold him up, so he sat down on the gravel beside Möbius's marker.

You could do with a good long rest, my boy! Möbius told him.

"You're right," Harry agreed. "But first I'd like to know if you can explain what happened to me."

I think I can, yes, said the mathematician. *You yourself have likened my strip dimension to a parallel plane, and this gate at Perchorsk leads to another; they are both gates between planes of existence. Both are negative conditions, blemishes on the perfect surface of normal space-time. Now: take two magnets and push their negative poles together, and what happens?*

"They repel one another," Harry shrugged.

Exactly. And so does the gate and the doors which you create in your mind. But the Perchorsk Gate is stronger, and so the repulsion is that much more fierce. When you used that door close to this sphere gateway, you were hurled across the Möbius Continuum like a shot from a gun! Your equations were warped out of focus; your body underwent stresses it could never hope to survive in the physical world; in three-dimensioned space you would have died instantly! The Continuum itself saved you, because it is infinitely resilient. Lesson: you may not impose your metaphysical *self upon*

346

the Gate. Go through it as a man, by all means, if you must; but never again attempt entry using the Möbius Continuum.

Harry frowned, then slowly nodded. "You're right," he said. "And I've been foolish—but that wasn't entirely my fault. I hadn't intended to use the Continuum in conjunction with the Gate, it just worked out that way. But my curiosity has worked against me. I *had* to see what this Gate looked like—see it with my own eyes. And by now there won't be a man in the entire Perchorsk Projekt who doesn't know what *I* look like! The next time I stick my nose in there, be sure someone will blow it right off my face."

What will you do?

Harry leaned back against the headstone and sighed. "I don't know. But I know I'm tired."

Go home, said Möbius. *Sleep, rest. Things will be that much clearer in your mind when you wake up.*

Harry said his thanks, his farewells, did as Möbius advised. He emerged back in Jazz Simmons's flat in a prone position two inches over his bed, gently fell onto it. Almost before his head hit the pillows he was asleep . . .

Chapter Eighteen
Zek Continues Her Story

IT WAS DEEP TWILIGHT NOW. A FEW BIRDS SANG HUSHED, warbling songs in the grass of the plain; the mountains marched cold on the right flank, dark in their forested roots and gold on their snow-spiked peaks; the tribe of Lardis the Traveller moved silently, no words spoken, with only their natural jingle, the creaking of their caravans and rustle of travois to tell that they were there at all in the shadows of the woods where they skirted the barrier mountains.

It was colder, too, and a racing moon sailed like a pale, far-flung coin on high, calling to the wild wolves of the peaks, whose answering calls echoed down with an eerie foreboding. The sun was a sliver of gold in the south, gleaming faintly far beyond the plain and silvering the coils of winding rivers.

Only Michael J. Simmons and Zekintha Foëner spoke, because they were hell-landers and knew no better. But even their speech was hushed. It would soon be sundown, which was not a time for making loud noises. Even strangers could sense that.

Jazz had built a light-framed travois; he hauled their kit bundled up in skins, carried only his SMG strapped across his back. Zek helped as best she could where the going was rough, but in the main he was well able to manage on his own. In just a few days his trained physique had attained new heights of strength and endurance.

A few miles back they'd picked up the main Traveller party and now Lardis's tribe was complete. Now, too, the sanctuary outcrop was only a short distance ahead; already its dome was visible, with the sun gleaming on it like some great, fleshless, yellowed skull in the middle distance. From here on, as they went, the Gypsies would cover their tracks, leave no sign to tell that they'd come this way. Oh, the Wamphyri knew their hiding-holes well enough, but even so they didn't care to advertise their presence here.

A few minutes ago Lardis had toiled up alongside Jazz and Zek, said: "Jazz, when the tribe's in and settled down, then meet me at the main entrance. Myself and three or four of the lads, we'll have a go at learning how to use these weapons of yours. The flame-engine, and your guns."

"And the grenades?" Jazz had paused for a moment, wiped his sweating brow.

"Eh? Ah, yes!" Lardis grinned. "But bigger fish next time, eh?" The grin had fallen from his face in a moment. "Let's hope we don't have to use them—any of them. But if we do—the silver-tipped bolts of our crossbows, sharpened staves which we've got cached away in the caves, our swords of silver which are likewise hidden, combined with your weapons . . . if it's our turn to go, at least we'll go fighting."

Then Zek had spoken up: "That's gloomy talk, Lardis Lidesci. Is something bothering you? We've just one more sundown ahead of us, and before the next one we'll be meeting up with The Dweller. That's what you promised your people. Surely all's gone well so far?"

He'd nodded. "So far, aye. But the Lord Shaithis has a score to settle. There was no bad blood before. It was the old game of wolf and chicken, as always. But now the chicken has clawed the wolf's nose. He's not

just curious or greedy any more, he's angry! Also—"
and he'd closed his mouth and shrugged.

"Tell us the worst of it, Lardis," Jazz had urged
him. "What's on your mind?"

Again Lardis's shrug. "I don't know—maybe it's
nothing. Or maybe it's several small things. But there's
a mist back there, and that's something I don't like for
a start!" He'd pointed back the way they'd come. In
the distance, to the east, a wall of grey mist rolled
down from the mountains, coiled itself shallowly on the
forests. It swirled and eddied, lapping like a slow tide
over the foothills. "The Wamphyri have a way with
mists," Lardis had continued. "We're not the only
ones who cover our tracks . . ."

"But it's still sunup!" Jazz had protested.

"In a very little while it will be sundown!" Lardis had
snapped. "And the great pass has been in darkness for
a long time now. Here in the lee of these forests,
there's shade aplenty."

Zek's hand had flown to her mouth. "You think
Shaithis is coming? But I've sensed nothing. I've been
scanning constantly but I've read no alien thoughts."

Lardis had breathed deeply, more a sigh. "That's
reassuring, anyway. And if he *is* coming, we'll meet on
our terms at least." He'd glanced up into the mountains. "But the wolves were howling, and now they've
stopped. And our own animals are quiet, too. See—
only look at Wolf, there!" Zek's great wolf loped a
little way apart; his ears were flat and his tail brushed
the rough ground. Every now and then he'd pause and
look back, and whine a little.

Jazz and Zek had looked at each other, then at Lardis.
"But maybe it's nothing," the Gypsy leader had grunted.
And with another shrug he'd gone on ahead.

"What do you make of all that?" Jazz now asked
Zek, his tone soft.

"I don't know. Maybe it's just as he said. Anyway,
the closer we get to sundown, the more nervy everyone

becomes. There's nothing new in that. The Travellers don't like mists, and they like their animals frisky. Anything else is a bad sign. The current mood: it's just a combination of things, that's all." For all her brave explanation, she hugged herself and shivered.

"Ever the optimist?" Jazz's smile was uncertain.

"Because I've come through a lot," she was quick to answer. "And because we're so close to the end now."

"Yes, you have been through a lot." Jazz began hauling the travois again. "And come to think of it, you never did get round to telling me how come the Lady Karen let you go."

"We've been busy," she shrugged. "Do you still want to hear it?" Suddenly the idea appealed to her. Maybe talking would calm her own nerves a little.

"Yes," Jazz said, "but first there are a couple of other things that have been bothering me."

"Oh?"

"Anachronisms," he nodded. "The Gypsies, this romance-language tongue of theirs, their metal-working. Unless there's a lot of this planet I don't know about— and I can't see how that can be, for one side's hot enough to fry eggs and the other would freeze you stiff—then these things I've mentioned are anachronisms. This world is . . . well, it's primitive! But there are paradoxes. Some of the things in this world . . . by comparison they're high-tech!"

Zek's turn to nod. "I know," she said, "and I've thought about it. If you talk to the Travellers about their history, their legends, as I have done, you might find an explanation. Something of one, anyway. According to immemorial sources, their world wasn't always like this. Wamphyri legends bear the Traveller myths out, incidentally."

Jazz was interested. "Go on," he said. "You talk and I'll save my breath for hauling."

"Well, the Traveller legends have it that once upon a time this planet was fertile in almost every region, with oceans, ice-caps, jungles and plains: much like Earth, in fact. And it teemed with people. Oh, it had its vampire swamps, too, but they weren't so active in those days. People knew about them and shunned them; local communities drew boundaries and patrolled them. Nothing living was ever allowed out. Vampirism was treated like rabies, the only difference being that if a man was ever vampirized they didn't attempt a cure. There is no cure. So they'd simply stake him out and . . . you know the way it goes . . .

"But in the main the vampires were kept down, and in those days there were no Wamphyri. The people weren't migratory; they had nothing to fear and so nothing to run from; their systems were mainly barter, less frequently feudal.

"Anyway, as far as I can make out they were maybe three to four hundred years behind us. There were big differences, of course; they hadn't discovered gunpowder, for one thing. Also, while they'd developed a complex language, they still hadn't made much effort to get it down on paper—or on skins. That's why most of this has had to come down by word of mouth, from one generation to the next. Of course, you can get big distortions that way: some unimportant things get exaggerated while others of real importance are lost entirely. For example, the heroes in the Traveller myths are all giants, who eat vampires for breakfast and don't even get stomach ache! But no one remembers who developed the metalworking skills, designed the first caravan, made the first crossbow.

"So that was the way this world was: like ours maybe three or four hundred years ago, but in many ways less dangerous, less warlike, less noisy. Mainly people lived in peace with each other, and apart from small territorial disputes they were left alone to farm, fish, and trade off anything extra which they managed to produce. There have been plenty of worse places, and worse times, in our own world.

"Oh, and perhaps I should mention: in that bygone time the world did have proper seasons, shorter days and nights, again pretty similar to our own planet. But then—

"Then something happened.

"According to the Traveller legend, a 'white sun' appeared in the night sky. It came through the heavens so fast it looked like a bar of fire; it glanced off the moon, speared down and blazed across the surface of the world! As it fell so it shrank, until finally it skimmed across the land in a huge ball of fire, like a flat stone bouncing on water, and came to rest back there beyond the mountains.

"But though it was small, this 'white sun,' its magic was enormous. It speeded up the moon in its orbit, changed the world's axis, brought into being geological stresses of awesome magnitude. It created these mountains, the frozen lands to the north, the deserts of the south. And for a thousand years after its coming, the surface of this world was more like hell than the friendly place it had been.

"The seasons were gone forever, the moon was now a demon flyer that called to the wolves, an estimated quarter-billion people were reduced to a few thousand. The continents had changed, mountains disappeared from where they'd been, were forced up elsewhere; the surviors went through a nightmare of tidal waves, storms, volcanic upheavals—you name it. But they learned to live with it, and eventually the world settled down. Except that now there was a Starside and a Sunside.

"Centuries passed. Who knows how many? Far Sunside became a desert, and Starside . . . well, you've seen it. Only the mountains and their Sunside foothills could support human life as we know it. People had settled there, started to rebuild, however slowly, crudely. They remembered a few of their skills, used them to start afresh. And meanwhile the swamps, mainly unchanged, had restocked with evil vampiric life . . .

"Explorers went over the mountains, through the passes, saw the frozen wastes beyond. Torrential rains, the howling elements and glacial ice had carved mighty stacks from the mountain flanks, but the land was all but barren. Men couldn't live there. *Men* mind you . . .

"Then there came the plague—a plague of vampires!

"The swamps overflowed with the damned things. They infested men and animals in unprecedented numbers. Bands of vampirized men roamed on Sunside, murdering by night and crawling into holes during the interminable days. Reduced to near-savagery by Nature's disaster, now this *un*-natural disaster reduced people further still. Then the tribes rallied, began hunting vampires, killed them as they had in the old days. They used the stake, the sword, fire; they dragged vampires screaming into the open, pinned them down for the sun to fry.

"Finally Sunside was safe again; the swamps became more or less quiescent; the plague was under control. But vampirized men had been driven north through the great pass. Long-lived, they fought with each other for the blood which sustains them. They discovered and lived off the troglodytes in their deep caverns on Starside. Then as they started to inhabit the stacks, so they became the 'Lords' of that dark hemisphere. They built their aeries, called themselves Wamphyri; and with the intelligence of men and the drive of the vampires within them, so at last they began to raid on Sunside. The people they victimized survived by becoming Travellers, and they're still travelling. That's the whole story . . ."

"This 'white sun,' " Jazz said after a while. "Are we talking about the sphere—the Gate—whatever?"

Zek shrugged. "I imagine so. It's a space-time gate, right? Not only a distortion of space but a bridge across time, too. Is it possible that what appeared here thousands of years ago was caused by the Perchorsk accident, and that the two are linked through the sphere? An anachronism, as you say."

"But what the hell was—*is*—it?" Jazz frowned. "Back at Perchorsk there was talk of black, white, even grey holes. And you said it tied in with Wamphyri legends, too. How do you mean?"

"The Wamphyri legends have it that the 'white sun' came from hell or a place that was hell to them, anyway. In other words, a world where the killing sun was a constant factor, a regularly recurring nightmare from which there was only brief surcease. Up until a time only a few years ago, the sphere we came through from Perchorsk out onto the plain of boulders on Starside was buried. It used to lie at the bottom of its crater, where only its upper surface was visible, beaming its white light up into the sky like a searchlight. It was maybe fifteen to twenty feet deep, surrounded by the crater wall. I had all of this from Karen."

"But just two years ago our time—"

"At the time of the Perchorsk accident?" Jazz was quick to note.

"Yes," Zek nodded, "I suppose so. Anyway, that was when a change took place. During sunup, when the Wamphyri stick close to their stacks, the sphere apparently elevated itself up from the bed of its crater until it was positioned as it is now."

"Explanation?"

Zek's shrug. "I certainly don't have one. But the Wamphyri saw it as an omen. Their myths have it that any change in the sphere—the gate to the hell-lands—is portentous of great changes in general. Changes they themselves might instigate."

"Such as?"

"Well, for a long time now they've talked of joining forces and waging war on The Dweller. If they could put aside their own petty squabbles long enough, maybe they'd do that. Also, *we* were something of a change in ourselves. When Chingiz Khuv started sending political prisoners and other 'undesirables' through the Gate as a series of experiments . . . it was the first time that the

355

Wamphyri had proof that the hitherto half-mythical hell-lands were real!''

Jazz was frowning, chewing his lip. "Something's wrong here," he said. "If the recent Perchorsk accident in our world caused the 'white sun' effect thousands of years ago in this one, why didn't we appear through the Gate all that time ago? Another anachronism? A space-time paradox? I don't buy it. It doesn't ring true. Now tell me this: how long have the Wamphyri been using the Gate as a punishment? When did they first start sending transgressors through it?''

Zek glanced at him. "Why do you ask?''

"Just a thought.''

"Well, as far as I'm aware, they've been doing it right through their history, for thousands of years.''

"See what I mean?'' Jazz was sure this was important. "Up until the time I left Perchorsk there had only been a handful of 'encounters'—of which only one was, or had been, a man. A creature of the Wamphyri, anyway.''

Zek shook her head. "No, he was true Wamphyri, that one. He was Lesk the Glut's heir, Klaus Desculu. He had Lesk's egg, but instead of going off and finding or stealing a stack of his own, he tried to usurp his father, Lesk. The Glut is insane; even the Wamphyri recognize that fact, that Lesk the Glut is not responsible. His passions are enormous! He brought Klaus to heel, punished him for ten years—submitted him to incredible cruelties—then banished him through the Gate. He was the one they hosed with liquid fire on the walkway. But I see what you mean. If the Wamphyri have been sending their malefactors through the Gate throughout their history, where have they been going? Not to Perchorsk, obviously, for Perchorsk didn't exist then.''

"Coming this way," Jazz mused, "from Perchorsk to here, there's only one exit—onto the boulder plain on Starside. But going the other way . . . is there more than one exit into our world? One at Perchorsk and another somewhere else?''

It was Zek's turn to be excited. "I've wondered about that," she said. "And it might explain away certain other things which have puzzled me—*and* you.''

"Oh?"

She nodded. "For instance, how is it that the Traveller tongue is so close to the Romanian of our world? And for that matter, how are the Gypsies *themselves* so close? What do you know of Earth's languages, Jazz? *Our* Earth, of course? It's obvious that you're something of a linguist.''

He smiled. "What do I know about Earth languages? Quite a lot, actually. I have qualifications in Russian. My father was a Russian. The Slavonic languages, yes, and something of the Romance tongues, too. That's how I picked up the Traveller *patois* so quickly. Why do you ask?''

"A theory of mine," she answered. 'My own knack with languages comes from my telepathy. Languages are easy if you've a rapport with your subject's mind. But the connection between the Traveller tongue and Romanian seemed so obvious to me. And of course the Wamphyri have the same tongue . . .''

Jazz saw what she was getting at and drew breath in a hiss. "The banished Wamphyri took their language with them into our world!" he said. "Zek, that's clever! But—''

"Yes?"

"But that's to suppose that the Latin tongue originated here, not in our world."

"That's my theory, yes. I also believe that some of those ancient, banished Wamphyri took their followers with them. The Szgany, Zingaro, Zigeuner: the Gypsy!''

"The Romance tongues spread outwards from Russia?" Jazz looked puzzled. "I can't see that."

"Who mentioned Russia?" she answered. "If there

is more than one exit in our world, why must they all be in Russia?''

"Romania?''

"That would be my bet, yes. Ask yourself this: where did the vampire legend arise from in our world? Where does it have its roots?''

"In Romania, of course.''

"And which nation has retained its own language almost entirely intact since time immemorial, despite being surrounded by countries with little or no linguistic relationship? Like Hungarian and the Slavonic tongues?''

"I see,'' he nodded. "By periodic injections of vampires and their followers, right?''

"It's possible.''

Jazz began to get hooked on the idea. "The more I think of it the more plausible it seems,'' he finally said. "The first Wamphyri migrated (were banished) to our world many thousands of years ago. They took their followers and their language with them: the Gypsies and their tongue, which is a form of Latin. They spread outward from Romania into all the lands around, but their heartland was Romania itself. Despite being conquered by Avars, Magyars, Goths, Gepidae and what have you, the language could only be diluted, not eradicated; for when the conquerors moved on there would always be new arrivals from this side of the Gate to reinforce the watered-down tongue. It explains why Romania is so isolated in its use of a Romance language. And as you say, it gives a real basis for Earth's vampire legends. But weren't Gypsies supposed to have come out of India? The Korakaram mountains?''

"Maybe the first of them through the Gate *went to* India,'' Zek answered. "Why not. They're travellers, aren't they? And from there they spread themselves throughout the world. Their urge to travel is simple to explain: it had been bred into them by the Wamphyri for so many hundreds of years . . .''

"So to sum up,'' Jazz said, "what you're saying is

358

this: that there's another Gate somewhere in Romania, through which the Wamphyri have been arriving in our world for millennia?''

"Never a great many of them," she answered. "But yes, that seems to be our conclusion. I hinted at it and you worked it out for yourself. It's plausible, as you said.''

"So why doesn't anyone know about this Romanian Gate? I mean, a thing like the shining sphere isn't likely to remain obscure for very long, now is it?''

"Ask me another," said Zek, with another shrug. "But from what we know of The Dweller, *he* certainly seems to have access to our world. And if *he* doesn't use the Perchorsk Gate—''

"Which Gate does he use?''

"Exactly.''

After a little while, Jazz said: "We've covered a lot of ground. So now, before I get too confused, let's go on to something else.''

"Like why Karen set me free?''

"If you don't mind.''

"Very well, it was like this:''

"I don't know how long I stayed in the Lady Karen's aerie. Time seems suspended in such places, numbed by horror. Not interminably lengthened, however, because so much of one's time is spent asleep—exhausted! To live in such a place drains a person, physically and mentally. Menace seems to lurk even where there is none; nerves stretch to breaking; massive as even the smallest room is, still the *feeling* is claustrophobic. Silent for hours, then ringing with the laughter of the Wamphyri, or perhaps reverberating with screams of direst agony, an aerie is like Satan's antechamber.

"And yet the Lady Karen became my friend, or as much a friend as any human being could ever hope to find in a vampire!

"Perhaps that's not so hard to understand. She had

been a simple Traveller girl. She remembered her previous life, knew the horror of her present circumstances, foresaw a future more monstrous yet. She had been a striking beauty in her tribe, and I myself was not without good looks. She found a kinship with me, read in my predicament echoes of her own. Also, she knew her vampire must soon take ascendancy. When it did . . . her actions would no longer be entirely *her* actions.

"If she hadn't been female—if this aerie had been that of one of the Lords—then things would have been very different. I wouldn't have been here telling the story now. Can you imagine what it means to be loved, physically loved, by one of the Wamphyri? 'Love' in the spiritual meaning of the word isn't part of their language, but in the physical . . .

"When a vampire takes a woman for his pleasure, Jazz—not for food, but for sex pure and simple—well, it cannot *be* pure and it is never simple! The things lovers do . . . nothing is forbidden between a woman and a man in love. But between a vampire and a woman, or between a *female* vampire and a man? They are *powerful* creatures! You have heard that old saying 'a fate worse than death'? Ridiculous, for what could be worse than death? But there, I'm sure I don't have to describe it.

"But Karen was entirely woman, and her female elements were emphasized by her parasite. There was nothing of the lesbian in her—not yet, anyway, though God only knows what she would be like later. So I don't suppose the thought of me as a sexual diversion even occurred to her. Not for herself, anyway.

"But her lieutenants, they wanted me.

"Oh, they had their own women—stolen Traveller girls—but they were dark and I was fair. My colours were so rare as to be almost unheard of. And I was a hell-lander. Better still, I could steal thoughts. Now, the true Wamphyri, born of a vampire egg, has a degree of telepathy—but their lesser creatures do not. Not unless such is deliberately bred into them or gifted to them by their masters. And so, all in all, I would make a highly desirable property. Karen feared that when the vampire in her was fully mature, then she'd lose what small degree of compassion remained in her. Following which my future would become much more unreliable, my unspeakable fate that much more certain. She did not want that for me.

"One day she said to me: 'Zekintha, there is something you can do for me; when it is done, if it is done well, then I shall take you to Sunside and leave you there for the Travellers to find. I see no reason why you should become what I have become, what I am still to become.'

" 'You offer me a way out of this place?' I answered. 'Only tell me what I have to do.'

" 'There's a truce,' she said. 'The Wamphyri have called a meeting. All the Lords shall gather in one place, under their many banners, to see if they can find common ground in a certain cause. Now, can you guess where they'll gather?'

" 'Here?'

" 'Indeed! In the aerie of Karen. That in itself—that they wish to hold their talks here—seems to me a highly suspicious thing. A very inauspicious thing. However, I shall make provisions. Now, what are your thoughts so far?'

" 'I know only what you have told me of these Lords, Lady,' I answered. 'Which is to say that I fear them greatly! I think that if you let the Lords Shaithis, Lesk, Lascula and the others into your castle, then you'll lose it. Of all the stacks, this one of yours holds a prime position, Karen, and they covet it. They know, too, that you have me here, and that I have magic. I am therefore desirable. Your warrior-creatures would pass down to him who killed you, and they are the finest warriors of all, for none could make warriors like Dramal Doombody. These are your own words, which I repeat to you. But if your castle and your beasts and I myself am desirable, you are more desirable still, Karen. They would make fine sport with you—with both of us—before making an end of it. But you are Wamphyri! You would last so much longer than me, and suffer so much more.'

" 'Are you finished?'

" 'For now.'

" 'Normally I would agree with you in everything you've said, but there are always two ways of looking at things. For instance, perhaps there is nothing inimical in this—not immediately, anyway. At least admit this: that if the Lords are to meet, then they need neutral ground on which to do it, even if it is only to agree to disagree! This would be the ideal spot, for they don't consider me their equal; I am merely renting them a room. Also, I said I would make conditions; by which I meant that I will take precautions against treachery. One: they must come alone, without their lieutenants. That shall be the first proviso. Two: no gauntlets.'

" 'What?' I was amazed. 'But, Lady, will they heed you? I mean, you really intend to order them to leave their battle-gauntlets behind?'

" 'For their own protection!' she smiled her half-human smile. 'So that they will not be tempted to brawl amongst themselves if their talks get heated. So . . . no gauntlets—or no admittance. Oh, they'll agree, for they're eager to get this thing underway.

" 'And finally, three: the meeting shall be right here in these chambers—this very hall—with one of my own warrior-creatures in each corner. Stalemate! if they attempt any . . . *act*, against me, then my creatures will attack! Remember, Zekintha, that for all his strength and his powers, a vampire is only flesh and blood. He *will* die in the right circumstances, under the correct conditions. And melting in the stomach acids of a warrior is one such condition. On the other hand, the Lords will know that if I call upon my creatures without

362

provocation, then they shall have the right to deal with me in their way: a stave through my body, decapitation, a bath full of blazing oil! As I said; stalemate. Now what do you say?'

" 'I still find it fraught.'

" 'So do I, but it's done. And I may even profit from it. Now look there—'

"Through the window the mountains were blackly silhouetted where a fan of golden sunlight faded behind them in the southern sky. 'Sundown,' I said. 'Soon . . .'

" 'Aye, soon,' she echoed me. 'When there's a pink rim all along those peaks, then they stir, mount their beasts, glide from stack to stack. They land in the launching levels below, proceed on foot upward through the body of the stack. One at a time, they shall come. My table shall bear . . . unconventional dishes. Suckling wolf in pepper, hearts of great bats floating in their blood, but blackened by the use of herbs, grassland game from Sunside, and weak mushroom ales from the trog caverns. Nothing to inflame their passions.'

" 'But what is your purpose, Lady?' I was curious— terrified, but curious. 'I know you wish nothing to do with these Lords. I know that you are . . . not like them. Could you not refuse them outright? Is there no other place suitable for them to hold their meeting?'

" 'Most of these men,' she answered thoughtfully, 'have never before set foot in Dramal Doombody's aerie—my aerie, now. I think Shaithis was a visitor, once or twice, in Dramal's youth when they had something in common. They used to hunt women together at sundown on Sunside, just the two of them. Not so much a friendship as a rivalry. But for the others it's an opportunity to see what I've got here. I know that they'd use the visit to study my defences against some future invasion. But if I turned down their request, refused to offer them my . . . hospitality, that would only provoke them, unite them against me.'

" 'You said you might even profit from their coming,' I reminded her. 'In what way, profit?'

" 'Ah, yes. And that's where you come in,' she answered. 'We Wamphyri have powers, Zekintha. You are not alone; I, too, have the ability to steal the thoughts of others. It is of course a talent of my vampire, transferring to me. As yet, however, the art is undeveloped, dubious at best. I can't always be sure that I read aright, and over any great distance it is not worth the effort. Also, because I am Wamphyri, they would know if I probed too deeply. Our vampire minds are similar, do you see? But *you* are not Wamphyri . . .'

" 'You want me to listen to their thoughts? And if they should discover me?'

" 'They will *expect* to discover you! What profit in owning a thought-stealer and letting her talent go to waste? But the trick is this; to sneak into their minds without them knowing, with your guard up lest they read yours! Discover you mentally? Possibly; but no real danger, as I've said, for they'd expect as much. But they will not discover you physically for we shall hide you in a secure place. And these are the things I shall desire to know:

" 'Their thoughts and plans concerning myself; whether their meeting here is entirely genuine or simply a ploy to seek out my weaknesses; *their* weaknesses, their uncertainties, if they have any. Look into each of their minds in turn, and see what you can see. Except I'd caution you: don't bother with Lesk the Glut. His brain is addled. His vampire is itself mad. How may one discover truth in a mind as mercurial as that? What?—he cannot make sense of his own thoughts, not from one moment to the next! But he has a strong aerie, and his strength is prodigious, else the others would have dealt with him long ago.'

" 'I shall do my best,' I told her. 'But as yet you

haven't explained the point of this meeting. What is it that brings them together like this?'

" 'The one they call The-Dweller-in-His-Garden-in-the-West,' she answered. 'They fear him. Him and his alchemies, his magics. And because they fear him they hate him! He dares set up his home there in the western peaks, midway between Star- and Sunside, without so much as a by-your-leave! He harbours Travellers, too, and instructs them in his weird ways. And any who dare go against him . . . ah, but *they* have tales to tell!'

" 'And shall you, too, set yourself against this Dweller?' I asked her.

"She looked at me with those blood-hued eyes of hers. 'We shall see what we shall see,' she said. 'Now go, sleep, rest your mind. Perpare yourself. When it is time I shall come for you, show you your hiding place. Do well, and I shall keep my promise.'

" 'I won't fail you,' I told her, and went off to my bedchamber. But sleep was a long time in coming . . .

"Then it was sundown. I started awake, heard Karen's footsteps. And she was hurrying!

" 'Come!' she said, taking my hand. That unnatural strength was in her fingers where they drew me up from my bed. 'Dress—and quickly! The first of them comes.'

"Vampirized Travellers—slaves, leeched to death and returned from that condition by reason of their converted physiologies, their altered organs and functions— had prepared the great hall. The table had been laid, and at one end had been placed the mighty bone-throne of Dramal Doombody. Raised up on a shallow platform, it seemed to yawn down the great length of the table.

" 'There,' said Karen. 'Your hiding place—*within* Dramal's great chair!'

"I might have protested, but she foresaw it, stilled my babble before it could pour out:

" '*Have done!* None shall sit upon the throne of

Dramal. I do this to honour the leper Lord, my father and master, whose egg is in me. *Hah!* So they shall suppose, anyway. Myself, I take the great chair at the other end of the table. Between us they are trapped! Their thoughts, at least. Too late now to make other arrangements. I'll brook no argument. Proceed with your part of our plan or get out. And I mean get out! If you're not with me you're against me. Find yourself new chambers within the aerie, or escape from it if you can. I shall not hinder you—but I can't say as much for the others.'

"She knew I couldn't refuse; her vampire was stirring in her, aroused by her excitement. Useless—indeed dangerous—to try to dissuade her when she was like this. I went to the bone-throne.

"God, what a monstrous chair that was!

"It was a cartilage-creature's lower jawbone, as I have said. Perhaps five feet long, the eye-teeth formed hand grips at the front, so that the user's arms would rest along the shining white cartilage ridges which in our jaws house our side or back teeth. Toward the rear of the jaw its sides rose up steeply to the hinge, but of course the upper half was not there. The flat, steep slope at the back of the jaw formed the chair's backrest, against which was normally set a massive red-tasseled cushion. At front and back, the four corners, knobs of cartilage protruded downward, making perfectly symmetrical feet; the whole piece had been intricately carved and arabesqued, like an enormous ivory. And like ivory, it too had once known life—of a sort. Entire, it stood upon its own small stage, beneath which was my hiding hole. I must crawl in from behind, where once had been the trachea, then sit up inside. In there I found a large cushion; I could sit there as in a canoe, upright, with my head and shoulders protruding through into the cavity under the jaw, and look out through the arabesques so artfully cut in the bone. The great red cushion would not obstruct my view for Karen had had it removed, so that I could view at will every face at the table. It's far easier to know a man's thoughts when you can see his face.

"And so they began to arrive.

"As they came I read their names in Karen's mind. They communicated briefly, mentally, in the fashion of the Wamphyri, exchanging names and boasts. First was Grigis, the least of the Wamphyri Lords. He made out it was a matter of priorities, but plainly he had been sent to test the way.

" *'Grigis is here,'* he sent, as he appeared from the stairwell. *'The Wamphyri honour me, Lady, as you see. My stature is such that I am first-chosen to enter your aerie. Alas, I see warriors there, all about the room. What is this for a greeting?'*

" 'For your protection, Grigis,' she told him. 'and for mine. When heads as great as ours meet, they might clash! But for now consider the warriors as decoration, a symbol of Wamphyri power. They have no instructions. While we and the other Lords are still, they shall be still. And now, welcome to my manse. You have entered of your own free will, and I freely welcome you. Be seated. The others are not far behind.'

"Grigis strode to a window, leaned out and made a sign. It was dark, of course, but that is nothing to the Wamphyri. I read in Karen's mind how a second flyer, warily circling, at once turned inward and sped for the launching levels. Then Grigis took his seat, on one side of the table and well away from the bone-throne. Grigis was of course true Wamphyri and awesome in aspect, but he was nothing special among the Lords; pointless to describe him further.

"So the arrivals proceeded: many lesser lights, but here and there a power among them. Menor Maimbite was one such. His blazon was a splintered skull between a pair of grinding jaws. Allegedly immune to kneblasch and silver, Menor was known on occasions like this to carry a small pepperbox of these poisons, with which to flavour his food. His head and the gape of his jaws were enormous even for a Lord.

"But after a dozen of them were in, welcomed, seated, and while they fidgetted and muttered low among themselves, then the mightiest of them began to show. Fess Ferenc, who stood eight and a half feet tall and needed no gauntlet, for his hands were talons; Belath, whose eyes were ever slitted, set in a fleshless face never known to smile, whose mind was cloudy and cloaked and totally unreadable; Volse Pinescu, who deliberately fostered running sores and festoons of boils all over his face and body, so that his aspect would be that much more monstrous; and Lesk the Glut, who, it was legended, in an attack of his madness, commanded one of his own warriors to fight him to the death! The story went that he'd got under the thing's scales where it couldn't reach him, eaten his way into its brain and so crippled it. But as Lesk left its skull through a nostril, so in a convulsion the beast had snapped at him. He lost an eye and half of his face, where now he wore a huge leather patch stitched to his jaw and temple. But to replace the missing eye, he had grown one on his left shoulder, which he kept bare, wearing his cloak thrown over the right. Lesk took a seat on the left, right next to my hiding place in the bone-throne, which caused me to tremble violently. But I managed to control it.

"Next to last came Lascula Longtooth, who had so refined and concentrated his metamorphic powers that he could lengthen his jaws and teeth at will, on the spur of the moment, which he was wont to do habitually, like a man scratching his chin. And last of all was Shaithis, whose stack was a fortress impenetrable, whose legends were such as needed no embroidery. Of them all, he might *appear* one of the least imposing. But his mind was ice, and every move he made, had made or would ever make was calculated to an inch. The Wamphyri might not greatly respect each other, but every one of them respected Shaithis . . .

"I had wondered at Karen's dress—or lack of it. If I'd been in her position, unwilling hostess to these monsters, I would certainly have buried myself in clothing, even in armour! She wore a sheath of a gown; it was of a white material so fine and clinging that every ripple of her flesh was visible. Her left breast—and she had beautiful breasts—was bare; her right buttock, too, or very nearly; with no undergarments the effect was shattering. But as the Lords had arrived, so her purpose became clear. Instead of casting about with their eyes and minds, *all* thoughts had immediately centred on Karen.

"Remember: these had been men before they were Wamphyri. Their lusts, however magnified, were the lusts of men. All of them, at first sight, lusted after Karen, which kept their minds from more devious work. I'll not mention the *things* I read in their vampire-ridden minds; as for Lesk the Glut, I refuse to even dwell upon what I read in his!

"And so they were assembled, and so after some small preamble, and after trying the food she'd had prepared for them, then the talks commenced . . ."

Chapter Nineteen

The End of Zek's Story—Trouble at Sanctuary Rock—Events at Perchorsk

BY NOW THE DOME OF THE SANCTUARY ROCK HAD RISEN UP to a towering two hundred feet or more. It was a light, patchy ochre—an enormous sandstone pebble lying on its side—protruding from a hillside that rose through pines, oaks, bramble and blackthorn. Above, the belt of trees was narrow, dark now, rising steeply to cliffs and mountainside; below, the forest spread downward into a thin rising mist, levelled out where the foothills met the plain, disappeared in milky distance. A faint light came from the south, like a false dawn. It wasn't dawn, however, but sundown.

Looking up at the rock as they followed flowing contours to its flank, Jazz asked Zek: "Have you been here before?"

"No, but I've been told about it," she answered. "It's wormy as some vast blue cheese, left forgotten on a shelf. There are tunnels and caves right through it, enough room for Lardis's entire tribe and twice as many Travellers again. You could hide a small army in there!" They paused fifty yards from the boulder's base where the hillside fell away and a great cave opened, watched the streams of Travellers entering, taking travois, caravans, wolves and all with them. In a little while orange lights became flickeringly visible (and were quickly hooded) in "window" holes higher up, where lamps or torches were lighted; and still Jazz and Zek stood there in the gathering gloom.

Lardis came looking for them, said: "Give them a little longer to settle in and choose their places, then I'll meet you in there—" he pointed, "—just inside the main entrance, which we call the hall. But if you like your air fresh, best get your share of it now. It gets smoky later. By the time you see sunup again, you'll be ready to barter your eyes for one good deep breath of clean mountain air!" He took up the handles of Jazz's travois. "Here, I'll take this the rest of the way."

"Wait!" said Jazz. He dipped into an easily accessible bundle, came out with two full magazines for his gun. "Just in case," he said.

Lardis made no comment, went off toward the cavern entrance where now moving lights flickered here and there.

"Lardis is right," Zek said. "They'll take some time to get themselves settled in and the place fortified. Let's climb up, behind the rock. We might still be able to see the rim of the sun from up there. I don't like it when the sun goes down."

"Are you sure you're not just putting something off?" Jazz answered. "Zek, I'll not hold you to any promises. I mean, I know you're right: this isn't our world, and so we're drawn together."

She linked arms with him. "Actually," she tossed back her hair, "I think I'd be drawn to you in any world. No, it's just a feeling, that's all. Those caves look totally uninviting to me. See, even Wolf would prefer to stay out here with us."

The great wolf padded along behind them where they climbed through trees along the steeply sloping base of the rock. For fifteen minutes they climbed, until Jazz said: "Far enough, I think. It'll take us just as long to get down again. This rock's bigger than it looks. Come sunup, then maybe we'll climb it to the top."

They found a ledge in the rock and sat there close together, Jazz with his arm around her. She leaned back against the coarse sandstone and toward him, sighed tiredly. "Why do they call you Jazz?"

"Because my middle name is Jason," he said. "And I hate it! Don't make any cracks about the golden fleece, for God's sake!"

"Jason is a hero of my homeland," she told him. "I wouldn't joke about him."

Wolf whined a little where he sat at their feet looking up at them. Zek snuggled closer.

Conscious of her warmth, and of her shape against him, Jazz said; "Zek, finish your story." It sounded abrupt, but he knew it wouldn't do to get caught up in something he couldn't control. Not now, up here with night settling fast.

"What?" she said, her tone surprised. Then . . . perhaps she sensed, or read, his thoughts. "Oh, *that!* It was almost finished anyway. But . . . where was I?"

A little angry with himself, angry with everything, Jazz reminded her . . .

"I'll make it short," Zek said, her voice a little cooler now. "Then we can get on back down.

"The Wamphyri Lords were there in Karen's aerie to talk about The Dweller. But Karen had been right: it wasn't only The Dweller that concerned them. They wanted Karen's stack. Shaithis wanted me, too, for my magic—God knows for what else! The rest of the bunch would dice for Karen; the winner would put her to whatever use; afterwards . . . she would be burned. They feared that her vampire was a mother. If it was and if she should vampirize her entire aerie—give all of her lieutenants eggs, and others to freshly selected, stolen Travellers—why then, with all of her 'children' in thrall to her, there'd be no stopping her! She had to go before things went that far.

"As for her aerie: Fess Ferenc, Volse Pinescu and

one of the lesser Lords were of a mind to produce their own eggs. With Karen out of the way they would do so; their 'progeny' would fight it out and the winner become Lord of Karen's aerie. The losers would remain in thrall to their masters until new opportunities presented themselves. Wamphyri 'children' in thrall, by the way, don't have an easy time of it; there's nothing a Lord enjoys more than using his own child, male or female, for his own satisfaction. The blood of one's own kin, especially of the vampire in him, is the greatest delicacy of all! If Dramal Doombody hadn't been done for, Karen's life would have been an unending nightmare.

"The deed itself—the taking of Karen and her properties—that was to come before her vampire reached full maturity and took ascendancy. Patently it was a slow developer, but the Lords knew from their history and legends that Ladies were hard to get rid of once they achieved full flower. The 'female of the species,' so to speak. So . . . she would be invited to join with the Wamphyri Lords in their attack upon The Dweller. Her forces would be used as cannon-fodder; when the battle was over, and without pause, her depleted units would be crushed in their turn, wiped out, and Karen herself taken.

"If she refused to join in the attack on The Dweller, that would be seen as a rebuke, an insult; it would warrant a full-scale, subsequent attack on her stack. But it was hoped she would join in, for if her aerie could be taken intact, undamaged—simply walked into—so much the better.

"All of this I got in bits and pieces from the minds of Shaithis, Volse, Menor Maimbite and one or two others. I dared not stay with any mind too long, in case they should become aware of me. But Karen had been quite right: in protecting themselves against her probing, they had left themselves wide open to me. I can tell you now, Jazz, that there are many hells. And if one of them is that place we were told about as children, where if we're not careful we go for our sins, then be sure that the others are the minds of Wampyri Lords! There's little enough to distinguish between them . . .

"Anyway, finally the meeting was over and Shaithis stood and made a closing speech. As best I can remember it went like this:

" 'Lords, and Lady:

" 'With one exception—the exception of one vote, that of our . . . *charming* hostess, who will, she assures us, give the matter her most earnest consideration—we are all agreed on a punitive expedition against The Dweller. The hour of that effort against our great and mutual enemy is still to be set, but until it is decided, all are to stand forewarned and prepared. We all have valid reasons to wish to be rid of him. Apart from the fact that he has set up house in our territory—I take it we are agreed that the mountains are ours?—very well; apart from that fact, and that he gives succor to Travellers, who are our traditional prey, some of us have more personal grievances.

" 'Some hundred sundowns past, Lesk sent one of his men to parley with The Dweller. Only to parley, mind you, as we have heard from the lips of Lesk himself, most lucid of Lords. The man did not return. Angered (quite rightly) Lesk sent a warrior to test The Dweller's mettle. The Dweller contrived to trap rays of the recently sunken sun in mirrors, with which he burned Lesk's warrior to a crisp! Lesk, whose reasoning occasionally differs from that of, er, less *sensitive* minds, sent a second warrior—but not directly against The Dweller. For Lesk had determined that The Dweller was a hell-lander, sent here to spy on us and provoke us, perhaps preparing the way for large-scale invasion. The idea became obsessive—that is, he was convinced of its logic—especially so considering that immediately after Lesk's initial attacks upon The Dweller, the Gate to the hell-lands was seen to rise up into the very mouth of its crater! Surely as preamble to the feared attack? And so he sent the second warrior directly *into* the hell-lands, through the gate, to let any would-be invaders see for themselves something of the might of the Wamphyri. Needless to say, the second warrior did not return. But then, no one ever has . . .

" 'Volse Pinescu, having heard of Lesk's losses, determined a more subtle approach: he activated and armed a hundred trogs to send against The Dweller's garden. They were to sack, burn, rape any women to the death and murder any men. They were raw, these trogs, with nothing of the Wamphyri in them; which is to say that while they did not much care for the sun, still its rays would not harm them. The Dweller's vile mirrors would not avail him here! But . . . they, too, failed to return. Apparently they were suborned: The Dweller found caves in which to house them, placed them under his protection!

" 'Grigis of Grigis, being the son of the much-fabled Grigis the Gouge, thought to enrich his struggling stack with The Dweller's wealth—perhaps even to steal his entire garden, which commands a lofty view, as we are all aware. Or maybe Grigis thought to do something more than this; for if he could gain some understanding of The Dweller's magic and his cursed machines, then his own currently—er, middling station?—his *circumstances*, let us say, would be that much more improved and enhanced. Indeed, with The Dweller's weapons at his command, the Lord Grigis might even lord it over all of us! But of course, we can be certain that this was not his intention. Alas, he lost three fine warriors, one hundred and fifty trogs and Travellers, two lieutenants. His stack is now inadequate to his needs. Let us be honest at least with ourselves: if not for the menace posed by The Dweller, one of us by now might well have found the resources to diminish Grigis's lot further yet . . .

" 'My own interest is easy to explain: it *is* interest pure and simple. Curiosity! I desire to know who this Dweller is. Wamphyri?—a new breed born of the swamps, perhaps? If so, how came he by his knowledge of weapons, machines, foul magic? What *does* he there, in his garden? And why are we scorned and so rudely ignored?

" 'This, then, is the plan:

" 'We *watch* The Dweller! Nothing more, simply that—for now. Covertly, in the darkness of sundown—however many sundowns are required—we watch him. How? Through the eyes of our familiar creatures. Through bats great and small. From below, in stealth, where trogs shall crouch in shadows and observe; from above, even so high as they may glide, where our flyers may relay his every move; in our very minds, with which unceasingly we *will* spy upon him!

" 'The extent of his garden, dwellers therein other than he himself, the locations of his mirrors, weapons, the numbers of his retainers—until we know as much of him as is required. And when we know all of these things and can concert our attack accordingly—'

" 'Then you strike?' This last from Karen. And all eyes turning her way where she sat at the head of the long table facing the bone-throne.

"Shaithis eyed her leeringly. 'Then *we* strike, Lady, surely? Unless you've already made up your mind not to be with us?'

"But she merely smiled at him, saying: 'Fear not, Lord Shaithis, for I shall be there.'

"A sigh went up. All were in accord. And the Lady neatly netted. So it appeared.

"Then they took their leave; Shaithis and Lascula being first away, then Lesk, Volse, Belath, Fess, Menor and all the rest, and lastly Grigis. The reverse order in which they'd arrived, leaving their least till last. And when Karen called me out of my hiding place, to attend her by a window, the sky was acrawl with them. They circled outwards, dark clouds of ill-omen in the lesser darkness, each swooping back to his own place, returning to his personal hell.

"I turned to her. 'Lady, you may not go with them against The Dweller!' And I told her all I had read in their minds.

"She smiled a strange, sad, knowing smile. 'But did you not hear me? I said I shall be there.'

" 'But—'

" 'Be still! Why, I could swear you actually *care* for me! Aye, and perhaps I care for you. So make ready what weapons you desire to take with you. If you need something, ask for it. Make provision of whatever I have to offer. Now I rest me. When I awake, before sunup, then I keep my promise.'

"And she did. She went with me for my safe conduct; we had a flyer each; she flew us direct over the mountains and down onto Sunside. And with the new sun rising she bade me farewell and raced her beasts home again. That was the last time I saw her. Watching her flyer out of sight, I couldn't help but feel sorry for her.

"Some time later Lardis and his Travellers found me, and now I've told you everything . . ."

In a little while Jazz said. "There are a couple of other things I'd intended asking you. One of them was about that warrior creature which caused all the destruction at Perchorsk. Well, you've answered that—it was Lesk's creature—but there are other things. The great bat, the wolf, the thing in the tank."

Zek shrugged. "Maybe the bat and wolf got through accidentally. Blinded by the light, the bat flew into the sphere. Like us, it was guided one way through the Gate. Similarly the wolf, which was old, nearly blind. As for the thing in the tank: it was a vampire. As coincidence would have it, it numbered among its ancestors both a wolf and a bat. In its metamorphic state, it was likely to take on characteristics of both. The slug characteristics are typical of its swamp origin. Maybe it entered the gate looking for prey. I don't know . . ."

Jazz blinked tired eyes, said: "Too deep for me. I begin to half understand, but then I bog down. I suppose I'm just weary. One last thing. What about the others from Perchorsk, the men who came through before you?"

"I wasn't told about them," she grimaced. "Khuv—the lying dog—didn't mention them! But I did learn about them from Karen. Belath took the first of them; mutated, he's now one of Belath's warriors. The other was a man called Kopeler. I used to know him."

"Ernst Kopeler, yes," Jazz said. "An esper."

Zek nodded. "He could read the future. When he came through the gate Shaithis's familiar bats saw him. Shaithis took him, but before he could make use of him Kopeler shot himself dead. If I'd been able to read the future, maybe I'd have done the same."

Jazz nodded his agreement, said, "It's time we got on down. I've still got a spot of weapon-training to do. And after that . . . I want you very much. That's assuming I can still manage it, of course." He grinned—but only for a moment.

Wolf, who had been still and silent for some time, began to growl low and throatily. His ears twitched nervously, went flat to his head.

"What—?" Zek stiffened, looked startled; and for the first time Jazz noticed how quiet it had gone, and the thickness of the mist where it rolled down from the mountains. Zek clutched at him, her eyes suddenly flown wide.

"What is it?" he husked.

"Jazz," she whispered. "Oh, Jazz!" She half-closed her eyes, put a slim hand to her forehead. "Thoughts . . ." she said.

"Whose thoughts?" Gooseflesh rose on his spine, his forearms.

"Theirs!"

Panicked shouts came echoing up to them; shock-ingly, an explosion tore the night; one of Jazz's gre-nades, left with Lardis. A weird, bestial roaring commenced: a primal sound. "What the hell—?" Jazz lifted Zek down from their niche in the rock, turned from her to begin making the descent.

"No, Jazz!" she cried, then clapped a hand to her mouth. And: "Oh, be *quiet!*" she whispered. More explosions followed, hideous screaming, then shouting in blunt, commanding tones. Following which all was a tumult of sounds—battle sounds, and desperate!

"They were waiting for us!" Zek hissed. "Shaithis, his lieutenants, a warrior, hidden away in the deepest recesses of the rock. And there are other warriors out here!"

Something huge launched itself from a position higher than their own. It throbbed in the thin mist that curled over the treetops, a dark shape speeding down the sky, trailing appendages which tore through the higher branches of the trees almost directly overhead. It, too, began to roar.

Jazz took his SMG from behind his back, automati-cally loaded up. "We have to help," he said. "No, *I* have to help. You stay here."

"Don't you understand?" she clutched at him, stop-ping him before he could get started. "It's all over! You can't help. That was a warrior, one of several. If you had a tank and crew you *still* couldn't help!"

As she spoke there came a last, booming explosion and dull orange fire blazed momentarily through the screen of trees and mist. There sounded a fresh bout of screaming: human screaming, nerve-shattering, from many terrified throats. Then through a barrage of lesser shouts and yelps, Shaithis's booming voice, reaching up through drifting cordite-stink and mist:

"Find them! Find Lardis and the hell-landers! As for the rest: destroy them all! But don't let the warriors glut themselves. I have been hurt and now I take my vengeance. Now it is *my* turn to inflict pain! Now find the ones I want, and bring them to me!''

"So much for Lardis's defences," Jazz groaned.

"He was ambushed," Zek sobbed. "His people didn't stand a chance. Come on, we have to get out of here."

Torn two ways, Jazz ground his teeth, turned his head this way and that. "*Please*, Jazz!" Zek dragged at him. "We have to save our own lives—if we can."

They couldn't go down, so they started up. But—

Before they could take more than two paces there came a hoarse panting from below, a scrabbling amidst the shrubbery. White-faced, Jazz and Zek shrank back into the shadow of the rock, stared at each other. A figure came reeling up through the trees, clawing at the base of the rock, thrusting itself from bole to bole. In Zek's ear, Jazz whispered: "A Traveller?"

Her face strained in concentration. The panting was louder, frightened, almost a sobbing. Jazz thought: *it has to be a Traveller*. He let the stumbling figure come closer, reached out from cover and grabbed him. At the same time he heard Zek's hiss of warning:

"No, Jazz! It's—"

Karl Vyotsky!

Vyotsky, seizing his one chance to make a break for it—or perhaps simply fleeing from the horror of what was happening below.

The two men recognized each other in the same moment. Their eyes bulged. Vyotsky's mouth flew open in a gasp of complete astonishment; he started to bring up his gun, drew breath for a mighty shout—which went unuttered. Jazz clubbed him in the throat with the butt of his SMG, tried to kick him and missed, slammed a blow to his face. Vyotsky's head rocked on his shoulders; he went crashing backwards, off balance, probably unconscious into brambles and mist-damp shrubbery. The ground mist rolled over him as he went sliding out of sight.

Jazz and Zek listened with bated breath, their hearts pounding. They heard only the hoarse, unending screams from below, a gigantic snuffling and bellowing, loud crunching sounds. And in another moment they started in again to climb.

They forced aching muscles to the limits of effort, drew level with the dome of the rock and climbed above it, ran waist deep through clinging mist and tearing undergrowth where the ground levelled out a little. Then they were climbing again, still not daring to pant too loudly, hearts and lungs straining as they forced weary legs to pump and tired arms to drag them through the foliage. But the sounds from below were gradually fading, and trees and mist both were thinning out.

"A vampire mist," Zek gasped. "They cause it to happen. Don't ask me how. I should have known, should have heard them in my head. But they knew about me and were shielding themselves. Wolf knew, I think. Oh!—where is he?"

She needn't have worried; the animal hounded her heels like a faithful dog. "Save your breath," Jazz growled. "Climb!"

"But I might have heard them, might have given a warning if I wasn't so tired. And if—"

"If your mind hadn't been on other things? You're only human, Zek. Don't blame yourself. Or if you must blame someone, blame me." Jazz dragged her up onto a shale-covered ledge in a slippery rock-face. They had come through the tree-line to the cliffs, the feet of the very mountains themselves. Clear of the mist, they could see a fading orange glow far to the south. It was the sun, and it was down. Sundown, and nowhere was safe now. But at least in the clean light of the stars they could see where they were going.

The ledge was wide but sloped outwards a little; it ran crookedly, steeply upwards. Echoing cries still rang from far below where the mist boiled as before; fewer screams now, mainly the signal calls of monstrous searchers and the answers of their fellows. Then—

Zek gave a massive start, drew air in a plainly audible gasp of terror. "Vyotsky—he's coming!" she said. "He's following us—and Shaithis himself is not far behind him!"

"Keep still!" Jazz grabbed her. *"Shh!"*

They listened, watched. Down below at the edge of the tree-line, the mist parted and Vyotsky came into view. He looked left and right but not up, started toward the base of the cliffs. Perhaps he thought they'd skirted the cliffs, and maybe they should have. But at least on the ledge no one was going to surprise them.

Jazz aimed his SMG, scowled and lowered it. "Can't be sure of hitting him," he whispered. "These things are for close-quarter fighting—street fighting. Also, the shot would be heard."

Again the mists parted and the awesome cloaked figure of Shaithis flowed out of them. He looked neither left nor right but inclined his head to stare directly at the fugitives. His eyes glowed like small fires under the stars.

"There they are!" the vampire Lord shouted, pointed. "On the ledge, under the cliff. Get after them, Karl. And if you'd be my man, don't let me down . . ."

As Shaithis glided forward, Vyotsky passed out of sight into the angles of the cliff face. Jazz and Zek heard shale sliding, Vyotsky's surprised yelp and his cursing. He was on the ledge and had discovered how slippery it was.

"Move!" said Jazz. "Quick—climb! And pray this ledge goes somewhere. Anywhere!" But if Zek did pray, then her prayers weren't answered.

Where the cliff was notched and bent back sharply on itself, the ledge narrowed to an uneven eighteen inches. In the "V" of the notch a chimney of rock had weathered free, leaning outward over dizzy heights. Behind the chimney scree had gathered, forming the floor of a cave. The stars gleamed down on the ledge, but in the deeps of the cave all was inky blackness.

Shaithis, too, was on the ledge now; his commands came echoing: "Karl, I want them alive. The woman for what she may be able to do for me, the man for what he has already done to me."

Edging along the ledge toward the chimney and the cave behind it, Jazz asked Zek: "Why hasn't Shaithis called up more help?"

"Probably because he's sure he doesn't need it," she groaned. Even as she spoke a knob of rock crumbled underfoot where she stepped, causing her feet to slip. Her legs and lower body shot sideways, out over empty space. Jazz let his weapon swing from its sling, grabbed Zek's flying hand. He dropped to one knee, raked the cliff with his free hand to find a hold. His fingers contacted, grasped a tough root in the instant before the girl's weight fell on him.

Zek was dangling now, one elbow hooked over the rim of the ledge, the rest of her kicking and swinging. Only Jazz's grip on her offered any stability at all. "Oh, God!" she sobbed. "Oh, my God!"

"Drag yourself up," Jazz groaned through gritted teeth. "Try not to put too much leverage on me. Use your elbows. Squirm, for Christ's sake!" She did as he said, came slithering up onto the ledge in front of him. He grabbed her belt, hauled her unceremoniously against the face of the cliff. "Now go on all fours," he said. "Don't try to stand up or you'll be over again. If we can just make that chimney . . ." *Oh, and then what?* But he refused to think about that.

Finally Zek crawled onto the scree beneath the overhang, collapsed face-down there and spread-eagled herself, dug her fingers deep into loose rock fragments and hung on. Jazz stopped, caught her under the arm and drew her upright. "We have to get under cover," he said, "otherwise—"

383

Ch-*ching!* came that unmistakable sound from behind them.

Jazz half turned. Vyotsky had appeared round the sharp corner. His cruel lips drew back from his teeth as he lined-up his SMG on the pair he pursued. But from behind him:

"Alive, Karl, do you hear?" Shaithis's voice warned, that much closer now. Vyotsky's eyes went wide with fear. He glanced back. Jazz took the opportunity to swing his own weapon in Vyotsky's direction, squeezed the trigger. To hell with keeping quiet!

The gun chattered, and whining bullets chewed at the cliff like metal wasps, hurling chippings in Vyotsky's face. Instinctively he fired back, and a lucky round snatched Jazz's gun from his hands, sent it spinning out over the abyss. As the sling was yanked from his shoulder, only the chimney of rock stopped him from being drawn after it.

Zek clutched at Jazz and they clung together. And—

"Step over here," said a cool, low voice from the shadows.

A figure was there, in the cave under the overhang, tall, slim, cloaked. Male, he wore an impassive golden mask over his face. Starlight gleamed on the gold. Jazz was struck with the thought that he looked like the Phantom of the Opera! "Who—?" he gasped.

"Quickly!" said the newcomer. "If you want to live."

"Stand still!" Vyotsky shouted, but Jazz and Zek were already moving to obey the stranger. As they stepped toward the cave, so he came out to meet them. Vyotsky saw him. Because of his cloak, at first the Russian mistook him for one of Shaithis's lieutenants.

The stranger held out an urgent hand to the pair, held up his cloak almost as if to shield them. He drew them toward him . . .

So much Vyotsky saw, but in the next moment . . . the Russian blinked, used his free hand to rub furiously at his eyes. They'd gone—all three, gone! But he hadn't seen them step back into the cave.

A huge hand fell on Vyotsky's shoulder and he froze. Shaithis's monstrous voice hissed in his ear: "Where *are* they? Did your weapon strike them? I hope for your sake it did not!" Vyotsky didn't look back, simply continued to gape at the empty ledge ahead.

"Well?" Shaithis's fingers dug into Vyotsky's shoulder.

"I didn't hit them, no," the Russian gulped, shook his head. "There was someone else. A man in a cloak, and a mask. He came . . . and he *took* them!"

"Took them? A man in a cloak and—?" Shaithis's breath was hot on Vyotsky's neck. "A mask of gold, perhaps?"

Now Vyotsky looked at him—and at once shrank back, cringing from the horror of his face. "Why . . . why, yes. He came—and he went! And they went with him . . ."

"Ahhh!" Shaithis hissed. "The Dweller!" His fingers were like the jaws of a steel clamp, crushing Vyotsky's shoulder. For a moment the Russian thought he intended to hurl him down from the ledge.

"It . . . it wasn't my fault!" he gibbered. "I found them, followed them. Maybe they slipped into the cave there. Maybe all three of them are there!"

Shaithis sniffed the air, his blunt snout quivering. "No," he finally said. "Nothing. No one. You failed me."

"But—"

Shaithis released him. "I won't kill you, Karl. Your spirit is puny but your flesh is strong. And there are uses to which good strong flesh can be put in the aerie of Shaithis of the Wamphyri." He turned away. "Now follow me down. And be warned: do *not* try to run away. For if you do that a second time it will make me very, very angry. I would give you to my favourite warrior. All except your quivering heart, which I would eat myself!''

Vyotsky watched him commence the descent, gritted his teeth and slowly lifted the barrel of his gun.

Without looking back, Shaithis said: "Yes, by all means do, Karl—and we shall see which one of us is caused the most pain.''

The Russian's tense expression slowly slackened, relaxed. How could you fight beings like these? What hope did any man have of ever defeating or even damaging something like Lord Shaithis? He let out his pent breath, gulped, put his weapon on safe and followed timidly on behind the other where he made his way down from the ledge.

Below in the woods a great wolf howled piteously— Zek's Wolf, who knew that his mistress was now removed from him and gone far away. He lifted his head and howled again, the cry rippling from his taut throat. Then he sniffed the air and looked north and a little west, across the mountains. She was there, yes. That was the way he must go.

Grey as the night, Wolf began to climb through the trees. Two figures passed him going down. He curled his upper lip back, writhing from his carnivore teeth. But he made no sound. They passed out of sight into the misty woods. Wolf let them go and continued on his way.

The siren call of his mistress was strong in his mind . . .

It was noon at Perchorsk, but in the metal and plastic bowels of that place it could be midnight and nothing would be changed. One change at least was occurring, however, and Direktor Luchov and Chingiz Khuv were watching as a team of workmen fitted pipes high in the wall of the perimeter corridor. The pipes were maybe seventy millimeters in diameter, made of black plastic, and might in other circumstances be conduits for heavy-duty electrical cable. But that was not their purpose.

"A failsafe?" Khuv said. He looked flustered. "But I know nothing about this. Perhaps you'd explain."

Luchov looked at him, tilted his head on one side a little. "You work here," he shrugged, "and I have no reason to keep it from you. I proposed this mechanism some time ago. It is simplicity in itself, and quite foolproof. What's more, it's cheap and very quick and easy to install—as you can see. If you follow these pipes you'll see that they go straight back to the loading bays inside the main-doors. There you'll find a fifteen thousand litre container on the back of a truck. The truck is locked in position with its brakes on, rotor arms removed. That, too, is a failsafe. The pipes connect directly to the truck and they're being laid throughout the Projekt."

Khuv's frown grew deeper. "I've seen the truck," he said. "It's a military supply vehicle, carrying chemical fuel for flamethrowers. Are you telling me that these pipes will carry *that* stuff? But it's highly corrosive! Man, it would eat through this plastic in a matter of minutes!"

Luchov shrugged. "By which time it wouldn't matter anyway," he said. "A failsafe only has to work once, Major, and that's the beauty of this one. Gravity fed, fifteen thousand litres of highly combustible fuel will rush downward through these pipes and circulate right through the Projekt in less than three minutes. As it courses along its way there are sprinklers. They will spray the fuel under pressure into every corner. Its fumes are heavy but they'll spread very rapidly. The Projekt has laboratories, boiler rooms, electrical fires, workshops, a thousand naked flames of one sort or another." He shrugged again. "But I'm sure you can see what I'm getting at. We can sum it up in one very descriptive word: inferno!"

A short distance away, Vasily Agursky had paused to listen. Khuv had noticed him and now he deliberately stared at him. Still looking at Agursky, Khuv said: "I take it this information is not sensitive? If it is, you should know we are being eavesdropped."

"Sensitive?" Luchov glanced along the corridor, saw Agursky. "Ah, but it *is* sensitive, yes! Everyone who works here in the Projekt will soon be aware exactly how sensitive it is. It would be criminally irresponsible for anyone to try to keep it a secret. There will be notices posted everywhere explaining the system in great detail. This is not a matter for the KGB, Major, but for humanity. It is not your sort of 'security' but mine— and my superiors'. And *your* superiors'!"

Agursky came closer, joined Khuv and Luchov. "If this system is ever used," he said, in a strange, emotionless voice, "The Projekt would be destroyed utterly."

"Correct, Vasily," Luchov turned to him. "That is its purpose. But it will only be used if another horror like Encounter One should ever escape from the Gate!"

Agursky nodded. "Of course, for fire destroys them. It's the only way we can be sure that nothing like that ever gets out into the world again."

"More than that," said Luchov. "It's the only way we can be certain that this place never becomes the focal point of World War Three!"

"What?" Khuv snapped.

Luchov rounded on him. "Oh? And do you think the Americans will sit still for a second of those nightmares launched from here into their airspace? Man, you know as well as I do that they think we're manufacturing them!"

Khuv drew air in a gasp, became suspicious in a moment. "Who have you been talking to, Viktor? That sounded very much like something the British spy Michael Simmons once said to me. I hope you haven't been interfering in things which don't concern you. I accept that this failsafe of yours is probably necessary, but I will not accept anyone meddling in my work!"

"Are you accusing me of something?" Luchov kept his anger under control.

"Maybe I am," Khuv's tone was icy. "We still don't know where you disappeared to for three hours when that damned esper ran amok in here. Is that it? Has Alec Kyle been talking to you?"

Luchov scowled, the veins in his seared skull pulsing. "I've told you, I don't know what happened to me that night. I suppose I was unconscious. Maybe it was an attempt to kidnap me—bungled, as it turns out. As for this—Alec Kyle?—I've not only never met him, I've never even heard of him!" Which was true enough, for the man he'd spoken to was called Harry Keogh.

Agursky had turned away, leaving them to their argument. Khuv watched him go, staring hard after his departing, white-smocked figure. Was there something wrong with the peculiar little scientist? Or . . . not wrong but different? Something . . . *different* about him?

"Aren't you interested how it's triggered?" Luchov asked, still glaring.

"Eh? Oh, yes, very interested. I'd also like to know if there's a failsafe for your failsafe!" Khuv's attention was back on the Projekt Direktor. "This place houses some hundred and eighty scientists, technicians, soldiers at any given time of the day and night, and it contains many millions of roubles worth of equipment. If there was an accident—"

"Oh, there'll be no accident," Luchov shook his head. "If it's ever used it will be a very deliberate act, I assure you. Let me tell you how it works.

"There's empty accommodation close to mine. That becomes the failsafe control centre, with access only to the officer on duty and round the clock access to myself. Oh, and yourself, too, I suppose, since you'll probably insist upon it. However, I shall expect you to make your name available for the duty roster, as mine will be."

"Control centre?" said Khuv. "And what will this control centre contain?"

"A closed circuit TV monitor panel with three screens. One will watch the Gate and the others the stairwell through the shaft and the exit from it into the Projekt proper. There will be evacuation alert klaxons, too, though I admit a man will have to be pretty nimble to get out once they start sounding. As for the failsafe mechanism: two buttons and a heavy electrical switch. Button one will sound the evacuation alert in the upper levels the *very moment* that the Duty Officer sees anything come through the Gate. Button two will only be used if the creature is of *that* sort, and if the electrical fence, flame-throwers and Katushevs don't stop it. The button will control subordinate machinery: the alarms will sound more urgently, and steel doors will close in the ventilator shafts. If and when the creature passes from the core area, through the magmass levels and into the complex itself . . . then the switch is thrown. This cannot be done accidentally, or until the two buttons have been pressed. The switch, of course, opens the stopcocks on the tanker."

"Huh!" Khuv grunted. "I note that your quarters— and the control centre—are not far removed from the loading bays and the main entrance."

"Your own quarters are similarly situated, albeit on a different bearing," Luchov pointed out. "We would have equal chances. So would anyone in that area, including your KGB men and parapsychologists."

Khuv grudgingly conceded that. "And you think it's a wise move to tell everyone just exactly how this failsafe operates? You don't think it will scare them witless?"

"I think it probably will," Luchov answered, "but I see no alternative. In the event of . . . a disaster, as many as possible should have the chance to live. And where the military is concerned: well, they are the only ones who can't run when the alarms start sounding. The

390

Katushev crews and the flamethrower squads. And here I'm afraid I begin to sound too much like you for my own liking—but at least they now have the ultimate incentive to stop any emergence from the sphere!''

Khuv pursed his lips, made no reply.

''And now that I have satisfied your curiosity,'' Luchov continued, ''perhaps you'd be so good as to tell me how your—experiments?—are proceeding? Have you had any message from those poor bastards you hurled through the Gate? Or have you simply written them off? And what about your investigations into this intruder affair. Do you know how he got in? What have you discovered about him?''

Khuv scowled, turned on his heel and strode away. Over his shoulder he called back: ''At this moment in time I have no information for you, Direktor. But when I have all the answers, and when they make sense, then rest assured that you will be among the first to know of it.'' He paused in his striding and looked back. ''But you are not the only one who has been busy, Comrade, and I have made certain recommendations of my own. So far you have only considered an invasion from the other side, but my imagination is more wide-ranging. In a few days you will more fully comprehend my meaning, with the arrival of a platoon of crack assault troops—under my command!''

Before Luchov could inquire further, Khuv had passed through a bulkhead door and so out of sight . . .

In his private quarters, Vasily Agursky stared at himself in a mirror on his toilet wall. He stared, and had difficulty in believing what he saw. As yet no one else appeared to have noticed, but then no one took a great deal of interest in him. But Agursky knew himself very well indeed, and he also knew that what he saw in the mirror was more than the sum total of his parts. Of *his* parts.

His first reaction, when he'd noticed the early changes,

had been to distrust the mirror, a distrust which had quickly turned to a strong dislike. Ridiculous for a man to dislike a mirror, but it was true, he did. He disliked *all* mirrors, probably because they reminded him of certain undeniable alterations, which he'd be only too happy to forget about.

The changes were . . . weird! He wouldn't have believed them possible.

He had positioned this mirror on the wall himself, so that his face would be exactly centered in the glass. But now he had to bend his knees a little to get the same effect. He had gained two or more full inches in height. That fact should have delighted him, who had always considered himself as being little more than a dwarf, but instead it terrified him. For he could actually feel the *ability* of his body to be tall! And if the vampiric growth continued—then someone would notice.

His hair, too, was undergoing something of a metamorphosis. Its dirty-grey down was darkening, showing signs of a long-delayed virility, and the halo was contracting toward the centre of his head's dome, filling itself in. No one had noticed that, either, but he supposed they must when finally the growth was complete. Why, already he looked—and felt—years younger. Felt ready now for . . . almost anything. And yet for a little while longer he must continue to play the part of the old Vasily. The old, despised, neglected and contemptuously treated Vasily . . .

Still gazing at himself, Agursky was surprised to feel a growl rising unbidden in this throat. It came up soft, purring from his chest, then thickened to a snarl. His lips curled back from his teeth—from his strong, white, animal teeth, whose canines had grown so as to interlock with each other more surely than they ever had in all his previous life—and he snarled like a beast! But he cut it off right there, took a grip on himself. For a moment there'd been a power in him like none he'd ever known before; and knowing where it came from, he knew too that he must control it. As long as he could.

For at the Perchorsk Projekt, they had this habit of burning things like Vasily Agursky.

Finally he took off his thick-lensed spectacles. The old curved lenses were gone now, removed from their frames and disposed of. In their place, flat discs of common glass which he'd cut in the workshop: "eyepieces for my instruments," as he'd explained it. No need now for aids to eyesight which had improved to an entirely incredible degree. Why, he could even see in the dark!

But in connection with his eyes, there was something else which might soon begin to show, though what he could do about that was quite beyond him to imagine. Contact lenses? By the time he could order and receive them it might well be too late. In a way that frightened him too, but in another way . . . it was fascinating.

Slowly he reached out a hand to the cord of the light-switch, gave it a single sharp tug. *Click!*—and the light went out.

But in the mirror two lesser lights had taken its place. Agursky couldn't suppress the strange smile, the wolfish grin, which spread over his darkly-mirrored features then. A smile in which the pupils of his eyes burned like tiny censers, filled with hell's own sulphur . . .

Chapter Twenty

Harry and "Friends"—The Second Gate

HARRY HAD SLEPT THE CLOCK ROUND, AND TOWARD THE end he dreamed. Not knowing he dreamed, it seemed to him he had always existed in this timeless, lightless limbo, and that now someone called to him from far, far away.

Harry! Harry! You're asleep, Harry Keogh—but the dead are awake! They've begged a boon of me—of me!—whom hitherto they shunned utterly. And I have agreed to talk to you: but when I sought you out, I discovered only a sleeping mind. Jumbled memories and dreams and intricate mind-puzzles. Pictures of an existence beyond existence! A strange thing, your sleeping mind, Harry, and not one with which I may readily converse. So stir yourself! Faethor Ferenczy offers his services . . .

Faethor? Harry snapped awake, sat bolt upright in his bed. Cold sweat drenched his brow, slimed his trembling limbs. A nightmare, yes: he'd dreamed that Faethor Ferenczy called to him in his sleep. A man shouldn't dream about creatures like Faethor, not even when they were dead and no longer capable of mischief. A dream like that was the worst possible omen. But—

A dream? The glutinous, far-away voice sounded again in Harry's Möbius-orientated mind. *A nightmare? Hardly flattering, Harry!* And Faethor's ancient, dead-undead mental chuckle came across all the miles between, came unerringly, tingling at the edges of Harry's still sluggish perceptions. But he was awake now, and the thing was no longer nightmare but reality. It was his business; it was what a Necroscope is all about; and now that he knew it was real it was no longer frightening. His limbs stopped shaking and he peered about the room. The blinds were drawn but slices of light made faded bands on the wall opposite the windows. An electric bedside clock said that the time was three in the afternoon.

"Faethor?" Harry said. "The last time I spoke to you was at your old place under the Moldavian Alps. At that time I got the impression I'd heard the last from you. Has something changed that? Anyway, I'm still in your debt, so if there's something . . . ?"

What? the other's dark chuckle was sly now, insinuating. *Something you can do for me? That's a fine macabre sense of humour you have there, Harry! No, there's nothing you can do for me. But perhaps there is something I can do for you. Didn't you hear what I said? Were you that deeply asleep? I said that the teeming dead have begged my assistance, and that I have agreed to help—if I can.*

"Eh? The dead, talking to you?" Harry slowly shook his head in astonishment. "There must be something they want pretty badly."

Aye, but not for themselves, Harry—for you! They've spoken to me of a quest, your quest, and asked for my guidance. And in this they've shown more wisdom than you. For who would know better the secret source of vampires than an ex-member of the Wamphyri himself, eh?

Harry gaped. The source of vampires! The place where they originated! The world in which they were spawned, to come through into this world—as they had now started to come through the Gate in Perchorsk!

"And do you know this secret source?" Harry couldn't

conceal the eagerness in his voice and thoughts. "Did you yourself come from that place?"

Myself? Was I once an inhabitant of that world of vampire legend? Ah, no, Harry—but my grandfather was.

"Your grandfather? Do you know where he lies, where his remains are buried?"

Buried? Old Belos Pheropzis? Alas, no, Harry. The Romans crucified and burned him a hundred years before your Christ. And my father: the last word I had of him was that he was lost at sea, somewhere off the mouths of the Danube in the Black Sea, in the Year 547. He was a mercenary for the Ostrogoths against Justinian, but of course he was on the wrong side. Ah, we Wamphyri were a fierce lot in our day! There was a living to be made, if you'd the stomach for it.

"Then how can you help me?" Harry was perplexed. "It seems to me that something like a thousand years separates your grandfather's era and yours. Whatever he knew about his origins—about this source world— must have died with him."

But there are legends, Harry! There are memories, stories Old Belos told his son Waldemar, which he in turn passed down to me. They are as fresh now in my mind as they were the day I heard them. I kept them fresh, for they were the only Wamphyri history I was ever likely to know. I was still in thrall to my father at that time. If Thibor, that ingrate, had ever spent his apprenticeship with me, then I would have passed the legends down to him. But of course he never did. Now, if you in your turn would learn these things—which might well provide the clues you need to complete your quest—then come to me in my place and talk to me, as we talked once before.

Faethor's voice was faint now. Killed in a bombing raid in the Second World War and burned to ashes, what was left had seeped into the earth where once stood his house on the outskirts of Ploiesti toward

Bucharest. It must be an effort for one such as he to speak across all these miles, after all this time. On the other hand, Harry was well aware of the devious nature of the vampire—of *all* vampires. To his knowledge they rarely did anything which was not of benefit to themselves. But there again, in the past Faethor had not been orthodox. Harry could never "like" or ever really "trust" him, but he did in a way respect him.

"No strings?" he said.

Strings? I'm a dead thing, Harry. Nothing remains of me but my voice. And only you can hear it—and the dead, of course, when they choose to listen. Even my voice is fading with the years. But . . (Harry sensed his shrug) *do as you will. I am merely respecting the wishes of the dead.*

Harry would have to be satisfied with that. "I'll come," he told the other. "But as well as hungry for knowledge, I'm plain hungry too! Give me an hour and I'll be there."

Take your time, Faethor answered. *I've plenty of it. But do you remember the way?* His voice was dwindling now, shrinking into deep distances of mind.

"Oh, I remember it well enough!"

Then I'll wait for you. And then, perhaps, the Great Majority will see fit to leave me in peace . . .

Harry washed and shaved, had a change of clothes, "breakfasted" and contacted E-Branch. He quickly told Darcy Clarke what he'd done, and what he was about to do. Clarke offered a cautionary "take care" and Harry was ready.

He used the Möbius Continuum and went to Ploiesti.

The scene was much the same as it had been eight years earlier: Faethor's house on the outskirts of the town was one of several burned-out shells lying half-buried in heaps of overgrown rubble, stony corpses in what was otherwise open countryside. It was dark here, around

6:50 P.M. Middle European Time, but there was still enough light for Harry to find himself a tumbled wall and take a seat. And he had remembered the way: he could feel Faethor's presence lying like a shroud on the place, albeit one which was slowly returning to dust. A very faint nimbus of light glowed on the western horizon, beyond the Carpathians in the direction of home.

All around Harry was desolation, made worse by the feel of winter in the air. He shivered, but entirely because of the chill he could feel slowly working its way into his bones. In summer this place would have a certain wild beauty, when the old bomb craters would be masked by flowers and unchecked brambles, and the skeletal walls covered with lush ivy. In the winter, however, the snow would bring the perspective back to gaunt, monochrome reality. The devastation would be obvious, incapable of disguise. It would always be a reminder, and that was probably why the Romanians would never rebuild here.

One of the reasons, anyway, Faethor agreed. *But I have always liked to believe that I was the main reason. I don't want people building here. Since Thibor destroyed my old place I've had several homes, but this was the last of them. This is where I am, so to speak. So now, when people come nosing around and I feel their footfalls—*

"—You sort of gloom over the place. You exert an influence, your aura."

You've noticed.

Harry shivered again, but still only from the cold. "How about your legends, Faethor?" he said. "I don't like to rush you, but I've never yet spoken to one of your sort who told me anything in plain, simple language! And time is precious. It could be that lives are at stake."

At "stake"? An unfortunate choice of words. Do you mean human lives? In that other world? Ah, but they always have been!

"I mean lives which are important to me. You see, I think people have found a way into that place, that source world. Some of whom are, or were, very dear to me."

He sensed Faethor's nod (for the fact is that people nod with their minds as well as their heads.) *So I have been informed—er, by the dead, of course. Very well, the legends:*

"Wait," said Harry. "First tell me what's in this for you? Oh, I know you've said there are no strings attached, but still I can't imagine you'll help me out of the goodness of your heart."

Faethor's chuckle grew into a laugh. Not a pleasant thing. *Ah!—but you know us well, Harry Keogh. Very well, I'll tell you:*

My grandfather, Belos, was exiled from his aerie, his world, his heritage, by the Wamphyri. He had grown too strong. They feared him mightily, and when their chance came they tricked, entrapped, expelled him. His lands and properties were stolen and he found himself here, in this world. He wasn't the first or the last, and if things don't change there may well be others still to come. Now I never knew Belos, who was dead before Waldemar passed on his egg to me, but I do know that if he had not been so badly treated then I would now be one of the Wamphyri in my rightful place—in the source world! When they expelled him they not only stole his heritage but denied Waldemar his after him and also mine. For that reason, and despite the years flown in between, Belos is worth avenging.

"You're going to help me find my way into that world for revenge?" Harry frowned. "I don't intend to look anyone up for you, Faethor. As I see it, it will be a case of in, rescue, retreat. I won't be staying there long enough to write off any old scores."

Oh? And you know all about this place you're searching for, do you? (A certain amusement in Faethor's tone.) *Get in, rescue your loved ones, or whatever, and get out again. As simple as that . . .*

"Something like that, yes." But Harry was less certain now.

Again Faethor's shrug. *Well . . . possibly. But I see it differently. For after all, you are Harry Keogh! And the fact is that in your use of your special talents you have been a dire force against vampires in this world. You've dealt with my treacherous son Thibor, with Boris Dragosani, Yulian Bodescu—the list is impressive. My feeling is that when you enter into the source world, then things are almost bound to happen. I believe that you are the catalyst which will change, perhaps even destroy, the old balance. So all I require of you is this: that if the time should come and someone should ask you, "Who are you?"—then you will answer him that Belos sent you. Is that too much to ask?*

"No, you have a deal," Harry agreed. "So now tell me what you know. First about Perchorsk."

Eh? (Surprise.) *I never heard of it.*

Harry quickly explained.

That may well be one way into, or out of, the source world, Faethor answered, *but it is not the only route. Now listen: this is what Old Belos told my father, which he in turn told me. The Wamphyri sent him into the hell-lands (this world) through a shining white door in the shape of sphere. Yes, the very duplicate of this sphere you've mentioned at Perchorsk. But Perchorsk is in the upper Urals, and Belos's exit-point was far removed from there.*

"So where did Belos surface?"

"Surface" is the wrong word. Rather he "descended." Inside the sphere he fell. He was aware of falling—as if into hell! It was as if he plunged down the throat of a great white luminous shaft whose walls were so far distant he could not see them. He fell, and yet at no great speed, or so he believed. And he must have been correct in that belief, for when he emerged he was still

400

*falling! He fell out of the sphere—the gate of entry—
into this world.*

"Where?" Harry was eager again.

Underground!

"Like at Perchorsk?"

*Unlike Perchorsk. Belos gathered his senses, looked
all around. The sphere he had fallen through was
imbedded in the ceiling of a great horizontal borehole,
over a ledge of smooth dripstone. Through the bed of
the bore rushed a black, gurgling river. Belos knew not
where it came from, nor where it went. All around the
sphere where it hung suspended, great holes were apparent in the ceiling—like these magmass holes of yours
at Perchorsk. Likewise in the ledge where Belos had
landed. The extent of the cave, and its ledge, was not
great. Where the river rushed from cave into darkness,
the gap between ceiling and water came down to a few
inches. The ledge was large enough for a man to walk
maybe ten paces this way, ten paces that, before it
narrowed down and smoothed into the glistening wall
of the bore. There was no way out. Or there was, if a
man had the stomach for it.*

"A subterranean sump!" said Harry.

*Exactly. The river might run for miles. It might never
surface at all! That was Belos's predicament . . .*

*Others had been there before him, and some of them
were still there. He found their remains, ossified. Things
he called "trogs," and "Travellers." even the skulls
and mummied remains of Wamphyri, who'd preferred
to sit here on the ledge and wither rather than risk the
unknown. But Belos's heart was bigger than that.*

"He dared the river?" Harry was fascinated.

*Faethor's shrug. What else could he do? First he
tried to re-enter the sphere, of course, but it rejected
him. When he held up his arms to plunge them into its
light, they were repelled. The Gate into the hell-lands
had closed on him. But to sit here with these others and*

stiffen into stone was not his way. He would go now, while he still had all of his great strength.

Now, Harry, I suppose you have heard this myth, how vampires fear running water?

"Next to you," said Harry, "I'm the world's greatest expert on vampires! Or as much of one as you'll find, anyway. You're going to tell me the myth stems from this underground river, which the Wamphyri had to overcome to make their way to the surface of this world, right?"

Correct.

"Thibor had a different explanation."

Faethor sighed. *Thibor didn't know, as I've explained. He could have learned so much from me, that one. But not knowing, he obviously invented an explanation. Devious, as you've said.*

"I've said that of all of you," Harry reminded. "But you've side-tracked. Get back to the point."

Very well, but the underground river is the source of that particular myth. A vampire is flesh and blood and bone, Harry. Immerse him in water long enough and he will die. Now let me get on:

Belos braved the river, was washed along downstream. At times his head was above water, but there were other desperate moments when the gap narrowed to nothing, so that he was pushed under. It seemed a long time before the ceiling receded, before natural light returned, glimmering at the end of the watercourse. Then came the resurgence, into a basin, which emptied itself into a sluggish river. But this time, as I've said, on the surface. Bedraggled and a little battered, coughing up the river water until he thought he'd dislodge his lungs, at last Old Belos was in this world!

The time—the era—was some three hundred years before your Christ. And the place . . .

"Yes?" Harry could scarcely contain himself.

As the crow flies: one hundred and seventy miles from the very spot where you now stand!

And indeed Harry was on his feet. "Where, exactly?" he asked.

Near Radujevac, on the Dunarea, Faethor told him. *Or on the banks of the Danube, as it might be better known to you. That's where you'll find this resurgence. It is the source of the legend, and the legend is the source of the Wamphyri! Will you go there now, at once?*

"Now? No," Harry shook his head. "Tonight I plan. I go there tomorrow." He stood there in the darkness and sighed.

A weight off your shoulders, Harry?

"Perhaps—or maybe it's just one more burden."

I have kept my part of the bargain.

"And I'll keep mine, if the time should come. Meanwhile, you have my thanks."

Aye, and those of the teeming dead. Hah! Talk about legends! But your own legend is spreading, Harry. And soon to spread much farther, I think. I bid you farewell . . .

Harry beat his arms across his body, loosening the stiffness in his joints and driving out the cold. Then:

"Goodbye, Faethor," he said. And as always, the Möbius Continuum was waiting to welcome him . . .

Harry's plans and preparations were the simplest of things, easily carried out. Back at E-Branch HQ he told Darcy Clarke what he required, and while the items were being assembled he brought Clarke up to date and went a little deeper into detailing what the boss of E-Branch already knew.

When he'd finished Clarke said: "Let's get this right. You're going to Romania, the Danube in the vicinity of Radujevac, where you'll travel upstream along the course of an underground river, right?"

"That's right."

"Somewhere up there you expect to find a Gate like

403

the one at Perchorsk, except there won't be anyone who'll shoot you dead on sight.''

"There might well be people there,' said Harry, "A handful, maybe, but they won't shoot at me. They won't be able to. If I know my business they'll welcome me; they may even have valuable information for me.''

Clarke looked at him and thought; *Dear God!—he's human but he's so bloody inhuman!* Out loud, quietly, he said: ''Dead people, right?''

''Corpses, yes. Maybe not even that. Maybe just memories of people.''

Now Clarke shuddered, long and visibly and violently. He was remembering the Bodescu affair, a time when he'd witnessed with his own eyes the unbelievable *extent* of Harry's power over the dead. Or rather, the result of their respect for him. In fact it hadn't been Harry who called up the dead that time but his son, the then infant Harry Jr. But Harry could do it too, when he had the need.

Finally Clarke steadied himself and continued. ''And having found this Gate, then you'll use it to go . . . wherever! To another world, the place where your wife and son are. And presumably Jazz Simmons, too.''

Harry nodded. ''And Zek Foëner, and maybe one or two others. If they're still alive, and you know I believe they are, then I should have some friends there—I think. But I may also have enemies. At least one, anyway: a KGB thug called Karl Vyotsky.''

''But assuming everything works out OK, then you'll speak to Brenda, Harry Jr., and when that's done you'll see who wants to come back with you?''

''Something like that, except I still don't know if there's a way back. Remember, I know that nothing from this world has ever got *back* here, and I know that nothing that's come here can ever go back there! Does that make sense? Anyway, that's the way it is.''

''In short, you're risking your life.''

"Do you want it done or don't you?"

"I want it done, yes; in my own way I'm as curious as you are. And the next thing I want is to see Perchorsk closed down. Even if they don't make those things there, still it's a time-bomb."

Harry nodded. "I feel the same way about it—but I have Viktor Luchov's word that nothing will ever escape from Perchorsk again. That's good enough for me."

Clarke gave a snort. "Harry, your word is good enough for me *any* time, but I'm just one small cog in a very big wheel. I don't suppose that anyone is going to take preemptive or any other sort of action against Perchorsk. Especially not now, in this new climate of 'political understanding,' but if something else *does* escape . . ." He threw up his hands.

"Then it would be right out of your hands, I know," Harry answered.

Again Clarke's snort. "Right out of control is more like it!" he answered.

"Well, and that's another reason for my going in," Harry was almost fatalistic about it. "To see if there's anything we can do about it—which is maybe better done from the other side."

The two were silent a while, then Clarke said: "Harry, the rest of your gear will take a little time to get hold of. But it's being done. It's very late now and I'm overdue for my bed. I'll catch a couple of hours and be here to see you off in the morning. Before I go, is there anything else I can do for you? And what will you do with yourself for the rest of the night?"

Harry shrugged. "Oh, I'm not tired," he said, "but I will try to get some sleep later. It's silly, I know, but I'd rather tackle that underground river during the daylight hours. I mean, I could go tonight, but I don't fancy that."

"Silly? What's silly about it?"

"Because day or night will make no difference down

405

there. It's pitch dark all the time. It's just that I'll feel happier knowing it's daylight outside. But anyway, before I do anything I have to speak to Möbius again.''

Lost for words, Clarke shook his head. Harry always had this effect on him. ''You know,'' he finally said, ''we're both part of the same world, you and I, but when you talk like that, so naturally, matter-of-factly—about the dead, and about these talents of yours, the Möbius Continuum and what all; the way you say: 'I'm going to speak to Möbius,' just like that—Jesus, it's like you're an alien! Or else it's like I'm a small kid again. I mean, I *know* what you can do, I've experienced it. But still I sometimes doubt my own senses.''

Harry smiled, open and honest. ''And you're the boss of E-Branch!'' he said. ''Maybe you've got the wrong job, Darcy.''

He waited until Clarke had left before he went to see Möbius . . .

In Leipzig it was 10:30 A.M. and the graveyard was locked for the night. But of course Harry didn't go in through the gates but through a door, went to see the man who'd taught him to unlock all such doors.

Harry, my boy, I'm glad you've come, said Möbius. *I've been doing some thinking about this conjectural parallel universe of yours.*

''It gets less conjectural all the time,'' Harry told him. ''Only its nature is conjectural now.'' And he quickly brought the dead mathematician up to date.

Fascinating! said Möbius. *And it confirms my own thoughts on the matter.*

''Well I have to admit it only baffles me,'' said Harry. ''There is light at the end of the tunnel, so to speak, but . . . I mean if there are two gates on this side, why does there only appear to be one on the other?''

Only one? What makes you say that?

''Faethor talked about a shining white door in the

shape of a sphere. *One* door. If there'd been two, wouldn't Old Belos have mentioned the fact?''

Well, whether he did or didn't, there are two, I assure you. Möbius sounded convinced. *Two on this side, and two on that. I can explain the principle very simply, without going into a lot of mathematical detail.*

"I'm all ears," said Harry.

Right, Möbius got down to business. *Let's consider these "gateways" a little less intensely, a little more basically. These "doors" which defy the physical laws of that state which we call space-time. We know there are several sorts, and that all of them warp the "skin" of this space-time dimension. Modern scientists readily admit of one such: the black hole. And they make guesses about another sort, which they've termed white holes. In fact a current theory has it that white and black holes are two ends of the same tunnel. The black sucks material in, and the white expels it. Agreed?*

Harry nodded. "So I understand," he said.

Very well. Now, even if the theory is wrong and they're not two sides of the same coin, there remains one factor common to both.

"Which is?"

That they're both one-way systems! Once you enter a black hole, you don't get out again. And once you're expelled from a white hole, there's no way back in. The way I see it, the same thing applies to your grey holes: this Gate at Perchorsk, and the second Gate which you believe lies somewhere along the course of this underground river.

"One-way systems?"

Each of them! Emphasis on "each." You go in through one, and you come out through the other!

It stopped Harry dead in his tracks. Finally he said; "That's brilliant! Once you use a Gate, it's out of bounds. Having passed you through, it won't accept you again, no matter which end you start out from. But a *second* Gate will! So all I have to do is find the

407

second Gate. In fact, I already know where it is! It's the Gate the Wamphyri have been using to send their monstrosities through to Perchorsk.''

Ah, but that's what *it is, not* where *it is,* said Möbius.

"It's a step in the right direction, anyway," Harry replied. Then he sobered a little. ''There is however one small drawback. If I come through that Gate into Perchorsk, they'll not only shoot me, they'll probably fry me, too!''

Ah—! but here Möbius could only shrug.

"Thanks, anyway," said Harry. "You've confirmed what I was already suspecting: that there *have* to be two Gates. The Wamphyri have been using one for thousands of years, and now they've started using the new one, which Luchov and his crowd inadvertently blasted into being at Perchorsk. It's the only explanation. So . . . if you'll excuse me now I'll be on my way. I have to say goodbye to my mother. She'd never forgive me if I did something like this without telling her.'' He sighed. ''She'll want to try to talk me out of it—even knowing she can't. But . . . she's like that.''

All mothers are like that, Harry, said Möbius, very seriously. *Good luck, my boy*.

But in fact, luck would have very little to do with it . . .

The next morning Darcy Clarke met Harry at E-Branch HQ in London, and while Harry checked his equipment, making sure he knew how to use it, Clarke took the opportunity to pass on a little information.

''About this subterranean contributary of the Danube,'' he said. ''Harry, it's a death-trap! I had it checked out overnight. Our man in Bucharest looked into it for you. The place is known well enough and we have its exact location. There are newspaper clippings concerning it, various bits of documentation. The locals have an immemorial dislike for it. In 1966 a couple of cavers took it on. It was summer and the tributary was running dry at the time. Four hours after they started in there was a flash flood up in the mountains. One body was washed out, the other lost forever. And these were experts.''

"And they were walking and swimming," said Harry. "I won't be."

"Eh?"

"I said I was going up to the watercourse, but I didn't say how."

Clarke gasped, "You'll use the Möbius Continuum?"

"Of course."

"Then why the wet-suit, aqualung and all?"

"Just in case."

Clarke fell silent for a moment, then said; "I was only trying to help."

"And I appreciate it," Harry told him. "But I know my own business best."

Ten minutes later he took up his gear in a waterproof kit-bag and went to Radujevac. From the outskirts of the town he caught a taxi into the countryside close to the location Clarke had given him. He paid his driver with money from the same source. With his bag over his shoulder he set off down a country track, eventually arriving at his destination. It was a wild place and there was no one around. Harry dumped his kit in a copse and covered the bag with dead branches, then returned to the site of the resurgence.

It was in the base of a cliff, overgrown with ivy, where limestone outcrops glistened with moisture. To the northeast stood the grey, forbidding Carpathians, and to the south sloping wooded countryside. Harry stood on the banks of the pool under the cliffs and looked again at the mountains, then down at the dark water where it gurgled into view from untold caverns of gloom. It issued from the mouth of a cave. This was the spot where Old Belos of the Wamphyri first entered our world. And others like him. And between here and those legendary mountains, somewhere underground, lay a gateway to an alien world. Now it was Harry's task to pin-point that Gate as accurately as possible before setting out up the river to find it.

He checked again that there was no one around, no one to see him take his departure. The place was silent, wooded, where only the birds sang and the cold water gurgled. But this time Harry was well muffled-up and didn't feel the cold.

He picked a spot in the foothills to the north-east, went there via the Möbius Continuum. The door from which he exited was the same as always: a "hole" in the universe, with nothing to distinguish it from hundreds of other doors Harry had used. Harry moved again, even closer to the looming peaks. But this time when he emerged, the "edges" of his door shimmered a little. It was the warning he'd been looking for, which told him he was close.

Very close, Harry, said a dead voice in his mind, surprising him. It felt like someone had come up close behind him and whispered in his ear.

"Do I know you?" He scanned the countryside around, looked down on distant towns, Radujevac, Cujmir, Recea. They were smoky, wintry smudges on his horizon.

No, but I know you. Your mother has been making enquiries on your behalf.

Harry sighed. "She means well," he said. "Has she disturbed you?"

Not at all. I'm happy to help. You intend to travel the length of the Radujevac resurgence, right? The voice was full of excitement, eagerness. Which was what gave its owner away.

"You were a caver," said Harry. "You died back in the summer of 1966, somewhere up that underground river."

That's me, said the other, a little sadly. *And I never did get to finish the job. My name is Gari Nadiscu, and if I'd made it the bore would have been named after me: the Nadiscu Route. It was a dream. Maybe you can finish it for me?*

Harry said: "Wait," and transferred to the Möbius Continuum. "Now talk to me," he said "I want to get closer to you." He followed the other's thoughts, emerged at the very foot of the mountains. And again the Möbius door shimmered, more than before, confirming Harry's belief that he was moving closer to the Gate.

"You didn't do badly," he told Nadiscu. "You covered, oh, maybe nine miles before that flood hit you! Are you still down there?" He glanced at the stony mountain soil under his feet. "I mean, is there anything left . . . you know? How did you get trapped? Your companion was washed out."

Trapped, answered the other, grimly. *That's the right word, Harry. I crawled onto a ledge. There was a crack in the wall. As the water rose I climbed deeper into the crack. Finally I got jammed, couldn't move. I was wearing a lung, of course. It was a bad time. I lasted as long as my air . . .*

"That must have been pretty terrible," Harry commiserated. But:

Don't waste time on that, said the other. *You've things to do. How can I help you?*

"Two things," said Harry. "One: what was the course of the river up to the time you . . . when the flood came? And two: how deep are you, as you calculate it, under the surface?"

Nadiscu supplied the answers and Harry thanked him. "I won't be looking for the river's source," he admitted, "for it's a different kind of source that interests me. But if it all works out I'll come back some time and tell you how far I got. OK?"

Thanks, Harry. I'd appreciate that.

Harry used the Continuum and moved on into the mountains, exiting on a steep, pine-covered slope. This time the interference was such that Harry knew he was almost there. Directly below him, at some great depth

411

in the roots of the mountains, the Gate to the world of the Wamphyri was waiting for him.

He calculated the distance to his starting point, fixed his location firmly in his head—his location not only the mundane world but also in the metaphysical Möbius Continuum. It was a sort of mental triangulation. And then he went back to the copse where he'd hidden his gear.

Half an hour later, dressed in wet-suit and aqualung, equipped with fins and a powerful waterproof torch, Harry slipped into the water and conjured a Möbius door. No shimmer here. He moved upstream, emerging in darkness with his flippered feet on a pebbly bed. The darkness was absolute and there was a current strong enough to cause Harry to lean against it. He used his torch to scan the way ahead, its powerful beam cutting the dark like a knife. On the next jump his feet were still on the bottom but the bore had narrowed down, the water was chin-deep, the way ahead convoluted.

And so Harry proceeded.

Sometimes he swam; at other times he was underwater, where there was no gap between ceiling and river; occasionally the bore was wide as a cathedral and the water shallow. Almost before he knew it he found Gari Nadiscu in the crevice where he'd trapped himself. There was very little of him left: a single flipper and an air tank half-buried in shingle, and a trapped thigh bone.

Harry could have come to Nadiscu direct, he saw that now, but there could have been hazards. The caver had been trapped in a tight spot; Harry hadn't wanted to emerge in a cramped, difficult location. Also, and more importantly, Nadiscu might have been too close to the Gate. Harry had experienced the danger in using the Möbius Continuum close to a Gate; it was to be avoided. No, he'd preferred his own way. If there'd been difficulties, getting out again would have been as easy as conjuring a Möbius door. And this way he'd got used to his system of sighting the way ahead and then jumping

412

there. Which was as well, for beyond this point the route was totally unknown.

Now: he and Nadiscu exchanged a few encouraging words, and Harry moved on.

Five minutes later, after a series of short jumps, Harry's exit door shimmered violently and seemed to bend back on itself. Harry emerged in deep water, swimming. He shone his torch ahead. The bore was almost circular, with maybe twelve inches between ceiling and water. He daren't use the Continuum again and so put all of his effort to swimming. The current wasn't much but still it made for hard work.

Then, ahead, Harry saw a faintly luminous arc of light. He switched off his torch and hooked it to his belt, using both hands to aid his flippered feet in forging ahead. The arc expanded and the light grew stronger. White light!

Harry emerged into the cave of the sphere and gratefully hauled himself up onto the ledge—*where he at once recoiled from what lay upon the moist floor!* It was a headless corpse, running rapidly to decay. The head, also sloughing flesh, lay some little way along the ledge. "Jesus!" Harry breathed. He had taken off his demand-valve attachment but now quickly replaced it to breathe bottled air. That was better. Then he examined the corpse more carefully—but without touching it. The severed spinal column was fat, reinforced with extra bone and sinew. It contained in effect *two* spines! Wamphyri! The head would likewise contain a composite brain, also turning to mush.

"Who were you?" Harry asked.

I was Corlis, of the Lady Karen's aerie, the other moaned. *Alas, I was too ambitious. Now go away—leave me to my misery.*

"Too ambitious?" Harry gulped. "So it would appear!" He glanced up at the sphere and quickly looked away. The light was unbearable. From a zippered pocket he took out dark goggles and put them on, then looked

413

all about. A little apart from the corpse lay a modern walkie-talkie radio, somewhat battered, its aerial fully extended. Harry stared at it, shook his head. He could see that it was a Russian model; beyond that it seemed pointless to conjecture.

There were various niches in the walls, together with the mouths of many magmass wormholes. When Harry saw what some of these contained, then he remembered Faethor's—or Belos's—story.

High up in the curved wall, one such sat with its shrivelled legs dangling over the rim of a magmass hole. The thing was mummied, where dripstone had fused its legs to the wall and commenced covering them with gleaming calcium. An eyeless skull, hideously misshapen, leaned out. Frozen in death, its gaping jaws were wolfish, toothed like a carnivore. The creature seemed to leer at Harry with a permanent, imperishable malignancy. He wasn't much worried; it had leered like that for a long, long time. *Vampire killer!* it suddenly accused.

Harry shrugged. "I can't deny it. But on that score, it seems you at least have no worries. Nor any of you here."

Now other voices joined the first: *Impudent pup!* And: *This is a private place of the Wamphyri—begone!* And: *Who are you, to disturb our sleep of centuries?*

"Sorry," Harry shrugged, "but I'm not dressed for conversation—polite or otherwise. But I'd better inform you: I know that to a man you're all exiles. You may have been high and mighty Wamphyri in your own world, but here you're just crumbling old dead things! That's how it goes. Now me, I won't hold your past against you, as long as you don't hold mine against me."

After a moment of blank astonishment: *You dare—!?* they cried in one voice.

"Now it's cold in here," Harry continued unperturbed. "So I'm going to pick up a change of clothing.

414

If by the time I return you're feeling more sociable, we can start over and no hard feelings. If not—'' again his shrug. ''It's your loss, as the teeming dead would doubtless testify—*if* they'd waste their time talking to such as you!''

Before they could answer he took up his torch and flippers, slipped back into the water. It was icy cold but it would only be for a moment. He let the river bob him downstream to a safe distance, then conjured a slightly warped door and floated through it. He fixed the location firmly in his mind, went back to the copse and his kit-bag.

There he took a long deep swig from a hip flask of brandy, tossed the flask away. He tied a fifty foot length of nylon cord to the neck of the waterproof bag, went back to the midnight river and exited the Möbius Continuum into the water at the required location. As the kit-bag sank he swam furiously for the cave of the sphere. Climbing back onto the ledge, he hauled in the kit-bag and quickly changed into warm clothes. The bag also contained a heavy, special-issue machine-gun, which he now checked against the possibility of damp or damage. Everything seemed OK.

Ahhh—! He was aware of a concerted mental sighing as he stood on the ledge and paused to wonder if he'd forgotten anything. *He comes and goes like a ghost! He has a deal of magic!*

Harry smiled. ''Oh, I've got some magic, all right,'' he agreed. ''But as for being a ghost . . . I'm flesh and blood, and it's you fellows who—''

Harry! said a different voice, a very frightened, very primitive, guttural, almost animal voice in his mind. *Be careful, Harry Keogh. It's dangerous to speak to the Wamphyri as you have spoken to them!*

Harry found the speaker—a squat, dwarfish aboriginal creature—crouched in a cramped cavity apart from the others. A stalagmitic sheath had almost completely enveloped him, so that it seemed to Harry he conversed with what was very nearly a stone statue.

"You're not Wamphyri?" he said.

Hah! The others were part-amused, part-outraged. *Him—that!—Wamphyri? A trog, you fool!*

"Trog?" Harry glanced from the trog to the others and back. "Oh, yes, I remember! I was told I might find a trog or two here. Travellers, too, perhaps?"

Travellers, too, Harry, said yet another voice, much more human. But it sounded very distant, that voice, very faint and fading. *Alas, we don't have the same durability as trogs and Wamphyri. I'm afraid we're little more than memories now.*

"So, several sorts of people from the world beyond the Gate," Harry mused. "And none of you willing to help me, eh?" He adjusted his goggles, tightened the strap of his weapon across his shoulder. "What, dead these thousands—or at least many hundreds—of years, you trogs and Travellers, and still the Wamphyri oppress you? I'd hoped to ask your advice."

He looked up, gazed at the glaring white surface of the sphere. If he reached up a hand he could touch it.

Only ask it! Several Traveller voices spoke up. *In our time we fought the Wamphyri. We staked them through their black hearts and burned them. But when they came to power, this is how they avenged themselves. Still, we have no regrets. So speak to us, Harry. We were not primitive, fearful trogs but men!*

There was pride in their fading voices—then sudden panic as Harry stood on his toes, stretched a straining hand toward the surface of the glaring sphere where its huge globe bulged downward from the ceiling. *HARRY —DON'T!*

Too late—his hand had touched the sphere, broken the surface of its skin. He tried to snatch the hand back, which was about as much use as asking a hurled stone not to return to earth.

Harry heard the grim laughter of the Wamphyri, the

groans of trogs and Travellers alike—felt himself grasped, drawn up, passed *into* the sphere. And in a moment the cave and gurgling river had disappeared from sight, and he floated up, up, weightless as a feather in a beam of white light, toward a different place—

—A different world!

Chapter Twenty-One

The Dweller—The Problem at Perchorsk—In the Garden

PERHAPS INSPIRED BY THE REACTION OF THE SPHERE-CAVE'S ossified inhabitants, Harry's first reflex was to panic. Instinctively, he came close to conjuring—almost attempted to fashion—a Möbius door, and only just retreated from that action in time to avert a disaster. God-alone-knew where, or how, he would end up if he tried to use Möbius mathematics here, *inside* the grey hole!

And so he floated, drawn irresistibly upward—or passed—through the Gate; and almost before he knew it . . .

. . . His resurgence was almost as big a shock as his entry; he passed through the skin of the sphere, then slid down its curve crashingly onto a jumble of stony debris between the sphere and the crater wall. For indeed he saw that the sphere was *inside* a crater, and directly overhead—*a second sphere!*

So that now Harry could see almost all of the picture. The jigsaw was very nearly complete. The Gate he had just traversed was the original. The one above, seated in the mouth of the crater, had appeared here simultaneously with the creation of its twin—its other "end"—in Perchorsk. Perhaps the presence of the first had somehow influenced the location of the sec-

ond, Harry couldn't say. Maybe Möbius would know.
Except—

If that decapitated corpse in the cave had come
through comparatively recently, and also the walkie-
talkie . . . were the Wamphyri now using the original
sphere as a dumping site? And why dump a radio? But
one thing was certain: they *had* passed through. They
had entered the sphere—*this* sphere—from this side.
And if they had found their way down here, then he
could make his way up. No sooner had the thought
occurred than he saw the magmass wormholes running
through the rock. They were everywhere, cutting
smoothly through the solid rock at all angles.

Under his duffle-coat, Harry still had his torch clipped
to his belt. He took the torch out, chose a horizontal
shaft and wriggled in. In a little while the hole turned to
the right, then bent sharply into a descent. Harry abandoned it, came out backwards. Other holes were no
better. But then, at his fifth attempt . . .

. . . He found a hole which climbed gently, not so
steeply as to cause him to slide back. In a little while it,
too, bent to one side, the left, following which it rose
marginally more steeply. Then it levelled out and swung
right. But beyond the level bend it shot almost vertically upward. Harry stood up, switched off his torch.
After the claustrophobia of the hole this was a little
better; for now it was as though he stood at the bottom
of a shallow well. Up there, strange constellations of
stars glittered brightly in a black, jewelled sky. He
reached up a hand . . . the rim of the hole was at least
twenty-four inches beyond his grasp.

He bent his knees, jumped. A hard thing to spring
upright and make any height in the confined space of
a hole two and a half feet across! Especially in a duffle-coat,
carrying a heavy machine-gun, with a spare magazine
and two hundred rounds in your pockets.

The gun!

Harry took the weapon from his shoulder, extended

the sling to its full extent. Taking the gun by the barrel, he pushed its stock up the smooth bore of the wormhole, hooked its pistol-grip over the rim. Then, wedging himself against the wall, he used elbows and knees to gain enough height to get his foot into the loop of the dangling sling. And after that it was easy. Gradually straightening up, he dragged himself out of the wormhole and hauled the gun up after him.

Panting a little from his exertions, he scanned the terrain. And just as it had affected Zek Föener, Jazz Simmons and other before them, so it affected Harry. Starside at sundown was—weird!

But while Harry observed Starside, so too was he observed. Keen-eyed shapes moved in the shadows of boulders to the west, and a flitting thing high overhead squeaked a cry beyond the range of Harry's ears to detect. Then the great bat, Desmodus, sped east, making for a distant stack, while on the ground a trog set off to lope westward, cupping horny hands to his Neanderthal face and sending a cry ringing ahead of him. The cry was heard, picked up, passed on. A straggled scattering of trogs spread out over many miles passed the eerie message down the line.

Almost at the same time the messages were received both in the stack and in The Dweller's garden. But where Lord Shaithis of the Wamphyri must order a flyer readied and descend to the launching bays, The Dweller was not dependent upon that sort of conveyance; he simply inclined his head and *listened* for a moment, turned his eyes eastward and sighed. The newcomer's identity could not be doubted; The Dweller would have known that mind anywhere, any time.

So, after all these years, finally *he* had come. And at such a time. Well, nothing for it but to welcome him; and who could say but that shortly he might be sorely needed? And so The Dweller simply *went* to Harry, where for long minutes he had stood, close to the glaring sphere, gazing on the world of the Wamphyri . . .

Harry was staring at the distantly rearing stacks, wondering about them just as Zek, Jazz and others had wondered before him. Suddenly . . . he was aware that someone watched him. He spun round and fell into a crouch, swung his gun up and cocked it. Some forty yards north of the sphere, out on the boulder plain, there stood a figure, motionless, watching. It was a slim figure, male from what Harry could see of it, and its face was golden, burning in the reflected glare of the sphere.

"Don't shoot!" the other called out in a young-old voice, holding up a hand. "There's no danger. Not yet."

There was something about the voice. Harry relaxed a very little, tilted his head on one side inquiringly. "Not yet?"

"No," said the other. "But soon. Look!" And he pointed at the sky to the east. Harry looked.

Dark blots were growing large in the sky. Two of them, with others mere dots far behind. They came from the direction of the stacks. One was winged, shaped something like a manta. The other was . . . a nightmare shape! Gigantic, it squirted through the sky like a squid. "I should think that's Shaithis," said The Dweller, pointing. "And the other thing, that'll be one of his warriors. And see behind them? More flyers, carrying a couple of his lieutenants."

"Wamphyri?" Harry guessed.

"Oh, yes. You'd better come over here."

Go over there? Harry believed he knew why: to be away from the Gate. He knew the voice, too. He *didn't* know it—couldn't possibly know it—but he knew it. He moved to obey, and the flying shapes came closer.

The two leading shapes, Shaithis aboard a flyer, and a riderless warrior, swooped down out of the sky. They began to circle, and Shaithis's beast sank lower, the wind of its great wings blasting dust and grit up from the plain into Harry's and The Dweller's faces. Its shadow fell on them as it shut out the stars, and Shaithis's booming voice called:

"Surrender! Surrender now, to the Lord Shaithis!"

"Are you ready, father?" said The Dweller. He held up one wing of his cloak.

Harry believed. No, he knew. The child he had searched for was eight years old, and this young man was at least twenty, but the two were one and the same. How didn't matter, not right now. Harry's whole world, his entire life, had been filled with things just as strange as this. Stranger.

"I'm ready, son," he answered, his voice catching a little. "But . . . does it work here?"

"Oh, it works. Except you mustn't use it too close to a Gate."

"I know," said Harry. "I tried it once."

Shaithis settled his beast to earth to the west, his warrior crunched down to the east. Other shapes loomed in the sky, almost directly overhead. "Ho, Dweller," Shaithis called, dismounting. "It seems I have you!"

"Let me take you to our garden," said Harry Jr. to his father.

Harry stepped forward, took him in his arms and hugged him. He felt his son's cloak close around him.

Shaithis, striding forward, jerked to a halt. Dust leaped up from the plain, formed itself into a devil that swirled in the vacuum that the two men had left behind. They were no longer there.

For long moments Shaithis stood, his flattened, convoluted snout sniffing the air. Then his great nostrils flared and his eyes blazed their fury. He threw back his head and roared. And as the plain echoed his cry, so he began to curse. And then he made his vow:

"Dweller, I *shall* have you!" he snarled. "You and your garden and all you possess. I shall have your magic, your weapons, your cloak of invisibility, your every secret. Do you hear? I shall have you, and the hell-landers, and everything. And when I have these things, then I shall use them to make myself the most powerful Lord there ever has been or ever will be. So speaks Shaithis of the Wamphyri. *So let it be!*"

The echoes of his cry, his cursing and his vow died away, and for a long time Shaithis stood there alone with his dark Wamphyri thoughts . . .

Ten days later:

At Perchorsk, Chingiz Khuz paraded, inspected and briefed his troops, "Khuv's Kommandos," as he had named them: a platoon of top-quality infantrymen from the famous Moskva Volunteers. Thirty armed men and machines, specially uniformed (or painted) in the colours of their task: black combat suits with white discs on the upper arms, plus the usual badges of rank with the hammer and sickle sigil blazoned over. Their vehicles—five light-weight, jeep-like trucks and trailers, plus three outrider motor-cycles, all for the moment waiting in the Projekt's loading/unloading bays—were likewise black, marked on their doors and panniers with the white disc of the Gate. They bore no number plates, carried no documentation. No requirement for such encumbrances where they were going.

For the next ten days these men would sleep in a converted Projekt warehouse here "on the premises"; they'd be briefed, given all available details of what they could expect, shown films of the same, and intensively trained in the use of one-man flamethrowers and three larger, trailer-transported units. Their mission: go into the sphere, through the Gate, and set up a base camp on the other side. They were in short an expeditionary force.

Each man was hand-picked; they left no loved ones behind, had few friends or relatives, were all volunteers as befitted the history and traditions of their parent regiment. And they were as hard as foot-soldiers come.

From the landing at the top of the wooden stairs Viktor Luchov watched Khuv strut, listened to his voice echoing up as he paraded before the platoon on the boards of the Saturn's-rings circumference, saw the goggled faces of the thirty where they stood at ease turning to follow him up and down, up and down, as he delivered his welcoming address.

Welcome—*hah!*

And would the hostile new world they were invading welcome them, too?—Luchov wondered. With *what* would it welcome them?

Finally the initial introduction to Perchorsk was over: Khuv handed over to his Sergeant-Major 2I/C; the men were fallen out, told to leave the core in an orderly fashion and return to their billets. They came up the steps single-file, passed Luchov and disappeared through the magmass levels. Khuv himself was the last to leave, and looking ahead up the steps he saw Luchov waiting for him. "Well," he said, as he came up the stairs to the landing, "and what do you think of them?"

"I heard what you said to them." Luchov's voice was cold, almost distant. "What difference does it make what I think of them? I know where they're going, and therefore that they're dead men!"

Khuv's dark eyes were bright, less than inscrutable. There was a fever in them, which while it told of excitement refused to hint at the source. So perhaps they were inscrutable after all. "No," he shook his head, "they'll survive. They are the best. Men of steel against entirely flesh and blood monsters. Self-supporting, working as a perfectly co-ordinated team, equipped with the best personal weapons we can give them . . . they'll do much better than just survive. Against the primitives we know exist through there—" he glanced down on the shining Gate, "—they'll appear as supermen! They're a bridgehead, Direktor, into a new World. Oh, a military bridgehead, I agree—but that's only temporary. One day soon," (and here his eyes narrowed a little, Luchov thought) "you, too, shall visit that other world, when they've made it safe for you. And who can say what resources will be found there? Who knows what wealth, eh? Don't you understand? They'll claim and tame that world for the USSR!"

"Pioneers?" Luchov hardly seemed impressed. "They're soldiers, Major not settlers. Their prime function isn't to farm or explore, it's to kill!"

Again Khuv shook his head. "No, their prime function is to protect themselves and the Gate. To open it up, keep anything else from breaking through to us. From the time they go in, this Gate becomes *literally*—one-way. From here to there. That's what I call security."

"And what about them?" Luchov's voice was colder than ever. "Do they know they can't come back?"

"No, they don't," Khuv's response was immediate, "and they can't be told. You'd better understand that: they can't be told. I have instructions for you on that matter, and on other matters . . ."

"Instructions for—" Luchov sucked in air implosively. "*You* have instructions for *me*?"

Khuv was impassive. "From the very highest authority. The *very* highest! Where those soldiers are concerned, Direktor, I am in charge." He produced and handed Luchov a sealed envelope stamped with the Kremlin crest. "As for not coming back: no, they won't, not immediately. But eventually . . ."

"Eventually?" Luchov glanced at the envelope, put it away. "Eventually?" he snorted. "How long do we need, man? This Gate has been here for over two years —and what have we learned about the world on the other side? Nothing! Except that it's home for . . . monsters! We've never even communicated with the other side."

"That comes first," said Khuv. "Field telephones."

"What?"

"We know sound travels through the sphere," said

the other, "and light—*both* ways! However warped the effect, men can talk and communicate with each other in there. These men will lay a cable as they go. It can be tested after they've travelled no more than a few paces! And if that doesn't work they'll set up temporary semaphore stations. At least we'll get to know what it's like through there. What it's like on the other side."

Luchov shook his head. "That still won't get them back," he said.

"Not yet, not now," Khuv grated, losing his patience. "But if there is a way back we'll find it. *Even if it means building another Perchorsk!*"

Luchov took a pace backwards, was brought up short when the small of his back met the handrail. "Another Per—?" His jaw fell open. "Why, I hadn't even considered—"

"I didn't think you had, Direktor." Now Khuv grinned, his face a grim, emotionless mask. "So *now* consider it. And stop worrying about these men. If you must worry, then worry for yourself, and for your staff. You'll find *that* in those orders, too. Once the bridge-head is established—you're next!"

Luchov tottered where he stood grasping the rail. He was furious, but shock had made him impotent as Khuv turned away. Then he found his voice, called out: "But oh how neatly you've escaped the net yourself, eh, Major?"

Khuv paused, slowly turned to face him. He was as pale as Luchov had ever seen him. "No," he shook his head, and Luchov saw his Adam's-apple working, "for that, too, is in the orders. You'll be happy to know that in just ten days time we part company, Viktor. For when they go through, I go with them!"

At the other end of the shaft to the magmass levels, out of sight round the corner, Vasily Agursky had been privy to all their conversation. Now, as Khuv's footsteps sounded on the boards, he turned and ran silently for the upper levels. He wore rubber-soled shoes, moved with the litheness of a cat. No, like a wolf! He loped, and revelled in the strength of his thighs as they effortlessly propelled him. Strong? Even in his youth he'd never known such strength! Nor such passions, desires, hungers . . .

But for all Agursky's speed and stealth, still Khuv caught a glimpse of him before he could pass out of sight. It was only that, a glimpse, but it caused the KGB Major to frown. On top of all his other worries, now there was this thing with Agursky—whatever it was. Khuv hadn't seen much of him lately, but whenever he had . . . he couldn't put his finger on it but something was wrong. And there he went, swift as a deer, head forward, silent as a ghost and just as weird.

Khuv shook his head and wondered what was ailing the strange little scientist. Wondered what had got into him . . .

The next morning, early, Khuv jerked awake to the clamour of alarms. In the moment of waking his heart almost stopped—tried to tear itself free and leap up into his throat—until he realized that these were only the general alert alarms, not Luchov's damned failsafe. Thank God—whom Khuv didn't really have any faith in, anyway—for that!

A moment later, as he hurriedly dressed, came the hammering on his door. He opened it to let in the unctuous Paul Savinkov; except that apart from the sweat on his fat, shining, frightened face, there was nothing at all slimy about him now. He smelled now not of grease but fear!

"Major!" he gasped. "Comrade! My God, my *God!*"

Khuv shook him. "What is it, man?" he snarled. "Here, sit down before you fall down." He shoved Savinkov into a chair.

The fat esper was trembling, wobbling like a jelly. "I . . . I'm sorry," he said. "It's just . . . just . . ."

Khuv slapped him, backhanded him, deliberately

slapped him again. "Now perhaps you'll tell me what's wrong!" he growled.

The white burn of Khuv's slim fingers came up like long blisters on Savinkov's face. His eyes lost their glaze and he shook his head, as if he was the one who had just woken up and not Khuv. Then—Khuv thought the man was about to burst into tears. If he did, Khuv knew he would hit him right in the teeth! "Well?" he rasped.

"It's Roborov and Rublev," Savinkov gasped. "Dead, both of them!"

"*What?*" Khuv knew he must be imagining this; it had to be some crazy dream. "Dead? How, for the love of—? An accident?" He finished dressing, slipped into his shoes.

"Accident?" Savinkov grinned like an idiot, but his features quickly melted into a sob. "Oh, no—no, it wasn't an accident. When it happened, their thoughts woke me up. Their thoughts were—*awful!*"

"Thoughts?" Khuv's mind, still not fully awake, sought for an explanation. Of course: Savinkov was a telepath. "What about their thoughts?"

"Something . . . something was attacking them. In Roborov's room. I think they'd been playing cards, gambling, and that Roborov was a heavy loser. He'd been to the toilet. When he came out . . . Rublev was nearly dead! Something had him by the throat! Roborov tried to pull it off, and . . . it turned on him! Oh, God —*I felt him die!* Huh . . . huh . . . he . . ."

"Go on, man!" Khuv gasped.

"He grabbed the thing and turned it around, and he saw it. He was thinking: 'I don't believe this! Oh, mother, help me! Sweet God, you know I've always loved you! Don't let this happen!' "

"Those were his thoughts?"

"Yes," Savinkov sobbed. "The rest of it was just background stuff, but it was Roborov's thoughts that really woke me up. And as he died—*I saw it too!*"

"What did you see?" Khuv took Savinkov's face between the flats of his palms.

"God, I don't *know!* It wasn't human—or maybe it was? It was a nightmare. It was . . . its shape was all *wrong!* It was like . . . like that thing in the glass tank!"

Khuv's blood ran cold. He gulped air into his lungs, released Savinkov's face. He grabbed his lapels and dragged him to his feet. "Take me there," he snapped. "Roborov's room? I know it. Were you there? No? Then who *is* there? You don't know? *Fool!* Well, we're going there right now!"

On their way, the alarms stopped clamouring. "Well, let's be thankful for that, anyway," Khuv grunted. He jostled Savinkov ahead of him. "At least I can hear myself think! Now, are you sure you can't remember who you told? I mean, did you simply forget *all* the procedures and come running straight to me? God, but if this is a wildgoose chase I'll—!"

But it wasn't.

Outside the door of Roborov's room a sleepy, nervous soldier stood on guard. He saluted sloppily as Khuv and Savinkov came into view. They rushed by him. Inside were two more espers, and a KGB man named Gustav Litve. All were whey-faced, shaken to their roots. Crumpled on the floor, there lay the reason. Or reasons.

Nikolai Rublev could be Savinkov's twin! thought Khuv, grimacing at what he saw. They were, or had been, much of a kind. But now there were differences, the main one being that Savinkov was still alive. And he was also intact.

Whatever it was that had killed Rublev, it had taken half his face from him. The fleshy part of the left side of his face was missing, flensed from the bone, from his ear to his nose and down to his chin. But it wasn't the work of a scalpel or knife. The flesh had been ripped off. In addition his throat was torn—*torn*, as by an animal—with the main arteries severed and exposed. Khuv thought: *where's all the blood?*

Perhaps he'd said something out loud, for his underling Litve said: "Sir?"

"Eh?" Khuv looked up. "Oh, nothing. Fetch Vasily Agursky, will you, Gustav? Bring him here. I want to know what kind of animal could do this, and he might be able to tell me."

Litve gratefully made for the door, called back: "The other's not much better, sir."

"Other?" Khuv's mind still wasn't on business.

"Roborov."

Khuv realized he'd been wandering. To make up for it he snapped. "He was your colleague, wasn't he?"

"Was, sir, yes," Litve answered. He went out.

Behind an overturned table, amidst a litter of bloodied paper money and cards, lay "the other," Andrei Roborov. The two espers were standing looking down on him. Khuv shoved them aside, took a look for himself. Roborov's face was a mask of sheer horror. His dead eyes bulged; his jaws gaped in a frozen rictus of terror; his tongue projected, blue and glistening. Mainly cadaverous in life, he was totally grotesque in death. From the ears up his thin head looked like it had been trapped in a toothed vise and crushed. The skull had caved in, and blood and brain fluid seeped from the cracks and the deep punctures of . . . teeth marks?

"Good Lord!" said Khuv; to which one of the espers added:

"Something bit his head like it was a plum! Major, look at his arms."

Khuv looked. Both arms were broken at the elbows, bent back on themselves until the bones had parted at the sockets. Whatever it was, it had found a simple and effective way of stopping Roborov from fighting back.

Khuv shook his head, felt his gorge rising. He could almost feel the pulse of the Projekt quickening as morning came and the place started to wake up. There was a

faint throbbing underfoot, like the heart of a great
beast. And within the beast, a lesser beast: the one that
had done this. Or perhaps, a greater beast? What *sort* of
beast? Not human, surely. But if not human . . .

There was a telephone out in the corridor. Khuv ran
to it and called the Duty Officer at Failsafe Concen. He
didn't let the man speak but rasped: "Have you been
sleeping? *Have you been asleep on duty?*"

"Who is this?" came a wide awake, alert voice from
the other end. Khuv recognized the voice: a senior
scientist on Luchov's team. A very responsible person.

"This is Major Khuv," he lowered his voice. "It
seems we may have an intruder. Certainly we have a
murderer in the place."

"An intruder?" the voice on the other end hardened.
"Where are you, Major?"

"I'm in the corridor close to KGB quarters. Why?"

"Do you mean an intruder from outside, or from the
Gate?"

"Well, obviously that's why I'm on the 'phone!"
Khuv snapped. "To find out!"

Now the other came back just as venomously: "In
which case it should also be obvious that your intruder
is from outside! If it was anything else—by now you'd
be burning, Khuv!"

"I—"

"Listen, I've got the screens right here in front of
me. Everything is normal down there, except they're all
a bit nervous because of those bloody alarms. Nothing,
repeat *nothing*, has come through that Gate!"

Khuv slammed the 'phone down. He stood glaring at
it. Something was loose in here. Maybe it had been *let*
loose in here. By whom? British E-Branch?

He ran back into Roborov's room, told the two espers:
"Out, leave all this. If you come up with something let
me know. But until then leave this to my investigators."

Savinkov was making himself as small and insignifi-
cant as he could in a corner. "You," Khuv said. "There

431

are three more KGB men stinking in their beds just down the corridor, a stone's throw from the scene of a double murder. Go wake the idle bastards up. Wake them *all* up! Tell them I want them here, now.''

Savinkov went.

Khuv ushered the espers out into the corridor and closed Roborov's door. Viktor Luchov had just arrived, looked bewildered, only half-awake. "Don't go in there," Khuv warned him, shaking his head. Luchov took one look at the KGB Officer's face and was sensible enough to take heed.

"But what's happened?"

"Murder—at least I think so."

"But don't you know?" Luchov gaped.

"I know two people are dead, and if their killer is human, then it's murder."

Luchov was waking up quickly. "Is it *that* bad? Have you checked with Fail—"

"Yes," Khuv cut him short. "To both questions."

"But—"

"No buts," Khuv interrupted again. "If it's something from the Gate, then it's invisible."

At that moment Litve returned with Agursky. Khuv's eyes went straight to the tiny scientist. Except . . . Agursky hardly seemed that small any more. He *slumped* a little, yes, but if he were to stand up straight . . .

Agursky had on his night things with a dressing-gown thrown over them. And he was wearing dark spectacles. "Something wrong with your eyes?" Khuv frowned.

"Eh?" Agursky squinted, peered at the Major through tinted lenses. "Oh, yes. It comes on now and then. Photophobia. It's with being down here, out of the natural light. All this artificial lighting."

Khuv nodded. He had more than enough with which to concern himself without worrying about Agursky's weirdness. "In there," he nodded, indicating the door to Roborov's room. "Two dead men."

432

Agursky seemed hardly concerned. He opened the door, made to go in. Khuv caught his arm, felt the tension in him. Strange, because it hadn't shown in his movements or his mannerisms. "I want you to tell me what killed them, if you can. Give me some sort of idea, anyway. Gustav, go in there with him."

While they were inside the room, Khuv told Luchov all he knew. Impossible to work if the Projekt Direktor was going to be prying into everything. Better to put him firmly in the picture right now, from square one. By the time he was through, Litve and Agursky had come back out of the room. Litve was still very pale; Agursky seemed his usual self.

"Any ideas?" Khuv asked him.

The other shook his head, averted his eyes. "Something terrifically strong. Immensely strong. A beast, certainly."

"Beast?" Luchov blurted.

Agursky glanced at him. "In a way of speaking, Direktor, yes. A human beast. A murderer. But as I said, a very large, very strong man."

Khuv said: "And the teeth marks in Roborov's skull?"

"No," Agursky shook his head. "His skull was smashed in with a hammer or something very similar. Yes, something like a small-pane hammer. But wielded with considerable force."

Remembering that garbage Savinkov had spewed out, Khuv scowled. "But I have an esper," he said, "Paul Savinkov, who says he 'saw' the killer. And he says it was something nightmarish!"

Agursky had started to turn away, but now he slowly turned back. "He *saw* this happen, you say?"

"In his mind, yes."

"Ah!" Agursky nodded his understanding. Then he smiled, shrugged half-apologetically. "Well, *my* science takes note of physical evidence only, Major. Metaphysics isn't my scene. Will you be requiring me any more? I have many things to do now, and—"

"Only one more thing," said Khuv. "Tell me, what did you do with the corpse of the dead creature from the tank?"

"Do with it? I photographed it, studied it to the point of stripping it down to cartilage and bone, finally destroyed, burned it."

"Burned it?"

Agursky shrugged again. "Of course. It was from the Gate, after all. There was nothing else to be learned from it. And . . . best not to take chances with things like that, don't you agree?"

Luchov patted him on the shoulder. "Of course, Vasily, of course we do. Thank you very much."

"If we do want you," Khuv called after him, "you'll be hearing from me. But with any luck we won't." To Luchov he said, "God, he gives me the creeps!"

"This whole place," Luchov muttered, "gives *me* the creeps!"

As Agursky went off, so Savinkov returned with Khuv's KGB operatives. They'd had civil police training, and since this now appeared to be a case of routine murder . . .

Khuv scowled at them. They looked ruffled, unshaven. He dressed them down, told them what had happened and what he wanted. They went into Roborov's room. By now Savinkov had disappeared, probably sneaked off before Khuv could find more work for him.

But as Khuv and Luchov made to return to the upper levels, so the telepath came back. He was reeling, sobbing, seemed totally uncoordinated. "Major—help! I . . . I . . . oh, *God!*"

Khuv pounced on him, grated: "What now, Paul?"

"It's Leo!" he gasped.

"Leo Grenzel?" The locator! "What is it with Leo?"

"I wondered why he hadn't picked up the presence of the intruder," Savinkov babbled, "and so I went to his room. The door was . . . it was open. I went in, and . . . and . . ."

Khuv and Luchov looked at each other. Their expressions were much the same: shock, disbelief, horror! Savinkov's reasoning was faultless, of course: Grenzel, if he was awake and well, should have appeared on the scene long before now.

Leaving Savinkov leaning against the metal wall, sobbing, Khuv and Luchov set off down the corridor at a run. Khuv called back: "No alarms, Paul! Only set them off one more time and the entire Projekt will take flight!"

In Grenzel's room it was a repeat of the same story. His spine had been broken, looked bitten through to the marrow and spinal cord. His sharp features seemed even sharper in death, and his huge, bulging eyes an even deeper shade of grey.

What had those esper's eyes of his seen before he died, Khuv wondered? And then he stilled the bobbing of his Adam's-apple and staggered out of the room, until he was no longer able to hear Luchov's throwing up into Grenzel's toilet . . .

The Dweller's garden was a marvellous place.

It was a miniature valley, a gently hollowed "pocket" at the rear of a saddle in the mid-western reach of the mountains. In extent the garden was something a little more than three acres in a row, with the length of its rear boundary against the final rise of the saddle, and its frontage where the saddle started to dip toward frowning cliffs. A low wall had been built there, to keep people from moving too close. In between there were small fields or allotments, greenhouses and a scattering of clearwater ponds. One of the ponds swarmed with rainbow trout, while some of the others bubbled with heat from thermal activity deep in the ground; hot springs, in fact.

Because of the abundance of water the place was lush with vegetation, but only a handful of species were unknown to Earth. The rest of the flowers, shrubs, trees

435

in the garden would have been perfectly at home in any English garden. Harry Jr.'s mother tended them, when she felt up to it. But usually his Travellers looked after the garden, as they looked after almost everything here.

Harry Jr.'s bungalow house was centrally situated, built of white stone with a red tile roof, its front perched over the wide mouth of a well that occasionally gave off streamers of steam. He swam and bathed in the pool regularly. His Travellers (no longer true Travellers, in fact, for they were permanent dwellers here themselves now) inhabited similarly constructed stone houses at the sides of the saddle, where the level ground met rising cliffs. All such homes were centrally heated, with a system of plastic pipes carrying hot water from a deep, gurgling blowhole. They had glass windows, too, and other refinements utterly unheard of before Harry Jr.'s time.

The Dweller (as all of his tenants insisted on calling him) had built greenhouses in which to grow an abundance of vegetable produce. Heated and watered from the springs, his crops were amazing. Also, he had found ways round the long, cold, dark sundowns. Plant species which would adapt already had, but others which wouldn't received artificial sunlight. The permanently running water drove his generators (small but incredibly powerful machines such as Harry senior had never seen or even dreamed of before), which in turn powered ultraviolet lamps in the greeenhouses—*and* electric lights in the houses!

"You've done . . . so *much!*" Harry Keogh told his son, where he walked with him along the edge of a plot shady with sweet corn grown tall. "All of this is nothing short of . . . astonishing!"

Harry Jr. had heard much the same thing from Zek Föener, Jazz Simmons, every Traveller who ever made it here; it was a common reaction to things he'd come to take for granted. "Not really," he answered. "Not set against what I'm capable of doing. Chiefly I wanted a place to live, for myself and for my mother. So it had to be *made* liveable. And what is it really but a strip of fertile soil some two hundred or more yards long by eighty wide, eh? As for the running of the place, the Travellers do that for me."

"But the buildings," Harry said, as he'd said it so often during the course of the past sunup. "Oh, I know they're only bungalows, but they're so, well, beautiful! They're simple but delightful. The great span of their arches, the delicate buttresses, the cut of the roof timbers. They're not Greek, not anything I can put a finger on, just *so* pleasing. And all built by these . . . well, by these cave-dwellers of yours!"

"The trogs are people, father," Harry Jr. smiled. "But the Wamphyri never gave them a chance to develop, that's all. They're no more primitive than your Australian bushmen, all considered. But on the other hand they're eager to learn. Show them a principle or a system and they catch on quick. Also, they're grateful. Their old gods didn't treat them too well, and I do. As for the architecture which so impresses you: well, that surprises me. Surely you realize that I'm not the designer? I got all this from a Berliner who died back in 1933. A Bauhaus student who never did make it when he was alive, but he's designed some beautiful stuff since then. I'm a Necroscope, like you, remember? All of the very simple, very efficient systems you see in use here were given to me by the dead of your own world! Don't you realize how far you could have gone, the things *you* could have done, if you hadn't spent the last eight years of your life tracking me?"

Harry shook his head, still a little dazed by what his son had shown him, by what he'd been told. "See," he finally said, perhaps a little desperately, "that's another thing. Eight years, you said. Now, in my mind you're a boy, an eight-year-old boy. In fact I've prided myself in picturing you that way, in imagining what you'd be like. It would have been far easier to think of you as a baby, which is how I remember you. But I made myself see you as you'd be now—or as I thought you'd be. And . . . and just look how you are! I still can't get over it.'' He shook his head again.

''I've explained that.''

''What, how you tricked me?'' Harry didn't try to disguise the bitterness in his tone. ''How you not only crossed the divide between universes but displaced yourself in time, too? You went back in time! Long before you were born, and long before I lost you, while *I* was growing up *you* were growing up too—here! Just exactly how old are you, anyway?''

''I'm twenty-four, Harry.''

Harry nodded, sharply. ''Your mother's now fifteen years my senior! Not that she'd recognize me, anyway. And . . . and you *have* looked after her. That was always one of my biggest worries: that she be looked after. But through all of those years I didn't know! Couldn't you have let me know, just once?''

''And prolong the agony, Harry? So that you'd always be there, just one step behind us?''

Harry grimaced, turned away. ''I noticed you've skipped the 'father' bit, too. You're a man, not the boy I expected. You wear that damned golden mask, so that I can't even see your face. You're . . . a stranger! Yes, we're like strangers. Well, I suppose that's the way it had to be. I mean, we're hardly father and son, are we? Let's face it, I'm not all that much older than you, now am I?''

Harry Jr. sighed. ''I know I've hurt you. I knew it all the time you were chasing me.''

''But you kept running?''

''I might have come back, but . . . oh, there were a lot of things. Mother wasn't improving; there were good places I could take her, where she'd be happy; many reasons for not coming back. One day you'll understand.''

Harry felt something of his son's sadness. Yes, there

was a sadness in him. He nodded again, but not so sharply now. For long moments he wrestled with his emotions. In the end blood won. "Anyway," he relaxed, took a deep breath, somehow managed to grin, "just how *did* you do it?"

Harry Jr. had felt the tension go out of his father, knew he'd been forgiven. He, too, relaxed. "Time-travel, you mean? But you did it too, and long before me—relatively speaking."

"I was immaterial—literally. I was incorporeal, all aura. You're flesh and blood. Möbius reckons it can't be done. It would create too many irresolvable paradoxes."

"He's right," Harry Jr. nodded. "In the purely physical sense—in any entirely physical universe—it can't be done."

"Are you telling me there are other sorts of universe?"

"You know of at least one?"

Harry felt he'd had this conversation before. "The Möbius Continuum? But we've already agreed that—"

"Harry," his son cut in, "I'll tell you. You took the universe you knew and gave it a Möbius half-twist. You did to space-time what your mentor had done to a strip of paper. And the ability to do that came down to me. But let's face it, you always knew I'd go one better than that. Well, I did. I took the Möbius Continuum *itself* and did to *it* what Felix Klein did to his bottle! That allowed me to break the time barrier and retain a physical identity, *and* come through to this place. But you know, this is only one place . . ."

Harry said nothing, just stood very still and absorbed what his son had said. There *were* more places, more worlds, an infinite number. Just as space and time were limitless, so were the spaces in between space and time.

Now Harry knew what Darcy Clarke had meant when he said he felt like he stood in the presence of an alien. Harry Jr. was *that* far ahead! Or was he?

"Son—" said Harry eventually, "—tell me: are you still vulnerable?"

"Vulnerable?"

"Can you be hurt—physically?"

"Oh, yes," Harry Jr. answered, and he sighed again. "I'm vulnerable, and never more so than now. In about one hundred hours it will be sundown again. And that's when I'll discover just how vulnerable I am."

Harry frowned. "Do you want to explain?"

"Just like the Wamphyri have their spies, so I have mine. And I get . . . a *feel* for what the opposition is up to. This place has been under observation for months, close scrutiny. Bats on high; trogs down below, on the plain; even Wamphyri mentalists trying to wriggle into my mind—as they've doubtless got into the minds of my Travellers. All of which corroborates things that Zek Föener has already told me. But what reads can be read, you know? What observes can be observed."

"An attack?" his father frowned. "But you told me they'd tried that before, with no success. So what's different now?"

"This time they're united," Harry Jr. answered. "This time they'll *all* come! Their combined army will be massive. Three dozen warriors; countless trogs; all the Lords and their lieutenants. Shaithis has stirred them up."

"But . . . you can get out of it," Harry was bewildered, saw no real problem. "You know the way—all of the ways! We can all be long gone from here."

Harry Jr. smiled a sad smile. "No," he shook his head. "You can, and the others, the Travellers and trogs—whoever wants to go. But I can't. This is my place."

"You'll defend it?" Harry shook his head. "I don't understand."

"But you will, father. You will . . ."

Chapter Twenty-Two

The Dweller's Secret—Karen Defects— War!

THE SUN'S DECLINING RAYS WERE STARTING TO FADE WHERE they turned the highest peaks gold when The Dweller, Harry Jr., called his meeting. He wanted to speak to everyone who lived in or was supported by the garden, and he must do it now, while there was still time. He stood on a balcony under the hollow eaves of his house and addressed guests, Travellers, trogs, making no distinction. His mother was there, too, for a little while, before she went indoors. Smiling, sweet, grey-haired and quite bereft of mind, but happy too in her ignorance. Harry Sr. couldn't bear to look at her, forgetting that in his Alec Kyle body she wouldn't recognize him. He was glad when she went inside. And anyway, to her it had all been so long, long ago.

"Friends, it's time for truths," Harry Jr. held up his arms and the low hubbub of voices was stilled. "It's time for you to make up your minds about certain things. I haven't deliberately misled you, but neither have I told you everything. Well, now I want to put that right. There are some of you here who have nothing to fight for. This just isn't your fight at all. You came or were sent here by the will of others. And I can just as easily take you out of it. Zek, Jazz, Harry, I'm talking to you.

441

"As for you Travellers, you can return to your travelling. The way is open to you: go now down the saddle and through the passes to Sunside. And you trogs: you can be down on the plain on Starside and hidden away in your caves—or in other, safer places—long before the Wamphyri strike. But you should all be aware that they *will* strike, and soon."

A low, massed moaning went up from his shuffling, bewildered trogs; Harry, Zek and Jazz looked at each other in dismay; a young male Traveller cried: "But why, Dweller? You are powerful. You have given us weapons. We can kill the Wamphyri! Why do you send us away?"

Harry Jr. looked down on him. "Are the Wamphyri your enemies?"

"Yes!" they all cried. And: "They always have been," shouted the same young man.

"And do you desire to kill them?"

"Yes!" again the massed shout. "All of them!"

He nodded. "Aye, *all* of them. And you trogs. There was a time when you served a Wamphyri Lord. Would you now turn against them?"

There came a brief, grunted discussion. "For you, Dweller, aye," answered their spokesman. "We know good from evil, and you are good."

"And you, Harry—father? You've been a scourge on vampires in your own world. Do you hate them still?"

"I know what they would do to my world," Harry answered. "Yes, I would hate them in this and any world."

Harry Jr. looked at them all, his eyes behind his golden mask flitting over them where they stood in a body. Finally his gaze fell on Zek and Jazz. "And you two," he said. "I can take you out of here, back where you came from. Do you know that? Any place in your world where you want to go. Do you understand?"

They looked at each other, then Jazz said. "If you

can do it now, then you can do it later. You saved us once, not so long ago. And we've faced the Wamphyri before. How can you think we'll run out on you?''

Again Harry Jr.'s nod. "Let me tell you how it is," he said. "Before most of you came here, at a time when I was beginning to build something here and had only my trogs to help me, I found a wolf on the hillside. His pack had turned on him, attacked him. He was badly torn, dying—I thought. I didn't know or understand the things I know now. I took the wolf in, healed him, made him well. Soon he was up on his feet again. Too soon, and I thought I had saved his life. *But in fact he'd been saved by the creature within him!*''

No one spoke. A hushed silence had fallen over the gathering. Harry Keogh found himself taking a step forward under the balcony, gazing fearfully up at his son.

"Father," Harry Jr. continued, "I told you there were reasons why I couldn't come back. Reasons why I must stand and defend my place. But all of you have told me how you hate and would destroy the Wamphyri. *All* the Wamphyri! So how can I ask you to fight for me?''

"Harry—" his father began, only to be cut short.

"This is how the wolf repaid me," said The Dweller. And he took off his golden mask.

Beneath it was the face of a young Harry Keogh; Harry knew now beyond any doubt that he gazed upon his own true son. But the eyes in his face were scarlet in the twilight!

A long, low sigh went up from the crowd. For long moments they stood and stared, began to mutter, to talk in breathless whispers. Finally the crowd began to break up, drift away in small groups. In a little while only Harry Sr., Jazz and Zek remained. And The Dweller thought: *They're here because without me they have nowhere to go.*

443

"I'll take you out of here now," he said.

"Like hell you will!" his father growled. "Come the hell down from there and explain. You might be The Dweller but you're also my flesh. You, a vampire? What *kind* of vampire that so many people have loved you? I don't believe it!"

Harry Jr. came down. "Believe it or not," he said. "it's the truth. Oh, I'm different, all right. My mind and will are too strong for it. I have mastery over it, I have it tamed. It takes me on now and then, but I'm always ready and always win. Or have so far, anyway. So the vampire works for me, and not the other way around. I get its strength, its powers, its tenacity. It gets a host, and that's all. But there are disadvantages, too. For one, I have to stay here on Starside, or close to Starside. The sunlight—real sunlight—would hurt me. But the main reason I stay here is because this has become my place. *My* place, my territory. No other shall have it!"

He looked at them with his scarlet eyes, smiled mirthlessly. "So there you have it. And now, if you're ready . . . ?"

"Not me," Harry shook his head. "I'm staying, until this is over, anyway. I didn't look for you for eight years just to leave you now."

Harry Jr. looked at Jazz and Zek. Jazz said: "You already have our answer."

Trogs came shuffling out of the twilight. Their spokesman said: "We were Lesk's creatures, and we didn't like it. We liked working for you. Without you we have nothing. We stay and fight."

Harry Jr.'s face showed his despair. The trogs may be fast learners, but they weren't much good with his weapons. Then lanterns came bobbing, together with a familiar jingling, from the direction of the Traveller dwellings.

Jazz and Zek tried to count heads; pointless, there

were as many as before. Maybe eighty of them. Not a
man, woman or child had run out.

"So," said Harry Sr., looking at them all where they
regrouped themselves, "it looks like we stand and fight!"

His son cold only throw up his hands in amazement.
And gladness, Harry thought . . .

An hour later at The Dweller's armoury, Jazz Simmons
had finished handing out German-made pump-action
shotguns and shells to the Travellers. The armoury was
well-stocked and there were weapons for everyone.
There were half-a-dozen flamethrowers, too, and Travellers who had been trained in their use. Harry Jr. was
there to point out that the shells for the shotguns were
probably the most expensive ammunition ever made;
their shot was pure silver. Though most of the equipment had been stolen (Harry Jr. made no bones about
it; he believed the manufacturers were well able to
stand the loss) he'd been obliged to order and buy these
shells. Jazz, ever practical, had asked how they'd been
paid for. With Traveller gold, he'd been told, of which
this world had an abundance. The Travellers considered
it pretty, and of course it was very malleable; on the
other hand it was much too heavy to carry around in
large amounts, and far too soft for serious metalworking. It made nice baubles, which was about as much as
could be said for it!

For himself, Jazz had chosen a heavy caliber machine-
gun, a Russian job firing a mix of tracer and explosive
shells. The weapon could be used with a tripod or
carried in both arms; it took a strong man to handle it.
Jazz knew the gun and had trained with it; it was
capable of laying down a deadly and shattering barrage
of fire.

"But still," he told The Dweller, "from what I've
seen of Wamphyri warriors, I'd say these things are
toys."

Harry Jr. nodded, but: "The flamethrowers are not

toys," he said. "And I assure you the Wamphyri won't like this silver shot! Still, I take your meaning. One warrior—even a dozen—but forty? Ah, but you haven't seen all my weapons!" He showed Jazz a grenade.

Jazz weighed the thing in his hand. It was as large as an orange and very heavy. He shook his head. "I don't know this one."

"It's American," The Dweller told him. "For clearing pill-boxes and foxholes. A very grim weapon: it shivers into fragments of blazing metallic phosphorus!"

Meanwhile, Harry Sr. had used the Möbius Continuum (for the first time in this world) to convey two very important Travellers to a nearby peak rearing high over most of the others. They knew their job and had practiced it on many previous occasions. In a hollowed out depression at the peak's crest, literally an "aerie" in its own right, great mirrors had been rigged on swivels to catch the dying sun's rays and hurl them down—or up—at any attackers. The Travellers also had shotguns and bandoliers of vampire-lethal shells.

As Harry dropped off his astonished charges and prepared to return to the garden, so his keen eyes spotted something approaching in the sky. As yet it was two or three miles east of the garden, but even at that distance its size and shape made it unmistakable. A flyer, like Shaithis's mount!

The Travellers had seen it too. "Shall we try to burn it?" they cried, springing to their mirror-weapons.

"One flyer?" Harry frowned. Instinct cautioned him against abrupt action. "Not unless it makes an attack on the garden."

He went back there, looked for Harry Jr. Instead he found Zek Föener, her eyes closed where she stood facing east and slightly north, one trembling hand to her brow. "Is something wrong, Zek?" Harry asked.

"No, Harry," she answered, without opening her eyes, "something's right! The Lady Karen is coming to join us. She wants to fight on our side. She has four fine warriors, but they're holding back until she calls to them. Now . . . she wants to know if it's safe for her to land.''

''She's not attacking us?''

''She's *joining* us!'' Zek repeated. ''You don't know her like I do, Harry. She's different.''

Karen was closer now, a mile at the outside but still wary, still holding off. Everyone in the garden had seen her. Jazz Simmons came hurrying, a shining brass belt dangling from the ammo-housing of his gun. ''What is it?'' he said.

At the same moment The Dweller had materialized. Zek spoke to both men, told them what she'd told Harry Sr. ''Harry,'' The Dweller turned to his father. ''Go and tell the Travellers to hold their fire. Let's see if she's genuine.''

Before anything else, Harry detoured straight to the peak where the Travellers manned their mirror-weapons. He passed on Harry Jr.'s message, then spread the word right through the garden and its defenders. Meanwhile, Zek had told the Lady Karen: *land in front of the wall, between the wall and the cliffs.*

Karen's flyer swept closer, swooped lower, swiftly grew larger in the sky. Far behind it, four dark shapes made spurting motions across the star-sprinkled indigo of the heavens. Tiny at this distance, still everyone knew how big they really were, knew *what* they really were. ''Here she comes,'' Zek breathed.

The flyer, turning face-on to a low night wind that moaned from the west, dropped lower. It seemed to hover for a moment, like a kite, then dipped down and uncoiled its nest of springy worm ''legs'' to the earth. It bumped gently down, lowered its wings for stability. The thing parked there, swaying and nodding hugely, gazing with vacuous disinterest first at the garden, then down the sweeping ramps of the mountains to the plain, then back to the garden. Karen dismounted, came to the

447

wall. She was dressed—or undressed—to cause consternation, as was her wont.

The two Harrys, Jazz and Zek met her there. It was Zek's impulse to hug her, but she held back. She saw that Jazz was immediately shaken, stricken by Karen's looks. Harry Sr., too: awed by Karen's beauty. It was an unearthly beauty, of course, for it was the work of her vampire. But what it had given her in looks, shape and desirability, it had taken from her in the bloody fire of her eyes. She was unmistakably Wamphyri.

Only The Dweller seemed unmoved. "You've come to join us in the coming battle?" His voice was unemotional.

"I've come to die with you," she answered.

"Oh? And is it that certain?"

"Certain?" she repeated him. "If you believe in miracles, pray for one! For myself, I don't care." And she told them her dilemma, reinforcing what Zek Föener had already made known, how whichever way she jumped the Wamphyri meant to be rid of her. "This way . . . at least I'll take a few of them with me!"

"What of your trogs, your lieutenants?" The Dweller pressed her.

"I activated my trogs, turned them loose," she answered. "My 'lieutenants,' as you call them, are faint-hearted dogs! Them I sent away. Maybe the Lords have taken them on. I neither know nor care."

"Your aerie stands empty?"

"Aye."

"You've sacrificed a lot."

"No," she tossed her head, "I have *been* sacrificed. And now you'd better make your final preparations. You can't hear them but I can, and they're on their way."

"She's right," Zek confirmed it. "Their minds are lusting for war, open to read like reading a monstrous book. They're coming!"

The Dweller nodded, pointed to the four dark shapes

squirting down through the darkening sky. "Your warriors, Karen—are they trustworthy?"

"They answer only my commands," she answered.

"Then station two of them at the back of the saddle, over the rise there," and again he pointed, "and the other pair down there, at the foot of the cliffs where the first trees grow. There they'll form our protection—some protection, at least—and they'll be well-positioned for launching, if the need should arise. And how will you fight?"

"In the thick of it!" She swept back her diaphanous cloak from her right side, took her gauntlet from her belt and thrust her right hand into it. Blades, hooks and scythes gleamed silver in the bright starlight where she flexed the deadly thing, adjusting its fit.

"Look!" Jazz snapped. "I see them."

It was impossible not to see them. The sky to the east was dark with dots large and small, like the approach of a small swarm of locusts. Except, while they were just as ravenous, they were not small and they were not locusts.

"Everyone to his station!" The Dweller cried. "Are those lamps in order?" For answer, all along the wall, Travellers turned on their batteries of ultlraviolet lamps, aiming them down into darkness. They cut the night with their hot, smoking beams. The light wouldn't kill vampire flesh, but they would hurt it greatly and blind Wamphyri eyes, however temporarily.

The Dweller caught the elbow of a passing Traveller. "What of your women and children?" he asked. "And my mother?"

"Gone, Dweller," the man answered. "Down toward Sunside, where they'll stay until they know the outcome."

Harry Jr. turned to his father and the others. He nodded grimly. "Then we're ready," he said.

"Just as well," Jazz Simmons answered, "for it's

already started.'' He inclined his head down toward Starside. ''Listen—''

Hoarse trog cries and the clamour of battle drifted up out of the shadows. The roar and blast of gunfire, too, from a handful of trogs whose learning skills had been able to accommodate weapons.

Harry Jr. said: ''Well, this was to be expected. The Lords have been massing their trogs along the fringes of these mountains for a long time now. There'll be many hundreds of them . . . but I may have their measure.'' He turned to his father. ''Harry, I could use some expert help.''

''Just name it.''

''When did you last call up the dead?''

Harry took a pace back from the other, his face falling. But then he slowly nodded. ''Whatever's in your mind, I'm ready when you are, son,'' he said.

They rode the Möbius Continuum down to the plain of boulders, materializing clear of the mountains and their shadows. Up in the gloomy foothills where they met the mountains proper, there they saw dust-clouds boiling up from what could only be furious fighting. Also, amidst the rumble and roil, the occasional flash and *crack!* of a discharged weapon. The two Harrys moved closer, taking a short jump that brought them to the very fringe of the fighting. And already it was clear that The Dweller's trog troops were on the retreat. A thin brave line of shuffling Neanderthals, they fell back under the massive assault of others just like them, driven ever higher into the sullen foothills. But in fact the Wamphyri trogs were not like them, because they were slaves and The Dweller's trogs were free. Which was why they fought.

When Harry Jr. saw how it was going he groaned. ''I'd like to save some of them if I can,'' he said.

Harry Keogh, Necroscope, closed his eyes and talked to the teeming dead of this strange world. ''We need your help,'' he begged of them. ''You down there, in the earth, under the soil and down where the roots twine. We need your help against a great injustice."

Things stirred in the ground, heard the desperate voice of a friend and tried to answer him. *Who? What? Help you? But how can we help?*

"Trogs!" said Harry Jr. "Before the Wamphyri, they roved over Starside at will. Thousands of them lived and died here. They were their own masters then, and this was their land."

"How about it?" Harry spoke to them as he always spoke to the dead, as his friends, his equals. Even as his peers. "If you're dust then you're beyond helping us, but if you can still hear me, if you can understand, then listen." He told them what was required. Harry Jr, too, answering the stumbling questions of the dead.

The Wamphyri, you say? Some of us served them in life. Many of us, many hundreds, died in their wars. False gods! Vile, terrible masters! But fight them? How? They'll destroy us again, a second time.

"You can't die twice," Harry and The Dweller were desperate. "Only your brothers can die; and they're doing it right now, dying, to hold back the troops of the Wamphyri."

Troops? You mean trogs like us?

"Trogs, yes," said The Dweller, "but slaves of the Wamphyri. Death holds no terrors for such as them. It is preferable to what they have now!"

The Dweller speaks truth, some of Harry Jr.'s own trogs, recently dead in the fighting, joined in. *We at least know you, Dweller, and we gladly rise up again!*

"What of the rest of you?" Harry Sr. cried. "Will you not also rise up? Wake up now, before it's too late. You have sons and grandsons and great-grandsons who are fighting even now. Join us in this last great battle against your immemorial vampire oppressors!"

In the cliffs backing these foothills, in ancient cavern burial grounds, the preserved, mummied bodies of a thousand trogs stirred, groped upward, tore free of the clinging soil. Under the trees, lone graves gave up their dead. Behind the massed Wamphyri trogs where they drove back the defenders, freshly dead cadavers sat up, forced their riven bodies to move, shuffled or crawled toward their vampire-controlled enemies. The stench of the pit filled the air. They came from the shadows, from mildewed graves and niches, from all their many resting places beyond life.

The Dweller's trog forces, when they saw what now battled on their side—even *though* they were on their side, hemming the invaders in all about—broke in terror and fled for their secret places. No matter, the grim army of the dead would do their work for them. And they *would* win, for as the Necroscopes had pointed out, they couldn't die twice.

Shrieks of terror split the night, wrenched from hundreds of Wamphyri-trog throats when they saw and understood what they were fighting. Sickened, the two Harrys turned away from the carnage. But—

"Son," said Harry Sr., grasping the other's arm. "Look!"

The sky was dark with Wamphyri flyers and warriors. They circled the garden, descending toward it. And some of the warriors were truly gigantic; any five of them, falling on the garden in unison, would totally obscure and obliterate it. Up there in the mountains, even now, a greater battle was about to be waged . . .

They took their own special route back to the garden.

Warriors had already landed below the cliffs fronting the wall, where the Lady Karen's creatures were now locked in hellish combat with them. Their shrieking and bellowing alone was deafening. Other warriors circled, looking for an opening in the ultraviolet searchlight beams which swept the sky and seared their hides.

Up on a certain peak, mirror-weapons blinked out as Lesk the Glut deliberately crashed his flyer down on the Travellers who sweated and swore and died there. But they'd seen him coming; before his flyer struck they had turned their shotguns on it, pumping shot after shot at both beast and rider right to the end. Lesk, wounded and more dangerous than ever, goaded his half-crippled beast to slither free of the peak, directed it in an insane suicide dive on the heart of the garden.

He was seen; smoking ray-beams converged blindingly on him; his flyer felt artificial sunlight eating at its hide, burning in its many eyes. It reared back from its headlong dive, pulled up, swooped low over the garden. Then someone threw a grenade, which exploded directly in front of the beast. With its spatulate head blazing, screaming like a safety-valve under high pressure, it swooped to earth, struck the wall and carried a great section of it away, and with it several defenders. The creature's huge manta body tore up the earth, somersaulted like a derailed train, hurled Lesk out of the saddle.

Other flyers swept down out of the darkness on the periphery. They crashed among the greenhouses and allotments, floundered in the pools. Down from their backs sprang lieutenants of Shaithis, Belath and Volse, to create carnage within the garden itself. Jazz Simmons saw them; he tracked them with tracers and streams of exploding shells. Two at least ducked away into the shadows and smoke, to commence their task of cold butchery on whichever Travellers or trogs they should come across.

Jazz saw Harry and his son on the balcony of the latter's house. They watched the battle. He breathlessly called up "How's it going?"

In the glare and sweep of hot beams, the booming of automatic weapons, howling of monsters and cries of men, it was hard to say. "We should be *in* this!" Harry said to his son.

"No," the other shook his head. "We're the last resort."

Harry didn't understand, but he trusted.

453

Zek came running, caught Jazz's arm where he stood by The Dweller's house. "Look!" she cried.

High overhead a warrior dragged some bloated, puffing, incredible *thing* through the sky. A second warrior, higher, was similarly burdened. Scything searchlight beams cut across them and Zek gasped: "Gas-beasts!"

"What?" Jazz gaped. He saw the bloated thing cut loose, begin drifting like some obscene balloon down toward the garden. The thing drifted a little northward, over the wall, where the battery of searchlights was concentrated. The beams picked it out, centered upon it, and it began to smoke. Puffing black evaporation and clouds of steam, it settled faster towards earth.

Jazz saw the strategy. "*No!*" he cried. Then he grabbed Zek, threw her down and hurled himself on top of her.

The gas-beast—a living creature, once a man—issued a hissing, high-pitched scream as its skin blackened and ruptured—and then it blew itself to bits with all the force of a thousand-pound bomb! The ray-gunners directly underneath it died instantly in the blast, their bodies and equipment flattened. At a stroke, one-third of The Dweller's defences had been wiped out.

A foul, stinking hot wind blew across the garden, and when it cleared Jazz helped Zek to her feet. The Dweller's house was still standing, but all of its windows and been blown in and half of its roof was missing. Harry and his son had ducked inside the space under the eaves in the moment before the blast; now they came out, white and shaken.

More warriors had landed at the back of the saddle. There they fought with Karen's creatures, overwhelming and quickly silencing them. But there were Travellers back there and they were armed with grenades; lobbing their deadly eggs, they gave the warriors blow for blow.

Lieutenants of the Wamphyri seemed to be ravaging in every quarter of the garden, their war-gauntlets drenched in Traveller blood. The night was covered with smoke and stench, split by shotgun blasts, made still more hellish in the surreal slash of searing light and long moments of total blindness . . .

Down by the shattered wall, the Lady Karen saw something coming up out of the smoke-filled depression. It crawled, but as it reached level ground reared up and charged! It was the mad Lord Lesk, bloodiest of all the Wamphyri, almost fully recovered and little the worse for his wounds and the tumble he'd taken. He saw Karen, rushed upon her full of nightmare intent.

She thrust aside a dazed Traveller and turned his lamp's beam full in Lesk's hideous face, blinding his eye. He cursed, clapped a hand to his face, came on and kicked the lamp from her grasp. Half-blind, he turned his left side toward her, glared his fury from the lidless eye in his shoulder. But as he swung his gauntlet, so his body turned with the swing and he again lost sight of her. She ducked under Lesk's arcing blow, tore away the flesh and ribs from his left side with one raking, razor-sharp swipe of her own gauntlet.

He cried out, staggered, gasped his amazement. He felt fumblingly with his free hand at the terrible damage to his body. His heart pounded like a great yellow bellows, plainly visible against the dark, pulsing sack of his exposed left lung. Travellers leaped on him, tried to trip him and drag him down. While he roared and raged, Karen stepped in and grasped his naked heart with her awesome weapon-hand. She cut the heart's pipes and tore it out of his body. He coughed blood, puffed himself up . . . and toppled like a felled tree! The Travellers fell on him like wolves, beheaded him, poured oil on his body and set fire to it. Lesk went up in flames.

Meanwhile:

A second gas-beast had come drifting directly toward The Dweller's house. The two Harrys fled the place, encountered a pair of Wamphyri lieutenants in their way. Their strategy in dealing with them proved their kinship: they let the grinning, gauntletted vampires close with them and charge, then ducked through Möbius doors. As their pursuers plunged into that unknown realm directly on their heels, so they closed the doors and exited through others. The lieutenants had simply disappeared; perhaps faint echoes of their screams came back, to be quickly drowned in the row and confusion of battle.

The mewling gas-beast over The Dweller's house was hit by a stray burst of gunfire. It exploded with a devastating roar, demolishing the place and sending out a great rush of vile stench.

Warriors were coming over the saddle behind the settlement. Another crashed down on the low structure housing Harry Jr.'s generators. The remaining ultraviolet lamps blinked out, leaving only a handful of lanterns and starlight to light the reeling night. The bellowing voices of the Lords Belath and Menor Maimbite sounded *inside* the garden! From overhead, the Lord Shaithis shouted down instructions.

Still reeling from the gas-beast blast, Harry clutched his son's arm. "You said we were a last resort," he breathlessly reminded him. "Whatever you meant by that—whatever's on your mind—you'd better say it now."

"Father," the other answered. "in the Möbius Continuum even thought has weight. And you and I, we're linked. Wherever we are in the Möbius Continuum, we know each other."

Harry nodded. "Of course."

"I've done things with and to the Continuum that you've never dreamed of," The Dweller continued, but innocently, without boasting. "I can send more than mere thoughts through it—as long as there's someone to receive what I send. In this instance, however, what I must send is dangerous. Not to you, but to me."

"I don't follow you." Desperately aware that the

battle was being lost, Harry licked suddenly dry lips, shook his head.

"But you will." Quickly The Dweller explained.

"I've got you," Harry said. "But won't it hurt the garden, the Travellers?"

"I'm not sure. A little, perhaps. Nothing serious or lasting. But you should get the Lady Karen out of the way." He went running back to the ruins of his house, found a shimmering metallic robe of foil where he'd stored it and put it on. It covered him from head to toe, with tinted glass disks for his eyes. "I've used it before," he said "out beyond the stars. Now you'd better see to Karen."

Harry had followed him, said: "Where will I find you?"

"Here. I'll wait for you."

Harry used the Möbius Continuum and went to the wall. Men with flame-throwers were hosing down a stricken warrior; Karen fought with a lieutenant, dispatching him even as Harry arrived. "Don't question this," he said. "Come quickly!"

He caught her up, stepped through a Möbius door, emerged down on the plain of boulders at a safe distance from the glaring sphere Gate. Dazed, she swayed for a moment and her scarlet eyes went round as saucers. "How . . . ?"

"Which is your stack?" he asked her.

She pointed and he caught her to him again . . .

Harry left her in her deserted aerie, returned to the garden. His son was waiting. "Do you understand?" The Dweller wanted to know.

"Yes," Harry nodded. "Let's get on with it."

They entered the Möbius Continuum and Harry Jr. moved away very quickly, across the mountains to Sunside and from there—

—To the sun! He stood off from that monstrous furnace in deep space, opened a Möbius door. Harry

457

heard his *hiss* of torment, also his directed thought: *Now!*

Harry opened a Möbius door on the garden, trapped and fixed it there, let his son re-direct and pour sunlight *through* the Möbius Continuum and out through Harry's door. The garden was at once bathed in intense, glaring, golden light!

Harry turned the door like the gun-turret of a tank, sending his shaft of concentrated sunlight sliding across the garden. The beam struck warriors where they ravaged forward across the saddle. It ate into them like acid, devouring their vampire flesh. For this was sunlight, but not thinned by distance, not diluted by atmosphere. It was the *essence* of the sun! The monsters melted, boiled away and slumped down into sticky black pools.

Ahhh! The Dweller's agony was a fire in its own right, burning in his father's mind. The beam shut off, gave Harry time to recoup, rest from the task of holding steady and controlling his Möbius door.

"Son?" his anxious thoughts went out along the Möbius way. "Are you all right?"

No! . . . Yes. Yes, I'm all right. Give me a moment . . .

Harry waited, conjured a door and looked out. He chose new targets: the Lords Belath and Menor where they came striding through a host of panicking Travellers, swatting them like flies.

Now!

Harry fixed the door, guided his son's sun-blast through it. The brilliant beam fell on Belath and Menor like a solid shaft of gold. It super-heated them, blew away their skins and flesh in writhing, stinking evaporation. As the Travellers scrambled wildly away from them, they exploded into tatters of smouldering vileness.

Harry turned his beam to the north, found a warrior in mid-air, descending toward the defenders at the wall. He shrivelled the thing before it could come too close, reduced it to a tarry fireball that fell well beyond the cliffs. Other warriors were overhead, and flyers with their startled riders. Harry swung the door horizontally, turned its beam into a giant searchlight. The sun shone *upwards*, from the earth!

Monstrous debris rained from the sky, and: *Ahhh!* Again the beam was shut off.

"Son! son!" Harry cried into the Möbius Continuum. "Let that be an end to it. They're beaten, moving off. Stop now, before you kill yourself!"

No! the other's Möbius voice was a shudder. *They must never recover from this. Go down onto the boulder plain, close to their stacks.*

Harry understood. He did as directed.

Now!

The Dweller's beam reached out and licked at the base of Shaithis's stack. It played there for a moment, blazed in across bony balconies and through cartilage windows, found the gas-beasts in their places. In an uncontrollable chain-reaction of living bombs, the stack's base exploded outwards, hurling rock, bones, cartilage carcasses and all far out onto the plain. The stack teetered, crumpled downward into itself, toppled. Falling, it flew apart; but before its gigantic sections could strike earth, already Harry had redirected his beam.

And one by one the aeries were brought crashing down on the shuddering plain, reduced to rubble, erased.

Twice more during the work The Dweller cried out and the beam was shut off. But in the end only the Lady Karen's stack remained. And:

Let it be, Harry Jr. whispered.

Father and son went back to the garden. They emerged as the smoke and reek were lifting, and as the dazed Travellers and their friends from a different world looked all about them and rubbed grime from stinging eyes.

The Dweller's cloak of foil had fused to his body. Smouldering, he swayed there a moment—a black and silver thing that groped blindly as it took a single pace forward—then crumpled into its father's arms . . .

* * *

In what would have been three days Earth-time the news was: The Dweller would recover! It was the vampire in him, which given time would repair the damage he'd suffered. But Harry Sr. knew he could never take his son, or Brenda, back to the world where they were born. Harry Jr. was Wamphyri; however different from the others, still he must stay here forever. Indeed he *wanted* to stay here. This was his place now, his territory which he'd fought and paid dearly for. And of course he could never be sure how things would go.

But . . . The Lady Karen was different, too. For the moment, anyway. Also, if what Harry had heard about her was true, she'd one day be more dangerous than all the others put together. He cared nothing for her, but he did care for his son. And an idea had formed in his mind.

Leaving The Dweller in the care of Jazz, Zek and the ever-faithful Travellers, Harry went to Karen's aerie. It was memorable when he left the garden, because for one thing there was gold on the peaks again, and also he had witnessed a strange reunion. Wolf, his paws bleeding, had made the crossing to find his mistress. No vampire in him, just a great deal of love and a lot of faith.

There'd been another, perhaps even more joyous reunion, too: along with Wolf had come a weary Lardis Lidesci and a handful of his people . . .

Chapter Twenty-Three

The Last Warrior—The Horror at Perchorsk!

FOLLOWING THE BATTLE AT THE DWELLER'S GARDEN, Shaithis of the Wamphyri guided his half-crippled, seared flyer for home. He fancied the creature wouldn't make it, not for all his goading, for it was burned all along its underbelly and dripping fluids like rain. He, too, had taken a dose of direct sunlight, but had been nimble-minded enough to throw himself down on his flyer's back, in the trench of horny ridges formed of its huge wing muscles.

The blast had come as Shaithis's creature was turning away from the garden after a trial landing run, and so he'd not been blinded; but still he'd felt the hideous, searing heat of the true sun, and so had known that The Dweller could not be defeated. His weapons were simply too powerful, beyond Wamphyri understanding and certainly beyond their control. Which, together with the loss of his lieutenants and warriors, had convinced Shaithis that the attack was a pointless exercise. Wamphyri losses had been devastating, and the survivors had come to the same conclusion as Shaithis, quitting the fight *en masse* and heading for home.

Down across the Starside plain they'd flown their creatures, many limping, all humiliated, and Shaithis had felt their hatred of him beating like hammer blows on his psychic Wamphyri mind. They blamed him for their losses, for he'd been the one who instigated the attack, their self-appointed leader in the abortive affray. Generals who lose are rarely fêted, mainly scorned.

On the way east, using the half-dome of the shining sphere for pharos and rolling in his saddle, Shaithis had seen Fess Ferenc and Volse Pinescu go down, fluttering out of the sky on flyers finally too weak to resist gravity's pull, and he'd watched them crash in clouds of dust far below on the moon-silvered plain. The Lords must finish the rest of their journey afoot, for Shaithis doubted they'd have strength for flight metamorphosis. He certainly wouldn't, if his flyer was to succumb. Still, walking had to be better than dying.

The Lords Belath and Lesk the Glut, Grigis and Menor Maimbite, Lasula Longtooth and Tor Tornbody were missing, along with many lesser Wamphyri lights. Of warriors there were none to be seen . . . no, Shaithis corrected himself, one—only one?—spurting through the sky eastward, acting of its own volition. Doubtless its master was dead, and now it returned to the only home it knew.

As for lieutenants: where were they? Gone—gone with the flyers, the warriors, the trogs—gone with all dreams of conquest and revenge. Only a dozen flyers left in all the sky, exhausted, gliding where they caught the thermals and desperate to conserve energy, carrying their Lords whole or crippled, bearing them back to their stacks and their . . .

. . . Their aeries?

Crossing over the glaring dome of the Gate, Shaithis had lifted his blackened face to peer ahead. And he'd seen the unbelievable, the unthinkable. Of all the mighty stacks of the Wamphyri, only one remained standing. And that was the stack of the treacherous Karen!

Fury galvanized him. Karen, that mother-bearing bitch! He hauled on the reins, lifted the head of his flyer and turned it towards Karen's stack. His creature tried: its manta wings pulsed once, twice, three times; pulsed feebly at the air, then quivered mightily and formed a shallow "V." The thing was barely alive. Its fluids were gone and there was nothing left to power it. The glide grew steeper, swifter, and nothing to be done about it. At the last moment Shaithis bellowed frantic mental commands into his creature's dull, dying mind, dragged on the reins until he thought they'd surely snap. The beast's head slowly came up and its wings adopted a more nearly aerodynamic profile. It swooped, levelled out, tilted to one side; the debris-littered plain became a dizzy, whirling, surreal kaleidoscope of rushing landscape. Then—

The creature's inner wingtip struck the stump of a stack, accelerating its spin. Its master was hurled from the saddle, felt bones break in his left arm and shoulder, tasted dust and his own blood where his face ploughed the plain and rocks broke his teeth. Long moments passed, silent except for Shaithis's pounding heartbeat, and the worst of the pain slowly ebbed. Finally, gasping and swaying, he staggered to his feet, shook his gauntlet-clad right hand at Karen's lone stack. He cursed it long and loud. Her aerie stood as a sure sign of her treachery. She was The Dweller's, bought and paid for!

A vengeful snarl twisted Shaithis's broken features more yet. Well, and when she returned from The Dweller's garden . . . *ah*, but then there'd be a reckoning! A reckoning, aye—long and lusty and bloody, bloody, *bloody*! And oh so very sweet!

He took a stumbling step in the direction of her stack —and froze. Descending toward that solitary needle of rock, that last Wamphyri aerie, was the warrior he'd previously noted. He groaned as it squirted in through the dark mouth of her launching bay. *Her* warrior! And while she lived it would defend her aerie to the last, against all comers, even against Shaithis of the Wamphyri himself.

How Shaithis raved then; ranted and raved, and no one at all to hear him but a flock of great bats, familiar creatures who doubtless questioned the whereabouts of their crevice colonies in the stricken Wamphyri stacks.

The moon raced on across the sky, and Shaithis grew quiet and became still. His shadow passed through the vertical and began to lengthen on the other side. When it was as long as Shaithis himself, then his shoulders slumped and he turned and headed for the shattered, far-flung ruins he'd once called home . . .

Weary and hollow-cheeked—with half of his body seared, several broken bones, and his face crushed and burned on one side—the once-great Lord Shaithis of the Wamphyri drew nigh the base of that mighty outcrop, that towering rock now gone forever, which had housed him for all of his five and half centuries. In the stump itself, there he'd had his workshops: the vast vats where with great cunning he'd forced and moulded metamorphic flesh, creating his warriors, flyers, gaslings, siphoneers and various types of cartilage creature. Down there, if the massy ceiling had not fallen in upon it, a freshly formed flyer was even now mewling and floundering in its vat. Once a Traveller, soon it would travel again, and at least Shaithis would have a mount.

There, too, he'd find his pit-things: metamorphosed Travellers and trogs, mindless criers in perpetual night, the raw materials of his warriors and the other creatures he'd made. Well, they could leap in their pits, wail and gibber, stiffen, eventually fossilize. He cared not at all.

Overhead, the last of the Wamphyri were silently flying north, heading out across the icelands for those dark regions on the roof of the world, where the sun never shone at all. When his flyer was ready, then Shaithis would join them there. The legends had it that if one crossed the polar cap and kept going, then that he'd find more mountains, new territories to conquer. No one in living memory had tested the legends, how-

ever, for the great stacks had been the places of the
Wamphyri, their immemorial homes. But . . . that was
yesterday. And now it appeared that the legends were to
be tested in full. So be it.

As Shaithis went to descend a shattered stairwell, his
good eye detected a movement in the rubble and he
heard a muffled moan. Someone here, alive, in the
ruins of his aerie?

Shaithis picked his way over tumbled blocks of stone
and bony debris, came to a tangle of shiny cartilage and
fractured rock where a hand and arm protruded from a
gap. The hand groped blindly about, clawed uselessly
at rough stone. From below came a half-conscious
moaning.

For a moment Shaithis was puzzled; a Lord, even the
lowliest lieutenant would have dug his way out by now.
But eventually he smiled a grim smile and nodded his
recognition of the trapped man. "Karl!" The vampire's
false smile disappeared as quickly as it had come.
"Hell-lander. Ah, but I've several large scores to settle
with hell-landers!"

He tore away blocks of stone and weirdly fused
cartilage masses, reached down into darkness and drew
Vyotsky out. His handling of the Russian wasn't gentle,
especially since both of Vyotsky's legs were broken
below the knees. He cried out: "No, no! Oh, God—
my legs!"

Shaithis shook him mercilessly until his agonized
eyes popped open. "Your legs!" he hissed. "Your
legs? Man, look at *me!*" He sat Vyotsky down on a flat
stone surface, let fall his cloak to expose his ravaged
body, slowly turned in a circle for the other's inspection. Trembling in his own extreme of pain, still the
Russian winced at the extent of Shaithis's injuries.
"Aye," Shaithis agreed. "Pretty, isn't it?"

Vyotsky said nothing, continued to hold himself upright where he sat by pressing down on the rock's

surface with the flats of his spread palms. In this way he kept pressure off his trembling, jelly legs.

"Now, Karl," said Shaithis, facing him squarely. "It seems to me that I remember a conversation we had, that time when we almost caught your fellow hell-landers, before The Dweller's intervention. You remember?"

Vyotsky said nothing, wished he could faint but in any case knew that he didn't dare do so. His agony was great, but if he collapsed now the odds were that he'd never wake up again. He gasped, closed his eyes as a fresh wave of pain burned upwards through his body from his shattered legs.

"You *don't* remember?" said Shaithis, in mock surprise. He lifted his gauntlet, clenched his hand, opened the weapon wide so that the Russian could see its dozens of cutting edges. A single blow from that would flense a man's entire face, Vyotsky knew, or crush his skull like an eggshell. "Well, I *do* remember," the vampire Lord continued, "and it seems to me I warned you then what I would do if you should ever again attempt to flee from me. I said I would give you to my favourite warrior, all except your heart which I would eat myself. Surely you remember that?"

Vyotsky's eyes were wide now and his lips trembled to match his straining arms.

"Alas," said Shaithis, "but I no longer have a warrior and so can't keep my promise. But I *would*, you may believe me! Except, of course, we do not know that you were fleeing. Ah, but I also remember telling Gustan that he was to carry you with him upon his flyer when we went to sack The Dweller's garden. Could it be that Gustan forgot my command? A shame, for I so wanted you to be there—to witness the way I would have dealt with the woman Zek and the man Jazz. On the other hand . . . perhaps you were hiding, waiting for us to leave before making a break for it?"

Vyotsky managed to shake his head in silent denial. "I . . . I . . ." he stuttered.

"Oh, indeed!" Shaithis nodded, smiling hideously. "I . . . I . . ." And as his smile once more slid from his face he reached down a second time into the space where the Russian had been trapped—and this time he drew out Vyotsky's SMG, and a leather sack containing provisions.

Again Vyotsky moaned out loud, closing his eyes and swaying where he sat racked with pain. But Shaithis only burst out laughing, slapping his thigh as at some rich joke—then abruptly stopped laughing, reached out with his gauntlet and slapped Vyotsky across the knees. For Shaithis—by his standards—the blow was the merest tap, light as the touch of a feather. It ripped open Vyotsky's combat-suit trousers, tore away his knee-caps in a red welter. He did faint then, toppling sideways off the flat stone. But Shaithis caught him up before he could further injure himself. Then—

Without further pause the vampire tossed him over his good shoulder and proceeded with him down into the black bowels of his workshops . . .

Below, it was not as bad as Shaithis had thought it might be. Parts of the stone and cartilage ceiling had collapsed here and there, and several of the protoplasmic things in their deep pits had been blocked in, so that their mindless cries were made faint by masses of fallen stone, but in the main all was in order. The larger vats were undamaged, and Shaithis's new flyer uninjured. It mewled when it saw him, bending its glistening, spatulate, armoured head in his direction. Soon the liquids in its vat would all be absorbed into it, and then its skin would form into membranous leather. After that a training flight, and finally Shaithis would be ready to undertake his great journey northwards.

Before then, however, there was one last task he must perform, one final act of vengeance in this place.

He had admitted to the hell-lander Karl Vyotsky that his warriors were all dead. Well, and so they were—but that was not to say he couldn't make another. Indeed, the making of warriors and other beasts was an art of the Wamphyri, and certainly Shaithis was a great artist. Moreover, he had the necessary materials right here. Ah, but this one would be *the* warrior!

In a recent experiment, Shaithis had created a small creature of such primitive slyness and insidious vileness that his creation had surprised even him. The small mind of a trog, with some subtle alterations, had governed the thing—if governed was the word—while its principal physical component had not been man-flesh but that of wild creatures. The tissues of a great bat and a feral wolf had featured strongly, together with protoplasmic flesh from Shaithis's pit-things. But twice the creature had escaped, which in the end prompted him to put it down and have done with it.

Indeed, it would not have been prudent to let it live —not *here*, anyway—not and chance the other Wamphyri Lords learning of it. For while Nature often gave wild creatures a vampire egg, it was generally deemed unseemly for the Wamphyri themselves to perform such experiments.

And yet Shaithis had done just that. Slighted by a lesser Lord, he'd challenged and killed him, and so earned the right to burn his remains. Instead he had brought the body here to his workshop, cut out the vampire within and transplanted its egg into his creature! But when he saw how uncontrollable was the thing, then he'd sent it through the Gate. It had seemed to him a grand jest: that his creature should take its own brand of hell with it into the hell-lands.

Ah, but that was before he realized just how hellish the hell-lands were! Shaithis little doubted now but that all his troubles stemmed from that unknown place beyond the shining sphere-gate; perhaps even The Dweller himself had his origin there. Which was why he would now create the WARRIOR of all warriors! And, who could say, perhaps it might even be the last warrior? Aye, and when they saw what he had sent them, then the wizards of that world would think again before sending their hirelings adventuring here.

So thinking, Shaithis tossed Karl Vyotsky's limp form down onto the great slab of stone which was his workbench, then went to fetch the other ingredients of his work and certain instruments with which to fuse them . . .

It was a long job; sunup came and went, and a new sundown was beginning; finally Shaithis was done. He inspected with some satisfaction the thing heaving and hissing where it waxed in its enormous trench of a vat, striding down the length of it and admiring the rapid formation of a deadly array of weapons. Then, into its groping, vestigial mind, he implanted those commands which would form its one aim, its single goal in life, and left it to fend for itself. Emerging in a very little while, the warrior would discover the pit-things and devour them, and find its way out of here. The exit might well be too small for it by then, but Shaithis could not doubt that this warrior would make it bigger.

In the interim he had tested his flyer; the beast was better than any before it, fit steed for the long journey ahead. First, however, Shaithis would gaze once more upon the face of that mother of all treachery, the beautiful face of the Lady Karen. He flew to her aerie and without hostility began circling it, calling to her in the way of the Wamphyri until she came to a window.

"So, Karen," he called, from where he rode a gusting wind, "then you are the last. Or maybe the first? Still, no matter, we are all undone because of you."

"Shaithis," she answered, "of all the great Wamphyri liars, you are the greatest. You even lie to yourself! You blame me for your troubles, or whoever else it takes your fancy to blame, when in fact you know that you alone have brought the Wamphyri to this end. And in any case, what care you for them? Nothing! You care only for the Lord Shaithis.''

''Ah, you're a cold, cruel creature, Karen!'' he nodded and scowled at her across an abyss of air.

''Merely accurate,'' she answered. ''Do you think I did not know your plans for me? The truth is that you underestimated, Shaithis. You underestimated me, The Dweller, everything. You were so bloated up with your own schemes and lust for ultimate domination that you considered yourself beyond defeat. Well, and now we see how wrong you were.''

He flew closer, all of his great fury visible in his partly-healed face; until she cautioned: '' 'Ware, Shaithis! I have a warrior. It's but the work of a second to launch him.''

He drew back. ''Aye, I have seen it. But do you call that a warrior? I doubt if it would have my measure, not if I was the whole man. Which I will be, one day.''

''Are you in a position to threaten?''

He glared at her, saw that a second face had appeared at her window. ''Ah, and you even managed to save a companion for yourself!'' he said ''A lieutenant lover to warm you through all the lonely time ahead, no doubt? But . . . I don't recognize this one. Now tell me, who is he?''

''I speak for myself,'' Harry Keogh answered. ''I'm a hell-lander, Shaithis. The father of the one you call The Dweller.''

Shaithis gasped, drew back further yet. But in a little while his courage returned. From what he knew of The Dweller and his sort, if they were desperate to have him dead, then he would *be* dead! Perhaps they were satisfied with what they had done. Curiosity overcame all, and Shaithis flew his beast closer. ''Tell me one thing,'' he called out, ''Why did you come here? To destroy the Wamphyri?''

Harry shook his head. ''That was the way it worked

470

out, that's all.'' And then he remembered a promise
he'd made. "Maybe you should ask instead, who sent
me?''

Shaithis nodded. "Say on!''

"His name was Belos,'' Harry said, "and he told
me: 'Tell them Belos sent you.' ''

It meant nothing to Shaithis, who had never been
much of a one for studying the legends and histories.
He frowned, shrugged, turned his beast away and headed
north. The winds carried back to them his final word:

"Farewell.''

But they knew he didn't meant it . . .

Chingiz Khuv, accompanied by two of his KGB men,
was on his way to the Failsafe Control Centre. It was
almost 2 A.M. and Khuv's shift would last for six hours,
when he'd be relieved by the next Failsafe Duty Officer. The wee small hours of the morning, but here in
the Projekt time didn't mean a lot. Except that it was
rapidly running down. For Khuv, for his commando
platoon, maybe even for the Projekt itself.

These were Khuv's thoughts as he marched the steel
and rubber corridors with his men flanking him. One of
them was armed with a machine-gun, the other had a
flamethrower. Khuv himself carried only his issue automatic, but the safety-catch was off where it sat snug in
its holster.

Eight days, Khuv thought. *Eight days of sheer hell!*
Tomorrow he had no official duties and could rest, but
the day after that . . . that was when he and his platoon
were scheduled to be on their way, through the Gate.
That in itself—the preparations, worrying about what
was waiting in there and on the other side—would be
troubles enough; but of course in the thirty-six hours
between times there would also be the small matter of
staying alive!

The Perchorsk Projekt had always been claustrophobic: its magmass levels had been eerie, frightening

places ever since the accident which spawned them, and there was always the fear of further nightmare incursions from the Gate; but at least the creeping horror of the magmass was a familiar one, and the dangers of the Gate were known and appreciated. Now, however, the entirely *un*known had entered into it, and someone or something was loose in the Projekt which struck and disappeared without trace, and which so far seemed quite invisible. It wasn't simply a case of stopping it, first it had to be found. For since the night of the triple murder . . . well, things had only got worse.

Now, to any outsider entering Perchorsk for the first time, it would seem a place of total madness. The main exit was guarded day and night by half a dozen men with a variety of weapons; people no longer moved about singly but in pairs or even threes, every face wore a strained look, with eyes hollow and bloodshot, their gaunt owners given to violent starts at every smallest unaccustomed sound. A terror had settled on Perchorsk, and there seemed no way to break its hold.

It had started with the deaths of the KGB men Rublev and Roborov, and the psychic locator Leo Grenzel; God alone knew where it would end. Khuv thought back on the string of murders since those first three:

A lab technician had been next, during a late night power failure as he was clearing up in his lab. Something had entered in the darkness, crushing his windpipe to a pulp and crumbling his face and forehead with what must have been a single terrific blow. It had looked as though a giant bulldog grip had been allowed to snap shut on his face and the front of his head. Agursky had given his opinion that it was the work of a maniac with a tool of some sort, possibly a portable power-vise from the workshops.

Next had been a pair of soldiers going off duty, leaving the core and passing through the magmass levels, where they'd encountered something which they shot at. The shots had been heard, of course, and the

bodies of the two eventually discovered. Their throats
had been torn out and they'd been stuffed into one of
the magmass holes. An examination had shown that
under the massive bruising many bones had been broken, and the spinal columns dislocated.

Then, the night before last, one of Khuv's remaining
four KGB men had gone missing and still hadn't been
found; and just three hours ago . . .

That one was one of the worst. The body of Klara
Orlova, a theoretical physicist working closely with
Luchov's team of scientists, had been discovered in one
of the ventilation shafts dangling upside-down from the
pulley cables. Her throat, too, had been ripped out.
And as with many of the other cases, there hadn't
seemed to be very much blood around.

Khuv had barely arrived at the scene of that one
when he was called on the double to the telepath Paul
Savinkov's room. The door, a light-weight timber frame
with a thin metal skin, had a fist-sized hole in it and
was hanging half wrenched from its hinges. Inside was
Savinkov, crumpled in a corner like a discarded doll
and hideously broken. Although the snapping of his
bones must have sounded out like a series of gunshots,
apparently no one had heard a thing.

But at least this time it was seen how the murderer
was wily as well as immensely strong and brutal. The
cable to Savinkov's telephone had been cut outside his room
in the corridor. The killer had been taking no chances that
he might try to summon help. Which seemed to prove
Vasily Agursky's theory: the murders were the work of a
powerful, cunning madman, or at least a human being.

By then, however, it had been time for Khuv to
prepare himself for his duty at Failsafe Control. He'd
left Gustav Litve in charge of the new cases and gone to
change into clothes suitable for the long shift ahead.
And now that shift was about to commence.

Approaching Failsafe Control, Khuv and his men
heard footsteps behind them, turned on their heels to

473

see Gustav Litve coming at a run. White-faced, he was thrusting a sheet of paper before him, waving it at Khuv. "Comrade Major," he gasped, drawing close. "This is it! I found it stuffed down the back of Savinkov's chair."

The paper was a little crumpled; Khuv smoothed it against the wall, saw shaky lines written in pencil. They said:

I've been checking all the staff one by one. I would have done it sooner, but Andrei Roborov saw it with his own eyes and what he saw wasn't human. So I thought it *must* be something from the Gate, something we'd missed. Then I thought: how is it that with all these espers we can't find the intruder? Maybe it was shielding itself psychically; maybe it was hiding behind its own mind-screens! But if it could do that, then I should be able to detect the shields. Grenzel would be proud of me: I found it! He would have done it better, of course—which is why it stopped him! How I did it: I found an area where there were *no* telepathic readings, where there was powerful psychic interference. It was the mortuary. I checked to be double sure, and found I'd been wrong. But then I got the same sort of reading in the accommodation area—in the scientific section. I narrowed it down. It's Agursky! He keeps the bodies in the mortuary. He must have been in there when I checked the place the first time. And he was in his room when I went there a few minutes ago. I managed to contact his mind—and I think he recognized me! But be sure, *he's the thing that Roborov saw!* My telephone is out of order. I think there's someone outside. If I listen at the

The note stopped right there. Khuv read it again, his eyes wide, skipping over the words. Something of the meaning of the thing sunk in and he felt the short hairs stiffen at the back of his neck. His blood seemed to turn to ice in his veins; but he forced himself to leap toward the heavy metal door of Failsafe Control and hammer on it, yelling:

"Viktor, open up for God's sake!"

Direktor Luchov was on duty. Red-eyed, he came to the door and opened it, was bowled backwards as Khuv burst in. "What in the name of—?"

"Read this!" said Khuv, thrusting Savinkov's note at him. "It's something of a dying declaration. Things are beginning to add up, making a monstrous sort of sense. Savinkov seems to be saying that there's a connection between Vasily Agursky and the thing he kept in that tank of his. I still don't know what it's all about, but I'm damned well going to find out! Now listen, Viktor: get on the phone. Let's have no alarms, for that would only alert him, but I want everyone looking for Agursky. God, I've known there was something weird about him for weeks, ever since . . . since . . ."

Luchov stared at him, said: "Since that time when he had his breakdown? When they found him down there in the thing's room? Poor Vasily, and he always seemed to me such a harmless little man."

"Well, he's not harmless now!" Khuv snapped. "Right, we're off to find him. Put the word about: if anyone gets to him first they're to hold him, by any means possible. And if they can't hold him they must kill him—also by any means possible." He ushered his men out of the room, called over his shoulder: "Search-parties in threes, Viktor. For God's sake don't let anyone tackle him alone!"

The mortuary was situated off the main perimeter corridor above the magmass levels. In its time it had housed the victims of the Perchorsk Incident, and for a while it had been a cold storehouse, but right now it was a mortuary again. And Agursky was the only one with a key. On their way to the place Khuv and Litve had separated from the other two KGB men; Litve had commandeered one of the Projekt's flamethrowers from its bracket on a wall, and the Major had equipped himself with a snub-nosed sub-machine gun taken from a reluctant soldier. They'd been to Agursky's laboratory and found it locked, with the lighted sign over its door proclaiming it "vacant." Likewise Agursky's room, which Khuv had opened with skeleton keys. Agursky could be anywhere in the complex, but they might as well try the mortuary. All of the bodies from the murders were down there, on ice, where Agursky had supposedly been examining them.

Word of the manhunt had not got down to the core, and the magmass levels were silent as usual. Khuv and Litve looked down there for a moment—down to where the lights were low and the wormhole-riddled walls moulded into weird shapes—before turning off along the short straight corridor through solid rock to the door of the mortuary. It was locked but it wasn't a security door; Khuv's keys opened it. They swung the door wide and stepped inside, and Litve went to put on the lights. They didn't come on. The light-bulbs had been removed from their fixtures in the low ceiling.

A little light filtered in from the corridor. Khuv and Litve stood just inside the open doorway, glanced at each other, then at the tables against the wall, and at the long narrow boxes on the tables. At the back of the mortuary machinery made a slow, regular breathing sound, sending frigid air circulating. Other than that there was no sound, no motion. The room was a giant refrigerator.

Litve primed his flamethrower, lit the pilot light. Its blue flicker threw the shadows back a little. "Major," Litve said, his voice nervous and echoing, "there's nowhere he could hide in here. Let's go."

Khuv tucked his elbows in and shivered. He blew into the palm of his free hand. "All right," he said, "but don't be in such a hurry." He turned in a slow circle, paused for a moment to watch his breath pluming in the air. Then he relaxed a little. "OK, we'll make for the—" and again he paused, listening intently. After a moment: "Did you hear something?"

Litve listened, shook his head. "Just the pumps back there."

Khuv stepped towards the makeshift coffins where they lined the walls. "While we're here," he said, "it might be a good idea to check on what Agursky's been up to. You don't know him quite as well as I do." He shivered again, but not from the cold. "He has funny ways with dead bodies, that one."

With Litve moving up beside him, he looked into the first casket. Klara Orlova had been brought down; white as a candle and stark naked she lay there. The gash across her neck, which went from ear to ear, looked like a black velvet choker. On a young girl it would have looked erotic—if one was unaware that in fact it was a fatal wound.

The two men stepped to the next box. The contorted face of a young soldier, still silently screaming, looked up at them. *God!* Khuv thought. *You'd think someone would have closed his eyes!*

The next box was empty, and as Khuv moved on Litve quickly crossed the room to where a box stood on its own on a separate table. It had a lid loosely laid on top, which he lifted down. On Khuv's side of the room, the next box contained the second soldier. His face was a raw red mess, completely unrecognizable. Two more boxes to go. Khuv made to move on, and—

Across the room Litve drew breath in a shocked gasp. *"Erich!"* he said.

"What?" Khuv strode over to where he stood. Litve seemed frozen in horror, but he was right, the man in the box was the missing KGB agent, Erich Bildarev. He was naked and of course dead; the ribs over his heart were crushed in, as badly as if he'd fallen on a bear trap. Khuv grasped Litve's arm, more for support than any other reason. His breath came faster, making a string of tiny plumes. At last he managed to gasp: "That's the last bit of proof we needed. Savinkov was right, Agursky's our man!"

Then, across the room, someone—something—said, '*Ahhh!*'"

"Jesus, Jesus!" Litve cried out, going into a crouch and whirling to look across the room. Khuv turned with him, his eyes bulging to penetrate the gloom. The last two coffins lay there, their contents as yet uninspected. But even as the two men clung together and stared, so there was movement. A tiny plume of air rose up from the first coffin, and another from the second. And Andrei Roborov and Nikolai Rublev sat up in their boxes and stared back at them!

Their injuries, visible even in the poor light, said that this could not be. But it could be, it was. Rublev's cheek was absent from the left side of his face, so that the left eye gazed from a bony orbit; the cadaverous Roborov's skull dripped pus and brain fluid, which crept like wax down his pallid cheeks. They sat there in their coffins, stared, then smiled—and their upper eye-teeth curved down like fangs over their lower lips!

Khuv tried to gasp, "Oh God—oh, my God!" but his tongue had stuck to the roof of his mouth. The eyes of the dead men—no, of the corpses, the *un*dead men —were pits of glowing sulphur cratered with blood, and they continued to smile.

"Burn them!" Khuv finally managed to gasp. "Quickly, man, burn them!"

"Oh?" said a sly, familiar voice from the door. "Then you must hope that your flamethrower is not one of the many which I have emptied!"

They looked that way, saw Vasily Agursky step back out into the corridor and close the door. His key grated in the lock. "Agursky, wait!" Khuv yelled after him.

"Oh no, Major," came Agursky's faint answer.

"You've found me out, and so there's no more time for waiting." His footsteps rapidly faded.

Meanwhile, Roborov and Rublev had climbed out of their coffins, Khuv saw them, ran for the door. Astonished that his legs obeyed him, he hoped his hands would do the same. As he went he took his keys from a pocket, trying to distinguish the right one from its feel.

At the door, fumbling with the bunch of keys, he glanced back. The two dead men (and for the first time Khuv thought of them as vampires) were advancing on Litve, their hands starting to reach for him. Khuv shouted from a sandpaper throat: "What are you waiting for, you idiot? Burn them! *Burn the fucking things!*"

Litve came out of his trance, aimed his weapon and squeezed the trigger. Nothing! The flamethrower hissed but that was all. The pilot-light flickered. "*Jesus!*" Litve screamed. He came scrambling, dodged Roborov where he went to grab him.

Khuv had tried half of his keys. In the near-darkness he couldn't make out which was which. He wrenched the ones he'd tried from the key-ring and hurled them down. Litve clawed at him, gasping: "Open the door! For God's sake open the door!" Khuv shoved him away, thrust his remaining keys at him.

"You open it!" he shouted. He cocked his submachine gun, turned it towards the vampires where they came almost mincingly forward out of the mortuary's shadows. Roborov's smile was malicious as he said:

"Why, Comrade Major! I do believe that this is the first time I've seen you in a real flap! Has something upset you?"

"Get back," Khuv shrilly warned.

"Back?" Rublev seemed to mimic him. "Have we offended in some way, Major? But that's too, too bad . . ."

They were almost within arms reach, and still Litve babbled and cursed while he tried to find the right key. Khuv fired, a deafening cacophony of sound in the enclosed space. He squeezed the trigger of his gun and kept it squeezed until the stink of cordite stung his eyes and clawed the back of his throat. Then he released it, and as the fumes cleared saw the two where his sleeting lead had picked them up and hurled them half-way across the room. They lay there moaning, but even as he stared in disbelief they were struggling to rise up again.

Litve gave a sobbing gasp—and the key he was trying turned in the lock. He yanked the door open, stumbled outside. Khuv was right on his heels. As the Major came he stooped to retrieve Litve's discarded weapon. Litve locked the door and both of them leaned on it, Khuv scowling while he checked the flame-thrower over.

"You can tell by its weight that it's loaded," he said. "What?" He pointed a shaking finger at the mix-lever on the stock. "Look! You were giving it too much air and not enough juice. Fool!"

He adjusted the lever, aimed the weapon along the corridor and fired. A jet of flame instantly roared out, white at its core and tapering to a shimmering blue tip. He killed the flame, said: "Now open the door."

Litve unlocked the door, kicked it open and stood back. Roborov and Rublev were on their feet, advancing. Behind them, the young soldiers were also out of their boxes. Khuv didn't wait for further developments. He turned all four to shrieking, crackling torches, burned them until they collapsed, melted them to bubbling, crumpled, stinking piles of fused flesh. Then, as Litve once more locked the door, he turned away and fought to retain his control. Fought desperately not to be ill.

"Grenzel wasn't in there," said Litve. That pulled Khuv out of it.

"That's right," he choked the words out, holding up a hand to his mouth. "Which means there are *two* of them on the loose!"

"Where to now?" Litve was in control of himself

again; and now that the immediate horror had been dealt with, Khuv's mind got back in gear and began working with its usual efficiency. Perhaps too efficiently. His bottom jaw fell open and he grabbed Litve's arm, then released him and set off down the rock corridor at a run.

"Where to?" he called back. "Where would you go if you were Agursky, or Grenzel? What would you *do*?"

"Eh?" Litve came running after him.

"We know what they are," Khuv cried. "He knows we'll burn him if we can. He can't let any of us live. There's only one place he *can* go!"

Of course. Failsafe Control!

Chapter Twenty-Four
Inferno—Harry and Karen

CHINGIZ KHUV AND GUSTAV LITVE RACED FOR THEIR LIVES, for the lives of all concerned, through the serpentine bowels of the Perchorsk Projekt and towards Failsafe Control. At any moment they expected, dreaded to hear the failsafe klaxons starting up; they realized what would happen when the klaxons *did* sound—the panic, horror, the mad, futile scramble—and mainly the nightmare of more than one hundred people waking, staggering from their beds, opening doors to see liquid death spraying from the sprinklers, and hear the roaring of a rushing, all-consuming inferno.

For if Vasily Agursky, or the thing he had become, got to Failsafe Control before them . . . it was obvious what he would do. Save himself and burn them. Burn the entire Projekt.

And yet, for all their terror, the two KBG men weren't without courage. Twice at telephone points, Khuv skidded to a halt and tried to phone ahead. On the first occasion the phone was dead, and on the second he noticed the cable sliced through, trailing its severed ends down the wall. Agursky had outmanoeuvred him. Litve, where he ran on, as he reached the scientific accommodation section, thought to re-check Agursky's room; on the way out he roared like a bull, kicked doors, screaming hoarse-voiced for everyone to "*Vacate, vacate, vacate!*"

Khuv, every forty or fifty paces, would pause briefly to fire a deafening burst from his gun into the ceiling; which he continued to do until the magazine was empty and he was left with only his issue automatic. But those shells he reserved. It was as much as the two men could do, for not only the telephones were out but also the everyday corridor alarms. Agursky had taken care of everything.

Finally they climbed a spiralling ramp to the upper level, where they encountered a lot more activity. Obviously Viktor Luchov had managed to pass on something of a message, for here at least the manhunt was underway. Maybe a dozen or more soldiers searched rooms, patrolled at the double in pairs along side corridors, used walkie-talkies to keep in touch and loud-hailers to muster people from their beds or their work. This last was against Khuv's advice to Luchov, but the Major was unsure which way events had moved since then. In any case, the measures were having an effect, however disorderly. Late-shift staff were spewing out from laboratories, jamming themselves in the corridors and tunnels, on the move without really knowing what they were doing or where they were going. Khuv and Litve couldn't talk to all of them; they simply howled their warnings as they battled a way through them.

"Get out!" they yelled. "The place is going to go up! Get out now or you'll all burn!" It worked, but only served to slow them down as the struggling crowd began to move with them, in the same direction. And it dawned on Khuv: in the crush of frightened people Agursky would be that much harder to spot. But as it happened, Agursky wasn't the one they had to worry about. Not yet.

Up ahead, with maybe only thirty metres to go to Failsafe Control, corridors converged at a bulkhead door. Khuv and other high-ranking Projekt officials had their quarters in one of these corridors; Luchov and various heads of his staff were accommodated in the other. Further into the complex, the corridors put out smaller branches which led inward and inevitably downward, but here at the end closest to the exit into the Perchorsk Ravine they came together, forming something of a bottleneck. Worse, there was the bulkhead door, of dense metal set in concrete, which when shut formed in effect an airtight seal. Ever since the introduction of Luchov's failsafe, the door had been kept permanently open, firmly clamped to the wall.

But now, as Khuv and Litve outdistanced the bulk of fleeing personnel and came round a bend where the corridors merged on the approach to the door, so automatic gunfire sounded from up ahead. Approaching a second bend more cautiously, they came in sight of the door, saw what the shooting was about and took cover in an alcove in the wall.

Leo Grenzel was at the door. He had unlocked two of the three clamps and was working on the third which appeared to be jammed. Every time he stepped into view to put leverage on the clamp, soldiers in the alcoves closest to the door would open up with their guns, driving him back under cover. The thickness of the door itself, and an alcove directly behind it, shielded him from the worst of their fire; but even as Khuv and Litve arrived on the scene they saw him hit, saw him stagger back out of view. In another moment he reappeared cradling a machine-gun, opened up and sent a hail of lead sleeting the length of the corridor. Two soldiers toppled screaming out of their alcoves where ricochets hit them. Their comrades dragged them moaning out of sight.

"You up there," Khuv called during the lull. "Who's in charge?"

"I am," a Sergeant stuck his head out, snatched it back as Grenzel opened up again. Khuv saw him briefly before he, too, ducked back: his white face and staring eyes, their glazed look. And he could well understand that look. It was unlikely that the Sergeant knew Grenzel *was* dead, but it must be very hard to him to understand why he wasn't! The soldiers kept hitting Grenzel but they couldn't put him down! As Grenzel appeared yet again at the door, tugging furiously at the last clamp, the damage he'd suffered was obvious.

He was lop-sided in his stance; *that will be from his snapped spine*, Khuv supposed. And he marvelled at his own ability to accept this impossible thing, just like that. A broken spine, and Grenzel still mobile, however awkward. But why not, for he was also dead! Nor was that the end of it. He was wearing white coveralls. They smouldered down his right side, where they hung in rags. Tatters of flesh hung with the rags, grey and red, but there was very little blood in evidence; these things didn't bleed too readily. There were three small holes in Grenzel's right shoulder, neat as the dots on a dice where a burst of bullets had printed full stops on his coveralls; but at the back the holes were the size of small apples, coloured a ragged, reddish-black. Grenzel hung his shoulder on that side, adding to his lopsidedness. His difficulty with the clamp was that he worked at it left-handed.

Khuv took Litve's flamethrower, called out to the men ahead: "Give me a burst of covering fire when I call for it—just a concentrated burst—and I'll deal with this bastard. But first of all, can one of you boys take out that light?"

"Are you sure you know what you're doing, sir?" a shout came back. "I mean, this one hardly seems human!"

How right you are! "Yes, just put out that light." Above the door was a lamp in a wire basket. On instructions from the Sergeant, one of his men shot it out. There was a *crack!*—a tinkle of glass—and the buckled wire basket was torn from its housing. The light in the corridor was at once reduced, turning the place to a smoky tunnel.

"When I yell 'now,' " Khuv reminded, "one burst and then keep your heads down."

Grenzel had vanished for a moment, but now he reappeared, stood half-silhouetted in the doorway. He had his gun with him, which he propped against the wall before returning his attention to the clamp. Behind Khuv and Litve the converging corridors were suddenly full of milling people; their hushed yet massed voices were like the susurration of a congregation in a great sounding church. Litve called back: "Stay still! Be quiet. Just wait where you are."

Khuv checked that his weapon was primed and ready for action. It was still fairly heavy, indicating that there was no lack of fuel. Then he shouted: *"Now!"* There came an answering burst of fire and Grenzel staggered back. Khuv crouched down, ran forward. Grenzel sensed or saw him, grabbed up his gun, fired a short burst and ran out of bullets. Khuv heard the *whip* and *buzz* of angry lead, heard voices back down the corridor cry out their agony. Then he opened up with his flamethrower, stabbed its blade of near-solid heat right at the yellow wolf-eyes burning in Grenzel's silhouetted face.

All shadows fled as the flamethrower roared. Grenzel was scorched, mawled like a run-over cat. He dropped his useless gun, and in the next moment Khuv was on him. He hosed him down with fire, burned him to a blistered crisp that burst into flame and stuck itself to the metal wall. Then Grenzel slid down the wall, toppled over and lay still. Khuv stopped firing, stood back. The flames gradually died down and Grenzel's remains hissed and crackled, issuing vile black smoke.

Then Litve came forward with the Sergeant, and Khuv told the latter: "See that all of these people get safely out of here. They're not out of the woods yet." Without waiting, he and Litve went on to Failsafe Control.

With frightened people hurriedly filing past them, they stood in the corridor and banged on the metal door. Luchov's voice, shrill, terrified, came through to them: "Who is it? What's happening?"

"Viktor?" Khuv answered. "It's me, Khuv, Open up."

"No, I don't believe you. I know who you are. Go away!"

"*What?*" Khuv glanced at Litve. Then he guessed what had happened. Agursky had been here. He banged again on the door. "Viktor, it *is* me!"

"Then where's your key?" All of the listed Failsafe Duty Officers had keys to this room.

Litve still had Khuv's keys. He took them from a pocket and handed them over. Luckily, Khuv hadn't thrown the Failsafe key away with the others down in the mortuary. Now the Major turned the key in the lock, pushed the door open—and at once gasped and stepped back!

Luchov stood there, eyes bulging, veins pulsing in the seared half of his head, aiming the hot muzzle of a flamethrower straight into Khuv's straining face. "God!" he gasped, lowering the weapon to point at the floor. "It *is* you!" He staggered back, collapsed into his swivel chair in front of the TV screens.

He was a wreck. A trembling, panting, completely terrified wreck. Khuv carefully took the flamethrower from him, said: "What happened, Viktor?"

Luchov gulped, started to talk. As he proceeded some of the wild, frightened look went out of his eyes. "After you left, I . . . I started to phone. Half the lines were out. But I got the guards on the entrance, in the ravine, and told them about Agursky. Then I got through to half-a-dozen other numbers, too, and passed on the message. I said everyone should evacuate, but as quietly as possible. Then it dawned on me how crazy that was. Agursky was out there somewhere and he'd see them leaving. He'd know the game was up and God only knows what he'd do! I managed to raise the military and told them to see to the evacuation, also to hunt Agursky down. I said the phones were out of order and that they should alert all the people I couldn't reach. I spoke to everyone I could, but so far I haven't been able to reach the core.''

Khuv and Litve glanced at the screens. All looked normal down there; faces were strained and nervous, but there was no sign of any unusual activity. ''What about Agursky?'' Khuv asked. ''Did he come here?''

Again Luchov gulped. ''God, yes! He came, knocked on the door, said he had to speak to me. I told him I couldn't let him in. He said he knew I knew about him and he could explain. He said if I didn't let him in he would do something terrible. I said if I did I knew he'd kill me. Then he said that he knew we planned to burn him, but that he was going to burn us—all of us! In the end he went away; but I thought: *if he kills any one of the Failsafe duty officers, and takes his key* . . .

''I had an automatic, but I knew that those two dead soldiers hadn't been able to stop him with their guns. So I waited a little while, sneaked out and took the nearest flamethrower. I came back and just as I was letting myself in . . . oh, *Jesus!*''

''He showed up?'' Khuv took the other's elbow.

''Yes,'' Luchov nodded, gulped. ''But you should *see* him, Khuv! It's not Agursky. I don't know what it is, but it isn't him!''

All three men exchanged glances. ''How do you mean, 'not him'?'' Litve asked, sure that he wouldn't like the answer.

''His *face!*'' Luchov's lips trembled and he shook his head disbelievingly. ''It's all wrong; and his head, the wrong shape. The way he moves—like a great sly animal. Anyway, he came at me at the run, loping towards me. He didn't have his dark glasses on and his eyes were red as blood, I swear it! I got inside, slammed the door and somehow managed to turn the key. And outside . . . he was a madman! He raved and threatened, hammered on the door. But eventually he went away again.''

Khuv shuddered. The whole thing was like a nightmare, getting worse all the time. Then Luchov's phone rang, causing all three men to start violently. Khuv reached the phone first, snatched it from its cradle. ''Yes?''

''Corporal Grudov, at the entrance, sir,'' an excited, tinny voice sounded. ''Agursky, he was here!''

''What?'' Khuv crouched over the phone. ''Did you see him? Have you killed him?''

''We shot *at* him, sir, but kill him? I'm sure we must have hit him, but he seemed to ignore us! So we went after him with a flamethrower.''

''But you didn't get him? Where is he now, outside?'' Khuv held his breath. He knew that Agursky mustn't escape.

''No, he ducked back inside. We burned him a little, I think.''

''You think?''

''It all happened so very quickly, sir.''

Khuv thought fast. ''Are the people out yet?''

''Most of them, but they're still coming. I've called up trucks from the barracks, else they'd all freeze out here.''

''Good man!'' Khuv sighed his relief. ''Now listen: let everyone out except Agursky. If he shows up again give him all you've got. Kill him, burn him, destroy him utterly! Have you got that?''

''Yes, sir.''

Khuv put the phone down, turned to the others. ''He's still in here. Him and us, and maybe a few stragglers. Oh, and the soldiers at the core, and whoever else is down there with them.'' He turned to Luchov. ''The first button sounds the klaxons, right?''

Luchov nodded. ''You know it does—if they're still working.''

489

Khuv reached across and pressed button number one. He gave Luchov no time to think or to argue. Simply did it. The alarms were still working: their monotonous yet nerve-wrenching howling started up at once. It was like the crying of some vast, wounded prehistoric beast.

"But what are you doing?" Luchov gasped.

"Getting those soldiers out of it," Khuv nodded at the screens. Down at the core all such niceties as orders went to the wall. Those men down there knew what the klaxons meant. And they'd had enough. Nerves could stand just so much, and then no more. In a matter of moments it was chaos, and panic-flight. The staircase was packed with fleeing men; the Katushev teams were scrambling out of their kit, running for it. A Sergeant-Major fired his pistol into the air once, twice, then holstered it and joined the rush.

Khuv laughed, slapped his thigh, punched Litve's shoulder. "Agursky can't get out," he said. "He's in here, probably wounded, and those men—heavily armed men—are coming up from below. And we're going down from the top!"

"You're right," Luchov gasped. "But me, I'm staying right here. If he comes back this way I'll make sure he doesn't get in here; also, I'm not chancing meeting him between here and the exit!"

"Good," said Khuv. "But we'll need your flame-thrower. Here—" He brought out his automatic and handed it over. "It's not much but better than nothing."

Luchov let them out into the corridor. "Good luck," he said, simply.

"You too," Khuv nodded. Then Luchov quickly closed the door and locked it . . .

Half-way between Failsafe Control and the magmass level, they met the soldiers coming up. They came at the stampede, until Khuv called out: "It's OK, you men. There's no problem. We have a maniac running loose, that's all. The scientist, Vasily Agursky. Has anyone seen him?''

"No, sir," the Sergeant-Major who had fired his pistol down at the core came to attention, saluted. "I'm afraid we all panicked, sir, and—"

"Forget it," Khuv said. "You were supposed to panic. That way I could be sure you'd get out of there fast, that's all."

"You see, sir," the other was at pains to explain, "the phones have been out for some time, so we guessed there was a problem. Then, when those klaxons started up—"

"I said forget it!" Khuv snapped. "Now get your men out of here—I mean right out of it. Out of the Projekt."

Litve grabbed his arm. "But they could be of assistance," he protested.

Khuv shook his head. "With them out of the way, anything else that moves has to be Agursky. And *anything* that moves dies! Let's go."

They proceeded to the magmass levels, checking rooms and laboratories as they went. And all the while the klaxons sounding, sounding, sounding, and their flesh crawling on them like they were covered in cockroaches . . .

Up in Failsafe Control, Viktor Luchov heard the pounding of booted feet as the core's military units vacated the Projekt. Well, at least they were out of it now. That left Khuv and Litve, and whatever else was down there waiting for them. Luchov glanced again at the silent, now motionless screens—especially the centre screen, which showed the core and the Gate—then returned to his private thoughts. Thoughts about Khuv. He had never much cared for the man; the KGB were a brutal lot. And yet now . . .

Luchov's thoughts froze right there. Gooseflesh crept on his neck. Something he had seen? He looked at the centre screen again. He strained his eyes, rubbed at them . . . but no, there was nothing wrong with his eyes.

On the centre screen a pale, gelatinous mass was visible on the curve of the sphere's dome, a slow-motion picture of something within. It hadn't been there ten or fifteen minutes ago—or maybe it had, and with so much going on he simply hadn't noticed it. Crazy! It was exactly what he was here to notice!

He stared harder, and yes—in a minute the thing had grown larger, starting to bloat up huge on the great curved screen which was the Gate. It was like . . . like Encounter One. But bigger. *Much* bigger! And it was moving faster than anything had ever moved in there before. If it *was* the same sort of creature as Encounter One, and if it should break loose from the Gate—

God! Luchov gritted his teeth, slammed a balled fist into his palm. *At a time like this!*

Khuv and Litve were still down there somewhere. They had thought to trap Agursky between themselves and the soldiers. And now who was trapped? At least Luchov could try to warn them. Khuv's own novel method should suffice.

He reached out a trembling hand and pressed button number two . . .

Down on the fringe of the eerie magmass levels, Khuv and Litve stayed close together, moving very slowly. There was darkness here, where even the well-illuminated areas were dark with implication. Even above the blaring, maddening klaxons, whose row was fading a little behind them, the heart of the Perchorsk beast could be heard thudding more loudly, seemed that much closer.

They moved cautiously down the wide timber stairway, Khuv's eyes raking the magmass on the right, and Litve's on the left. The pilot-lights of their flamethrowers threw weird, blue-flickering shadows, making faces and threatening figures of the disturbing magmass fusions.

Khuv adjusted the strap of his flamethrower across his right shoulder, and metal parts chinked together. The sound was amplified by the magmass, and despite the incessant klaxons came echoing back seemingly from all directions. Another sound, having its origin elsewhere and rising to drown it out, came back with it: stuttering, almost chattering laughter!

"Behind us?" Khuv whirled to look back, eyes wide so as to miss nothing.

"No," Litve's voice was a whisper where he crouched, "in front of us—I think."

"It's hard to tell," said Khuv, beginning to breathe a little faster. "He could be anywhere."

"But he's just one," Litve was starting to shake, his voice, too, "and there are two of us. For God's sake don't get separated from me, Major!"

They turned right and followed the wooden path— an artificial and entirely familiar road through this alien landscape—into the heart of a magmass cavern, where the echoes of their footsteps resounded louder yet . . . and that was when the pitch and frequency of the alarms increased from a repetitive, mindless blaring to a definite cry of warning!

"What the hell—?" Litve gasped.

"That was Luchov," said Khuv, "telling us that something isn't right. Shit—we know that already!"

The laughter came again, and this time there was no mistaking its source: behind them. Also, Khuv recognized the voice as Agursky's beyond any shadow of doubt. So did Litve, apparently. "He's tracking us," he whispered.

"Let's find a vantage point," Khuv moved faster, heading for the stairwell through to the core. That was the only way to go now, down to the core itself. But with still thirty or so paces to go to the final descent, Litve grabbed Khuv's elbow.

"Look!" he croaked.

Khuv looked back. From behind a leaning magmass

nodule, a shadow had fallen on the walkway. One that moved. Closer still, there was more movement: Khuv's and Litve's startled eyes went together to a heavy-duty cable where it snaked along the mad flow of the magmass wall. The cable jerked; its loops between staples contracted as something hauled on it. Almost before the meaning of this could dawn, there came a cry of combined pain and frustration from behind the same magmass nodule. The shadow on the walkway was highlighted, emboldened by flaring blue illumination and a shower of sputtering sparks. And it was a monstrous shadow!

Incapable as yet of movement, the two watched. The shadow—a *single* shadow—began to split in two. There came a rending sound, like sailcloth tearing, as the two halves of the shadow struggled to break apart —struggled and succeeded. Two of them now: one of which seemed human, and the other the size and roughly the shape of a dog, except it was *not* a dog. Then both of them moving back a little, merging with the shadow of the nodule, and a further moment of struggling with the power cable. There was more electrical sputtering and a second shower of sparks . . .

And the lights went out!

The two men backed toward the shaft going down to the core. Their legs were jelly but they forced movement out of them. A faint wash of light came from behind them, over their shoulders: residual light from the sphere-gate, shining up through the shaft. But along the walkway where they'd been, all was now night.

"If he—it—they are going to come," Litve stuttered, "then it has to be along this walkway."

Khuv's throat was too dry and tight to answer, but he thought: *That's right*. They were both wrong. The thing from the tank, or rather metamorphic vampire material from the core of the thing in the tank—not dead but subsumed into Agursky, and now released to even up the score, two against two—didn't have to come that way at all. It came *under* the walkway!

494

Almost at the mouth of the shaft, where the walkway turned sharply to the left and once more descended as stairs, the thing struck. Something coiled up over the handrail, wrapped itself clingingly around Litve's waist, dragged him screaming through the shattering rail. He was there, beside Khuv, and he was gone. His flame-thrower put forth a single blast of flame, and looking down Khuv saw what had him. The thing from the tank, yes: a great flat tentacled leech now, which smothered Litve's face and the upper half of his body like a mass of leprous dough, while its many-jointed ''limbs'' wrapped him and crushed his body like so many pythons! And eyes in the surging filth of the thing, staring up unblinking at Khuv where he choked and gurgled on the walkway.

Litve's flamethrower went clattering; Khuv knew that was the end of him; he aimed his own weapon and sent searing flame blasting into the heaving obscenity where it threshed on the magmass floor. Screaming his rage and terror, he burned it—burned it—burned it. Until the white heart of his torch turned yellow, hissed, crackled into silence, until the pilot-light itself went out.

Then came Agursky's chuckle again, and through the reek and the smoke Khuv saw him coming. He saw him closing with him, his hands elongating, reaching . . .

He dropped his empty weapon, ran, stumbled, went flailing down the stairwell into the heart of the place; and down the stairs from the landing onto the boards of the Saturn's-rings perimeter. Agursky came close behind, chuckling, flowing, inexorably pursuing. Khuv looked back and saw him: the impossible gape of his jaws, the nightmare of his bone dagger teeth meshing like a mincer in the cavern of his mouth. He screamed and raced for the nearest Katushev cannon.

"Shit, *shit!*" he screamed, and: "Oh, God! Oh mother of—" He leaped up onto the Katushev's platform, slid into the gunner's chair, traversed the assembly to face

Agursky where he loped after him. But . . . he had no idea how to fire the thing!

Before Agursky could reach him, he leaped out of his seat, fled across the rings and onto the gantry bridging the gap to the sphere. The power was off and the gate in the electrical fence open; Khuv ran through it, reached the spot where the boards were scorched and blackened. The Gate was the only route open to him now, but better that than—

He skidded to a halt, threw up his hands before him to ward off . . . something he couldn't believe, something from the mind of a raving lunatic! He stared at the sphere and his eyes bulged, popped in his white mask of a face. Agursky had seen it, too, and he was likewise brought up short. And a third pair of eyes had seen it, had indeed been watching it for some time.

Up in Failsafe Control, Viktor Luchov waited no longer but threw the failsafe switch. He opened the floodgates to hell—because he had to, and for Khuv. For Khuv, yes, who even now turned his face to the closed circuit TV monitor and pleaded with him, begged him to do it. "Do it!" the Major's face screamed silently at Luchov from the centre screen. "For God's sake, Viktor, if you know the meaning of mercy—*do it!*"

Volatile liquids rushed and sprinklers commenced spraying all through the Projekt; plastic pipes began to blister as the liquid flowed faster; thousands of litres of the stuff flowed into the heart of Perchorsk, becoming vapour where it was exposed to air. Forced by the weight of fuel in the huge tanker, dragged downwards by gravity, it quickly saturated the complex, began to gush from an outlet into the core itself.

The core: where now Agursky knew he was finished and closed with Khuv, reaching for him. But the Major was no longer concerned with Agursky, only with the *thing* that was breaking through the screen of the sphere, only with the heaving, pulsating monstrosity of hooks and teeth and claws which wore the vast, bloated, nightmare distortion of . . . *of Karl Vyotsky's face!*

But this was not, could not be, the Vyotsky who had gone into that other world; it was so radically *different* that its passage through the Gate in the reverse direction had not been forbidden. It half-emerged, saw and fell upon the figures on the gantry and devoured them, and in the next moment was itself devoured. Somewhere, the deadly vapours had reached a naked flame. Incendiary fires raced through the Projekt in an unstoppable chain-reaction. The entire place detonated—exploded—like a vast bomb!

Viktor Luchov, gasping and almost fainting from his exertions, was hauled through the wicket-gate onto the marshalling area in the ravine under the cold night stars. They hurried him away from the giant doors, which in a little while were blown off their rollers like so much scrap metal. A shaft of fire roared out, bending like a waterfall to strike the dammed waters, sending clouds of steam boiling upwards.

Perchorsk was no more . . .

From the time of his early childhood, when he was maybe eight or nine years old, Harry Keogh remembered one especially bad dream. It had been repetitive, bothering him through many long nights, and even now —especially now—was not forgotten.

Where the idea had originated, he couldn't say. It might have come from some ancient medical book, or from the mind of one of his long-dead friends, may even have stemmed from a flash of precognition. But he could still remember it in detail. The long hall, brick walls, and the heavy wooden tables set end to end; the starving man stretched out on his back, lashed to the end table; his head firmly fixed between blocks of wood, a leather strap across his forehead to keep it tilted back, and his jaws propped wide open.

He lay there, conscious, skeletal, chest heaving and

arms and legs straining where they, too, were lashed, and men in long white coats and a woman with a long-bladed hatchet watching him and nodding among themselves, tight-lipped. Then the men, (doctors, maybe?) standing well back, and the woman with the hatchet laying her weapon down on the table farthest from the wretched man. Her departure through an arched doorway, and her return with a large plate of rancid fish.

The pictures were very vivid: the way she carefully took a piece of putrid fish and smeared it from directly in front of the man's face, all the way along the centre of the joined-up tables to the last one, before dropping it on the plate with the other stinking remnants. There was a screen at that end, where now she took her position, seated there with her cleaver in her hand, patience itself as she looked through a peephole in the screen and waited for it to happen. The way her eyes fixed upon the gaping mouth of the racked man.

Then the worst part of the dream, when the cestode came out of him, its segmented, ribbonlike body inching laboriously from his convulsing throat, writhing where it followed the fish-stink in its search for food. Blind, the tapeworm, but not without senses of its own, and not without hunger; its head flat on the table but swaying this way and that, creeping forward, and the hooked segments coming into view from the man's choking throat, one by one, releasing their hooks within him and venturing forth into daylight. For while the man was starving because of his worm, *it* was starving because of the doctors who hadn't fed him for five or six days!

Harry remembered it so well, that dream:

The *length* of the thing, covering first one six-foot table, then two, three, until it had been feared that six tables would not be enough. Twenty-five feet of it when at last the forked, scorpion tail appeared, trailing mucous and blood behind it. And at that one of the doctors had tensed, started to inch silently forward.

And the man on the table gurgling and gagging; the cestode worm creeping warily forward, but more avidly as the fish-stink thickened; the woman with her cleaver poised, waiting, her teeth drawn back from her lips in almost savage anticipation . . .

The parasite reaching the plate and its leech-head gorging . . . the cleaver flashing silver in those practiced female hands, shearing through the soft chitin and primitive guts of the thing . . . the doctor slapping his hand over the man's mouth, as the frantically writhing rear sections of the worm tried to wriggle back into him.

Which was always the point where Harry used to come yelping awake.

He came awake now, to the Lady Karen's voice asking some question of him where they sat facing each other across her table; and he hoped he'd been able to keep the canvas of his mind shielded from her, so that she had not read the vivid thoughts painted there. "I'm sorry? My mind was wandering."

"I said," she repeated herself, smiling, "that you've been my guest through three sundowns, with another on its way soon, and still you haven't told me why you came—came willingly, of your own volition, into my aerie."

For my son. "Because you were a friend to The Dweller in a time of need," he lied, keeping his mind-voice to himself, "and because I'm curious and desired to see your aerie." *Also, because if I can find a cure for you I might be able to cure him.*

She shrugged. "But you've seen my aerie, Harry. Almost all of it. There are some things I have not shown you because you would find them . . . unpleasant. But you have seen the rest of it. So what keeps you here? You won't eat my food or even drink my water; there's really nothing here for you—except maybe danger."

"Your vampire?" he raised an eyebrow. *Your ces-*

tode, with its hooks in your heart and your guts and your brain?

"Of course—except I no longer think of it as 'my vampire.' We are one.'' She laughed, but not gaily— and a snake's tongue flickered behind her gleaming teeth. And her eyes were of a uniform, very deep scarlet. "Oh, I fought it for a long time, but uselessly in the end. The battle in The Dweller's garden was the turning point, when I knew it was over and accepted that I am what I am. It was the battle and the *power* and the blood. Waiting, watchful, quiescent until then, that's what woke it up and brought it to ascendancy. But I mustn't think of it that way, for now we're the same creature. And I *am* Wamphyri!''

"You are warning me?'' he said.

She looked away, gave an impatient toss of her head, looked back. "I am telling you it were better if you went. The Dweller's father you may be, but you are innocent, Harry Keogh. And this is no place for innocence.''

Me, innocent? "When I fell asleep in my room,'' he said, ''—when I sat by my window and watched the gold fading on the distant peaks, before the last sun- down—and woke up with a start, I dreamed you were standing over me.''

"I was, or had been,'' she sighed. "Harry, I have lusted after you.''

After me? Or after my blood? "How?''

"In every way. My host is a woman, with a wom- an's needs. But *I* am Wamphyri, with the needs of a vampire.''

"You don't *have* to draw blood.''

"Wrong. The blood is the life.''

"Then by now you must be starved of life, for you haven't eaten. Not while I have been here.'' He had taken his meals in the garden, travelling to and fro via the Möbius Continuum. But they'd been more snacks than meals proper, for he had not wanted to leave her alone too long, had not wanted to miss . . . anything.

When she spoke again her voice was cold. ''Harry, if you insist on staying . . . I cannot be held responsible.'' Before he could answer she stood up, swept out of the great hall, disappeared from view in that regal way of hers. Harry had not followed her before, had not spied on her in any depth. But the time had come and he knew it.

''Where is she going?'' he asked the long-dead cartilage creatures where their corpses fashioned the stack's decor. A carved bone handrail following stairs between the upper levels answered him:

She descends, Harry, to her larder. Her hand falls on me even now.

''Her larder?''

Where like Dramal Doombody before her, she keeps a number of trogs in store, hibernating.

''She told me she had set her trogs free, sent them home.''

But not these, the handrail, once a trog itself, answered. *These are for fashioning, and in times of siege for eating!*

Harry went there, two levels down, saw Karen flow in through a dark niche doorway and followed her. A trog had been activated, brought out of its cocoon. Harry stayed in the shadows, guarded his thoughts. He watched Karen lead the trog to the table. The creature, shambling, only half-awake, enthralled, lay down, bent back its ugly prehistoric head for her.

Her mouth opened—gaped! Blood dripped from her gums where scythe-teeth sprouted to poise over the creature's sluggishly pulsing jugular. Her nose wrinkled, flattened back on itself, and her eyes were crimson jewels in the twilight room.

''*Karen!*'' Harry shouted.

She snapped upright, hissed at him, cursed him long and loud—then swept by him in a fury and was gone.

There was no putting it off any longer; knowing what he must do, Harry went again to the garden . . .

He trapped her at sunup while she slept in her windowless room. He put silver chains on her door, which he left open no more than four or five inches, and arranged potted kneblasch plants whose stink sickened even him. Their smell woke her up and she cried: "Harry, what have you done?"

"Be calm," he told her from outside, "for there's nothing you can do about it."

"Oh?" she raged, rushing all about her room. "Is it so?" She sent commands to her warrior: *Come, free me!* But there was no answer.

"Burned," Harry told her. "And the trogs in your larder activated, all fled. And your siphoneer—that pitiful, monstrous thing—dead from the water which I poisoned in your wells. Your gas-beasts, too, themselves poisoned with unbreathable gasses. Now there's just you."

She wept and pleaded with him then. "What will you do with me? Will you burn me, too?"

He made no answer but went away . . .

He checked on her, every three or four hours returning to test the chains on her door, or water the kneblasch plants, but never letting her see him. Sometimes she was asleep, moaning in her red dreams, and at others she was awake, raving and cursing. Harry slept in the aerie only once at that time—and on that occasion woke up to find himself at the door, called there by Karen! It strengthened his resolve.

Another time: she was quite naked, telling him how she loved him, wanted him, needed him. But he knew what she needed. He ignored her lustful, luscious writhings and went away.

Five more sunups came and went, and Karen sank

into delirium. And when it was sundown again she slept and could not be brought awake. It was time.

Harry cleared away the kneblasch but kept the chains on the door; as before, he left only a small gap. Then he went to the garden and fetched a piglet, which he slaughtered into a golden bowl. He made a thin trail of blood from the door of Karen's room, into the great hall, where he laid the bowl on the floor in the centre of the room. The poor creature lay there, stiff in an inch of its own blood.

And then Harry waited, sitting in the shadows, quiet as never before and guarding his thoughts. And it was just as his dream, but worse. For this time he was there, and he was the one with the cleaver. Except it wasn't a cleaver.

Eventually the vampire left Karen (how, by what route, Harry neither knew nor wanted to know) and began to follow the bloody trail. Swaying its head this way and that, it entered the hall, inched forward towards the bowl. It was a long leech, corrugated, cobra-headed, blind, with many hooks. And it had pointed udders, a great many of them, along its grey, pulsating underbelly.

It sensed the blood, came on faster—then sensed Harry! It began a hasty retreat, curled back on itself and wriggled like a blindworm. Harry stepped into the Möbius Continuum, stepped out again at the door of Karen's room. The vampire came crawling, saw him, but too late. He aimed his flamethrower and burned it. Dying, it issued eggs, a great many of them, which rolled and skittered, vibrating across the floor towards him. Sweating, but cold inside, Harry burned them all. Until all that was left was the awful smell, and the screaming.

Karen's screaming . . .

Exhausted, Harry slept. He slept in the aerie, because there was no longer anything there to fear. He dreamed that Karen stood over him in her white gown—that gown she had worn so revealingly for the Wamphyri

Lords—and explained why he was the most miserable of all men. His victory was ashes. She had *been* Wamphyri, and now she was a shell. He thought he had won, but he had lost. When one has known the *power*, the *freedom* the magnified *emotions* of the vampire . . . what is there after that? She told him she pitied him, for she knew why he had done what he had done—and he had failed. And then she said goodbye.

He woke up, looked for her. No longer Wamphyri, she had taken the chains from her door, escaped. He searched the stack top to bottom, came and went through the Möbius Continuum until he was dizzy, but he couldn't find her. Eventually he went out onto her high balcony and looked down. Karen's white dress lay crumpled on the scree more than a kilometer below, no longer entirely white but red, too.

And Karen was inside it . . .

Epilogue

In the garden, the damage done in the fighting had been very nearly put to rights. Travellers worked at it during sunups, and trogs through the dark sundowns. And meanwhile the message had gone out: the Wamphyri are no more! Streams of Travellers, entire tribes, were en route even now, coming here to celebrate and worship at the feet of their saviour. Jazz and Zek, and Wolf, too, had gone home, conveyed to that distant place by The Dweller, who had then returned.

And all in all, The Dweller was well satisfied with his work.

But . . . feeling a burning on his neck, Harry Jr. turned from where he supervised the rebuilding of the wall, turned to glance at a rising hummock of ground a little way apart. Someone stood there, someone who watched him intently, silently. Someone whose mind was sealed tight as a limpet to its rock. Harry Jr. frowned, peered for a moment through the holes in the golden mask, then smiled. It was only his father.

He waved and went back to work . . .